THE VICTIM

"It's the girl. Sample. Something to do with Sample."

Peter was nodding enthusiastically. "She would be about the right age. Thirteen or so."

"Twelve."

"Well, they start earlier these days. Puberty," he explained. "A young girl, virginal, about to enter womanhood, has enormous power. We see it in poltergeists, you know. Many belief systems honor, fear or try to harness the power, according to their individual beliefs. Kellogg may have been appointed some task relating to Sample and failed to carry it out."

"What sort of task?"

"Well, judging by Kellogg's punishment, I'd say he was to have sexual intercourse with the girl. Then probably sacrifice her."

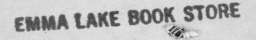

WHITE SPIDER

JOYCE WOLF

LEISURE BOOKS   NEW YORK CITY

A LEISURE BOOK

Published by

Dorchester Publishing Co., Inc.
6 East 39th Street
New York, NY   10016

Printed in the United States of America

PROLOGUE

He stumbled again, falling heavily to his knees this time.

The ragged sound of his breathing filled his ears. Years of too many cigarettes. And fear.

A hot stench of crushed weeds rose up from the ground and wrapped itself around him. He was fighting to catch his breath. Just hearing himself breathe like that was enough to scare him, and Jesus, so loud you could hear him half a mile away. There was no covering sound here, just the quiet night.

He strained to hold his breath and listen. Nothing. Just the sound of wind in the trees.

He rocked back on his heels and scrubbed the stickiness of the weeds clinging to his palms against his jeans. He sucked at the thick air and blinked hard, wiping the back of his hand against his eyes to get rid of the sweat.

Quiet.

Only that was wrong, wasn't it? There should be night noises. Crickets. Frogs. He should be able to hear a car now and then passing on the nearby road.

Kids would be leaving the bars now, heading home or out to the quarry or here to the riverbank for some serious drinking or a private spot to make love. In the

summer there was always somebody out on the riverbank, even in the loneliest hours of the night.

Some part of his mind kept yammering at him that
he should have stayed on the road, should even turn
back now. But senseless panic had driven him from
the car when it just shuddered and died and refused
to start again. He ran into the woods like a hunted
animal looking for cover, and now he was afraid to go
back.

When a wave of fresh fear hit him he lurched to his
feet, running instinctively to escape the shadows of
the trees. He was pushing towards the light reflected
off the river. Not far. Just there.

But he moved with the clumsiness of panic, and
trees loomed up in his path like the nastier surprises
in a funhouse. He reeled into them, skinning his face,
staggering through undergrowth that tore at his
clothes with thin, greedy fingers. And he fell again,
gasping too loudly in a night that was too still. Terror
crashed through him, but he couldn't keep moving.

His gasping became words that ebbed out as unconsciously as blood.

"*Pleasepleaseplease . . .*" He rolled onto his hands
and knees, head hanging, swinging like a bear swings
his head in pain.

"*Ohgod, ohshit, ohjesus . . .*" And he was trying to
get up, but his legs betrayed him as they shook and
folded beneath him.

And then he heard it.

Some kind of obscene snuffling sound. Some *thing*
that rustled through the undergrowth, shifting
through the shadows. Something that paused. And
listened. And knew he was there.

He tried once again to thrash to his feet but he fell.

Then he saw it.

And it saw him.

1

When her telephone rang Nora was out of bed and halfway across the room before she realized why she was up. Without the sound she stood there, lost, until it rang again and she turned in the direction of the shrill jangling.

Usually Nora took a perverse pleasure in being the most near-sighted person she'd ever met. Just then, without her glasses or contact lenses, she felt the old frustration. She wished she could see well enough to at least find the damn phone and stop its clamoring.

By the fourth ring she'd zeroed in on it, almost tripping over it where it lay in the middle of the bedroom floor, abandoned in the chaos of unpacking. She snatched up the receiver like a prize.

"Hello?"

"Nora? Did I wake you?"

"Simon?" Her ex-husband. Nora Durant squinted around the darkened room, still out of touch with reality. A crack of light shone under a drawn window shade and she moved toward it, carrying the phone. From the brightness of the light it must be well into morning.

Simon breathed with calm patience. "Yes. Listen, if I woke you up, I'll call back later. When you're awake.''

"I'm awake now," she snapped. Funny how much he could irritate her in just a sentence or two. She reached for the shade.

"No, this is important. I want to talk to you when I've got your full attention." Pompous, pompous. He wasn't that pompous when they were first married, was he?

"Simon, I'm wide awake. You have my full attention. Where are you?" She kept tugging at the shade, trying to ease it up without letting it make a telltale sound.

"At my office, catching up on some work. Pennsylvania. That's where I live, remember? I'll call you back."

"I *know* where you live . . ." Although, actually, he moved so often she sometimes had to stop and think about it. "Harrisburg."

"I couldn't tell. I never hear from you."

Nora pressed her lips together and eased the shade up another two feet.

"I don't suppose you've seen the newspaper?" Simon said it with the vast superiority of someone who always got the news first.

"Today's? No." The shade was fully up now and Nora carried the phone back to the bed, feeling around on the night table for her glasses. "Why?"

On her last birthday Simon's birthday card had arrived with an enclosed newspaper clipping, an article about his testimony at a Congressional hearing. But it was a first for him to call her when he got publicity.

"Ah," he answered, sounding uncomfortable.

"What is it? Is something wrong?" Then he did have her full attention. She knew how Simon sounded with bad news.

Silence. Then he drew a deep breath. "It's Ted Kellogg. Kate's, uh, boyfriend. He's dead."

˙ Nora frowned at the phone. "What are you talking about? He can't be. Anyway, how would you know? You're hundreds of miles away." Indiana, Nora thought fiercely, I'm in Indiana. She, too, moved often. It took an effort sometimes to recall where she was.

"It was in this morning's paper," Simon answered, sounding both defensive and accusing. "I just wanted to make sure you weren't mixed up in it."

Now he was beginning to sound wounded. Most of his calls over the two years they'd been divorced followed the same pattern. He started off bitter, restrained, sarcastic—just checking, he said, to make sure she was still alive. She was always surprised. He was always wounded.

"I don't understand." Nora tried to keep her tone reasonable. " 'Mixed up' in what? And why would Ted Kellogg be in a Pennsylvania newspaper. He lives here."

"It's one of those things newspapers pick up on through the wire service. Murder, pretty gruesome." Simon now was sounding self-satisfied and a little smug.

It's being a lawyer that did it to him, Nora thought irrelevantly. She refused to think about what he had just said.

"Tell me what you're talking about," she demanded, part of her flinching at the harshness in her voice. She always sounded so shrewish when she spoke to Simon. Actually she now was frightened.

"*Dateline: Stony Cliffs, Indiana,*" Simon read in oratorical style. "*The mutilated body of a man identified as Ted Kellogg, 36, was found in the early morning hours at the outskirts of the small college town of Stony Cliffs. The body was discovered by two college students at a popular picnic area on the bank of the Black River. Authorities have not yet released information on the exact cause of death.*

" 'I've never seen this kind of mutilation before,' said Deputy—"

"Stop it!" Nora cut him off. She couldn't stand to listen to his rhetorical delivery of the details. There was silence for a few moments on both ends of the telephone line, then Nora cleared her throat, tightened her grip on the receiver and challenged Simon.

"But you said murder. Couldn't it have been some sort of accident? The article doesn't say murder!"

"It does in the next paragraph. You didn't let me read that far."

"I don't want to hear it," Nora interrupted quickly. "Just give me a minute." She stared at the blank bedroom wall.

Simon waited only seconds before starting in again. "Look, Nora, I just wanted to make sure you were all right. I know you've been spending a lot of time with Kate and that Kellogg character." Nora made a choking sound.

"Face it," Simon continued, "Ted Kellogg was a real creep. He was a bum who drank too much, used every kind of dope he could mooch, used Kate, just pretended he was a writer. One trashy novel, six years ago, that's the only thing he ever finished. Some supposedly metaphysical masterpiece that he probably wrote stoned out of his mind." Simon had said it all before, at least half a dozen times. He was droning on into his lecture voice.

"Simon, I really don't want to hear it," Nora told him. "In fact, I don't want to talk to you at all right now. I'm going to hang up."

"I guess there are a lot of things we can't talk about." Simon sounded wounded again.

Nora took a deep, even breath. "Please. I appreciate your concern, but I just want to get off the phone. I should call Kate."

"I think you ought to just stay out of it. If she needs

anything, she'll call you."

"My god, Simon, she's my best friend and I'm not about to desert her. You know what Kate's like; she may be too upset to call. God knows what she could be doing."

Simon insisted, "She can take care of herself."

"Simon, good-bye," Nora said firmly, but she could never quite manage to hang up first.

"Just call me if you need anything," he answered with a trace of unguarded warmth.

"I will," Nora told him.

"Well, I don't believe you, but I don't suppose there's anything I can do about it. You could be starving in the gutter and you wouldn't call me, would you?"

Nora waited.

"Good-bye, then." Finally, Simon hung up.

Nora replaced the receiver in slow motion, absent-mindedly, not thinking of anything in particular. She pushed shoulder-length brown hair out of her face and anchored it behind her ears, looking around the room for something to put on. Her short, white, cotton kimono hung on a doorknob and she wrapped it around herself, then wandered, still lost and unthinking, to the second set of windows in her second story corner bedroom.

Nora was taller than most women and many men. Most of her height was in dancer's long legs that flowed with unconscious grace under the kimono. She'd given up years ago, after high school, wanting to be just two inches shorter. She accepted her height, was fond of her long, shapely hands, and pleased with her gray-blue eyes. Usually quirky humor shaped the expressions on her mobile face. Now, she was wide-eyed with the stunned look of someone who has just driven past the scene of a train wreck.

She moved around the room still caught in a languid dreaminess, opening drawn shades and pushing back

sheer curtains for more light and a view of the street
below.

Everything looked remarkably normal. The August
sun was high and bright in a clear blue sky dotted
with clouds as fat as puppies, the way summer skies
always seem to be in winter memories. Gilbert Street
with its canopy of sugar maples and sycamores
stretched toward the campus downtown and the
Black River, less than a mile away. The houses
crowded together, shoulder to shoulder, dowdy and
battered but still hanging on to middle-class dignity.
Most were clapboard, one or two stories in faded
green or brown or weathered white. Half a block
down and across the street, two freshly painted
houses side by side announced new, optimistic
owners. One was cream with rosy peach trim, the
other a smoky blue with black shutters and white-
painted gingerbread trim.

Directly across the street a pale little girl of about
five pushed colorful plastic trucks through the shaggy
grass with her younger brother. Next door to them the
elderly neighbor's bowlegged, barrel-bodied brown
mutt leaned against a peeling wooden porch, panting
heavily in the heat.

The view still seemed new to Nora, although she'd
moved into the rambling, three-bedroom half-double
almost a month ago. When it looked bone-deep
familiar at odd, startling moments, it was because
memory overlaid the view with the ghosts of other
streets in other towns. Stony Cliffs looked like at least
fifty other midwestern college towns, half a dozen
that Nora had lived in. It was a small, slow river town
surrounded by farm land. The college—Stony Cliffs
College or SCC as everyone called it—was the town's
main business.

Nora discovered, to her disappointment, that the
name of the town had nothing to do with its geo-
graphy. Though the town had the soft, rolling hills of

a river valley, the cliffs were more than twenty miles away. The name was a twist of fate, an old joke on the town's founding father.

Town folklore had it that Stony Cliffs got its name in 1838 from a surveyor passing through. Josiah Gilbert's General Store and blacksmith shop had been the only buildings on the site near the Black River and they served about twenty families that lived nearby. Josiah Gilbert had fond hopes of building a town around his store and calling it Gilbertsville or Gilbert's Corners and he greeted the surveyor like a long-lost brother. But Josiah was too generous with his hospitality and home-brewed liquor. The surveyor left the next day with a powerful hangover and no recollection of his host's name. Still, a few miles from Gilbert's store the surveyor ran across a sign. "Stony Cliffs," it said. But the arrow and the rest of the legend that pointed to cliffs 25 miles away had broken off in a hailstorm two winters back and no one had bothered to replace them. The surveyor marked the spot on his map and carefully printed Stony Cliffs below it, and Stony Cliffs it stayed. Josiah Gilbert was never a popular man.

Stony Cliffs had its heyday around the turn of the century and kept growing through the 1920s until the Depression nearly finished it off. Many of the gracious old homes were shabby now, cut up into rooms for a transient student population, and only the houses outside the radius of the original town were decent enough for the old town families and the college faculty and staff.

Downtown Stony Cliffs ranged along the top of the ridge of hills on the riverbank. Most of the small stores and restaurants were built or renovated in the 1940s and 1950s. A few were newer, remodeled in the late 1970s, but the wide sweeps of glass and concrete tended to look out of place in the rows of honest brown brick and sandstone, embarrassed as a gaudy dresser at a Baptist social.

The downtown area took up only seven or eight square blocks, but a new shopping center and multiple cinema complex two miles out in what was recently a cornfield held newer shops and restaurants. The SCC campus was centrally located, part of the downtown area, and it rambled over the hills on the Black River with ivy-covered brick and limestone halls and a scattering of concrete and glass buildings at its outskirts—a new science building, the new art school and museum with a twisted, rusty sculpture 20 feet high in the front courtyard.

Central to it all was the Black River. It flowed thick and slow through the town and campus, bisecting the town and college grounds. In the spring, summer and fall it was the center of social life for SCC. Students were always there in warm weather—alone, in small groups or even in full classes lounging on both long banks. They sunbathed or meditated between classes, played guitars or frisbee, slept, studied, necked, ate, drank and watched the clouds roll by.

In another month Nora would officially be on the faculty of the college, teaching a basic writing course and a class in myth and folklore. Now she was strictly on probation with a light course load and no guarantees. Her salary was correspondingly low and the place she rented showed her place in limbo.

There were fine lines drawn between town citizens and college people. Some neighborhoods belonged to the town, while others were segregated to the college. Most of the faculty, the ones with money to spend, lived at the outskirts of town in the brick and stone suburbs of big, solid homes. A few faculty families had infiltrated the old Victorian neighborhoods, renovating the fine old clapboard houses, carefully painting the gingerbread trim and pruning the overgrown lilac bushes that draped the iron fences out front.

Young students lived in dorms or in the fraternities and sororities. After sophomore year many moved out to rent rooms in the rundown areas around the campus. Nora lived in one of the better married-student neighborhoods, an area where young families mixed with elderly townspeople and no one had a kind word to say for anyone else.

In a month, she still hadn't unpacked much. She hadn't lived in the same place for more than six months since leaving graduate school. Simon was ambitious and mobile and they'd changed cities and parts of town almost constantly. Once on her own, Nora had drifted, but now she meant to settle in for a while. If not in this house, then at least in Stony Cliffs.

Kate Hall had lived here for five years with her daughter Sam—short for Sample, a family name. Kate had always spoken well of Stony Cliffs, or as well as she spoke of any place. And Nora had been lucky to get her one-year teaching appointment with the possibility of a longer contract in the future.

Nora was still standing at the window wrestling with shock and discomfort at the idea of calling Kate when the phone rang again. She knew who it would be before tentatively answering on the second ring.

"Nora?" It was Kate, her voice ragged and hoarse.

"Kate. I heard . . . Simon just called me."

"That vulture. My god, Nora, what they did to him." Kate trailed off, then added, "I need a favor."

"Of course, anything. You want me to come over?" Hearing Kate's voice made it all more real. The feeling of dread and obligation evaporated, but pained sympathy took its place.

"No," Kate answered sharply. "No. I couldn't cope with making conversation or dealing with another person right now. Not now. I need to be alone for a while." Nora heard Kate take a deep drag on a cigarette. "I think I want to get stinking drunk."

"Oh, Kate," Nora said, feeling helpless.

"Oh, hell, I'm not going to. I'd probably just throw

up. The thing is, I'm being a really lousy mother right now. Lousier than usual. And Sam needs to be around somebody who's halfway normal."

"I'll come and get her, then. I'm probably qualified as halfway, at least. She'll be fine with me for the rest of the day and we'll head back there to do something about dinner. Are you sure you'll be okay, though?"

Kate laughed, a strangled sound that caught in her throat. "Yeah," she said, and hung up.

After hanging up on Nora, Kate stood staring at the phone, knuckles white, clenching the receiver still held to her ear. She punched a rapid number. The phone was answered on the first ring.

"You bastard," Kate hissed. "What have you done?"

Forty-five minutes later Nora was driving away from Kate's with 12-year-old Sam slumped in the front seat. Sam's square, pale knees, bare and vulnerable, stuck out from baggy khaki shorts, and chunky calves disappeared into white gym socks. She wore a yellow "Save the Whales" T-shirt at least two sizes too big. Round tortoise shell glasses perched on her nose like a baby elephant in a circus delicately balancing on a rubber ball. Thick, straight brown bangs hid her forehead and her heavy hair swung forward to hide her face as, chin buried in her chest, Sam stared straight ahead out the window.

Nora fidgeted uneasily as she drove in a lengthening silence. She'd never gotten to know Sam well, seeing the girl only for brief visits passing through while she moved around the country. And Sam had only been back in Stony Cliffs for a week, returning from a month long stay with Kate's parents in Memphis.

What do you say to a 12-year old kid whose mother's lover has just been brutally murdered, Nora wondered in growing panic.

"Sam," Nora finally blurted, "I keep trying to think

of something really mature and wise and comforting to say to you right now and I'm damned if I can think of anything.''

''That's okay,'' Sam said, polite and resigned.

''Well, it shouldn't be,'' Nora insisted. ''Do you mind talking about it? Because I think we should. It's too easy to let sad, dark thoughts get trapped inside of you until they turn into a sort of barrier, a cloud that turns everything around you dark.'' The cloud, Nora thought, had been wrapping itself around her ever since Simon's call.

Sam didn't answer and Nora shot a quick, frowning glance at her. The girl had slumped further down in her seat, head turned away now toward the side window.

''Sam . . .'' Nora started again when the girl abruptly stiffened, shot up straight and rigid, staring blindly ahead, hands in fists at her hips. Her voice rang out like Cassandra pronouncing the fate of Troy.

''He was torn apart! Torn in pieces and they'll never be able to put him back together again and things will keep happening and happening and everybody's going to die!''

Sam gasped and panted like a marathon runner, then collapsed in her seat. Her hands suddenly cold on the steering wheel, Nora edged the car over to the curb, put it in Park, then turned to Sam without any idea of how to reassure the girl.

''Everything's going to be all right, Sam,'' Nora fell back on. ''I know what happened to Ted was terrible, but it's over now. Nothing else is going to happen. The police will catch whoever did it.'' Please God, Nora added silently, let them catch him soon.

Sam's lower lip jutted out and she reached a finger forward to draw a small circle in the light coat of dust on Nora's dashboard.

''The cops came this morning.'' She crossed the circle with a line. ''They wanted to talk to my mom

about . . . about him. But she threw them out." Sam
looked at the tip of her finger, then used it to push her
glasses up her nose.

"Kate threw them out?" Nora echoed.

Sam nodded, chin bumping her chest. She sat up
and turned to regard Nora. "She got real mad. You
know how Mom is. But they said they'd be back."

Nora could picture it. Kate's temper. When Nora
had first known Kate in their college years she had
sometimes envied her capacity for sudden rage and
drama. It had seemed so poetic, that passionate intensity. What she didn't envy were the tears and depression that always followed. In the last few years, the
always available well of anger had seemed to be
sealed off, tightly contained behind sharp movements
and hard grins that someone who didn't know Kate
might interpret as friendly.

In a way Nora was glad that Kate had let loose of the
iron control enough to get furious. But even if that
meant antagonizing the police?

"She was hysterical," Sam explained matter-of-
factly, "but she calmed down again."

Nora hadn't seen Kate when she arrived to pick up
Sam. The girl had been sitting on the front stoop
waiting for her. Self-contained, arms tightly wrapped
around her knees, Sam had looked deserted and as
forlorn as the house itself perched at the top of its own
small hill. Rambling, two stories, peeling paint that
was once white and now a soft, weathered gray, Kate
Hall's rented house was now a sad shadow of lost
grace. The wraparound porch looked almost ready to
collapse, and the lawn, Nora noticed, needed mowing
again.

When Nora had pulled her battered green Datsun
up to Kate's house, Sam had already jumped to her
feet. She reached for the passenger door before the
car had fully stopped and climbed in without a
greeting.

"She said she's sorry," Sam had recited staring out the front window. "She doesn't want to talk to you right now." No question of who "she" was. Kate had thoroughly withdrawn. With a small surge of guilt, Nora had been relieved to postpone seeing Kate until later. Now she wondered if she shouldn't insist on going back to make sure Kate was all right.

Sam seemed to guess the direction Nora's thoughts were taking. Offhand, like a mother talking about her petulant teenager, Sam now announced, "She'll be all right." She bounced impatiently. "Hey, do you think we could do something about breakfast? I'm starving."

"So am I," Nora suddenly realized. "Pancake house?"

When Sam agreed, Nora pulled the Datsun back onto the quiet street. They drove in silence through pockets of bright hot sunlight and pools of shade. On the cracked sidewalks small children peddled dusty, dented bigwheelers up and down and a few students in shorts and tank tops ambled in the direction of downtown and the river.

"Tell me what happened when the police came," Nora suggested as she and Sam were finally settled in the family-style pancake and waffle house. They had both ordered enormous breakfasts and Nora sipped a cup of coffee heavily loaded with cream and sugar.

Sam was examining the packets of sugar printed with pictures of state birds and flowers. She shrugged and pushed the packets into a pile.

"I was having this dream and the doorbell woke me up," she said. Nora hoped urging Sam to talk about it was truly as much for the girl's sake as for her own. Sam told her story without emotion, like talking about a boring day at school.

Knowing that Kate could sleep through nearly anything, Sam had put on a robe and gone down to answer the door on the third ring. It was about 6:30

and she couldn't imagine who it would be. There had
been two uniformed policemen, deputies from the
sheriff's department. They had refused to speak to
Sam, asking firmly but gently to speak to her mother.
Nora could imagine how they felt, faced with small,
earnest Sam in her pink chenille bathrobe, blinking
solemn and wide-eyed at them from behind
enormous glasses and tousled bangs.

With repeated shaking Sam finally had managed to
awaken Kate. She'd never enter the bedroom when
Ted was there, but he'd left the day before. To visit
friends in Bloomington, he said. Kate's face, Sam told
Nora, "looked funny" when the girl told her the
sheriff's deputies were downstairs.

Curious, and not knowing what else to do, Sam had
stood on the stairs halfway down, listening.

While the sheriff's deputies told Kate that Ted's
body had been found early that morning on the banks
of the Black River, she stood frozen. He was dead,
they told her, and appeared to be the victim of foul
play. Then one of the cops had asked her what her
relationship was to the dead man. That's when Kate
went berserk.

"She just flipped," Sam reported coolly. "She
started hitting the cop and screaming at him. Swearing, all kinds of stuff. They grabbed her and tried to
calm her down, but it didn't do any good. Then, when
one guy said he was going to call an ambulance and
have her taken to the hospital, she just stopped all of a
sudden."

She'd be all right, Kate had told the deputies,
abruptly calm, but they eyed her suspiciously. "Like
she was crazy or something," Sam said. When she
insisted she was fine the deputies followed her into
the kitchen. Sam heard water running and the
murmur of conversation. She had moved a few steps
farther down the stairs when her mother and the
deputies returned. Kate had stopped crying. She was

smoking a cigarette and telling them that she'd call her own doctor for "something." She'd talk to them later, Kate kept insisting. Come back later, Kate had said, turning a pointed look at Sam. The deputies followed her gaze, looking embarrassed as Sam stared back at them, then turned to Kate, nodding reluctantly.

"They'd be back, they told Kate, later.

"I'm sorry, kiddo," Nora told Sam when she finally finished. Nora reached across the table to lay a hand across one of Sam's tightly clenched fists.

Sam jerked her hand away. "I'm not!" She glared at Nora. "I'm glad he's gone. He was a creep. A rotten creep."

"Sam, you don't mean that!" They hadn't been close, Sam and Ted Kellogg, but Nora never thought there had been bad feelings between them. It must be shock, Nora reasoned. Anger at Ted for dying. Blaming Ted was easier than accepting the ugly fact of murder.

"Honey . . ." but the girl cut her off.

"I don't want to talk about it any more, okay?" Sam challenged. Her face shone pink with anger and stifled panic.

Nora looked at the tense lines of the girl's thin shoulders, drawn high and square like Kate's before rage.

"Okay," she said gently, meeting Sam's glare. "We'll leave it alone." For now, she added silently to herself.

The waitress, arriving with their breakfast, broke the moment's silence with the clatter of heavy plates shoved across the Formica table between them.

They ate in silent concentration. A few times Nora tried to start a conversation on safe topics, but Sam politely discouraged her with short answers. Nora finally got the message.

Only once during that day did Sam show any

emotion again. They had gone for a walk through the
large city park to the new art museum on the banks of
the river. Inside the museum they stopped to sit on a
low stone bench in front of a murky abstract painting.
It was a break more to rest their feet than to admire
the painting. On the massive canvas in front of them,
tortured faces, half-formed, were tangled in dizzy
swirls of deep reds, browns and tainted greens.

"Ugh," Sam said when they stopped in front of it
and Nora agreed, but it was the only unoccupied
bench in the air-conditioned gallery. They sank grate-
fully onto the cool bench with eyes averted from the
painting's silent screams, watching the few other
people who had taken refuge from the afternoon heat.

Nora felt the air subtly change as, beside her, Sam
suddenly stiffened. She didn't move. She didn't make
a sound, but tension shimmered from her taut body
like waves of cold.

Nora turned to find the girl transfixed, eyes pinned
to a spot on the bench. She followed the line of Sam's
sight to find a small white spider poised, almost invisible, on the gray stone bench. It had the pale,
unhealthy look of things that lived underground. Its
tiny legs cut strong, sharp angles, still as sculpture,
nearly transparent.

The spider lifted its delicate legs and moved a few
elegant steps closer to Sam.

The girl's breathing was audible now, coming in
dry and trembling gasps as though she were drowning
slowly in a vacuum. She didn't blink.

Nora looked at her, then back to the spider. With a
suppressed   shudder   she   reached   forward   and
brushed it lightly off the bench.

"Aargh," she said to break the spell. "I realize
spiders are great for the environment, sound ecologi-
cal bug control, but they give me the creeps. Somehow they seem so intelligent." She watched Sam
curiously as the girl blinked, took a deep breath and

shook her shoulders free of tension. She looked at Nora with something like an appeal, began to say something, then shut her mouth on it. Nora waited, but Sam's eyes fled back to her hands clenched in her lap.

"Well," Nora said and stood up.

Sam nervously scanned the floor, then jumped to her feet.

"Can we go to a movie or something?"

"Sure," Nora agreed. "Air-conditioning, buttered popcorn and a chocolate bar, coming up."

By unspoken mutual consent they avoided movies with any hint of violence. And movies with impossibly happy families. They finally settled on a mild comedy about a group of high school misfits who manage to triumph over the "popular crowd" and come into their own with goofy grace.

When the lights came up at the happy ending, Nora was swamped in tears. Sam was stony-faced.

It was nearly 5:00 when the movie let out and Nora decided it was time to take Sam home.

Time for both of them to face Kate.

2

A dented, dull white 1976 Chevy sprawled at the curb in front of Kate's house when Nora and Sam pulled up. Charlie Luther's car. Sam marched around it, head in the air, and Nora glanced curiously inside at the back seat littered with empty beer cans, crumpled wrappings from fast food burgers and fries, battered sections of two by fours, odd pieces of pipe and old clothes.

Sam strode quickly up the front walk and the screen door banged behind her as Nora trotted up the porch steps. Once inside, the girl disappeared up the stairs and Nora stood in the entryway feeling abandoned. Kate and Charlie Luther silently sat in the living room, each in a separate world, while a Mahler symphony ebbed, mournful and scratchy, around them.

The room was crowded with furniture—overstuffed, sagging nylon armchairs, a plump couch in faded blue corduroy, mismatched coffee and side tables piled high with magazines, newspapers, paperbacks, beer cans and overflowing ashtrays. Bookshelves lined the walls, some being metal utility shelves, others elaborate piles of bricks and boards. Worn paperbacks and torn hardcover books spilled from the shelves along with rocks and bottles of sea shells. Tattered art prints, posters, and watercolors and pastels by both Sam and Kate were tacked in confusion over the faded flowered wallpaper.

Kate sat in a high-backed rocking chair under a tarnished brass floor lamp with a red scarf draped over its paper shade. Her disheveled red hair shone in bright contrast, the curls and waves caught in tortured formations around her pale face. Bruised blue shadows smudged Kate's closed eyelids and her long lashes cast delicate shadows on her childlike cheeks. She wore an old blue chenille robe loosely closed over a floor length cotton nightgown. One hand lay limp and defenseless in her lap while a cigarette burned close to her knuckles. The other hung casually around the neck of a half-empty bottle of tequila propped on the rocker's seat. Kate's head lolled against the afghan hung on the rocker's back as she swayed the chair forward and back in time to Mahler's heavy cadence.

Charlie Luther sprawled on the floor in front of her, head propped on a pile of cushions taken from the couch. He was small and slight with a child's thin, strawberry blond hair and pale, freckled skin marked with a complex tracery of faint creases and wrinkles. Faded T-shirt and torn jeans completed the picture. Nora had never seen him wear anything else. His pale eyes were closed behind wire rim glasses, and he seemed to be gently asleep.

Neither Kate nor Charlie stirred when Nora stepped into the room.

"Jesus, Kate," Nora breathed, surveying the chaos. She moved forward again when the long ash of Kate's cigarette fell into her lap. "Kate," she said more loudly, stepping carefully over debris towards the rocker.

Kate's eyes opened and she blinked rapidly unfocused, lost in her own living room until she centered on Nora. Like a French mime her face was

distorted in silence, mouth stretching open, corners
drawn down to crease her cheeks, eyes squeezing to
slits, eyebrows fleeing up. Nora reached her, took the
cigarette and bottle from her loose hold and went
down on one knee in front of the rocker. They hugged
in fierce silence until Kate abruptly pulled away,
throwing herself back against the rocker. Nora leaned
back on her heels as Kate started driving the rocker in
a hard, steady rhythm, scrubbing tears from her face
with quick, rough movements.

"So," she said brusquely. She reached down and
picked up the bottle of tequila, held it up to eye the
level of liquid and took a straight swig. Then she held
the bottle toward Nora and cocked her head.

Nora shook her head and stood up, still silent,
waiting.

"So you're back," Kate announced. "There's still
some beer left, I think. In the kitchen."

"No thanks." She shook her head again and raised
an eyebrow. "What the hell are you doing to
yourself?"

"Obliterating," Kate enunciated carefully. "I am
working on obliteration." One side of her mouth
curled up in what could have been a smile or a smirk.

"Hey . . . Nora!" Luther spoke suddenly from the
floor. "*Qué pasa?*"

"Hello, Charlie," Nora said coolly. Ordinarily she
didn't dislike Charlie. He was harmless, occasionally
pathetic, occasionally entertaining. He spent most of
his life high on something. An old friend of Ted's, he
had adopted Kate and Sam as a homeless stray dog
would adopt a family.

"Where's the kid?" Charlie asked peering around
the room as though Sam were hidden somewhere in
the chaos.

"Upstairs." Nora turned back to Kate. "Kate, don't
you think you ought to get dressed?"

Kate glanced down at herself in mock surprise.

"Why?" she pulled the front of the robe more tightly around her. "Everything's covered. Right, Charlie?"

"Take a nice hot shower and we'll do something about dinner. You'll feel better."

"What the hell do you know about how I feel?" Kate snapped.

Nora stared steadily down at her.

"Oh, okay. What the hell." Kate sketched a salute to Nora with the bottle of tequila then carefully lowered it to the floor. She stood up cautiously, leaning on the swaying arm of the rocker for support like a passenger on a small boat in a rough sea. Standing straight was a small triumph. She took an unsteady step forward, then gained momentum and moved towards the stairs as Nora watched.

Kate stopped at the door to the living room and turned.

"Don't leave, okay?"

"I'll be here," Nora answered.

She and Luther watched as Kate slowly climbed the stairs, hand over hand on the railing. Charlie swung up to sit cross-legged and reached for a cigarette.

"She just can't take this shit," he muttered at Nora's back.

Nora turned to look at him, lips pressed closed against a quick reply. Charlie's thin fingers trembled as he lit his cigarette. The narrow shoulders drooped, curling protectively around his chest.

As far as Nora knew, Ted had been Luther's only friend. Charlie knew a lot of people, but few of them seemed to tolerate him the way Ted had. Nora had always thought Ted allowed Charlie to follow at his heels like an anxious dog because it boosted Ted's ego. She always defended Ted to Simon for Kate's sake, but Nora allowed herself to realize now that she had never thought much of Ted herself.

Kate's stubborn vision of Ted painted him as a tortured artist, a brilliant, angry writer too impatient and too sensitive to play the games of a trivial world, a world that conspired to keep him down.

He was, Nora thought, a parasite with bitter illusions of talent. And Charlie Luther was his loyal, spaced-out shadow.

Nora's eyes drifted from the empty stairs to Charlie's back where his pointed shoulder blades angled against his shirt. He started to turn towards her and she quickly looked away, not wanting to meet his eyes. Instead, she began to do the only thing she could to put order back into the universe. Tidy up.

Nora reached for an overflowing ashtray and a cloud of ash flew up while two crushed butts, smoked down to the filter, tumbled onto the floor. Behind her Charlie Luther scrambled to his feet.

"Hey, Luther's Handy-Dandy Clean-Fucking-Up Service is on the move!" Charlie announced and disappeared into the kitchen.

He returned moments later with a brown grocery sack and Nora emptied the ashtray into it. For minutes then they circled the room emptying ashtrays, picking up beer cans and gathering the scattered pages of a newspaper. It was the afternoon newspaper, the *Stony Cliffs Centurion*, and its headline screamed out the news about Ted's murder. But it was the subhead that caught Nora's attention. *Devil Cult Connection Investigated.*

> "Police are investigating a possible connection between the mutilation-slaying of Ted Kellogg, 36, and the satanic cult led by Victor Sears, 37, a Stony Cliffs man who committed suicide earlier this year.
> "Two witnesses, names withheld by the sheriff's department, stated that Kellogg was a member of the satanic cult which allegedly disbanded after Sears was found dead in his farmhouse home. Deputies discovered Sears' naked

body last May while responding to an anonymous phone tip. The former SCC student had
hanged himself in his loft bedroom.

"Sears' naked body was found hanging from a
black silk rope on which was pinned a quotation
from Aleister Crowley, leader of a European
demonic cult in the 1920s. The note read, 'Do
what thou wilt shall be the whole of the law.'

"Crowley, who called himself the Great Beast
666, was a self-proclaimed magician dubbed by
the popular European press 'the wickedest man
in the world.' Crowley gained notoriety for
founding devil-worshipping cults that used
drugs and bizarre sexual practices to communicate with Satan.

" 'There is no evidence at this time that Sears'
so-called devil cult was involved in the Kellogg
murder,' stated Sheriff Roy Finnerty. 'We're
simply investigating a possible link between
Kellogg and Sears.' "

Nora was suddenly uncomfortably aware that
Charlie Luther stood beside her, studying the newspaper article she clutched in her hand.

"That's such bullshit, man," he exploded as Nora
swung her head to look at him. Charlie bounced
rapidly from foot to foot, twitching his thin shoulders.
He jabbed the paper with his index finger. His fingernail was chewed down to the quick.

"Bullshit," he repeated. "Victor was looking for a
higher state of consciousness. He was a real smart
dude. He had his Ph-fucking-D. in philosphy, right?
Anybody with any brains is looking for something.
Rolfing, TM, EST, yoga. So Victor was into Crowley,
so what? He was a poet. He moved on the astral
plane, see? It was a search for the freedom of the true
self, man, not this voodoo crap."

"You knew Victor Sears?"

Charlie jittered back a step and flicked a squinty
eye at her, then studied the ground. "Everybody

knew Victor. He'd been in S.C. for about a hundred years. Victor always said he was three years older than God." Charlie snickered, then shot a hard look at her. "He was one of those genius kids who go to college at twelve or something. Yeah. I think he was about fifteen when he got here, then he just stayed. *Everybody* knew him," Charlie repeated.

"So Ted knew him?"

"Yeah, yeah, of course." Charlie shifted from foot to foot.

That meant, Nora reasoned, that Kate must have known Victor. But if she had, she'd never mentioned him. A devil cult? It seemed unlikely that even Ted could be involved in something like that, but an esoteric search for the self and "do what thou wilt" would have been the sort of thing that appealed to him. It would have made a great excuse for his failure to find a steady job or to at least finish the Great Novel he'd supposedly been working on for years.

Stop it, Nora chastised herself, you're beginning to sound like Simon.

"But could this cult have had anything to do with what happened to Ted?" Nora persisted.

"There wasn't any cult!" Charlie shouted, snatching the newspaper from her hand. "It's bullshit, man, I'm telling you. It sells papers. The cops like the idea. It's an excuse for them not to work too hard, just an excuse to hassle anybody they don't like or their tiny minds can't figure out!" Charlie's fair face flushed deep red and a twisted vein stood out on his high forehead. He shook the crumpled newspaper in a tightly clenched fist, strangling it, beating the air as he glared at Nora. "Those assholes don't want to find out what really happened to Ted!"

Nora stared back at him as tense silence swelled in the room. Then a quiet voice swung them both around.

"What did really happen to Ted, Charlie?" Kate

said it low and lilting, soft as a rattler's first warning.
"What happened to him?"

3

It was nearly midnight when Nora finally returned to the double she rented. Clapboard, vintage 1920s, it teetered on the shabby edge of disrepair in the unforgiving daylight. But in the night the heavy canopy of trees filtered the streetlamps' blue glare to soft shadows, shifting patterns of light and dark. It was a kinder light, a light that blurred edges and hid flaws.

Patterns of shadow shifted over the sprawling house as the leaves rustled and whispered in the night wind when Nora climbed out of the Datsun. The slam of her car door jarred the stillness of the deserted street and she looked around guiltily. Up and down the street few lights still burned. Her own half of the house was dark, and so was the half inhabited by Mrs. Roberts, her landlady. Mrs. Roberts had been gone for nearly a week, off recuperating in parts unknown with unspecified health problems. She had warned Nora to expect frequent absences. Mrs. Roberts had swiftly accepted her as a tenant, snatching her up like a robin seizing a worm, when she might have rented the three-bedroom place to a group of students for a much higher monthly sum. Instead she wanted someone who'd look after the place, someone she could count on. "Keeping an eye

open," she called it. Her nephew would be around
occasionally to handle any yard work or repairs.

The nephew was overdue, Nora thought as she
walked toward her front stoop. The lawn was nearly
as shaggy as Kate's untended patch. Dandelions
glowed in the shadowy lawn and, seen closer, the
house had a wistful, neglected air. Nora's footsteps on
the walk sounded too loud, calling too much attention
to her in the still night. The only other sounds on the
deserted street were the high-pitched sawing of
crickets and the metallic whir of cicadas, the sound
rising and falling like a tide. Night breathed around
her like a sleeper about to wake.

At the dark front door Nora fumbled with her keys,
casting quick looks over her shoulder. She had the
uncomfortable feeling she was being watched, but no
one was in sight.

This time last night, she thought, Ted Kellogg was
still alive.

Nora gave a quick shiver, snapped the key in the
lock and shoved the door open. She closed it firmly
behind her. Once inside the deeper dark of the living
room she had to pause and wait for her eyes to adjust.

Despite her best intentions, she still hadn't fully
unpacked, and boxes and odd pieces of furniture
dotted the room in a changing pattern. More chaos.
The room was uncommitted, unfamiliar. Black
shapes loomed up in the shadows, unidentifiable. She
found herself listening hard to the closed space,
spooked by the feeling that she wasn't alone.

"You're scaring yourself, you idiot," she said aloud
and took a tentative step forward. Then she gasped,
heart and stomach lurching to her throat. In the far
corner of the room a sullen red spot of light flashed at
her. She let out her breath, remembering it was only
the answering machine. She must have a message
waiting.

Uncertain in the dark, Nora moved cautiously,

gingerly feeling her way. She stuck out a hand, barely able to see it in the dark, feeling for a lamp across the room on the table near the couch. The skin on her bare arm prickled in the cool night air, anticipating a touch. She jumped when her hand finally brushed the pleated shade and grabbed at the lamp as she almost overturned it.

Light. She squinted against it as it flooded the room and glowed down into the lamp's glass base full of sea shells. Curves and scallops of soft pink, sea-washed white, deep browns and grays caught the light. Once upon a time, Nora thought, she knew what beach each shell was gathered on—the islands off Florida, Washington State, British Columbia, North Carolina, Maine. Now, they all blended together in a confused mosaic, like the rest of her past.

"Oh, shut up," she snapped at herself. Then she smirked. "You're going to have to stop talking to yourself," she said, earnestly addressing the lamp.

Nora looked around the rest of the room and frowned. In its own way the place looked as bad as Kate's had. She wouldn't sleep for hours, Nora reasoned, so she ought to try and make the place a little more livable. But first she wanted a glass of wine.

On principle she'd refused to drink anything at Kate's. It had been a long, uncomfortable evening. Most of the time Nora had taken refuge in cleaning, making soup and sandwiches for Kate, Charlie, herself and Sam, who'd finally, silently, come downstairs. Then, while Kate rocked and rocked, eyes closed and distant, the rest of them had played an endless, grim game of Scrabble.

Ted's name was never mentioned.

Nora moved through her living room turning on every light, fighting the dark and the creeping, nagging feeling that something or someone else was there. She moved through the dining room, turning up the dimmer, and on to the kitchen, flipping the switch for the overhead light. Nothing. Silly, she jeered at herself.

Every light downstairs was blazing when Nora crossed back to the living room, a generous glass of white wine in hand.

There was a lot of tape to rewind on the answering machine. That meant a lot of messages. I'm so popular, she preened, mocking because she couldn't imagine who would call her. Kate was the only friend she had in Stony Cliffs. She shrugged and pressed 'Play.'

"Beep . . . This is Dr. Ellicott. Please telephone my office. I'd like to speak to you regarding your class plans." Oh nuts, Nora grimaced. Stiff and formally old-fashioned, Dr. Ellicott was the head of her new department and made Nora feel, in the few times she'd talked to him, about as professional and competent as a gangly twelve year old. The top of his short-cropped white head barely reached her chin and she imagined he resented her tallness. Besides, her class plans were still vague and unsettled.

"Beep . . . Miss Durant, this is Sheriff Finnerty. I'm calling about the murder of Ted Kellogg. We'd very much like to talk to you so I'd appreciate it if you'd give me a call as soon as possible. The number's 699-9000. We can use your cooperation on this." Of course they'd want to talk to her. In the back of her mind, Nora had expected all along to hear from the police, but she'd pushed the thought away. They'd want to talk to her because she'd known Kate and Ted for years. What could she tell them? Nothing, as far as she knew. Certainly nothing about Victor Sears or the so-called devil cult. Damn.

"Beep . . . Nora, this is Simon. I want you to call me. Call collect. That way, you won't have an excuse not to call. If you don't call I'm simply going to have to call you again, so why don't you just make it easier on both of us.

You know I just want what's best for you.'' Good old
Simon, it's probably driving him crazy not being here
to tell everybody what to do. Nora took a deep
swallow of wine.

"Beep . . .'' A long hollow silence followed the tone
and Nora reached for the Stop button. Her finger was
an inch away from it when a man's voice breathed
her name.

"Nora . . .''

Her hand flinched back from the machine and she
waited, listening for more. But that was all. Just her
name in a stranger's voice that rolled melodically
with the careful shaping of his lips, as though he held
her name on his tongue, tasting and sampling the feel
of it. She felt suddenly cold and watched again.
Frowning, she backed the tape up to hear the voice
again.

'' . . . what's best for you. Beep . . .''

Only silence followed Simon's message. Nora
waited, puzzled, and turned up the volume on the hiss
of blank tape. She rewound the tape, listened through
the whole of Simon's message and waited. Again, the
tone of the machine. Then only silence.

"Swear to God, Finnerty, the hair on the back of my
neck stood up. Hell, I never used to believe that.''
Deputy Vern Snider shook his head in wonder.
"Damned if it didn't, though. Real slow like. Just
crawled right up my neck when I saw what was left of
that guy. Thought I was gonna puke. You ever seen
anything like that?''

Vern and Finnerty sat in an unmarked patrol car
parked half a block down from Kate's house where a
single light burned in the living room.

Finnerty grunted a noncommittal reply. Vern
whistled to himself between his teeth.

Sheriff Finnerty was big. It wasn't so much that he
was tall, although he was a little taller than average. It

was his dense stillness that made him seem big as a
tree. You got the feeling things would bounce off him
—boulder, bullets, hard words. Yet he could move
with quiet grace. You never heard Finnerty coming,
and that was one thing that kept all his men on their
toes.

His hair was chestnut, shot with gray and closely
cropped to keep it from curling. His gray eyes looked
sleepy, but they never missed much.

"Sheriff? You ever seen anything like that guy?"
Vern persisted.

Finnerty grunted again, a negative this time. One
big fist rested on the steering wheel, solid and
smooth-carved, seeming as all of a piece as a wooden
Indian's. He slowly straightened his fingers, staring
out at the night. Vern fidgeted beside him in the
passenger seat, not daunted by Finnerty's silence.
Finnerty was mostly quiet.

Not Vern, though. Vern had a ready tongue born in
him like his red farmer's tan. He was medium height,
skin tight on his bones, with big elbows, big, raw
knuckles, and a thin-bladed beak of a nose with high
curving nostrils. Vern's dark hair was always well-
greased and his sideburns were at least half an inch
longer than regulations permitted, but Finnerty
usually let it go without comment. When Vern really
got on his nerves, Finnerty could usually shut him up
by telling him to do something about his redneck
cheek fuzz.

"I never seen anything like it, not even in Nam.
Him all neatly laid out like on a cross. But with his
guts all ripped up and his hands and feet . . . Jesus!"
Snider had said it all before half a dozen times or
more since they'd been called in the night before.

Although he wouldn't admit it to Vern, Finnerty's
hair, too, had prickled and risen on the back of his
neck. The worst, most bizarre touch in the mutilation
murder was what the killer did with Kellogg's hands

and feet. They were severed, roughly torn at the ankles and wrists. Kellogg's midsection had been torn open from crotch to throat, the breastbone split like a chicken's, and from the gaping wound protruded his bloody hands, outstretched as though in supplication. His wrists were wedged into his open chest. And his feet were still in heavy workboots. The toes of his boots were buried in the wet tangle of intestines with the stumps of his ankles resting gently on his hips. His balls and penis were neatly sliced off and lay on the ground between his legs. Kellogg's tongue was cut off far back in his throat. So far, there'd been no sign of it, either discarded at the site or hidden in Kellogg's entrails.

Finnerty hadn't been able yet to talk with the two kids who found the body. The girl was hospitalized under heavy sedation. She was a student at SCC from out of state and her parents had flown in to be with her. She was suffering from shock and her parents refused to let Finnerty talk with her, the girl's doctor backing them up. The boy was local, at home now with his family but under a doctor's care. The kid had taken to his room and refused to talk with anyone. His parents thought it was just a matter of time. He'd be better real soon, his parents insisted. Finnerty wasn't counting on it. Besides, he didn't think the kids would be able to tell him much.

Like kids had been doing for years in Stony Cliffs, they'd hit the bars, drinking until closing, then picked up a six-pack and headed off for a private picnic in the woods. It was just their bad luck the spot they picked was already occupied. By Kellogg.

"You are one hell of a cold bastard, Finnerty," Vern started in again. "Don't it at least give you the creeps to think about what happened to that guy?"

"Vern," Finnerty said, low and distinct, "it scares the shit out of me. Now, will you just shut up for a while?"

Vern raised his eyebrows and pursed his lips in a
silent whistle. In fifteen years in the department with
Roy Finnerty, Vern had never seen him shaken, never
seen him shocked or even surprised. If Finnerty was
scared, anything was possible. He furrowed his brow,
rolled the news around in his mind a few minutes.

"Sheriff, you really think this Luther character did
it?"

Finnerty gave a sharp snort. "Vern, you don't know
shit from shinola, do you?"

Vern kept his mouth shut. If Luther wasn't a
suspect, why were they sitting out here watching for
him?

A soft rustling sound from the shadows caught
Vern's attention. It came from the crest of the short
hill that formed the front yard of the old home they
parked near. An overgrown lilac loomed at the top of
the hill and something dark moved in the shadows
that pooled at its base. Vern twisted around, trying to
see it better, feeling a chill tease lightly along the
length of his spine.

The dark shape moved to the top of the hill, to the
edge of the shadow. Vern's face cleared. It was a dog,
a big, black mutt, massive as a Lab, sleek and short-
haired.

"Hey, fella," Vern called softly into the night's
quiet. "Hey, dog, c'mere." He reached an arm out of
the open car window and snapped his fingers.

Finnerty glanced over at him and shook his head.

"Pup. Hey, pup." Vern gave a low, coaxing whistle.

The dog glided down the hill, smooth as a cat. He
stopped on the sidewalk, measuring the car with cool
eyes green as a spring leaf catching the morning sun.
He turned his head up toward Vern, nodding and
grinning, and his eyes flashed flat gold in the dim
angled light.

"That's a boy," Vern encouraged.

The dog moved closer, light on his feet, deliberate.
He stopped a yard from Vern's outstretched fingers.

Vern looked into the dog's eyes and his grin slid down
his cheeks. He had that instant, odd loss of time you
get looking down from a tall building. A slow shudder
started at the base of Vern's spine. He tore his eyes
away and shot a look at Finnerty, but the sheriff's
eyes were closed, head back and resting on the seat.

Vern looked back at the dog who watched him
steadily, then paced to the back of the car. The dog
raised his leg and shot a golden stream at the car's
rear tire.

Before Vern could react he disappeared around
behind the back end.

"Hey," Vern blustered. "Well . . . goddamn."

Finnerty cracked one eye and looked sideways at
the deputy. Vern was sitting quiet, looking straight
ahead, then he tensed, attention on the street.
Finnerty followed his stare. Charlie Luther was
leaving Kate Hall's house.

"Time to get on it," Finnerty said.

Kate closed the door slowly behind Charlie. She
leaned her forehead against it, breathing deep, eyes
closed, the palms of both hands pressed flat and tight
against the smooth painted wood.

"Ted," she said once, softly.

"Hey, Mom."

Kate swung around at the sound. Sam stood at the
top of the stairs in a floor length nightgown Kate had
made for her. Tortoises and hares chased each other
over its surface in random profusion.

"There's a spider in my room." Sam said it with a
bright, defiant lilt. It took Kate a moment to realize
that Sam must be afraid of it. She wanted Kate to
take care of it, but hesitated to show that kind of
weakness. Sam hated to act "like a kid." She'd never
been frightened by bugs before, but if she were
frightened by anything at all now, Kate couldn't
blame her.

"Okay," she finally called back. "I'm on my way

up to bed. Let me just turn out the lights down here and I'll be right with you.''

Poor kid, Kate thought, turning off the lights. And she's got me as a mother. Poor kid.

When Kate got to Sam's room the spider was gone. They checked, gingerly, to see if it was hidden somewhere on the bed, under it or on the wall nearby. There was no sign of it.

Nora woke late the next morning with a dull headache. She had spent hours the night before unpacking and sorting boxes of books, papers, photocopies of articles, back issues of magazines, research for the articles, books and other things she hadn't yet written, and scant copies of the few things she had managed to see through to publication.

She always had ideas for things to write. Ideas fascinated her like bright bits of colored glass. She'd pick them up, one at a time, and turn them over, examining them to see how they caught the light, how they colored the world. Then another fragment would catch her attention with a hint of undiscovered answers. She'd discard the piece she held without thinking and reach for something new while the debris of past discoveries piled up around her.

Like the ghost of Jacob Marley, she'd thought the night before, I'm doomed to drag around my own chain, forged link by link with my own hands. He dragged around ledgers, bills, and cash boxes. I drag around notebooks full of scribblings on the standing stones of Cornwall, Arthurian legend, and archetypes in myth. Not, as Simons is fond of pointing out, practical.

Still, she mused that morning, head buried under her pillow, it pays the rent sometimes.

Stony Cliffs College was dedicated to the liberal arts and humanities in the broadest sense of the word. According to Simon, who could always be counted on to be overwhelmingly practical, SCC was a mecca for crackpots and a haven for students with no particular skills or ambitions—students whose parents were happy to foot the bills for Johnny or Susie to get any college degree.

Nora defended the place to him and, occasionally, to herself on the idealistic grounds that pure knowledge has value in itself. She didn't tell Simon that one of the other teachers in her department taught a course called "Peripheral Fiction: Pornography and Comic Books." She didn't tell Simon a lot of things. And she was dreading having to call him back.

He would, of course, want to know how things stood in Stony Cliffs. How Kate was taking Ted's death, for one thing. Kate, Nora and Simon had all met in college and Simon had actually dated Kate first, a short summer fling that had ended abruptly, but on friendly terms, when Simon switched his attentions to Nora. Back then, Simon had been an eager idealist, romantic and ready to change the world for the better. All three of them had been wide-eyed innocents, eager for adventure, for passion, poetry and learning the fine art of living. That was before Kate had started drinking, married and divorced twice and settled in with Ted Kellogg, before Simon let ambition reshape his values, before he developed a sneering contempt for most of the rest of the world—and before Nora started drifting.

This is going to be home, Nora told herself. This is where all the pieces come together. Like the course she'd be teaching.

Dr. Ellicott had accepted her proposal for a course based on a multidisciplinary synthesis. She'd be teaching a class that would look for connections between archetypes in folklore, myth and fairy tales from half a hundred sources, times and cultures from ancient Persia to medieval England. Everybody wanted heroes. Everybody knew who the bad guys were and how to tell good from evil. The war between darkness and light raged on a thousand battlefields—

in the cave of the Cyclops, in Sherwood Forest, at Midgard and the gingerbread house of a witch.

It all seemed so simple, the dark against the light, with no confusing grays in-between. And the light would always win while the prince and princess lived happily ever after. The surety she couldn't count on in her own life, people had been dreaming of since history began.

Tying all the pieces together made an ambitious project. Ideas crashed over her like waves and she woke in the middle of the night sometimes with sudden insights and jotted down frantic notes. Other times she jolted awake in a cold sweat, close to panic and wanting nothing but to forget the whole thing.

She'd signed a contract, though, and made a commitment, and she planned to stick to it. It was some comfort that, besides the course she would design, Nora would teach a basic writing course. Nothing fancy, just how to string words together to make sense. It seemed a great many of the students searching after pure knowledge had problems simply putting nouns and verbs together and making coherent paragraphs. They couldn't spell either. Simon had snickered at that but, for once, let it ride.

Nora was doing her best to ignore the daylight when her phone rang. It was Sheriff Finnerty reminding her with a careful touch of reproach that he had left a message for her the day before.

"I'm sorry I haven't gotten back to you," Nora apologized. "It was late when I got in and I'm not actually up yet. Besides," she challenged, "I'm not sure there's really anything I can tell you."

"Why don't you let me decide that? Can you be at my office about noon?" Finnerty asked with weary patience.

Nora agreed. There didn't seem to be any way to avoid it.

She replaced the receiver slowly. Where, in the battle of light and dark, did Ted Kellogg belong?

4

Nora arrived at Finnerty's office a full fifteen minutes early after changing clothes twice. What was the proper attire for police interrogation? She settled on simple white cotton slacks and an embroidered white on white Indian blouse bought in a London flea market.

Like a sacrificial virgin at some Aztec rite, she thought, climbing the broad limestone steps to the sheriff's headquarters.

The deputy at the front desk eyed her like the maitre d' at an exclusive restaurant sizing up an unsavory customer.

Officious little twit, she thought as he led her to Finnerty's office. He reminded her of her Aunt Charlotte.

"Since you're early," he informed her, "you'll have to wait until the sheriff can see you."

A small waiting area outside Finnerty's office held two worn plastic chairs. Nora lowered herself into one of them. The other was occupied by a man in his early thirties who watched her with appreciative interest.

Nora felt her face growing slowly warmer as she met his eyes. She liked his looks—thick, dark brown hair a little on the long side, high, broad cheekbones, soft green eyes with long lashes and deep laugh lines. He was wearing pressed blue jeans, a crisp white shirt and a tan corduroy jacket.

"Looks like Finnerty's really stacking up the witnesses," he said, leaning back and crossing his arms on his chest. One corner of his mouth crept up. "Either he's busy making startling discoveries or this is a ploy designed to make us stew in our juices, meditate on our transgressions and spill the beans before he has to resort to hot lights and rubber hoses."

Nora laughed and shook her head. "I hate to ruin your theory, but I think I'm just early. I decided I'd rather sit here and be nervous than stay home and be nervous."

"Ah," he sighed, "I suppose I may have judged Finnerty too harshly, although that is his style. But I'm glad you enlightened me. Otherwise I might have had to be grateful to the sheriff for providing me with someone to talk to while I brood on my sins. I, by the way, am Michael Justin." He leaned across the narrow space, arm outstretched for a handshake.

Nora extended her own hand. "Nora Durant."

His hand was warm, dry and firm, and his touch sent a small shock up Nora's arm that landed with a half-pleasurable, half-fearful jolt in the pit of her stomach.

Oh, stop, she admonished herself, feeling all of 12. She barely restrained herself from checking his left hand for a ring.

"Nora." Michael Justin tried the sound of it, and for a passing instant Nora was reminded of the voice on her answering maching. Her name had been spoken once, then, she had decided, somehow erased by a malfunction of the machine.

He asked a question that gave her a different kind of jolt.

"Was Ted Kellogg a friend of yours?"

She found it oddly difficult to answer honestly.

"Not exactly, although I suppose I should say yes. I've known him for a few years. He was living with a very close friend of mine so I knew Ted, but not really very well. I haven't seen much of them in the last few years."

"Kate Hall."

"Yes. You know Kate?" Kate had never mentioned Michael Justin, but Nora was beginning to realize that there was a lot about Kate's life with Ted Kellogg that she knew nothing about.

"We'd met a few times, Kate and Ted and I, but I can't say I knew them well. We shared a mutual acquaintance. Finnerty, in his inimitable way, has invited me here to beat a dead horse."

Nora raised her eyebrows and made a restrained inquiring face.

Michael Justin snorted. "It's this nonsense about the so-called devil cult. Victor Sears was my half-brother."

"Oh." Nora looked hard at her lap. "I'm sorry."

"So am I," he said abruptly. "Oh, don't worry, you haven't trodden on painful territory. Victor and I shared the same mother, but that was about the extent of it. He was a few years older than I and we never connected much. He was always busy being a genius. I was bright, but not in Victor's league, thank God. We went to different schools, had different friends, different lives, never had much to say to each other on the few occasions we did spend time together. We were not, as they say, close." He rocked back in his chair, eyes on the ground, lips pressed tight, silent for a moment. Then he looked up at her with a quick grin.

"Hey, do you always have this effect on people? I'm on the verge of telling you my entire life story and the ups and downs of my family's fortunes. Would you like to hear about my Great-Aunt Gertrude?''

Nora pulled a serious face and leaned towards him.

''Yes,'' she said earnestly.

''Ha! Serves me right!'' He looked openly delighted and Nora felt her face grow hot again. She smiled back at him.

''What are you doing at the Inquisition?'' Michael asked. But before Nora had a chance to answer, Finnerty's door crashed open.

A woman who looked vaguely familiar to Nora stood in the doorway, her back turned to them.

''Up. Yours.'' She pronounced it succinctly and swirled on her heels with a flourish, taking two long steps with her head high before she did a double take at Michael and stopped abruptly in front of him. One hip was slung out, blonde head cocked to one side like The Other Woman in a Bette Davis movie.

Carole Salant, Nora remembered. She was a friend of Ted's and, Nora supposed, of Kate's. A sliver of profile was turned toward Nora, revealing a strikingly lovely face with the pink and white prettiness of a china doll. But her dark eyes, almost black, shiny as jet, were disconcerting in the delicate face. Her neck was long and slender as a ballet dancer's, a startling contrast to her bloated body, puffy flesh too generous for her small bones.

''Well, well,'' she crooned down at Michael.

He looked up at her, Nora thought, like Tweetie safely in his cage batting his eyelashes at Sylvester. ''Not getting along with the sheriff?'' His tone was dry and coolly amused.

''They're such a bunch of assholes,'' she said. ''Victor, again. Is that what you're doing here?''

Michael nodded once, sharply.

Nora looked curiously from him to Carole Salant and back again. He didn't like her, that seemed clear. But was there something else? The air between them seemed heavily charged as if they were playing some game she couldn't quite follow.

Salant's hip jutted out another two inches like a hash house waitress waiting for an order.

"Of course, you and Victor never did get along. You'd think Finnerty would realize asking you anything about him would be useless. But the world is full of assholes with tiny minds."

Michael leaned back farther in his chair. "I'm sure Finnerty was interested in your . . . opinions. And you and Rick were good friends of Kellogg's, weren't you? The sheriff's certainly practical enough to pursue current affairs."

"What the hell is that supposed to mean?" Salant shifted her weight to the opposite hip, shoving it out and settling into it like a fighter pilot settling into the cockpit.

Michael was all surprise and innocence. "Not a thing."

Carole studied him, bottom lip pouting out.

"You're still damn cute," she finally decided.

It was an exit line and she swung around to leave, but paused again, frowning down at Nora. Nora had quickly dropped her eyes to her lap.

"Hey," Carole narrowed her eyes, "you're that friend of Kate's, aren't you?"

Nora looked up and answered too quickly. "Yes." She felt like she'd been caught eavesdropping. "Nora. Nora Durant."

"Right. So how's Kate? Have you seen her? And the kid, what's-her-name?"

"Sam. They're doing all right. As well as you could expect, I suppose."

"If it was my old man," Salant said, "I'd be drunk on my ass for a week." She started to turn away, dismissing Nora quickly. "Tell her I'll be by sometime," Carole said over her shoulder. "Me and Rick."

The sound of her footsteps faded behind her and Michael broke the uncomfortable silence.

"Would you believe that Carole Salant was once a girl genius? It's true," he nodded, encouraging belief like a storyteller at the children's hour. "Story is our Miss Carole was offered the chance to come to SCC on a scholarship when she was just fifteen. But Carole had more sense than that. She stayed in high school, breezing her way through with straight A's and developing her social skills. Before she finally came to SCC on a full scholarship she'd been voted queen of her senior prom and Miss Altoona, Indiana. That was before she blew up like a balloon, victim of bad habits learned in college. The lovely Miss Salant, with a face like a madonna and eyes like a seasoned trader in snake oil." Michael paused and scrubbed his chin with a fist. "I'm not fond of her, you may have guessed."

"I don't really know her," Nora hedged.

"You're lucky," Michael countered just as Finnerty appeared in his open doorway. He and Finnerty exchanged nods and Michael stood up, then smiled down at Nora.

"I've enjoyed meeting you, even though I didn't let you get a word in edgewise. Would you like some revenge? Once we've both been grilled, I'd like to take you to lunch. I'll wait for you, faithfully. Parked on Finnerty's doorstep. Then I want you to tell me all about yourself and I promise to keep my mouth shut."

"Then you'll have a hard time eating," Nora smiled.

"Ah! It's a date, then. Good." He turned to face Finnerty, patiently waiting in the doorway. "After you, Sheriff."

Michael was in Finnerty's office for less than twenty minutes. He gave her a broad wink as he came through the door and muttered, "Piece of cake," through the side of his mouth as she passed by him on her way into the office.

Finnerty was only a few inches taller than she was, but he made her feel small, outweighing her by a hundred pounds and dwarfing the crowded office. He indicated a worn brown leather chair to her and edged his bulk around a massive wooden desk. The desk was overflowing with loose papers, folders and notepads. A giant-sized soft drink cup sweated condensation in a soggy circle on a pile of forms. Finnerty settled behind the desk in a creaking chair, rocking back familiarly and lacing his big fingers together over his chest.

The sheriff's questions were simple, and he seemed, Nora thought, almost bored. She caught herself wishing she could surprise him, provoke some reaction, but she had nothing to tell him. Finnerty asked, matter-of-factly, about subjects that 48 hours ago would have seemed ludicrous and unthinkable. Devil worship. Satanic cults. What did she know about them? Nothing. Only what she'd read in last night's paper. She'd never heard of Victor Sears before yesterday. She knew Carole Salant only slightly. She could identify only a few names Finnerty rattled off. They were people she'd met through Ted and Kate. Charlie Luther? Yes, she knew him.

Nora carefully kept any opinions about Ted and Kate's friends to herself. They were hangers-on, hangers-around, people with master's degrees and unfinished novels who worked odd construction jobs for enough money to pay the rent and get high or drunk on a regular basis. They were people, like Carole Salant, who had started out in one direction, then took easy, sleazy slides to small, bitter places. Carole worked in a dry cleaning store and bitched about what life owed her. Nora knew that Carole had dropped out of SCC to follow a boyfriend in a rock band. When the band broke up Carole drifted into commune living in Colorado and California in the

early 70s. She had drifted back to Stony Cliffs a few
years ago.

"How about Alex Thomas?" Finnerty asked.

Nora frowned. The name was familiar, but not
through Ted and Kate. He taught in her department
and she'd met him once at a faculty get-together a
couple of weeks ago. The shoes he'd worn to the
casual party cost more than the combined total of
everything she had on. The price tag on his full outfit
probably equaled half the cost of her wardrobe, if not
more.

"We've met. He's in my department at SCC."

Finnerty nodded. Probably he already knew that.
"But you never saw him at the Hall house?"

Nora shook her head. Alex Thomas a friend of Ted's
or Kate's? It was hard to imagine.

Finnerty nodded again. He nodded at everything
she said, including her finally voiced protest about
the absurdity of Ted's belonging to a satanic cult. He
didn't disagree with her, just kept nodding. Finnerty
didn't seem to expect much from her and Nora felt
obscurely disappointed.

"Well, thank you for your time, Miss Durant,"
Finnerty finally said, standing up to indicate the inter-
view was over and Nora was dismissed.

Nora stayed in her chair. "Do you have any idea,
yet, of who might have done it? Or why?"

Finnerty took two steps around his desk and
stopped. "We're working on it. When we come up
with the killer, you'll read about it in the
newspaper."

Nora stood up, but didn't begin to leave.

"Do you think it's over?" she persisted. "Will there
be any more killings?"

Finnerty gave her his first real look of interest.
"Why do you ask that?"

Things will keep happening and happening. Sam's
voice echoed through her thoughts, and she realized

she'd been hearing the girl's words in the back of her mind all along. *Everybody's going to die.*

Nora shrugged and shook her head.

Finnerty regarded her thoughtfully for another few moments, then his face resumed its carefully blank mask. "Don't worry, Miss Durant, we'll be taking care of it."

He moved another step closer, willing her to move on.

Nora stood her ground. "Do you think . . ." she began, surprising herself with her own question. "Do you think Kate or Sam might be in any danger?"

The ghost of a frown crossed Finnerty's face. His eyes drifted up to study the long hairline crack that crossed the ceiling of his office.

"Are you going to do anything to protect them?" She was stubborn now, playing the irresistible force to his immovable object.

Finnerty let his gaze wander back to her face. His eyes were hooded, like a hunting falcon at rest, the flicker of interest blown out of them.

"It's something to think about," he finally conceded. But as he said it, Nora suddenly wondered if the sheriff hadn't been planning on it all along.

5

"Hey, wait for me!" Marching out of the sheriff's office, working hard to retain her dignity, Nora traveled a few more steps before swinging around to face the voice.

"Your lunch date, remember?" Michael Justin stood grinning at her. "The one that talks so much?"

Nora felt her tense shoulders ease down two inches and the tight band across her forehead loosen. Something's going to happen, she thought, and she liked the idea even though she felt suddenly girlish and vulnerable.

"Hi," she said, smiling, and the smile felt foolish but she didn't particularly care.

A B-movie leer dropped over his face and he twisted into a dark alley crouch, edging towards her, squinting over his shoulder at Finnerty's closed door.

"Didja get the rubber hoses?" he stage-whispered.

Nora laughed. "No, no rubber hoses, no thumbscrews, not even a bright light shining in my eyes." She shook her head ruefully. "Guess I'm just not good stoolie stuff. I didn't have much to tell him, certainly nothing he didn't already know."

"You should be grateful," Michael said seriously. "It's a sad, sorry business. Ugly. They're just grasping

57

at straws now or they wouldn't be dragging in this
business about Victor. I wish to hell they'd let the
poor bastard rest in peace. If he can find any peace in
death, it'll be the first he's ever had."

Nora frowned with him in sympathy. He stood
close to her, scowling over her shoulder into some
private vision.

"So," he asked, face suddenly clearing, "are you
hungry? I'm starving." He examined her face. "Are
you one of those sparrowlike eaters who orders the
dieter's special and chews every mouthful of lettuce
religiously fifty times?"

"I suppose I should be ashamed to admit it, but I
adore food. Great sinful globs of starch, things with
sauces, mounds of cholesterol . . ."

"Wonderful! A woman after my own heart. I knew
we were destined to go places together. How do you
feel about lasagna?"

They settled on a restaurant Nora had heard about
but never visited, chattering nonsense about food as
they swept past the deputy guarding the front desk.
Pushing through the heavy wood and glass door to the
steps at the front entrance they both stopped, squinting at the bright sunlight and gasping for breathable
air in the August heat.

"Mine," Michael said, pointing across the parking
lot at a dusty red and white VW van. "We'll leave
your car and I'll bring you back here, yes?"

"Sure," Nora agreed and they moved together
towards the van, comfortably matching each other's
pace.

The interior of the van was packed with a cheerful
mess—torn cardboard boxes full of books, clothes, a
gray fedora, a white Panama hat, photographer's
lights, videotapes, cameras, a TV monitor, folders,
notebooks and miscellaneous litter. Michael unlocked
and slid open the door on the passenger side. A rush
of oven-hot air hit them and they stood in respectful
silence, surveying the crowded interior.

"I suppose you're compulsively neat," he said mournfully.

Nora slowly shook her head. "No-o-o. On the messy side. But the proportions here are close to awesome."

"I have excuses," Michael explained, lending her a hand up. "Do you want to hear them?"

Nora smiled down at him. "I suppose I'd better."

Michael Justin, it turned out, worked part time for the local public television station as a producer and host/director for a weekly program. He was also a faculty member at SCC, an associate professor in the department of communications.

"I play," he explained as the van lumbered out of the parking lot, "and people pay me for it. Once upon a time I thought I'd go to Hollywood and make Important Films. I got sidetracked," he shrugged, "but I've managed to do pretty much what I wanted. Oh, my God, I'm talking again! Stop me!"

But they talked in the van and then at the restaurant. Grimaldi's was part of the trendy "Victorian" Century Center a few miles from downtown Stony Cliffs. A hundred years ago the Century Center had been a massive brick warehouse and icehouse. In the late 1970s developers hired by the expanding town had transformed it into a shopping mall for small, fashionable clothing shops and closet-sized stores that specialized in period jewelry, collectibles and bathroom and kitchen decor. Grimaldi's narrowly escaped being precious. It inhabited the converted cellar of the Center. Cool and stone-walled, Grimaldi's served hearty Italian food on red and white checkered tablecloths with chilled bottles of chianti and frosty pitchers of beer. There were no windows in Grimaldi's. It stayed in a constant twilight, an oasis of escapism from time and place. It could have been anywhere, anytime. It was the perfect place for conversation over a lingering meal.

"We weren't 'from' anywhere," Michael told Nora midway through their lasagna. "My father, Victor's stepfather, was an over-the-road truck driver with problems of temperament. He found it difficult to work for anyone, so he changed jobs a lot and we moved from place to place, state to state. Take your pick. We lived in Colorado, Nebraska, Texas, California, Illinois, Missouri. Victor landed here early on. The boy genius. He settled in while I passed through places. When my parents died—both of them, two years ago in a car accident of all things—I moved here. In search of family, I suppose, Victor being all that was left except for an aunt and uncle I haven't seen in twenty years out in Arizona." He stabbed thoughtfully at his lasagna. "We never found sibling bliss, Victor and I. I suppose you've deduced that. But I stayed. I'm fond of the town. Gainfully employed and not, at the moment, looking for anything else."

They were trading life stories and it was the only time in their two hour lunch that Victor's name was mentioned. They talked about Kate and Ted, but only in Nora's past. For that brief span of time the present faded, and violence and murder didn't exist. Then Nora started feeling the uneasy tug of conscience, the kind of responsibility for Kate she used to feel when they were in college together, as though Kate were too fragile and too full of unbalanced passion to take care of herself. In contrast, Nora felt earthbound and motherly. Solemn. Adult. It was selfish, too, she knew. For years, Nora's ties to people had been fleeting, always temporary as first she and Simon, then she alone, had moved from place to place. In Stony Cliffs, Kate and Sam were her only anchors, the real contacts that tied her to the world of human life and emotion. Without them she was completely adrift. With them, especially now when she felt she could be involved with the process of consolation and healing, she felt more solidly a part of the world. She might be needed, and the idea made her feel stronger.

She cared about Kate and Sam and that made her feel a part of something. The feeling was like balm to her, soothing and reassuring after so long being an outsider, an observer of human events.

For Simon, she was a different kind of anchor and she recognized that. It was one of the reasons that they'd stayed in touch. They were like two lost children wandering in the big, cold world, keeping tabs on each other, comforted by the contact.

"I ought to be getting back," she told Michael and he didn't protest.

When they parted at the police parking lot, he didn't mention seeing her again. But she knew she'd hear from him. Some things she was sure of.

Less than two minutes after Nora Durant left his office, Sheriff Finnerty buzzed Tom Robbins, the deputy on the front desk.

"Who's on the Hall house?" Finnerty barked at the intercom without preamble.

"Bobby Hunt and Phil Jenkins," Robbins replied.

Finnerty snorted. "Both of them?"

Crackle. The intercome static obliterated Tom Robbins' deep sigh. "Yessir. I thought . . ." He let it drift, sounding reproachful.

"Okay," Finnerty informed the intercom sharply. "Make sure they keep their eyes open."

"Of course. Sir." Tom Robbins stared at the intercom with the soulful, offended look of a bloodhound whose dignity has been impugned. Finnerty didn't need to see him to know the look was there. He slid his finger off the intercom button, joined his fingers in a steeple over his chest and leaned back in his chair.

On Finnerty's desk was the preliminary autopsy report on Ted Kellogg. Still no sign of the missing tongue. Nature of the weapon used not identified. Finnerty grunted to himself and pushed the protesting chair back another inch. He started to rock, squinting

up at the crack in the ceiling, and pushed the chair on
its creaking springs back and forth, back and forth.

Sun-stained shades, tattered and frayed along their
margins, stretched to the window sills in Charlie
Luther's one-room apartment. The windows themselves were tightly closed. The room was still and
airless.

Seams of light seeping in from the bright afternoon
left the room a dull gray. It was drab anyway with its
old furniture carelessly chosen and placed—an old
dresser draped with discarded clothing, a small,
wooden kitchen table with two mismatched chairs,
an overstuffed arm chair that once had a white background with a brown plaid design but was now uni-
formly stained gray, an old portable TV balanced on
two stacked wooden crates of books, a single mattress
in the corner of the room and over it, hanging from a
string thumbtacked to the ceiling, a fly strip so full of
insect remains that there was room for no more.

Charlie Luther was crouched on the mattress,
wedged as far as he could force himself into the angle
where the walls met. His arms were wrapped tightly
around his knees, knuckles white on his fair, freckled
hands. Charlie Luther was fully dressed. The square
black toes of his cracked boots sent a pleated fan of
wrinkles over the gray sheets. His eyes were open,
staring at nothing in particular. There was a light
sheen of sweat on Charlie Luther's face.

Two things were moving in Charlie Luther's room.
The black layered fly strip revolved slowly in some
otherwise imperceptible stirring of the air.

And an oily drop of sweat slid on a slow path down
Charlie Luther's face. It traced a channel down his
temple, poised on his cheekbone, then slid to his
cheek, wound through the pale stubble to his jaw and
then fell to the damp shoulder of his T-shirt.

There was only one thing moving in Charlie
Luther's room.

6

Kate's house was less than a mile from the sheriff's office, more or less on the way to Nora's own apartment. As she drove down Kate's block, Nora could hear the racket from the house as far away as the intersection.

Sam was out front fighting a massive power mower up the steep incline of their yard. She was hauling it, edging backward up the hill, sliding back a step for every step she took, accompanied by roars, whines and ominous coughs from the motor.

Faintly over the din of the mower, Nora could hear the crashing crescendos of Beethoven's *Ode to Joy* spilling from the open windows of the house. Nora stood on the sidewalk, watching Sam's Herculean efforts with a rush of fondness. The girl's lips were pressed tightly together and her glasses were in imminent danger of sliding off her nose.

When Sam slid down two steps instead of one step carefully inched backward, Nora trotted up the hill behind her and reached an arm around each side of the girl to add her grip on the handle to Sam's.

Between the two of them they manhandled the mower backward up the hill.

"Thanks," Sam grunted. She pushed her glasses

back up her nose with a practiced index finger. Her face was shining red.

"I'll give you a hand with the rest of this part," Nora stated, sure that Sam would insist on doing it herself. "Walk it down yourself and we'll both haul it back up." She stepped back and tried to look like she'd take no nonsense.

Sam opened her mouth to argue, then shrugged her shoulders and turned back to maneuver the machine down the short, steep slope. When she started backing, Nora joined her and they pulled it, more smoothly this time, up the hill.

They worked together in sweaty, companionable silence under the mower's roar until the grassy slope was neatly trimmed. Then Sam turned to Nora with a stubborn set to her face.

"Thank you for helping me," she said politely. "Now I've got to finish mowing the rest of the yard and return the mower to Mrs. Panzer next door."

Dismissed, Nora managed not to smile. Sam would be irritated as hell, Nora thought, if she knew how cute she looked right now.

Nora watched Sam's ruler-straight back march the length of the yard behind the mower, then she turned up the path to the house.

Knocking or calling out would have been useless. Beethoven blasted through the screen door, volume so high that the sound seemed almost tangible in the still, hot air. It even managed to nearly drown out the sound of the vacuum cleaner droning in the living room.

She opened the screen door, moving cautiously into the chaos of Kate cleaning house.

Furniture was pulled away from the walls and shoved helter-skelter into the center of the room. Fat stuffed chairs turned upside down waved stubby wooden legs in the air like misshapen ostriches, while couch and chair cushions huddled on the floor. Books were off their shelves, and pictures were taken down. Dust rags, cans of cleaners and polishes were generously scattered around the room.

In baggy shorts and an oversize shirt tied around her midriff, Kate was attacking the back of the couch with the vacuum cleaner. Nora surveyed the place in awe.

Kate's head snapped up suddenly, sensing someone in the room. She was scowling with furious concentration.

"Hi," Nora mouthed at her over the din and waved.

Kate mouthed a greeting back and reached down to switch off the vacuum although Beethoven still surged over them.

"Can I do anything?" Nora shouted.

Kate frowned, businesslike, surveying the room like a foreman overseeing the building of the pyramids.

"Plants!" she finally decided, sweeping a hand wide to take in the room. "Pooch!" She pointed vigorously to the open front door, then shrugged. "They need help!"

Nora nodded and shaped an okay with her fingers. Kate switched the vacuum back on.

For the next 45 minutes Nora rescued plants from the wreckage of the living room and trotted them outside for emergency treatment. Showers of dead leaves flew behind her. Kate had always been death on plants. On the porch Nora puttered peacefully, watering, pinching back sickly vines of Wandering Jew and half-dead ferns, picking a few cigarette butts out of the dirt. While she worked her mind kept drifting off to Michael Justin, images of him laughing and how he looked when he was serious.

He'd been married, too, he'd told her. A marriage when he was young that had lasted less than two years. She was idly tamping dirt around the roots of an African violet when Sam broke into her half-thoughts. The girl clomped up the porch steps and dropped to sit Indian style a few feet from her. Nora looked up and smiled, then turned to study the yard.

"You're done!"

"Yeah." Sam started plucking dead and dying leaves from a grape leaf ivy. From inside the house Judy Garland belted and warbled her best from a scratchy album "*Clang, clang, clang went the trolley . . .*"

"Looks like a good job."

Sam frowned modestly and nodded. She picked up a handful of papery leaves and began rolling them between her palms, still frowning.

She wants to talk about something, Nora decided, biding her time and wondering if asking questions would help.

Sam broke the silence. "You ever have any dreams?" she asked it with elaborate casualness.

"Sure."

Sam opened her hands and let the leaves drop. "Nightmares?"

"Sometimes. Everybody does. People dream all the time, you know. We just don't always remember them. Some of them are bound to be nightmares."

"I know, I know," Sam answered testily. "REM and all that stuff. Rapid eye movement," she explained loftily.

"Sam, are you having nightmares?"

Sam began tracing a pattern in the pile of brown and yellowed leaves. Then she took a quick breath and looked up, searching Nora's face. "I had one last night. I had one the night . . . the night it happened, too."

"So did I," Nora remembered. "The night Ted was killed."

"What was yours?"

Nora's forehead furrowed. She'd forgotten she had a nightmare that night until Sam mentioned it. The feeling of the dream came back to her now—threat, fear, something that stalked her. The details were more elusive.

"A house," she said slowly, nodding with the memory. "A big old house, isolated, as though it were out in the middle of a swamp. The house was alive somehow, or something in it was watching me. I'm not sure. Nothing much happened really. It was just the feeling that someplace that ought to be safe was dangerous, wasn't what it was supposed to be. And it wanted something from me, but I don't know what." She shrugged. "It doesn't sound like much, I guess, but I was scared stiff."

"So what happened? How did it end?"

Nora shook her head. "I was upstairs packing. I was alone, it was night, and the house was watching so I had to pretend I wasn't scared. Then I heard doors closing downstairs and something thudding on the stairs. *Thump. Thump.*" Nora rubbed at the top of her head with a fist, then turned both palms up to the air, puzzled. "I don't know. There's some kind of gap and next thing I know I'm outside watching the house burning."

Sam grunted. "I wish I knew how you got out of it."

"So do I," Nora laughed. "What about you? What did you dream?"

Sam had been watching Nora's face as she talked. Now she turned away to pluck at the grape ivy.

"You're in it," she said slowly. "I can't remember mine very well either. Just bits and pieces, all mixed up. And somebody was after me."

"Do you know who?"

Sam shook her head. "But it wasn't a house."

"What *do* you remember?" Nora prompted.

"The dark," Sam answered firmly. Then, more hesitantly, "I was outside, I think, and there were things all around me, big things that kind of hung over me. Some of them were moving around so I

couldn't get past them when I tried to run, and I kept
hearing this whispering. They were saying my name,
hissing, real creepy. *Ss-s-s-sample. Ss-s-s-sample.* And
there were eyes like an animal's eyes, watching me.''

She shifted, drawing her knees up to her chest and
wrapping her arms protectively around her bare legs.
''Then the next part is where you come in.'' She
looked at Nora. ''We were in this long skinny
hallway. It was dark, and we were running and we
got to this stairway that went straight up. Only it was
so dark we couldn't see the top. The stairs were those
metal kind, like a ladder, you know, with open space
in between them that your leg could slip through. And
we started to run up the stairs and they went on
forever until we couldn't see the top or the bottom
and then there was this big clang from in front of us,
like a big metal door slamming and I turned around to
look at you, but you were gone.''

Sam fell silent and began to study her knees. She
picked with half-hearted interested at a scab on one
knee and Nora began to wonder if she was finished,
but she wasn't. ''And then . . . and then *he* said my
name.'' She looked up at Nora. ''And I couldn't move
because something was holding my ankle. So I looked
down and there was this hand. Just a hand, all bloody.
And I screamed and woke up.'' Sam hugged her knees
tighter and laid her cheek on them.

Nora looked at the careful part in Sam's straight
brown hair, the pale scalp pink with the heat. Who
called Sam's name?

''He?''

The girl's voice was soft and muffled. ''Ted.''

''Ah,'' Nora murmured, as though she knew what
she were talking about. ''Pretty scary,'' she agreed.
''And pretty natural, I'd think.''

Sam turned her head to rest her chin on her knees
and regard Nora. ''How?''

Nora shrugged. ''Death is scary. Especially violent

death and especially when it happens to someone we know. It scares me."

Sam considered it, nodded, and then said, "But I had a nightmare on the night he got killed, too."

"Coincidence. I had one myself, remember?"

The girl shook her head stubbornly. "It means something."

"Like what?"

Sam picked up her shoulders and dropped them with finality. She was gazing over Nora's head, face closed.

"What did you dream then?" Sam shook her head slightly, still looking past Nora. "Come on, Sam. What did you dream?"

Sam heaved a small sigh, as if humoring an adult. "Green eyes. Dark. Something moving around in the dark, whispering. Kind of like the dream I had last night. Then I was in my room and I opened my dresser drawer and they were in there. His hands. Just his hands and they moved." Sam shuddered and turned her eyes to Nora's face. The closed look was gone, replaced by fear. For once Sam's face was unguarded. Without her small, stern adult look she seemed terribly young.

Whatever Nora would have said was lost when Kate suddenly swept through the screen door onto the porch.

"Whew!" she breathed, hands on hips looking down on them. "Break time. Obviously you two are already indulging." She moved to a wicker rocker, threw herself into it and lit a cigarette, propping bare feet on the porch railing.

"How's it going in there?" Nora asked.

Sam turned her attention back to a Wandering Jew.

"I'm considering dumping all that garbage and living Japanese style. What do you think, Sam? We'll paint everything white, toss a couple cushions on the floor and have one vase to contemplate. Hey! You finished the grass, terrific!''

Sam grunted without looking up. ''It's time somebody did.''

''Well, you can do me another favor, as long as
you're feeling industrious. We're out of window
cleaning stuff. Take this,'' Kate held out a five dollar
bill, ''and go down to Kroger's and get some, will you?
And while you're there get something we can reward
ourselves with . . . watermelon, ice cream, something
like that. Your choice, okay?''

Sam reached out and took the bill, nodding.
''Now?''

''Right. Before I lose my momentum.''

Sam stood up, brushing off the seat of her baggy
blue cotton shorts.

''Not a big rush, though,'' Kate added. ''I've still got
plenty of other stuff to keep me occupied until you get
back.''

''Are you staying for a while?'' Sam asked Nora.

''Sure. I want some of this reward stuff.''

Sam nodded again and trotted down the porch
steps. ''See ya,'' she said over her shoulder to the two
of them.

Both women watched her go in silence.

''She's a good kid,'' Kate said when Sam was
halfway down the sun-speckled block. ''She knew I
wanted to get rid of her for a while.'' Nora inched
around to get a better view of Kate. ''I want to ask you
a favor.''

What Kate wanted was Nora's help in packing up
Ted's clothing and other belongings still in the
bedroom they had shared. She couldn't face doing it,
she said, but couldn't stand seeing his clothes hanging
in the closet every time she opened it and his shaving
cream in the bathroom and all the other reminders.

''I'll go through the stuff with you,'' Nora agreed.

Kate shook her head, blowing out a stream of
smoke. ''No. I can't handle it. I know that's weak and

stupid, but I'm feeling halfway stable today and I'd like to stay that way."

"I might not be able to tell, with some things, what's his and what's yours," Nora warned, eying the loose man's shirt Kate wore. "And, besides, don't you think there'll be some things you'll want to keep?"

Kate threw her cigarette butt over the railing onto the freshly mowed lawn and turned to smile crookedly at Nora. "You're so practical. Okay, maybe. If you get most of it, I'll come up later. Will you?"

Nora dropped another load of shirts on the rumpled sheets of the double bed. The tiny closet was like the clown car in a circus, pouring out more and more clowns, more and more clothes than you'd ever expect from the cramped space.

She stirred around the mess on the bed and extracted a worn tweed sports jacket. That, at least, had to be Ted's. A gaudy Hawaiian shirt and an oil-stained gray work jacket with one torn sleeve were added to the pile of heavy work pants. Then she started checking sizes on the stack of blue jeans.

Kate was small and fine-boned. Ted had been just over six feet, slim in the hips but broad-shouldered. She started making guesses at whose shirts were whose, based on size and memory. She remembered Kate in the red and black Pendleton shirt, Ted in the green Army sweater. After a while she had a considerable pile of clothing she guessed to be Ted's. It was time to start piling it in the boxes Kate had supplied, but first, Nora thought she ought to check the pockets for anything like bills, checks, cash, or letters.

It made her uncomfortable, intruding on a dead man's privacy. But then, this whole thing made her uncomfortable.

She dropped cross-legged to the floor and arranged boxes and clothes around her in piles, gingerly rummaging pockets, sorting, folding and finally putting the remnants of Ted Kellogg's life away.

And where the hell is Kate? Nora wondered.

Many of the pockets were empty except for shreds of loose tobacco making a soft grit in the seams. Some held crumpled gum wrappers and empty cigarette packs, small change, a lighter, empty and half-empty matchbooks from most of the bars in town. She made a small mound of the trash—the stubs of movie tickets, a receipt from the dry cleaner's where Carole Salant worked, an occasional scrap of paper with scribbled notes in Ted's handwriting, or what she assumed was Ted's handwriting. It was a tense and careless hand. The letters were loosely connected, the lower loops of g's and y's driven forcefully long, sharp and aggressive.

One note held lines Nora recognized from Yeats' "Second Coming." They sprawled across the torn sheet of creased white paper at random, running first across then down the margin.

"Things fall apart," she read, making it out with difficulty.

"The blood-dimmed tide is loosed, and everywhere the ceremony of innocence is drowned."

And a few words staggered across the bottom of the page like the signature on a letter. They were printed in shaky capitals and the pressure of Ted's pen had pierced the paper in more than one spot.

"ITS HOUR COME ROUND AT LAST."

She held it a moment and for the first time since she heard of Ted's death, Nora felt the slow settling of sorrow, a sense of the man who wasted what he had of life and died too soon.

She crumpled the sheet into a ball, rolled it tight between her palms and dropped it on the pile of gum wrappers and matchbooks. In the other pocket of the same denim jacket that held the Yeats, she found another folded sheet of paper. On it, Ted's handwriting was neater, more like a schoolboy's copying an assignment. She read the quote through once, frowning, then read it again.

> "He possesses great courage, incredible cunning, superhuman wisdom, the most acute penetration, consummate prudence, an incomparable skill in veiling the most pernicious artifices under a specious disguise, and a malefic and infinite hatred towards the human race, implacable and incurable."

> J. Weyer, 16th c.

It was carefully lettered in black ink, but at the bottom of the page a few lines were added in pencil, scrawled again, more unintelligible than ever.

> *The terror by night. The black fire. The Dweller in the Abyss. Prince of Light, Prince of Wantons.*

She was hunched over it, deciphering the lines, when a sound in the doorway made her start. Nora looked up quickly, feeling her face blush with something like guilt. Sam stood there, staring blankly at the piles of clothing. She looked at Nora.

"I'm glad you're here," she finally said and turned and walked away.

Without looking at it, Nora crushed the paper in her hand and dropped it on the pile of debris.

She was reaching again for the denim jacket when she gasped and flinched away from it.

A small white spider crouched on the faded denim, tiny eyes watching her, seemingly full of malice.

It's just a spider, she told herself. There's no reason it should be any more frightening than a ladybug.

She leaned towards it, studying the alien face, trying to make out the tiny features. But it rushed a few steps towards her and she shied back. You're so silly, she told herself, what can a little bitty spider do to you?

But she reached gingerly, eyes on the spider, for the jacket and gave it a sharp snap and shake.

"Go away," she said aloud. "Get lost, you little creep."

Rocky Road was Sam's favorite ice cream that week. They gathered on the front porch to eat it when the day turned still and deep gold in the heat of late afternoon. Nora, Kate and Sam split the half gallon in even, enormous portions and ate with gusto, slowly and silently stuffing themselves far beyond sensible consumption.

Kate rocked steadily in her porch rocker, while Nora and Sam perched at either side of the front steps like stone lions guarding a library. They stared across the street like visitors to the zoo, watching families in the summer evening.

Across the street and two doors down was a man still in his twenties, belly already gone soft and pouchy, stretching his Budweiser T-shirt to reveal a crescent of pale flesh above his cutoffs. In one hand he held a long fork and poked with concentration at the burning coals in his barbecue grill. The other hand held a can of beer in a foam liner. Up the street a dull yellow Pinto pulled into a driveway. Two small boys clambered out the passenger door and a pregnant woman heaved herself out of the driver's side. She was struggling with an overflowing sack of groceries and the two boys ran round her in circles shrieking at a glass-breaking pitch.

"Jeremy! Adam! Behave!" the woman shouted with no noticeable effect.

Kate, Sam and Nora watched her, spooning their ice cream, as she waddled to the front door of the house, balanced the bag on a hip, and managed to open the door with one arm and a foot.

"I'm warning you!" she shouted over her shoulder as she disappeared into the house.

"Well," Kate observed, "some things don't change. The neighbors never used to talk to us, and they still don't."

Sam made an unintelligible noise.

Nora clattered her spoon against the bottom of her bowl, scraping up the last of the melted ice cream. She swallowed it, made a face at the bowl and plonked it down beside her on the step.

"I think I'm going to be sick."

Kate snorted.

"Now that your house is so damn clean I feel awful about the way mine looks. A disaster area. Wreck of the Hesperus," Nora mourned.

"Well," Kate carefully eyed her last spoonful of Rocky Road, "I know a great dwarf you can borrow. Hard worker. Strong like a bull."

Nora and Sam looked at each other.

Nora got a crafty look. In a bad Brooklyn accent she whined, "Oh, yeah? So when can I get hold a dis dwarf?"

"How about tonight?" Kate said. "Rent-a-dwarf. Take her home with you and squeeze a few more hours work out of her while you're both still able to work up a cleaning frenzy."

Nora didn't answer immediately, waiting to hear the real reason behind Kate's suggestion.

Kate settled her empty bowl on the porch railing and shook a cigarette out of her pack. "I've got some people coming over tonight and Sam wouldn't be interested in hanging around." She turned to face Sam. "The study group."

Sam jammed her spoon into the small mound of ice cream still in her bowl and let it drop. She stood up and started for the door.

"I'll go pack some stuff."

"Nora, I hope it's okay with you," Kate said belatedly.

Nora shrugged. "If Sam doesn't mind a sleeping bag on the floor. But what's this about a study group?"

"Some people Ted and I got together with," Kate answered vaguely.

"But what did you study?"

Kate grimaced. "Ideas . . . ideas." She exhaled a long stream of smoke. "Bullshit, actually. Oh, Nora, you look so dismayed."

Nora tried to look neutral and attentive.

"Jesus. I know Ted was full of shit. But I loved him anyway. He was such a dreamer, like Peter Pan. And he was brilliant, you know." Her chin went up another inch. "He wanted so much."

Kate rocked furiously, inhaled a long draw and blew it out.

"These people, the study group, were friends of Ted's and wanted to come over. I think it's going to be damn dismal, but I feel like I owe it to him. So why not? It won't kill me. But Sam has always been pretty uncomfortable with them and she really likes you. You don't mind; do you?"

Nora shook her head. "No, I don't. I like Sam, too."

They sat in silence for a few moments, then Nora ventured a casual comment.

"I met someone who knows you today. Michael Justin."

Silence. Nora looked up at Kate. She was scowling, eyes fixed across the street.

"Kate? You know him, don't you?"

"Yes. I know him."

"But?"

"But what?" Kate shrugged. "That's all."

Nora watched her profile, waiting for something more.

"You don't like him," she finally decided.

Kate's scowl got deeper. "I didn't say I didn't like him."

"You didn't *say* anything. Speak to me. Tell me what that face means."

"Oh." Kate's rocking slowed and her eyes wandered up to the porch ceiling.

"I suppose it's Victor Sears," she finally admitted. She turned to look at Nora. "Ted idolized him, you know."

"No, I don't know! I never heard of Victor Sears before I saw his name in the paper yesterday. You never mentioned him or a study group or a devil cult or . . . oh, my God. Is *that* who those people are?"

"Oh, shit." Kate swung the rocker around to face Nora, violently banging it against the floor. She pointed herself at Nora like the prow of a ship.

"What do you think? Do you think I'd be in some devil cult?"

The dweller in the abyss, Nora thought. *Prince of Wantons*. Slowly, she shook her head. "Not you."

"But Ted?"

"I don't know," Nora said. Kate snorted and threw herself back in the rocker setting it into agitated motion.

"Kate," Nora appealed, "I'm not sure of a lot of things right now. I feel like I know you even though it's been years since we've spent much time together. I care about you. I never did get to know Ted, though, not really. And there are so many things in your life here that are new to me. I used to know everything about your life. Now I don't."

Kate made a noncommital noise, rocking.

"Devil worship sounds ridiculous. Something out of a bad movie. But I'm not ready to make statements of absolute faith about a bunch of people I don't know in a so-called study group you suddenly spring on me."

Kate shook a cigarette out of her pack and lit it. She blew out a long stream of smoke. "I suppose you ought to know something about what's going on here."

"It would help."

Kate kept rocking, smoke drifting around her like a cloud.

"Victor Sears." She said the name as thought it were a key to some locked section of her life, as though it held some puzzle she had yet to define. "Victor."

Nora settled herself against the porch rail, waiting, watching Kate.

"He was like a guru. Charismatic. Dangerous, I suppose. Victor collected people. Disciples. Admirers. He enjoyed being adored. And Ted was one of the people who adored him." Kate shook her head.

"Victor was a genius, there's no question of that, and articulate, the most eloquent speaker I've ever heard. He could talk for hours, constructing incredible theories that somehow wove together abstract ideas from Plato and the Babylonians to Machiavelli and Carlos Castenada. He knew something about almost everything, or could convince you he did, and he had a delicate, intricate skill, a way of creating fantastic notions that linked a whole world of ideas and insights into some strange structure."

The long ash on Kate's cigarette dropped into her lap and she brushed it off. "Of course, after listening to Victor for an hour, following him and agreeing with everything he said . . . always so clear, so lucid . . . you couldn't retrace the logic. Couldn't even remember exactly what he said. It was like studying a snowflake. Just when the pattern's angles and curves begin to make sense, it melts. Gone, like cotton candy."

Kate rocked in silence. Across the street, Kate's neighbor slapped hamburgers onto the grill.

"Ted was fascinated," Kate went on. "Hell, he was jealous. Victor was the only person Ted had ever met who could out-think, out-talk and out-bullshit him. He didn't resent Victor, though. He worshipped him. They all did."

"The study group?" Nora asked.

"Yeah. Victor's group."

Kate lapsed into silence and Nora turned the new information over carefully.

"But how did the sheriff and the newspapers get the idea that Victor led a devil cult?"

Kate snorted, then choked on the smoke from her cigarette, face flushed, coughing.

"Aleister Crowley," Kate croaked and coughed harder.

Nora waited.

"Aleister Crowley," she started again, pronouncing the name as though that explained everything.

"So?" The name had sounded familiar to Nora when she saw it in Kate's newspaper the night before. The Great Beast 666, the paper said. The wickedest man alive.

Kate rubbed the back of her hand against her forehead, pushing at the fine beads of sweat that gathered. "So Victor thought Crowley was some misunderstood martyr, too far ahead of his time to be appreciated. Crowley called himself a magician, but basically it added up to using kinky sex and drugs to find a 'higher spiritual plane.' Just Victor's style. Fuck your life away and reach nirvana." Kate raised her cigarette to her lips, screwed her face up at it and tossed it in a wide arc over the railing to the lawn.

Nora watched it land and settle in the fresh cut spikes of grass, sending up a thin stream of smoke like the caterpillar's hookah.

"Erotic magic, right?" Kate pushed off in the rocker with a short burst and then froze the motion. "A great excuse for screwing around. Crowley died in 1947, the same year Victor was born, and Victor loved to drop little hints that he might be Crowley reincarnated. Mostly, though, Victor liked being Victor. He was incredibly vain, a little God on wheels, but so . . . I don't know . . . convincing and magnetic. I don't know," Kate repeated and half-laughed, self-mocking. "Charles Manson. James Jones. He was one of a kind was Victor." Kate shook her head, some kind of bewilderment passing over her face, making her look years younger. And lost.

Nora watched her silently. Maybe I really don't know her at all, she thought, and the thought frightened her.

"Anyway, he used Crowley like the ultimate reference, adding his own little touches. What people like Charlie Luther and Carole Salant got off on was that Crowley preached that everyone's true self is a great and mysterious secret. All you have to do is find it, and bingo, every man and woman is a star, quote, unquote."

"Charlie Luther and Carole Salant?"

"And Ted."

"Oh."

"Oh, hell." Kate reached into her pocket for her cigarettes, then shoved the pack back in and started rocking.

Did Ted adopt more than the general philosophy? Kinky sex and drugs? Nora could never ask, but she had to push back a sense of relief that Ted was out of Kate's life. He was dead. Leave it alone.

"What Victor was really selling," Kate said, firm and locked in her own stream of logical explanation, "was power. Power for the powerless. You hide from the world and the hell with jobs and money and other people. You're superior. You're a star. You know the secrets of yourself and the secrets of the universe."

She slipped into silence and they both sat, islands in the August heat, with the only sound the distant roar of a neighbor's lawn mower.

"But Michael . . ." Nora broke the quiet, suddenly remembering what had started the conversation. "What's the connection? I mean, I know Michael was Victor's half-brother, but that doesn't explain what you've got against him, does it?"

"Oh, for heaven's sake," Kate snorted. "Who said I had anything against him?"

"There's something," Nora insisted.

Kate smothered a groan, pulled out a cigarette and lit it. She exhaled the smoke in a stream thin and tight as wire. "I suppose," she finally said, "I suppose Michael just makes me uncomfortable. He wasn't around much, and when he was, he indulged Victor, like a little kid playing magic. Ted thought it was just because Michael was too straight to understand anything, too insensitive. Ted said he wasn't spiritually well-developed enough to appreciate Victor. It pissed him off, too, that Michael seemed to have this contempt for the rest of us. A condescension. Arrogant in his ignorance, Ted said."

"But I think Michael really cared for Victor. He told me he'd moved here to be near him. I know it didn't work out, but I think Michael was more sad than contemptuous."

Kate grunted, a noncommittal noise with an overtone of disbelief.

"Where did you meet him?"

"Ah," Nora said, immediately uncomfortable. "At the sheriff's office."

Kate's gaze came down and pinned her. "Shit!"

She should have mentioned it sooner, Nora thought, though it would have been awkward at any time.

"Shit! They're questioning you about me and about Ted?"

Nora shrugged. "It's routine. It's what they do. If they don't try everything they won't find out who killed Ted."

Kate didn't act as though she heard her.

"And if you met Michael there it means they're dragging this devil cult stuff up again. Jesus."

"Sheriff Finnerty ran through a list of names. Charlie Luther, Carole Salant, Alex Thomas . . . some others I didn't know."

"Well, we're the devil cult, of course, Victor's study group. It's ridiculous! They're harmless." Kate glared at Nora as though the sheriff's suspicions were somehow her fault.

"They were Ted's group, really. I was just tolerated as a visitor. But I knew all of them and I knew Ted. There was nothing involved that could have anything to do with what happened to Ted!"

Kate was taut, aimed at Nora like a threat.

She sounds like she's trying to convince herself, Nora thought.

"They've been meeting over here since Victor died," Kate said more matter-of-factly. She leaned back in her chair. "Sam doesn't like them very much, which is why she took off like a shot when I mentioned they were coming. But they were like Ted's family. I may not be real fond of the in-laws, but I owe it to Ted, like having a private wake." She looked suddenly close to tears. "I may have to get plastered to get through this."

Kate's eyes were on the cracked paint of the porch ceiling and Nora tried to force Kate to look at her and hear her. She let all her concern, her worry, her caring about Kate and her fears for her fill her voice.

"Kate, you can't go on like this."

Kate's eyes traveled down to meet hers. One side of her mouth twitched and she snickered.

"Oh, hell, you know what I mean," Nora muttered, flushing a little, hearing how corny it sounded herself. Then she snickered, too, and they were both laughing, silly, giddy laughter that swept over them in waves. Whenever one subsided, out of breath, the other snorted or hooted and it started again. It went on for minutes until finally they were quiet, weak and cleansed.

"Whew," Kate said when it was finally over, "I really have missed you."

"Me too," Nora told her.

Kate mopped at her eyes. "Have you heard anything more from Simon the Magnificent?"

Nora groaned. "He called and left a message on my machine yesterday, but I haven't gotten back to him yet."

"Let him wait." Kate gestured imperiously. "It'll do his domineering soul some good if you don't leap to respond."

Nora fidgeted, feeling old guilts surface. "He does love me, you know. He's worried."

"That is not love," Kate declared. "That's obsession. Ownership. Simon simply can't face the fact that you're an independent person with a life of your own. He can't stand not directing every move you make."

"Oh," Nora hedged, "he's not that bad." She might echo Kate's judgment to herself, but she didn't enjoy hearing it. Besides, she still felt old ties of loyalty to her ex-husband. Simon still believed they might get back together again in some rosy future. It didn't matter to him that she kept denying the possibility. He had his own peculiar brand of tunnel vision and she was firmly pinned at the end of the tunnel. She'd escaped, she thought, but she'd been running away, not toward anything. Now, Nora thought, and about time, she was beginning to feel strong and capable and free again. And Michael Justin had brought a new and very interesting set of feelings unexpectedly into her life. I'm a survivor, she told herself. Things really will turn out all right.

"What about Steve?" she asked now. "Do you ever hear from him?" Steve was Kate's first husband, Sam's father. Flamboyant, handsome, charming Stephen Hall was a theatre major when he and Kate met and married in college. The marriage lasted two years, then Steve left Kate and six-month old Sam "for his career."

Nora had seen him on television in a shampoo commercial the year before.

Kate snorted. "A postcard last month. He's in a TV pilot, something about lawyers, and the jerk wants us to watch for it."

Kate had loved him extravagantly. When he left her, he left with a black eye and Kate had ended up on a month-long binge that sent her to a hospital to dry out. That's when Sam had first started long visits to her grandparents.

"The crud," Nora agreed.

"Men," Kate said.

"Life," Nora summed it up and Sam threw open the porch door, duffel bag in hand.

"I'm ready," she announced, then scowled, puzzled when both women burst out laughing.

7

Paul Vronski concentrated on slowing down his breathing. He allowed the oxygen to flow into his lungs like a warm tide, expanding his inner universe with peace and well-being. Then he exhaled through a timeless eternity, filling his mind with images of serenity—the tranquility of stone, the stillness of a lake.

The leaf unfolds in the sun, he recited to himself, gradually lifting his head from where it rested on his knees. Eyes closed, he placed the backs of his hands on the top of his thighs and concentrated on nose breathing, thinking only of clouds. Then he opened his eyes. Still focused inward, he didn't register the piano across the stretch of carpeted living room or the ceiling-high shelves of books on herbs, natural healing, yoga, meditation and a dozen other subjects he had devoted himself to studying over the years. Peace, he repeated to himself, peace. Then one nostril involuntarily dilated while his upper lip curled ever so slightly.

Franny was cooking hamburgers again.

Sighing, he unfolded his long, lean legs to stand and drift into the kitchen.

Paul stood behind his wife, watching over her

shoulder as she turned and prodded the sizzling meat spattering grease in the pan. He eyed it with a distant distaste and turned to search the refrigerator for the makings of his own dinner—carrots, cabbage, onions, peppers. Clean foods. In a habitual, graceful motion he reached for his grater and salad bowl.

"I'll be taking a bath in chamomile and maybe some rosemary before we go," he announced.

"Right," Franny acknowledged absentmindedly.

"I think you ought to join me. It's a calming influence."

"Sure," she answered, flipping burgers with practiced ease.

Cybele, their four-year old daughter named for the Roman goddess of fertility and the mysteries of earth magic, marched into the kitchen behind her father. She looked with interest at the hamburgers her mother was frying, then moved to stand beside her father, watching him grate carrots, bouncing her slender body against his long leg.

"Daddy poops a lot!" she pronounced gleefully.

Carole Salant lounged in the wing chair Rick's mother had given them after changing her mind about consigning it to Goodwill. One leg hung over the chair arm. She only wore a "satin" polyester robe in the heat and kicked her hanging foot impatiently up and down, studying Rick asleep in his work clothes on the couch.

"Hey," she called, then tossed a folded newspaper in the direction of his head.

The loose pages hit him in the face and he sleepily opened an eye, face buried in the crook of his elbow.

"We ought to get our asses in gear," she told him.

Rick yawned and dug the fingers of both hands into his curly brown beard, clawing at his chin. He rolled onto his back, arching against the couch in a full stretch.

"Shit," he said distinctly, rubbing at his crotch with both hands. Then he rolled up, swiveled to face Carole and stare with interest at the white skin between the gaping lapels of her robe, the blue veins of her breasts and the nipples just out of sight.

"Sure, baby," he answered, standing up and walking towards her. "Sure," he repeated and put his mouth on hers, sliding one hand inside the inviting robe.

Alex Thomas glanced up at the digital clock precisely centered on his walnut Regency desk. The contrast never failed to please him, the careful eclecticism of ages in the things he chose to place around him—an Art Nouveau lamp with a trio of naked, nubile nymphs supporting a seashell shade, the classic French Regency desk, the clean lines of the ebony digital clock, the medieval iron dagger he used as a paperweight for his class syllabus.

Alex carefully marked his place in *The Golden Ass* with an intricately worked leather bookmark and glanced out his window at the campus, quiet in the golden, late afternoon light. He stood, automatically fingering and shaking out the crease in his white, pleated Brioni slacks, and brushed manicured finger-tips through his layered, deep blonde hair. He carefully patted the top of his head, gratified, once again, that his hair still felt thick and healthy. It sprang back with a carefully constrained vitality.

Tonight, he thought, maybe the khaki Lauren shirt, the loose-fitting linen pants. Definitely casual, he thought, but not without style.

He methodically packed his reference books, mono-grammed leather notebook, datebook and small pile of file cards into his Gucci briefcase. Yes, he thought, definitely casual. After all . . . he didn't verbalize the rest of the thought, but allowed his upper lip to curl slightly in disdain. Things do change, he finally con-

cluded, reaching out to caress one of the nymphs with
a languid touch before switching off the desk lamp.
Things certainly do change.

Stiffly, slowly, Charlie Luther turned his head
towards the small electric alarm clock on the floor
beside his bed. Almost time. He looked down at his
fingers, clawed in a grip around his knees, willing
them to relax and straighten. Stiff, he pushed his
booted feet along the sheets, stretching his legs,
watching, detached, as his pillow toppled off the
mattress to the floor and his boots left streaks of gray
on the sheet. He inhaled, working his legs and getting
the circulation back, then lurched forward onto his
hands and knees. Almost time. He lowered his head
to rest on the mattress. Almost time.

Kate waved Nora and Sam on their way from the
porch. She waited until Nora's car was out of sight
before she went into the house and poured herself
half a tumbler of bourbon. She checked the clock, ten
minutes fast, in the kitchen. Almost time. Kate
swallowed nearly all the bourbon in one swift, head-
long rush. Almost time.

"Oh my God!" Nora yelped as they got near her
place, "Dr. Ellicott! Nuts, I forgot all about calling
him back."
"Who's he?"
"My boss, sort of. Peter Ellicott, Ph.D. He's the
head of my department and he left a message on my
answering machine. I should have called him back."
"Ellicott. I know who he is. He's the one with the
crazy sister."
"What?"
"That's what Nancy Wick said and her father
teaches there, too. Nancy said her father said that Dr.
Ellicott's sister was as crazy as a bag of rocks and

she's always going somewhere. You know," Sam shot her a significant look, "*going* somewhere."

"Well," Nora said as she swung the Datsun to the curb in a wide loop, "if she's anything like Dr. Ellicott, it's hard to believe."

They were on the walk up to the porch, Nora rushing ahead, Sam trotting after her with the self-satisfied smirk of someone who never forgot to return phone calls.

"Dr. Ellicott," Nora explained, fumbling her key into the lock, "has no sweat glands. I think he was born with a crewcut and bow tie, speaking impeccable English. I am definitely in trouble."

But the phone call to Dr. Ellicott went more smoothly than she'd expected. They spoke briefly, setting up an appointment for later in the week to go over Nora's plans. For once, Nora thought, he sounded halfway human, almost friendly in a courtly, formal way. She did want to find out more about his sister, though. If he actually had one.

Things are looking up, Nora thought as she hung up the phone with satisfaction.

"Good." Sam nodded her approval as Nora turned away from the phone. "You sounded real cool, very professional."

"Thanks. Now, about this professional housecleaning stuff. Where do you propose we start?" Nora smiled down at her. Sam was scowling at the boxes of pots and pans still unpacked in the kitchen.

What had happened between Ted and Sam? The thought surfaced unexpectedly. But the bond of trust forming between her and the girl was still so fragile, Nora didn't want to snap it by pushing. Maybe we'll talk about it later.

The study group arrived at Kate's in singles and pairs, drifting in from the night quietly, barely disturbing the thickening blue dusk. The crickets and cicadas were tentatively beginning their nightly chorus. A few moths circled the streetlights that had flickered into life. Across the street and two doors down, the last coals of the barbecue glowed a deep, sullen red. In the purpled shadow of a clump of shrubs across the street, a black dog waited, watching the people going into Kate Hall's house through golden eyes.

Almost time.

8

The silence in Kate's house had stretched for twenty minutes or more. They seemed to be waiting for darkness to drown them. It surrounded the house like a violet sea, seeping in at the open windows, washing them all with quiet. They moved a little in it, unsure, uncomfortable. The study group waited.

In one corner Carole Salant and Rick Cummings passed a thin joint back and forth. Alex Thomas had taken Kate's rocker, keeping up a subdued movement, theatrically lit from behind with the brass floor lamp, a red scarf hung over its shade. The rosy light made a golden nimbus around his tawny lion's head. He was smiling, lips in a soft curve.

Paul Vronski knelt beside the couch lighting an oil lamp with a wooden kitchen match. He moved with a ceremonious grace, large, luminous eyes catching the light. He had a gentle, mystical face, the face of a saint in the gold light of the flame, shadows marking high cheekbones. When he replaced the glass chimney he turned to smile at Franny, delicate and beautiful in the lamp light with hair as pale and soft as their daughter's floating around her face.

She was looking off into the distance, frowning slightly like a plaster martyr brooding on the sins of

91

the world. Franny was wondering if their teenage babysitter would manage to get Cybele into bed on time for once.

Kate was in the armchair with a full ashtray, a half-empty glass and Charlie Luther arranged at her feet.

"Shall we begin?" Alex Thomas asked, dropping it into the silence like a rock in a pond.

They all turned to look at him.

When Victor died it was unspoken but understood that Ted Kellogg would move into his place as their central figure—not as a replacement, but as the most verbal, most aggressive in the group. They had been like a spring with the tension suddenly released. Their focus was gone. They even bickered about some things and might have fallen apart entirely, drifted away, except for Ted. He held them together. He was the loudest among them, if not the most powerful. No one had Victor's power. Certainly Alex Thomas didn't, but now he was the only one willing to break the silence among them. It was a declaration of sorts. No one was especially pleased with Alex's self-election, but none of them was willing to offer a challenge.

Alex looked at them, one by one, a rite of approval.

Carole Salant's eyes glinted, almost feral in the dimness. Her lips curved up, the tip of her tongue flickering out to touch her upper lip, pink and moist. Rick's eyes were closed. He inhaled, wrapping himself in smoke, oblivious.

Franny half-smiled nervously, like a debutante trying to do the right thing at a party of Hell's Angels. Paul Vronski nodded dreamily, adrift in his own peace.

Charlie Luther was studying the floor, rocking his upper body in small jerky motions. One shoulder twitched occasionally.

Kate bent to pick up her glass and drained the rest of the bourbon, refusing for a time to look at Alex, feeling his steady gaze on her. Finally she met his eyes, appraising him until, in wry submission, she raised her empty glass in a mock salute.

They were ready to begin.

9

After two nights spent catching a few hours of restless dozing on his office couch, Finnerty had finally made it home.

He intended to let the Kellogg case percolate in the back of his mind while he finally got a hot shower and a warmed-over dinner from the Golden Dragon. The hours of questioning and reading reports had told him nothing, except that something was scaring the crap out of Charlie Luther, something he wasn't telling them. Yet.

Finnerty retreated to his den, his sanctuary and the only room he spent much time in since Shirley had left him nine years ago.

"Well, Roy Finnerty," she had said, pink face a harsh contrast to her cherry red lipstick, "now you got what you wanted. I'm darned if I know just why you married me in the first place since you never did want a real wife. You just go on back in there and brood like you always do. You won't be seeing me again."

He had watched her drive away in her white Chevy convertible, then gone back into their little box of a brick tract home to finish off most of a bottle of Scotch they'd gotten for an anniversary present. And he didn't much care for Scotch.

Finnerty had seen Shirley again, after she married Bob Owens, riding around town in the red Toronado Bob had bought her. Within a week of his old man's passing, Bob Owens started transforming the family chain of grocery stores to sleek supermarkets with plant boutiques and girls hired part-time from the college to pass out slivers of cheese and sliced kiwis. Shirley always waved when she saw Finnerty. Bob was a big man on the Chamber of Commerce, and rumor had it he might be mayor some day.

There were no rumors about Finnerty, not even about him and May Kwan. Her brother owned the Golden Dragon where she worked and had a small apartment over the restaurant. May had a closed face and guarded eyes. She didn't talk much, but she always opened the door when Finnerty knocked. The arrangement suited him, though he never knew how May felt about it.

Settled in his leather easy chair, Finnerty popped the top on a can of beer, took a long satisfying draught and felt the tension beginning to ease out of him. Few people were ever invited into Finnerty's den. Vern Snider had never seen it although he liked to fool himself that he and the sheriff were friends. Chances are it would have confused the hell out of him. Finnerty's den was the one place where he indulged his private obsession.

It started when he was a young deputy. He'd driven up to Chicago for a Bears game with a bunch of the guys, but had to take the bus back early for duty that night. With a couple hours to kill, Finnerty wandered the Loop and drifted, self-consciously but curious, into the Art Institute. He was pleased to find that some of the paintings appealed to him. He liked the bright Van Goghs and sensuous Gauguins, the round women with their soft eyes and generous hips. He liked the big stone Buddhas with their secret smiles.

But there was one room Finnerty couldn't get enough of. A room of glistening steel, that mixed death with pride and cold beauty, contained implements of war inlaid with gold and silver and graceful curving blades designed to hack through armor and flesh. It was a display of Renaissance weapons in their foolish grandeur and cruel efficiency.

The polearms fascinated him. They were slim wooden staffs, twice the height of a man, topped with two feet of thrusting steel, blades, spikes and spurs designed to pierce and tear. He read their names in fierce concentration, lips moving silently to shape the foreign sounds. *Guisarme. Partisan. Fauchard. Halberd.*

He studied the daggers and swords, tracing the intricate engraving on flat blades and the elaborate hilts inlaid with jewels and ivory, gold and silver damascene shaping delicate designs. Distracted, he moved up and down the aisles, discovering something new with every pass—the bone-inlaid crossbows, mail armor, heavy-flanged maces, fanciful helmets with horses' heads and Biblical scenes of inlaid gold.

He spent hours pacing that room, nearly missing his bus. Afterwards, the images of the weapons with their deadly beauty, their lethal intricacy, haunted him. In his off-hours he started making trips to the library and the local museum to learn more about the weapons and the minds that shaped them. He became engrossed in the fierce rivalries of the Italian city-states, the splendor and ritual of their wars and intrigues.

Finnerty's den was a showplace of his obsession. Over the years he had gathered reproductions of Renaissance paintings that depicted massive battle scenes, hunts and banquets, portraits of the *condottieri*, the great generals, ship models of the sleek Venetian war galleys, a drawing of Cesare Borgia's sword etched with illustrations of Julius Ceasar's con-

quests, Leonardo da Vinci's sketches of flying
machines and submarines, parachutes and ideal
cities. Books lined the walls—richly illustrated
volumes on history and art, weapons and architec-
ture, scholarly explorations of philosophy, transla-
tions of every work by Machiavelli, Dante, Lorenzo
de Medici, Castiglione, da Vinci and others.

Beer in hand, Finnerty sprawled in his chair, eyes
wandering familiarly over a poster reproducing the
painting of a tournament in Florence's Piazza Santa
Croce. A richly ornamented crowd of knights dis-
played their dazzling armor and weaponry as much as
their skill. Horses and men were packed together in a
heaving, muscled, gaudy spectacle. The knights'
names were embroidered in gold on their horses'
trappings and servants ducked underfoot to help
guide the charging, frantic animals in the crush of
bodies. Wealthy merchants in their red robes hung,
watching, over balconies and viewing stands while
the rich ladies of the city looked on demurely from
side balconies and the poor of the city crowded
around the wooden blockades, peering through knot-
holes or standing on stools and benches.

The faces of those now long dead always touched
something in Finnerty. He felt he knew them, their
disappointed love affairs, sore feet and upset
stomachs, their pride and determination. But all the
hopes and fears, ambition and innocence was dust
now. Their stories were unsolvable mysteries. It
should have put something like Kellogg's case into a
vaster perspective. One death among so many should
be just a speck of dust drifting onto a vast mound of
forgotten lives, fleetingly mourned. But for Finnerty
it didn't work like that. For Finnerty it was just the
opposite. Those hundreds of lives that had slipped
away unrecorded and unregarded made it that much
more important for him to create order, sense and
justice in every part of the world he could touch.

From what he had learned of Kellogg, Finnerty didn't think his death was much of a loss to the world, except that he had been alive and had been human and therefore of value. That much of Renaissance thinking, the humanism, had become part of Finnerty, satisfying some hunger that had worked in him all his life.

Finnerty believed in right. He would die for it.

Bobby Hunt and Phil Jenkins sat, cramped, bored, occasionally bitching out of half-hearted habit, in an unmarked Ford outside Kate Hall's house. They had watched the procession of visitors enter with mild interest and a few crude remarks. Now it was dark. Time had limped by and nothing was happening. They didn't expect much to happen and couldn't figure out why, precisely, Finnerty wanted the place watched. The arrival of the visitors had made them each wonder, strictly to himself, if there was some truth to this satanic cult crap. Afraid of sounding foolish or chickenshit, neither of them brought the subject up.

After a while, Bobby Hunt broke the latest long silence.

"Keep an eye open for me, will ya? I gotta take a leak."

The next time they spoke was after things started happening.

Michael Justin was editing tapes that evening, putting together samples from projects turned in from students last year to show this year's crop examples of technique. His mind drifted now and then to Nora Durant. He had already decided to forget about the standard waiting period before calling. He didn't want to wait before talking to her again. She touched some part of him he thought was buried under years of casual affairs. She captured his imagination.

On the screen in front of him Victor's face suddenly appeared and Michael's breath stopped until he remembered that one of his students had been a follower of Victor's. The tape project intercut a Rolling Stones concert, close-ups of the wheels of speeding trains, a hawk's flight and pounce on a sparrow and Victor, shot like a music video. Strange images and "Jumpin' Jack Flash" barraged the senses, always coming back to Victor, his face in close-up. Victor. Sardonic, sly, full of secrets, Victor gazed back at Michael with green-eyed irony.

"You knew, didn't you? You bastard." Michael spoke out loud, looking at his half-brother for one long moment before stopping the tape.

He took the tape out of the machine and reached for another.

Nora and Sam had cleaned industriously for more than two hours before they called a halt for the night. After they devoured a quick batch of spaghetti they rewarded themselves with Sara Lee cheesecake and a game of Scrabble. In the background, Crosby, Stills and Nash sang for Judy Blue Eyes. *"Don't let the past remind you of what we are not now . . ."*

Listening, Sam cocked her head. "Old guys," she pronounced knowledgeably. When Nora spluttered, indignant, she added, "They're okay, though."

Nora was crouched over her rack of letters, looking for a way to use her J that would include both a triple letter and double word score when Sam interrupted her concentration with a matter-of-fact remark.

"It's starting now," Sam said casually.

Jump. Nora moved the wooden pieces around. *Jumper.*

"What is?" she asked, absent-minded.

After a few seconds Sam came back at her. "What is what?"

Nora looked up at Sam. The girl was studying her

letters, then looked up to meet her eyes.

Nora signed, mock patience. "You said, 'It's starting now,' and I said, 'What is?' "

"No, I didn't. I didn't say anything." Sam scowled.

"Yes, you did," Nora insisted. "Maybe you were just thinking out loud."

"No! I didn't say anything! I didn't." She said it loudly, an edge of panic in it, and Nora studied her a moment, then shrugged.

"My mind was wandering, I guess. It happens in old age." But Sam had said something, Nora was sure. *It's starting now.*

They had gathered in a circle sitting on the floor of Kate's living room. The scarf-draped lamp was off and the oil lamp lit the room, filling it with moving shadows. Clusters of candles added pools of soft light. Votives, pillars and tapers perched on bookshelves, tabletops and window sills. Their scents of sandalwood, bayberry and clove mingled in a hot, rich mixture. Outside, the air was nearly still and no breeze trembled through the windows. The candle flames burned straight, tall and unflickering.

The circle of seven sat cross-legged, knees touching, hands joined. Carole Salant held Alex's right hand with Rick to her right, then Franny, then Paul Vronski. Kate sat between Paul and Charlie Luther. They had been sitting silently for some time, meditating, searching for unity, reaching for power.

Kate had frowned when Alex suggested the phrases. Meditation, okay. But power? She kept silent, though, waiting to see what came next.

"Blessed be." Alex spoke and a small, quick current of tension swept around the circle. Every hand tightened its grasp.

"Blessed be thy feet that have brought thee in these ways. Blessed be the pangs of love. Blessed be the desire of men. Blessed be thy womb that bore us.

Blessed be thy breasts, formed in beauty. Goddess . . ."

Paul Vronski's hand tightened around Kate's. It seemed familiar to them all, this droning chant, but it was new to her. She had been marginal, now she was part of them, and she wasn't sure she wanted to be. She looked at their faces, eyes closed, concentrating.

"Blessed be," Alex said. "Through your grace I know power. I know your gifts. You have seen strange things, the hand of death, the shapes of woe, mad dogs and the corruption of the flesh . . ."

A vibration that was not quite a sound began to build below the level of her hearing—a sense of oppression, a hollowness that thrummed a low echo.

"Stop." Kate's voice came out as a faint croak, barely audible. She felt as though a hand squeezed her throat closed, as Charlie Luther's grip crushed her hand, through pain to numbness.

"Raven, eater of the dead, the unseen who walks by night, comfort me. Touch me. Warm your icy fingers."

Carole Salant's shoulders began to move restlessly. A quick twitch. Lift, drop. She shuddered and Kate stared, watching a wave of motion writhe down her soft body.

"Pangs of love, throes of passion, grant that I am born again in your white heat . . ."

Carole's head dropped back, exposing her long white throat. She started to work her hips, moaning low in her throat.

"Touch me with power. Touch me with life."

Salant was grinding her buttocks into the floor, twisting her upper body. Her head lolled back, then forward, rolling side to side. Her moans grew louder. Kate felt sick, nauseated. Cold sweat trickled on her forehead, but she couldn't move. She looked at Alex. His face was blank, mouth opening and closing like a puppet's.

"Bring me madness," he said. "Bring me glory."

The long, thin flames of the candles went squat. The room grew a fraction darker. Carole moaned and shook.

She was working harder now, grinding at the floor, a frenzied pumping that shook her breath out in ragged gasps. The deep humming grew louder.

"Bring me the seasons of the flame. Lord of Darkness, take me . . ."

Carole cried out, head back, abandoned, a long, wild cry, her face contorted. Kate closed her eyes but felt she was falling in the darkness, and they burst open. Alex still chanted on, his voice firm, full of power, not quite his, not quite human.

The candles flared, then flames, impossibly high, danced in a wind Kate couldn't feel.

"Pangs of love, unity, death, rebirth. Take me."

"Take me," Charlie Luther muttered softly and Kate felt a cold whisper of icy air brush her cheek. At the window the curtains lifted and dropped, lifted still higher, dropped again.

"Hecate, *anteia*—the meeter. Hecate, *einodia*— she who appears on the way. Touch me with your sure and icy knowledge. Show me the road . . ."

The air moved around them now, alive. It trailed its fingers across Kate's face, touching her lips and throat, and she shook her head, trying to pull away. The sound in the air reverberated in her bones. Paul's hand in hers was clammy. His grip was relentless.

"Infernal, terrestrial, celestial . . . She of the crossroads, moon of a thousand forms, companion of the darkness, guide me."

Rick jerked and shivered. "Hecate, Isis . . ." he breathed and the words came out in clouds of icy vapor.

Two of the candles flared up, then died. Behind Kate the room grew darker yet. The curtains flapped and twisted with a life of their own. Franny's fine blond

hair blew up from her shoulders and settled to flutter
like a trapped butterfly.

"Queen of the night," Alex chanted, "companion of
the Prince of Wantons, consort of Bal, Bel, Tammuz,
holder of the keys, Kore of the underworld, wife of
the horned god, the antlered man, show me the secret
places. Touch me with dark knowledge, lead me in
your husband's ways."

And Franny's pale head snapped back, her eyes
staring open.

"Dark one, wanderer, we open a place." Alex
shouted it almost, voice battling the dark hum of
sound around them, the wind that whipped around
them, battering them now from every direction.

Franny's Indian cotton dress flapped in the wind,
pressing tight against her body. Her mouth opened as
if she would scream, gaping like a cave, but no sound
came out. And then they heard it.

Kate squinted into the wind, staring at her,
watching Franny's frozen face as the sound came out.

It started faint and distant, a sound that might have
been a half mile away. Agony, a tortured howling, a
man's voice impossibly far away. But coming closer.

And Kate watched Franny's face, a face that didn't
move. She didn't even seem to be breathing and yet
the scream kept coming. She was stone, a channel, a
hole in the mountain for the oracle's voice. The
scream built in volume, fluttered, twisted, working
its way to her throat. It reached her in a last wracking
rush, a bellow winding up a scale of pain to a pure,
unearthly shriek that stopped short, slicing the air
with silence.

And in the silence they heard a heavy crash from
upstairs, a boom that shook the house and rattled the
windows in their frames.

Through it all Franny still hadn't moved. Her
mouth still yawned open and now from it came the
barking of a dog. Kate's empty glass, abandoned on
the floor behind her, shattered.

Far away, it seemed, Kate heard a pounding on her front door.

"Police! Open up in there!"

Kate couldn't move. She was cold, so cold. And the wind kept blowing. Overhead another crashing boom shook the house. It was near the head of the stairs, she thought dreamily.

Three more candles flickered and died. The dark was moving in.

Out on the porch Bobby Hunt and Phil Jenkins had their guns drawn. Phil held the screen door open. Bobby kicked at the closed front door again, shouting, then reached for the doorknob.

"Jesus!" He snatched his hand back and shook it in pained surprise. It was like grabbing ice. He thought he'd left some skin behind. From inside the house each thought he could hear a train whistle and they traded puzzled looks.

"Window," Bobby Hunt said.

Franny started to shake, a strange howl pouring out of her.

Charlie's hand started to jerk and twitch in Kate's. His body shook like a rag doll's. "Huh-huh-huh-huh . . ." he breathed and each breath made an icy puff of vapor.

An open window slammed down, then another. One by one all around the house the windows crashed shut. From upstairs came the sound of glass shattering. Then a heavy crash ricocheted from the wall of the stairwell.

"Yes-s-s-s . . ." Carole Salant hissed in the flickering dark.

And finally a hoarse scream broke free from Kate's cold panic.

"NO!" she shouted it with all her strength. "NO!" And she found somewhere the strength to try and pull free of Charlie Luther's crippling hold, yanking away from him, twisting her hand in his cold, wet grip.

A stench began to fill her nostrils as the room filled

up with a thick, cloying odor. It was all rot and corruption, sweet, sickly. Kate coughed, gagging on the stink.

The candles were all out now, only the oil lamp still burned. With a high-pitched crack its chimney exploded. A flying fragment sliced Rick's cheek above the beard and slivers pelted Paul's back.

Another boom sounded in the front hallway. It blended with the sound of the men shouting and banging from outside.

On the floor before them in the center of the circle, a puddle of water began to form, coming from nowhere. Slowly, the puddle grew and the stench got stronger.

Kate had worked her hand an inch out of Charlie's grip, past the big knuckles. She was getting free, but not fast enough. One finger of the puddle began to extend toward her and the thought that it might touch her made Kate panic and scramble back. Charlie was staring down at it in dull fascination.

Kate shouted and with a tremendous heave threw herself back, out of the circle, free of Charlie's grip, but the sound was lost in the crash of the front door as the two deputies finally broke it in. A blast of cold air made them both stagger, but they recovered fast and dropped to a ready position, the points of their guns sweeping the room.

When Kate broke free of the circle the others all sprang back, jolted, as though an electric charge had hit them. Kate scrambled to sit up, to protect herself against she didn't know what.

Two of the candles lit of their own accord, she thought, confused.

"Jesus," one of the deputies said.

Franny Vronski curled slowly into a ball and began to sob softly. Paul leaned over, after a moment, and began to stroke her hair.

"It's all right," he crooned, "Everything's all right now."

"What the hell's going on here?" a deputy said and Kate just stared at him blankly. All of them were silent except for Paul and Franny, until Carole Salant suddenly screamed, a short, sharp, strangled bark, and threw herself backward. Her head hit the hardwood floor first with a sickening thunk and she began to convulse, arching and writhing on the ground, heels drumming against the floor while for long seconds they all stared at her.

Bobby Hunt moved in quickly, holstering his gun, grabbing a throw pillow from the couch to put under her head and stop its awful thumping against the floor.

"Call an ambulance," he snapped at his partner.

Jenkins surveyed the room suspiciously one more time and holstered his gun. "Where's the phone?" he snapped at Kate.

She waved toward the hall behind him. "On . . . on . . ." she croaked, words refusing to come out. But he turned and saw it on the hall table.

"Get some light in here," Bobby Hunt barked, and Kate hoisted herself to her feet as slowly as an accident victim. She staggered, then reached a lamp.

The scene in the bright light was sad chaos. Wax had splattered on the walls and furniture. Ashes and cigarette butts had blown from the overflowing ashtrays to leave a fine dust across the room. Fragments of glass from the shattered lamp chimney and drinking glasses scattered the room.

Blood traced a path down Rick's cheek and disappeared into his beard. A deep red stain soaked the shoulder of his workshirt from blood that trickled through his beard.

Paul was curved protectively over Franny. She lay still in a tightly curled ball, quiet now.

Charlie and Alex sat, pale and oblivious, staring at the puddle of water stretching between them on the wooden floor.

Kate followed their stare.

In the center of the puddle in a small jumbled heap
lay three green plastic mermaids.

"He's here now," Sam said in that dead-calm voice.

"Who? Who's here?" Nora sat beside the girl on her
upstairs landing outside the bathroom door feeling
her forehead, cool and damp, and talking to her
without getting a response.

It began downstairs when they were playing
Scrabble.

"It's starting now," Sam had said, matter-of-factly.

But she didn't remember saying it when Nora asked
her what was starting. And she disappeared into herself for long minutes while Nora watched, not sure
what to do.

"Sam?" she had asked and touched the girl's
shoulder.

And Sam had wrenched away from her like a rabbit
caught in a trap. Then she vomited.

"Gross!" she said then, sounding, at least, like
herself. "I'm so embarrassed!"

But Nora assured her and sent her upstairs to wash
her face while she cleaned up. When Sam failed to
reappear, Nora followed and found her sitting on the
landing, rocking herself gently.

"Sam?"

"He's here now," was all Sam said.

"Who? Who's here?" Nora asked her.

But Sam wouldn't answer. And afterwards she
denied saying it.

It was after eleven when Finnerty's phone rang. He
had drifted off in the leather armchair, but from long
practice he was instantly wide awake at the sound of
the phone.

"Finnerty," he answered.

"Sheriff, this is Bobby Hunt. We've got a situation
down here at headquarters. I think maybe you ought
to come in."

"Fifteen minutes," Finnerty replied and hung up.

At close to midnight Nora's phone rang. She snatched it off the hook quickly, hoping it wouldn't awaken Sam who slept beside her.

"Oh, so you're still alive." Simon barked at her with the acid sharpness of worry. "You could have returned my call."

"Simon. I'm sorry if you've been worrying, but a lot has been happening."

"Such as?"

Nora was keeping her voice low, but Sam had started shifting restlessly in her sleep. "Look," Nora murmured, "I really can't talk now, but I promise I'll call you in the morning. At your office, okay?"

"Why can't you talk? Is there someone with you?"

"Yes," Nora hissed, then she covered the receiver and her mouth with a cupped hand. "Sam," she whispered.

After a moment of silence Simon answered, sounding relieved, almost hearty. "Oh, Kate's daughter. She's staying with you?"

"Mmm-hmm."

"Well, of course you can't talk freely in front of her. All right, call me tomorrow then. Nora, I really do care about you, you know."

"I know."

"Goodnight, then."

"Goodnight." Sweet dreams, she almost said from years of the habit.

When she reached out to hang up the phone it rang as soon as she placed the receiver in the cradle. She snatched it up mid-ring, thinking Simon must have forgotten something.

"Yes?" But there was only a hollow silence, a distant static.

"Hello?" she questioned more sharply.

More silence, then a man's voice, not Simon's. It breathed in her ear as close as a lover.

"The girl," it said.

"Who is this?"

Silence without even the sound of breathing. Then, faint and far away, a dog's long-drawn moonlight howl.

Nora slammed the phone down, rubbed her ear hard against her shoulder and scrubbed her hand against the sheet that covered her as though some corruption clung to her from the touch of the phone.

"What?" Sam muttered.

"Wrong number," Nora told her. *The girl.* "Go back to sleep."

It was 3:00 a.m. when Calvin Russell sat up in bed beside his wife Tildy. Moonlight made the thin wisps of white hair that stood up, sleep-rumpled, on his head look like a crazy halo.

Calvin smoothed down his hair, lifted the flowered sheet and slid his feet down to feel around for his slippers. When he stood up he was slow and stiff, favoring his bad back. He twitched the sheet back into place and brushed a hand over it, nice and tidy. His robe lay on a straight-back chair next to the bed. Tildy had given it to him for their 32nd anniversary and he kept meaning to get her to fix the ripped seam of the pocket.

Robe wrapped loose and tied around him, Calvin Russell started shuffling to the door, old leather slippers flapping against his shiny callused heels. He made his way down the hall and the long narrow stairs to the kitchen without bothering to turn on any lights, all the way to the back door.

Errol met him there, tail wagging like a plume. Errol Flynn, one of the best retrievers in the country, named after the movie star, followed his master to the barn. His tail wagged even harder when Calvin came out of the barn with his double-barreled shotgun.

But Calvin ignored him, shuffling and flapping his

way back into the house, back through the kitchen, up the stairs, into the bedroom.

Tildy was still snoring gently. By moonlight he held the barrel of the gun a few inches from her blue-rinsed head.

"Bitch," he said. And then he fired both barrels.

At 3:00 a.m. Finnerty was still at his desk, reading and rereading the statements of the group picked up at Kate Hall's house. Bobby Hunt had wanted to hold them on some charge, any charge—disturbing the peace or creating a public nuisance—but Finnerty just snorted, shook his head at the crazy lot of them and, after getting their statements, sent them home.

The sheriff had spent time with all of them except Carole Salant who'd been taken to St. Francis Hospital with convulsions. Not one of them had made a damn bit of sense, including Bobby Hunt and Phil Jenkins. Frozen doorknobs. Windows that closed themselves.

Finnerty scowled down at the statement made by Alex Thomas. His eyes felt dry and gritty and reading was an effort. Just a word here and there jumped out at him, like "possessed." Thomas had said that, looking embarrassed and defensive. But he'd also looked secretly pleased with himself, excitement making the eyes shine in his cold face.

They started a group meditation, Thomas had told him, and Thomas had led a prayer. But something seemed to take him over. He didn't know where the words came from, had listened to his own voice as to a stranger and couldn't stop the flow of words. Talking in tongues, Finnerty's Aunt Cissy would have called it, but Finnerty didn't mention that.

All of their stories matched up. They all agreed that Thomas had sounded strange, chanting while they sat in a circle holding hands. Carole Salant had moaned and shuddered, then become quiet, seeming all right until afterwards.

When Franny Vronski talked about Carole, one of
her pretty pink lips had curled in disdain. Carole
liked attention, was all Franny would say. About her
own part, Franny was no help at all.

It was cold, she remembered. Then she got lost.

Lost? Finnerty had questioned gently, as though he
were speaking to a young child.

Franny looked like a child then—pale, eyes wide,
small hands twisting and working in her lap. She
nodded at him like a little girl telling her father about
her nightmare, big eyes fixed on his face.

Lost. She felt like she was far away, somehow floating above them all, seeing the room and her own body
from high in a far corner of the room and at the same
time simply somewhere else, not with them at all. She
saw the wind blowing on her, but couldn't feel it. She
couldn't really hear Alex because of the roaring. It
was a sound like thunder in deep caves and it was
made of a thousand different sounds. It was people,
shouting, crying, screaming. It was dogs that barked
and howled, wolves, foxes, lions. Birds that shrieked,
wild animals that bellowed, the sound of wind and
water, all beating around her. She was being drawn
away into the dark and she couldn't get back.

The stenographer took it all down, pencil scratching
dutifully on paper, the only sound in the silence when
Franny stopped, until Franny broke down. She
sobbed and shook, huddled in on herself in Finnerty's
brown leather chair, until Finnerty called Paul into
the office to take his wife home.

The others reported the pounding, the wind, the
cold, the water appearing on the living room floor.
What caused it? No one had an explanation. Who shut
the windows? Nobody, according to them.

Finnerty didn't like it.

Sam was up before Nora, banging pots in the
kitchen.

Probably, Nora thought, grimacing and clamping a pillow over her head, Sam didn't realize that not everyone slept as heavily as Kate. Unless this was Sam's unsubtle way of getting some company. She's a good kid, but she's not nearly as tough as she'd like to be. Sam wanted to be strong and self-reliant, feeling she had to take care of Kate. What Sam doesn't know yet, Nora thought, is that Kate's much better at taking care of herself than she seems to be.

She'd have to have a long talk with Kate about Sam, Nora decided. The girl needs help. The nightmares, the sudden vomiting, the things she said and couldn't remember saying, were obviously cries for help, more help than Nora or Kate could give her. Maybe she should see a counselor, some kind of child psychologist or psychiatrist. There were bound to be some in Stony Cliffs. They probably made a fortune out of the screwed-up kids of the oddball faculty.

Tsk, tsk, she admonished herself, *you're* one of the oddball faculty now. Sighing, she tossed aside the pillow and sat up squinting at the nightstand beside her bed, feeling around for her glasses. She found them marking a place in the notebook she always kept beside the bed in case inspiration hit in the middle of the night. She stared at them, puzzled, since she didn't remember opening the notebook the night before. Curious, hesitating, she put the glasses on and looked at the notebook. The page held an almost illegible scrawl—illegible, but her own handwriting. She reached for it gingerly, as though paper snakes would jump out at her. Or something worse.

Cunt, she read, *I will take you both.*

And she felt cold and obscenely invaded. She read it again and again until it turned into gibberish. She studied the handwriting, sure it was hers but hoping it was someone else's. Wondering, trying to remember writing it, she picked up the pencil. But she had no memory of writing anything at all.

Slowly, Nora tore the sheet from the notebook. She

folded it carefully, then tore it into small pieces.

Kate didn't fall asleep until after dawn. Deputy Bobby Hunt had drive her home, then gruffly volunteered to tour the house with her, checking every room. For what, neither of them was certain.

Probably, Kate assumed, the sheriff thought she or someone in the group had done it all with mirrors and dimestore magic tricks. Maybe Bobby Hunt was looking for hidden equipment or an accomplice lurking in a closet or under the bed. But she didn't care what the sheriff or his deputies thought of her. She was frightened, more frightened than she wanted to admit, and simply grateful to have company going through the house, surveying the damage, listening for strange sounds in the night.

They found nothing, only the wreckage they'd left behind when they went to the station. And a small puddle of water in her bedroom.

"You got a leak somewhere?" Bobby Hunt asked her.

But Kate just looked at him. There was no plumbing anywhere near the puddle.

The deputy shone his flashlights in closets and into the crawlspace of the attic where a stretch of silvery cobwebs made it clear no one had entered in years.

"There's a basement, too," Kate had informed him drily and Bobby had shot her a quick look trying to read her intentions.

Wordlessly, he turned and trotted down the stairs. Kate followed him, then led the way to the kitchen and the door to the basement. She opened the door for him but didn't accompany him down. He returned a few minutes later, shaking his head.

He seemed to feel a little sorry for her by the time he left—the spook lady with the crazy people holding shows in her living room. Pity was dangerous, Kate thought. She was beginning to feel enough of it for herself. She met his softness like a Dead End kid, face carefully arranged.

"Well," he had said, leaving, "we'll be keeping an eye on all of you."

To Kate it sounded half like reassurance, half a threat. She nodded him out as he carefully propped the broken front door in place.

"*Ciao*," Kate said, with a little wave. Then she turned back to what was left of her home.

It was quiet with that middle of the night stillness. The sick smell still lingered, but she had to force herself to approach the windows that had slammed themselves shut. She touched them gingerly, feeling the flesh on her fingers try to crawl away from the contact.

But the windows opened with no more difficulty than, with years of layers of paint and warping, they ever had. And they stayed open. She took deep breaths of the night air, comforted by the steady rhythm of the crickets and the distant scream of a nighthawk.

Then she turned to the mess of wax and ashes and glass. She cleaned doggedly for hours, leaving the puddle with its tiny centerpiece for last—three green plastic mermaids, the kind of whimsical ornament restaurants propped in a glass of tropical drinks.

She mopped up the water around them and finally, admitting to herself that she was afraid to touch them, she scooped them up in a paper towel. Reluctantly, ready for something to happen, she looked at them and they, green and silly, looked foolishly ordinary. She studied them for a long time. Mermaids?

Eventually she threw them into the garbage with the shards of glass and wax scraped off the tables and window sills.

The house was filled with pale pre-dawn light and the morning sounds of birds before Kate gathered the courage to go upstairs alone.

Brisk, efficient, refusing to look at the closet that seemed to draw her attention with a presence of its own, refusing to credit her feeling that small, dark things scuttled out of sight at the corners of her vision, she mopped up the water on the bedroom floor. She finally sank, fully dressed, onto the bed.

"Ted," she said aloud, then started to cry.

Michael Justin called Nora just as she and Sam were finishing the breakfast Sam had cooked. His voice on the telephone was already reassuringly familiar and yet it held the promise and mystery of the unknown. They made a date for a late lunch, speaking only briefly, their conversation punctuated by small laughs and silences. Both were reluctant to hang up and seconds passed after they said their good-byes before Nora finally replaced the receiver. At first she didn't realize that Sam was watching her with interest. When she turned to find the girl studying her she felt a quick hot blush flood her face.

"Geez," Sam observed, "you must be in love."

"Oh, come on!" Nora laughed, coming back to the table. "I just met him."

"Yeah, but you should see the way you look."

Nora pulled her chair out and sat down, feeling her face grow hotter. Then she grinned, picking up her fork and shaking it at Sam. "Just you wait," she said. "Another couple years and you'll find out how dippy *you* can get." Sam made a face at her. "Oh, yes. Dippy. Probably over some football player or something."

"Gross!" Sam cried, face contorting even more to indicate the pure impossibility. Then she sobered.

"I'm never going to fall in love," she said, firm and resigned.

Nora matched her sudden seriousness. "Oh, I hope you do, kiddo. But I hope you do a damn good job of picking who to fall in love with."

* * *

"Sheriff!" Tom Robbins, the desk sergeant, woke Finnerty from an uncomfortable doze on his office couch at a little after 9:00. "We just got a call you better know about."

10

"Probable murder-suicide," Robbins told the sheriff as he swung his legs to the floor with a soft grunt. "Ralph Cooksey called it in."

Tom Robbins had his best official face plastered on, but underneath, Finnerty could tell, he was just about squirming with excitement. These things just didn't happen in Stony Cliffs.

Finnerty reached down to slide a brown shoe over the heel of his swollen foot, irritated that his belly was in the way. He gave the shoe and Robbins equal looks of disgust.

"Go on," he barked, one shoe on, the other in the process.

Robbins glanced down at his notes, more for show than for prompting. "Calvin Russell and his wife Matilda. They have a 120-acre farm about five miles out of town on Route 40. Apparently one of the neighbors, a Mrs. Hodder, arrived at the farm about 8:15 this morning to put up some preserves with the Russell woman. For a church bake sale."

Finnerty grunted, both shoes on now, and glared up at the deputy.

"She found the Russells' dog dead on the back porch and the door open. When she went looking around inside she found Russell dead in the living room and called the emergency number.

"I clocked the referral call in here at 8:27 and sent Deputy Cooksey over since he was nearby. Ralph just called in. Upon searching the house, he found Mrs. Russell dead in her bed. At least, he thinks it's Mrs. Russell. The victim appears to have been shot in the head at close range with both barrels of a heavy gauge shotgun."

Finnerty stood up, resisting the impulse to stretch. He tried shaking some of the wrinkles out of his pants, fingering the crease. "And Calvin Russell?"

"Seems to have reloaded and shot himself."

"You call Doc Paulson?"

"Yessir." Robbins almost saluted. Of course he'd call the medical examiner before waking the sheriff. "And I've got Walt Eberhart waiting for you with a car. I assumed you'd want to inspect the scene."

"Yeah." Finnerty rubbed at his face, trying to get the circulation moving, trying to rub away some of the tiredness, wishing he could think. "You mind if I get some coffee on the way out, Deputy?"

Robbins looked at his feet, annoyed with himself for not thinking of it, while Finnerty brushed past him.

Finnerty slammed the car door and took in the scene around him, ignoring Walt Eberhart who stood on the other side of the car shifting from foot to foot and gawking.

The graveled parking area was crowded with cars. Finnerty spotted Ralph Cooksey's car, but didn't see Doc Paulson's silver Ford. A dark-blue, late model Chrysler was parked there. The neighbor's, Finnerty guessed.

It was a storybook day on a model farm. The house was old, but well cared for, white clapboard with a gingerbread porch. Geraniums stood tall in the window boxes surrounded by a nodding crowd of petunias, white flower borders surrounded the house. Finnerty recognized marigolds and other flowers in bright red and blue. Morning glories, open to the day's bright sun, climbed a trellis near the porch. Across the graveled area the barn stood, painted bright red, fresh and ready to open its doors and let out a herd of contented brown and white cows and a happy farmer like an illustration in a kid's book.

On one side of the barn stood a vegetable garden, its rows neat and lush. Trim green pasture swept away from the barn, bounded by an orderly white fence. Finnerty took a deep breath of the clear country air, fresh and not yet thick with August heat. He turned to the house.

Ralph Cooksey was standing on the porch near the screen door, waiting for him, looking steadily in his direction and not at the thing that lay at his feet.

It was the dog, Finnerty saw when he got to the porch. The animal was stretched out on its side, lying in a pool of dark blood where flies already swarmed around the thickening puddle. The dog's head had been neatly severed, the high-domed skull crushed. His front legs were cut through like kindling, chopped through the long bone above the first joint.

"The blow to the head would have come first," Finnerty said, thinking aloud more than relaying information to Cooksey and Walt Eberhart fidgeting behind him. "The rest of it was done after."

A long-handled axe lay on the porch near the dog's body, blood marking its bright head.

Finnerty jerked his chin at it. "Get prints on the handle, Deputy," he said without looking back at Walt.

"Jesus, Sheriff, why'd he cut off the legs?" Walt asked, as though there was a logical explanation.

Finnerty ignored him. He stepped carefully onto the porch, avoiding the thick puddle of blood, waving a

hand in front of his face to ward off the flies that
swarmed up, startled. Cooksey stepped to one side,
holding the door open for him.

A plump woman, middle-aged, gray-haired, sat at
the kitchen table with her back turned to the porch.
She turned only her head when the door opened,
staring over her shoulder at the sheriff like Lot's wife.
"Mrs. Hodder?" Finnerty asked and the woman
nodded. "I'm the sheriff, Roy Finnerty. I'd like to ask
you some questions." He moved around to lower his
bulk into one of the kitchen chairs of tubular metal
with padded, yellow vinyl seat and back. The yellow
matched the sunny yellow and white plaid of the
table's Formica top. Mrs. Hodder's strong, round
forearms rested on the table, both hands clenched
around a bundle of tissues. Her eyes were red-
rimmed, pale blue, and filling again with tears.

"Just a couple questions, Mrs. Hodder," the sheriff
told her and she nodded again.

Finnerty drew the story out of her slowly. She and
Tildy—Mrs. Russell—had planned to spend the day
putting up tomatoes, green beans and relish for a
church sale. First Baptist was planning a new addi-
tion. She thought maybe something was wrong as
soon as she drove up. It was so quiet, she said, and
Errol, that's the dog, always comes barking when cars
pull up.

When she found Errol like that on the porch she
was afraid for Calvin and Tildy, thinking of that
fellow who got killed up at the college, feeling
suddenly sick to her stomach. She called through the
open back door, got no answer and finally let herself
in.

She found Calvin in the living room with his
shotgun.

"I was afraid," she told Finnerty. "I hope God for-
gives me because I didn't have the courage to find out
if maybe Tildy was still alive and I could do something to help her."

"She was shot in the head, Sheriff. Dead for hours," Ralph Cooksey cut in. "Upstairs."

Mrs. Hodder gave a sharp gasp and clutched both fists to her mouth, watery eyes squeezed tight shut in a plump face like a raisin swollen with baking.

"There was nothing you could do, Mrs. Hodder," Finnerty reassured her. "You did the only thing you could, calling us."

Finnerty asked her a few more questions, then made arrangements for one of his deputies to take her home and bring her car back to her later. He heard Doc Paulson's car pulling up as he hoisted himself out of the kitchen chair to find the living room.

The Russell living room looked like it had been a comfortable place—plump chairs, a round couch covered in an Early American print fabric with a pile of throw pillows, a rust and brown recliner with the beginnings of permanent indentations at the head and seat. A knotty pine coffee table was covered in magazines.

But at the center of a brown and blue braided rug lay Calvin Russell's body. And his blood, brain, bone and hair spattered the china figurines on their glass shelves and splashed across the wood-framed prints of ducks and rabbits.

Calvin rested on his side, an old man in cotton pajamas and a pale blue robe, curled around a shotgun. His face was hidden, turned down into the blood-soaked rug. A leather scuff slipper still hung from one pale foot with shiny yellow calluses on its naked heel. The other foot was bare, the slipper lying near by.

From the position of the body—one arm and a thigh draped companionably over the shotgun—Finnerty guessed the old man had sat on the floor with the barrel of the gun in his mouth, the stock propped against the floor. The force of the blast would have thrown him over and onto his side. A spatter pattern of gore marked the wall behind him.

"Holy cow!" Doc Paulson and Burt Johnson, the photographer called in by the sheriff's department for special cases, stood in the entryway to the living room. Burt immediately started taking pictures. The medical examiner was still gawking.

"Jesus," he muttered, then started stepping gingerly around the body to stand beside the sheriff.

Doc Paulson was a kid. Some years back Finnerty had started feeling old when the doctors he saw around seemed younger and younger. But Paulson, the new medical examiner, was the hardest yet to get used to.

He came to Stony Cliffs as an eager stranger straight from his residency in family practice at Indiana University. Tall, skinny and blond, he had pale blue eyes that popped slightly behind round, wire-rimmed glasses. His fine hair was so pale it was almost white, and his skimpy mustache was invisible at a distance. Paulson was fine-boned, his chest curving in on itself. His Adam's apple was prominent. He wore faded jeans most of the time and Hawaiian shirts or T-shirts with the names of rock groups or portraits of Beethoven and Mozart.

When he first arrived in S.C. he was made medical examiner by virtue of being the only doctor around who'd accept the post. He told Finnerty to call him by his first name, Randy. But Finnerty politely insisted on calling him "Doc."

From what the sheriff heard, the kid was popular. Soft-hearted, easy on his fees, he treated the farmers' bursitis and backaches with a combination of remedies that included yoga and biofeedback. In Finnerty's experience with him during the past year and a half, the kid was thorough, efficient once he got over "gee-whizzing" and usually able to come up with some sensible answers.

Now, shaking his head, Doc Paulson moved towards Calvin Russell's sprawled body tentatively.

His beat-up running shoes stepped gingerly on the braided rug. He leaned sideways, long hair dangling like a silky sheet, pop eyes blinking behind the round lenses that flared to brightness in the flash of Burt's camera, craning down to see Calvin Russell's ruined face.

Finnerty walked around the body, eyes on Johnson as he slowed the pace of shooting, looking for just one more before the body was disturbed. Finally, he looked up at Finnerty, nodding that he was through. Doc Paulson glanced up at Finnerty, then moved in on the corpse. Paulson touched it lightly on the shoulder.

And the body flipped violently onto its back like a great fish out of water.

The three of them jumped away from it.

"Jesus!" Paulson yelped. "I just barely touched it!"

They stared at it, waiting to see if more would happen. One of the legs, the one that had rested on top of the gun, slid slowly from its twisted posture to lie limp and flat on the floor. They waited, but the body lay still.

"Muscle spasm?" Finnerty asked, frowning.

"I don't know." Paulson's hand hesitated in the air over Calvin Russell's white stubbled jaw. "Well," he finally said and squatted next to Russell to start the examination.

Finnerty looked up at Burt Johnson. "There's another one upstairs," he told the photographer. He left the room with Johnson close on his heels.

Nora decided to drive Sam home before calling Simon that morning. It was mid-morning when they walked out the front door and onto the porch and both stopped, admiring the day, taking deep breaths of the rich air.

Without thinking Nora sighed, sounding, even to herself, moonstruck.

Sam groaned. "You *are* in love."

Nora narrowed her eyes in mock threat, shaking her finger at the girl. "Sample, as I recall, you are extremely ticklish."

Sam shrieked and jumped, running off the porch with Nora close behind. Nora chased her up and down the yard, across the street and back and twice around the car before she yelled "Truce!"

Panting, Nora leaned against the Datsun without having laid a finger on the girl. "Let that be a lesson to you."

Pink-faced, Sam was grinning at her, walking around to the passenger door. "Ha," she said, sliding one bare leg into the car.

And then she screamed, the terror in her voice real this time.

"What is it?" Nora threw open the door on the driver's side.

Sam was brushing furiously at her leg, face contorted, hopping away from the car. She looked up at Nora, panic on her face.

"Spider web."

"Ugh," Nora sympathized. It seemed to her, though, that Sam's fear had much more in it than the nasty surprise of a spider web on bare flesh. She chattered over the roof of the car, waiting for the color to come back to Sam's face.

"It's because we forgot to roll up the windows." Nora leaned into the car, waving her purse over the passenger leg well and seat, brushing through the fragile strands of web catching the sunlight. "I get everything," she continued, climbing into the driver's seat. "Moths, these weird little black and orange beetles, spiders. We're lucky it didn't rain last night, or we'd both be sitting in puddles."

Nora leaned over, looking up at Sam still standing at the curb. "Come on, Sam," she said gently.

Sam hesitated, then climbed carefully into the car.

"Next time," Nora told her, turning the key in the ignition, "remind me."

Kate was on the front porch when they drove up, and Nora shifted the car into Park but didn't turn off the ignition. As Sam clambered out, Nora opened her door to stand beside the humming, sputtering car.

"Gotta get back," she called to Kate, "but I'm coming by later this afternoon, okay?"

Kate waved and Nora, taking that for yes, climbed back into the car and made a U-turn on the empty street. The radio had been playing soft rock music in the background, but suddenly it emitted a sharp burst of static. "Rats," she said. The Datsun was slowly disintegrating. She slapped the dashboard.

The static cleared for a moment and a soft, deep voice came through with a single word.

"Nora," it said.

Nora gasped and the car swerved towards the curb. Gooseflesh rose on her arms and Nora stared at the radio, then gave a nervous giggle.

"Silly," she said to herself.

She must be imagining things.

11

When Nora called Simon's office it seemed to her that the woman who answered the phone hesitated seconds too long when she asked for Simon.

"Just a moment," the anonymous woman told her and put her on hold with Muzak bubbling "Raindrops Keep Fallin' On My Head" too loudly in her ear.

"Mrs. Durant?" A man's voice, not Simon's, interrupted the mindless flow of music.

"Yes?"

"This is Hal Townsend, an associate of your husband's."

"Ex-husband," Nora corrected automatically. And premonition hit like a fist in her gut. She was having a hard time breathing.

"Isn't Simon there?"

He cleared his throat. "I'm afraid there's been an accident."

Nora stared at the kitchen clock. "Accident?"

"Yes. Very late last night and only Simon's car seems to be involved. Apparently he lost control and ran off the road on a very hilly stretch of highway. The car turned over and there was a fire. The state police are working on it, but they haven't been able to locate the body in or around the wreckage. I'm sorry.''

"But it's impossible . . . I just talked to him last night. How . . . ?"

"We don't really know the details yet. But I'll be glad to keep you informed about what's happening at this end. How do I reach you?"

Woodenly, Nora gave him her phone number. Half-formed questions, disbelief, protests that it couldn't be possible swarmed through her mind, but she couldn't shape a coherent sentence, so she simply hung up.

"This is terribly unfair to you." Nora sniffled, then blew her nose into one of the tissues Michael Justin had silently handed her.

"Just the opposite," he said and something in his voice made her stop crying to watch his face. "I know we've just met, but I already feel like there's something very special here. I want to know you, Nora. I want to know all about you, and though I'm sorry the way I'm finding out is because you're in pain, I'm glad I could be here. Do you understand that?"

She nodded at him, solemn.

"You're so lovely."

Nora groaned. "Right now I'll bet I look goddawful."

"Well," he grinned at her, "your nose is a little red. But I'm talking about inside."

"Ah." Nora waved a tissue at him like a flag of surrender. "Stop. I'm getting embarrassed."

If she had thought about it, if she had been able to think about anything at all, Nora would have called him to cancel their lunch date. But she'd still been standing at the kitchen phone, mind an idiot blank, when his knock at the door brought her back to the world.

She had stumbled through a vague excuse, telling him they'd have to change plans, but he wouldn't leave it at that. He wanted to know why and she'd told him. She told him about Simon's death and, more than that, all her feelings about her life as it had been with him, as it was now—the complex twining of guilt and responsibility, old resentments and slow-growing independence. She admitted that some small part of her was relieved that Simon was finally and irrevocably out of her life, even though she was horrified to hear herself say it. And mostly there was pain, a simple sorrow.

Michael had helped and comforted, prodding her with questions, handing her tissues, getting her a glass of water, and now, as they sat in her kitchen, making a pot of coffee.

"I really am sorry," Nora apologized again, self-conscious now that the storm of emotions had passed. "It's just . . . everything is so strange lately, ever since . . ."

"Moving here?"

She shook her head. "Since Ted died."

He carefully carried two mugs of coffee to the table. "Or to be more accurate," he emphasized, "was killed in what seems to have been a particularly ugly, brutal way. That alone would be enough to shake anyone who knew him. It must be especially hard on you since Kate's your only tie to this place. So far."

Nora nodded, stirring sugar into her coffee. "It's been tough for her. And for Sam."

"I really liked them, you know. Kate and Sam. I would have liked to know them better, but I never much cared for Ted and I don't think Kate thinks much of me."

Nora made a soft, demurring sound, looking only at her coffee.

Michael, watching her, raised a shrewd eyebrow. "I hurt Kate's pride," he said. "I let my feelings about Victor, my frustrations, badly affect how I saw and treated his little group of followers. They had nothing

to do with it, really. Nothing to do with shaping
Victor. I was just looking for a brother who never
really existed."

They sat in companionable silence, each wrapped
in private thoughts and losses. Nora kept coming back
to the random, sinister events of the past two days.
Since Ted's death it seemed as though the curtain of
reality had shifted, giving her an unwanted glimpse of
chaos. One by one the incidents added up to fill her
with unease, a terrible sense of foreboding. At the
core of it was Ted, flirting with some darkness in
himself.

But there were rational explanations for everything,
she argued. Ted's ominous scribblings were sad and
sick, but not dangerous. A loser with pretensions to
poetry, he'd picked up or written scraps and phrases
that glittered with twisted power, sullen hatred, and
destruction. He thought he was a writer, so he wrote.

And Sam, sweet Sam, was a child whose life was
falling to pieces. She needed help, a little girl in pain.

The voice on the phone was a bored teenager,
amusing himself. Her name on the radio was a trick of
her own hearing. The ugly message in her own handwriting must have been written in her sleep, a sign of
her own emotional chaos.

Rational explanations, but they didn't satisfy her.

"Listen," she said brightly, breaking the silence,
"There's something else, as long as I'm unloading on
you."

She told him everything. The notes in Ted's
pockets, Sam's strange behavior, the voice on the
phone, the note in her own handwriting. Spoken
aloud, matter-of-factly, they lost their ominous edge.

He listened to her solemnly not, as she was afraid
he might, interrupting to scoff or bully sense into her.
When she was finished she threw up her hands with a
little shrug that said, "There, you take it now." And
one by one he gave her the same rational explanations
she gave herself.

Nora felt relieved just talking about it, and the string of explanations were reassuring even if they still left her with some lingering unease.

She was afraid it had all just started.

As soon as Sam saw her mother she knew something had happened.

Kate's white face glowed like a ghost in the shade of the porch. She had smudges like purple bruises under her eyes. She looked sad and small and more tired than Sam had ever seen her.

Sam stopped at the bottom step, frowning, feeling the barriers slam down like iron walls to protect her from her mother's weakness. Kate was in her wicker rocker and Sam glared suspiciously at her. Neither of them spoke. Then Sam saw the splintered front door propped against its frame. She shot a quick look at Kate, then marched up the porch steps and into the house.

Still silent, Kate followed her into the hall, stopping a few paces behind her as Sam surveyed the living room, searching for clues.

"It looks different," Sam announced, not sure what had changed. The house seemed somehow soiled, used and discarded like yellow-stained sheets or old men with shabby coats and broken teeth.

Sam sniffed the air, wrinkling her nose in distaste.

"And it stinks in here." She turned to confront Kate.

"What did you do this time?"

But Kate only shook her head, slowly. When her eyes started to fill with tears Sam turned away from her to pace around the room like a tiger exploring a new cage. Then she circled back to stand before her mother. Kate had lit a cigarette, her shoulders set high and square like a teenager caught cutting classes.

"What happened to the front door?"

Kate's chin went up an inch. "Cops broke it in."

But as she said it Kate suddenly seemed to remember

who was the mother and who the child. Softer, she
said, "Sam . . ."

"Why?" the girl wailed.

"Honey, it's hard to explain."

Mouth tight, chin set, Sam waited for an explanation.

Kate shook her head, shrugging. "The study group
was here," she said. "We were meditating, sitting in a
circle, holding hands when Franny Vronski started to
scream. She was all right, nothing happened to her,
but she started to scream and suddenly some deputies
from the sheriff's department started banging on the
door. Charlie and Paul Vronski were holding my
hands too tightly so I couldn't get up and answer the
door soon enough. And the deputies broke it in.
That's all."

Sam's eyes narrowed, watching Kate's face. She
didn't believe that was the whole story. There was
more. Something ugly. But her mother wouldn't tell
her.

"Liar!" she cried. "You're all a bunch of weirdos!
Spooks!"

Kate slapped her, hard, across the face. Then,
horrified, she stared at the reddening mark on Sam's
face.

"Baby, I'm sorry." Kate moved towards her, hands
coming up to hold her, but Sam jumped back, out of
reach.

"Don't you touch me!" she shouted and ran out of
the room leaving Kate alone with the faint sick smell
of corruption.

Finnerty paced in the overly air-conditioned
corridor outside the hospital morgue where Dr.
Randy Paulson was performing a methodical autopsy
on the remains of Calvin Russell.

The sheriff had hovered, hulking but light-footed,
over the medical examiner and the technician who

assisted him, watching with cool professional interest. He knew how to stay out of their way, but he'd barked occasional comments and requests for blood tests, a search for abnormalities in what was left of the brain, asking questions until Paulson had politely commented that he might be more comfortable outside.

Surprised, Finnerty hadn't argued. He stepped out to the comparatively fresher air of the corridor where the fluorescent fixtures cast a sickly green-tinted light and the air was chilly and antiseptic. And he paced, like an expectant father.

So far, the autopsy had uncovered nothing unusual. Calvin Russell had eaten a pot roast dinner some eight or nine hours before death, followed a couple hours later with a helping of canned peaches. He appeared to be in good health for a man of 67. Finnerty wanted the doctor to look for brain tumors, glandular disorders, Alzheimer's. Something to explain a mad act. Thinking about it now, he realized that Paulson would have considered the possibilities himself. It wasn't like him to start telling the medical examiner how to do his job, Finnerty thought. Not at this early stage, anyway. The sheriff guessed the last few days were getting to him. He needed sleep. He needed to solve the Kellogg case and have peace and order back in Stony Cliffs.

Finnerty had put Walt Eberhart and Phil Jenkins on duty looking for information about Calvin Russell. They'd come back to him already with some background. It seemed that Calvin Russell had lived all his life just outside Stony Cliffs as an unremarkable farmer and family man.

Russell had worked his farm for almost 40 years. His finances were solid and as stable as a small farmer's ever were. He and his wife were regular churchgoers. Calvin belonged to the American Legion and the Kiwanis. He liked hunting and fishing. He'd

never been in trouble with the law and his only police
record was for a parking ticket issued seven years ago
and promptly paid.

The Russells had two grown children, a son and a
daughter, both of whom lived out of state. They'd
been contacted and both were due in that afternoon.
Finnerty wasn't looking forward to the interviews.

It seemed to him that the job of sheriff, after almost
15 years, fit him like a worn leather jacket, molded to
his shape. At times it had become suffocatingly
familiar, a matter of rote and routine where the warm
satisfaction of peace and order lost its glow.

Now, suddenly, that had changed. Finnerty's life,
his county's life, was contaminated by inexplicable
violence, complicated by mysteries. Things seemed to
be falling apart around him and for the first time in
his life Finnerty began to question his ability to come
up with the answers himself. So he waited, allowing
himself only a little impatience, for the kid, Doc
Paulson. He had questions, not only about Calvin
Russell, but about Ted Kellogg.

Charlie hadn't gone home when he had left the
sheriff's office. There was no comfort at home. No
safety. Instead he walked the streets of the town,
invisible as a ghost, a shadow wandering in the darkness.

Hungry for company, the light and sound of people,
he avoided them, hanging around the edges of life like
a scruffy stray cat who's been chased too often. He
watched the bars empty and the last rowdy groups
stagger away down the dark streets, hooting and
throwing empty beer cans. And he hid in the
shadows, paced the unlit alleys with his boots on the
concrete ringing back hollow echoes from the brick
walls.

Charlie stopped once at the big glass window of
Donelly's Bar. It was closed and empty now, just a

blue-shaded bulb burning somewhere in the back room. He found himself plastered against the cool glass, arms outstretched with nothing to grip, trying to hold it like a drowning man clutching the sheer base of a cliff, cheek pressed against the smooth coldness. He was crooning something to himself, something tuneless like a child's song.

Charlie Luther wanted peace. He wanted to go back to the time that seemed so long ago, a time of drinking beer and getting stoned with no hopes, no dreams and no nightmares.

His arms slid slowly down to his sides, palms skidding against the glass. He turned his forehead to the window and butted his head softly against its unyielding surface. He butted harder, rocking back and thudding his pale forehead against it. And again, harder, making the sheet of glass shudder and vibrate.

Charlie Luther arched his back, dropping his head back like a stone in a slingshot, and paused, legs trembling, palms gone cold and damp. No more nightmares, he thought. But the strength sluiced out of him like water down a rain gutter and he fell, disjointed, to his hands and knees, collapsing on the sidewalk in front of Donelly's bar.

He stayed that way a long time, until he knew suddenly that he wasn't alone and his head swung up like a dying steer scenting water in a drought.

The sidewalk stretched empty in front of him, pools of light from the streetlamps illuminating the deserted downtown like an abandoned stage set. Mouth hanging loose and open, eyes blinking, Charlie swung his head to stare across the street at the Indiana movie house, the J. C. Penney store, the alley entrance. And there, at the edge of a pool of light stood a big black dog. Broad-shouldered and sleek, the dog stood studying the man, eye level, across the empty street.

The corners of Charlie's mouth stretched up in a

vacant grin.

"Doggie," he said.

The dog took a measured step forward, eyes flashing green in the shift of light.

Charlie sank back on his heels, covering his face with his hands and moaning low in his throat. Then he shambled to his feet and began to run, weaving and staggering down the street.

12

It wouldn't hurt, Nora decided after Michael left, to spend a few hours working through her class plans, preparing for her appointment tomorrow with Dr. Ellicott. With piles of notes and books fanned around her on the floor, Nora lost herself in fairy tales with a small sigh of satisfaction. She was skipping the grimmer tales and going in search of the fool—the man with a thousand faces, Silly Boots, the youngest brother, Jack, who sold the family cow for beans, the cobbler who boasted of killing seven flies at a blow and got recruited to kill giants.

Boots in all his guises, Nora had decided, had a lot in common with the Fool of the Tarot deck, the only card without a number but a vital member of the major arcana. He was a silly young man, gaily dressed, pictured standing at the edge of a precipice, smiling, seemingly unaware of the abyss that stretched at his feet. Pack slung over his shoulder, he's ready to start a journey, his life, choosing between good and evil.

Like Boots, Nora thought, studying the card in the Tarot deck she'd owned since college. In fairy tales he's the unambitious brother who sits by the fire, warming his feet in the ashes, until he suddenly decides to seek his fortune. Then, out on the road, he's the silly creature who gives all his belongings to needy strangers or stops to help an ant carry a heavy load. In his foolishness he wins friends and receives aid from animals, wizards and old wise women. He's the suitor who wins the Tsar's daughter, the unknown knight whose horse climbs the glass mountain to win the hand of the princess.

The fool of fairy tales was always one of Nora's favorite characters. There were girls, too, who fit the fool's role, like Gerda who tracked Kay to the home of the Snow Queen or Beauty who loved roses and the Beast. And the Fool was her favorite card in the Tarot deck. She knew most card readers placed the unnumbered Fool at the beginning of the arcana's cycle symbolizing the first steps taken in the evolution of the spirit. But some placed him at the end. Following fulfillment, he goes out seeking. And she liked the picture of the Fool, blithely crossing mountains.

Now she was looking for other parallels, other figures in the Tarot deck that related to archetypes in folk and fairy tales. And they were there, she thought, excited, shuffling through the deck. Maybe enough to structure a section of readings. Nora congratulated herself. Order strikes again, she gloated, and Dr. Ellicott should be pleased. He used the Tarot in his own courses, Nora remembered, something about belief systems.

Here was the Hermit, the wise man who has reached the peak of the mountain and shines a lantern down on the trail for others to follow. Here were the Emperor, strong, stern ruler of his kingdom, and the Empress, the fruitful female principle, warm and golden mother figure, and the mysterious High Priestess, keeper of secrets. And the Magician. Nora studied the card. He was the prideful man who draws power from nature and the world of the spirit to serve his own ends, the man who imposes the force of his will on all things to shape the elements of life to his desires.

And here was the Devil.

Ralph Cooksey was taking a breather on the Russell's back porch, lounging in a green metal lawn chair with a back shaped like a scallop shell. His feet were propped on the porch rail and he had poured himself a cup of tepid coffee from the thermos Phil Jenkins had left behind.

It was the dog that bothered Ralph the most. He eyed the patch of blood still drawing flies in the heat of the early afternoon.

Then a flicker of movement out by the barn caught his eye. He swung his boots down from the railing and carefully put the plastic cup on the porch floor without taking his eyes from the barn. He craned over to get a better view and spotted a man, pale hair glowing in the sun, ambling in a circle like a dog searching for a scent.

Cooksey stood up, one hand automatically going to his holstered gun. The guy, ragged and wild looking in faded T-shirt and jeans, lurched to one side, falling against the barn. He leaned there for a while, time enough for the deputy to unholster his gun and start down the porch steps.

They met midway between the house and the barn, Cooksey blocking the intruder's path. He was a skinny little guy, Cooksey saw, a head shorter than the deputy. He didn't seem to see right, the way he kept blinking, his eyes looking watery. He wasn't looking at Cooksey and didn't seem able to focus. He staggered a little on the path.

Cooksey, feeling as big and solid as a mountain or a linebacker, blocked the little guy's way to the house.

"You got business here, mister?" The gun was held ready in Cooksey's hand, but he had it resting lightly cradled in the holster, ready to draw.

The scrawny trespasser ignored him, looking over his shoulder at the house as he'd look over a fence. He tried stepping around the deputy, but Cooksey shifted to block his path.

"Hey!" Cooksey said, "I'm talking to you. What are you doing here?"

The little man stepped back the other way and Cooksey blocked him again.

"What's with you? You on something? What do you want here?"

In the pale, blank face something struggled to surface. Watery blue eyes blinked and drifted to Cooksey's face.

"Ted," he finally said.

"And you can't get anything out of him at all?" Finnerty was asking Deputy Sheriff Ralph Cooksey an hour later.

Finnerty was back in his office, sprawled in his creaking leather chair with Cooksey lounging in the chair across from him.

Cooksey snorted, feeling cheated that Finnerty hadn't been as pleased with him for bringing Charlie Luther in as he figured the sheriff should be.

"Nope. Not till he comes down from whatever it is he's high on, I'd guess."

As far as Cooksey was concerned he'd just broken the case. Both cases. Charlie Luther was obviously some kind of crazy-ass bastard. Cooksey'd been pleased as hell to find out who the skinny little guy was—some psycho tied in with this Satan shit who'd already been pulled in twice. Perfect.

Just being around the Russell farm made a connection clear as day to Ralph Cooksey. Luther must have been the one who killed that Kellogg character. And he must have murdered the Russells with some sneaky bastard way of making it look like Russell did it. Luther also looked crazy enough to chop up that dog.

Finnerty's lips were stuck out in a pout, his big hands laced across his gut. He started trying to make sense of it, fitting the pieces together, talking to himself, though Ralph Cooksey thought the sheriff was confiding in him.

"Luther left here about one this morning and Doc Paulson placed the Russells' time of death somewhere between two a.m. and four a.m. So that would fit, if Luther'd driven out there. He couldn't have walked. Or could he?" Finnerty focused on the deputy.

"Check it out, Deputy."

"Sheriff?"

Finnerty contained a sigh. "Luther's car. Find out what he was doing with it last night after he left here. Get a make on the tire treads—any irregularities or distinguishing features. Take soil samples. Check the ground around the Russell farm for a match on the tread. If you don't know the routines, Deputy, maybe you better start brushing up on your old textbooks."

Cooksey's mouth flapped once and he heaved himself to his feet with exaggerated stiffness, then he decided to air his complaint. "I was suppose to go off duty an hour ago, Sheriff."

Finnerty just squinted up at him.

"Well," Cooksey finally said, petulant as a kid. He hooked his thumbs in his belt and studied his shoes before meeting Finnerty's eyes again.

"So when do I get some time off?"

Finnerty reached his clasped hands back around behind his head, leaning back farther and making the chair screech.

I hope it breaks on the bastard, Cooksey thought. But kept his face as straight and honest as a Boy Scout.

"Ask Tom Robbins," Finnerty told him. "He's having himself a hell of a good time passing out special assignments. I believe he has a chart all made up just waiting to fill your name in, Ralph. So you tell him you've got some special duty and let him figure it out.'' Finnerty gave him a cold look that reminded Ralph suddenly of his father. "There's three people dead. We're all going to do what we need to do until this town gets back to normal and we're sure we've got our killer. And we've got the evidence to get the bastard convicted.''

"Yes, sir,'' Cooksey told him. He wasn't nearly so pleased with himself now for bringing in Charlie Luther. He'd just managed to make more work for himself and it would probably turn out to be a dead end anyway. His luck was like that.

Ralph Cooksey left Finnerty's office promising himself to start looking for a better job soon. Selling cars, maybe.

One floor down, in a basement holding cell, Charlie Luther was alone, curled in a tight ball lying on his cot. His head twitched up suddenly, like a turtle's poking out of its shell. Someone had called him, he thought, but he looked around the cell and no one was there.

He couldn't remember how he'd gotten there, in fact, didn't remember much of anything since he'd left the sheriff's office some time before. He had left, hadn't he? He thought he remembered walking through town. And after that? Darkness. Confusion.

Charlie thought he heard his name again. But it was inside his head, he realized. It had to be, because he was alone here. All alone, except for a little white spider crouching on the frame of his cot.

Nora checked the clock when the phone rang, startling her out of her absorption with her scholastic plans. It was nearly 6:00, Nora realized wonderingly. When she heard Kate's voice on the other end she felt a pang of guilt. She'd intended to call. There were so many reasons she had to talk to Kate.

Kate issued a terse invitation to dinner and Nora hesitated in answering, wondering if she should tell

Kate now about Simon's accident or wait until she got there. But Kate took her slowness in answering as the start of a refusal and she added an appeal in a tight voice.

"Sam spent the day locked in her room," Kate said. "She's not speaking to me. If you're here as referee, maybe the kid will at least eat something."

Sam had seemed to be in such a good mood this morning. But nothing was the way it seemed any more.

"Why isn't she talking to you?" Nora asked.

Kate's answer was short and sharp. "Some things happened here last night," she said. "Sam's pissed at me for getting involved."

"What things? Something to do with those friends of yours?"

Kate snorted, "Friends."

"Well? What?" Stubborn silence from Kate's end forced Nora to completely lose her patience. "Goddammit, Kate, will you just cut the crap and tell me what's going on?"

Kate made a sound that could have been a laugh, a gasp or a sob. Quietly, then, she said, "I'm scared. I don't know what to do. Will you come?"

Nora sighed, rubbing her forehead. "Of course. I'll be there in half an hour."

Nora found herself almost reluctant to tell Kate about Simon's death. She wanted to protect him, and herself, from Kate's usual derisive comments and she told the news woodenly and briefly. But Kate surprised her with immediate, sincere sympathy.

I should have known better, Nora thought. We're friends.

They sat on Kate's front porch absorbing the last sunlight and drinking iced tea. The warm light made the tea glow amber in the tall glasses and shone on the lemon rinds bobbing and surfacing against the glass.

They had talked for a while and been silent for even longer when Kate finally began telling Nora about what happened at her house the night before. She told it simply, without dramatic detail and even without much emotion, but somehow that made it all seem even more bizarre.

As Kate talked, a cold, slow shiver started at the base of Nora's spine and worked its way up to the prickling hairs at the base of her neck.

When Kate finally finished Nora began asking her questions, looking for logical explanations.

"Did you figure out where the water came from?"

Kate shook her head.

"Has anything unusual happened today?"

Another negative.

"Have the windows ever closed by themselves before?"

"No."

"Have you talked to anyone else that was here last night?"

Kate hesitated, then answered with a noncommittal hum.

"Well?"

"What is this, the Inquisition?"

Nora stared steadily at her, swirling ice and tea in her glass.

"Okay, yes. I did. Okay?" Nora raised her eyebrows. "Alex Thomas. I talked to Alex Thomas."

"And what did he say?"

"The stupid son of a bitch wants to try it again!" Kate exploded. "Alex says he 'felt the power' last night. He thinks he's on the verge of some monumental breakthrough to the Other Side. The jerk." Kate lit a cigarette and blew a long thin stream of smoke into the still, heavy air. "If he really believes he called 'something' up last night, you'd think he'd have sense enough to leave it alone."

Nora watched her friend's carefully blank profile.

"And what about you, Kate? Do you think something was called up last night?"

Kate took another drag on her cigarette, grimaced and threw it over the porch rail watching the trail of smoke arch out over the lawn.

"I don't know what I think," she finally answered. "I really don't."

They sat for a while longer in silence, studying the cracked paint on the peeling porch, squinting at the sun as it set, flamboyantly blazing orange, behind the hilly line of trees at the end of the far stretch of Kate's street.

"Alex Thomas is in my department," Nora said after a while, conversationally. At the single faculty function Nora had attended, Alex Thomas had stood out, as exotic as a carnivorous plant, even among the disparate mixture of SCC faculty types.

He was nothing like the classic eccentric professors. Dr. Ellicott was one of those—scholars who wore mismatched socks and cared passionately about Minoan civilization. Some of the faculty were relics left over from the Sixties—earnest poets and philosophical scientists. Either they were mellow and hung out, or they hid and grew old, hunched over books and typewriters through the middle of a thousand nights, growing gray on artificial light and cigarette smoke. And now, of course, there was the New Wave, whatever that meant. As far as Nora could tell it meant having a hard face, sharp edges and as much disdain for the past as every group before it had had.

Among the mixture of types, Alex Thomas was an anomaly.

"I think he has his nails done," Nora observed.

"Alex has everything done," Kate told her, and they both snickered.

"Why did you call him?"

"To find out what the hell is going on. But he doesn't know any more about it than I do. I thought

. . . I don't know what I thought. I suppose I was hoping he'd tell me he had it all under control, that he'd somehow rigged the wind and the sounds and the smell. And I think I might have believed him even though it all happened in my house and I know better than that. I wanted to believe him, but the bastard wasn't cooperating. He wouldn't tell me anything I wanted to hear.''

"Did you tell Sam about all this?''

"All Sam had to do was take one look at me, her degenerate mother, and the bashed in front door and she pulled some of her own conclusions. I told her Franny was screaming, that's about all.''

"We need to talk about Sam,'' Nora told Kate, and then she began from the beginning.

Upstairs in her room Sam lay on her bed on top of the flounced white cotton bedspread staring at the ceiling. She was watching slanting patches of light creep imperceptibly slowly across the white desert of ceiling, watching as the reflected sunlight turned gold, then disappeared and the room sank into quiet blue dusk.

She was aware of the voices of her mother and Nora, the sound drifting in through her open window like the sound of birds and crickets and wind in the trees.

What she listened to was something different—a voice that called her name, she thought, calling from far away, like someone lost in a maze of caves. She lay on her bed, listening carefully to the faint sound of her name called over and over again.

"Hecate, Isis . . . She Who Meets, She Who Leads . . . Shiela-na-Gig . . .''

Alex Thomas sat alone, cross-legged on a wool Persian rug of brilliant oxblood that covered the highly polished hardwood floor of his converted carriage house apartment. The stone carriage house over-looked the Black River on the outskirts of town, isolated in an area too hilly for any use but secluded home sites.

Drapes were drawn against the fading sunlight and the shadowy great room loomed like an elegant cave. He sat before a fat green candle, staring at its flame, chanting to himself, feeling like a hermit, a wise man, a shaman. He was waiting for the night, waiting for a return of the power so great it had swept away all his weary sense of himself.

Alex Thomas sat chanting, like a child working magic spells with his lucky charm, waiting for oblivion. Waiting to be taken.

In the corners of the room, the dark was gathering.

A dozen glossy 8x10s of Calvin Russell covered Doc Paulson's desk—Calvin curled around his shotgun, a close-up of his hands, the shotgun stock between his legs in their cotton pajamas, a view from behind of Calvin's shattered skull.

Finnerty heaved a sigh of exasperation and tossed the photo he was holding back onto Paulson's desk. Paulson was holding his wire rim glasses in one hand using the other to massage the deep red marks in the bridge of his nose where his glasses rested.

"So it must have been self-inflicted," Doc Paulson said, patiently repeating the same conclusion they'd reached time and again.

"We can't find anything that says different," Finnerty admitted.

It made for a neatly self-contained crime, the murder-suicide, and that, at least, should have been a relief. But it was like an itch Finnerty couldn't scratch. It felt wrong, smelled wrong. All the facts made Calvin Russell a good man, well-balanced, content with his life, healthy for his years. There were no warnings for his violence, no signs of instability or depression. Nothing.

Doc Paulson hooked one wire earpiece over his ear and tilted his head to work the other one into place. "Killing the dog seems to indicate psychosis," he remarked mildly, not for the first time.

Finnerty grunted.

"Irrational behavior," Doc Paulson explained, fluffing his thin hair over his ears. "Who knows? He may have thought he had a reason for killing his wife, but the dog? And the mutilation after death would certainly indicate emotional disturbance."

"Beats the hell out of me," Finnerty said. "I don't think we'll ever know what went on in Calvin Russell's mind last night."

Doc Paulson shook his head. "Sometimes I doubt if we ever know what happens in anyone's mind."

Finnerty suddenly took a hard look at the young doctor. He sounded as bone-weary as Finnerty felt and his skin was so pale it was almost translucent.

"Where are you on the Ted Kellogg case?" Paulson asked now. A tic twitched at the bottom lid of his left eye and he rubbed at it like a sleepy kid.

Are you having nightmares? Finnerty wanted to ask. The sheriff was—confused dreams in his broken sleep on the office couch. Instead, he asked the doctor a different question.

"You studied psychology, didn't you? In medical school?"

Paulson gave him a wan smile. "My undergraduate minor was psychology. And some background in psychiatry is a requirement in a family practice residency. Why?"

Finnerty frowned, chin sunk into his chest, slouched in the chair across the desk from Doc Paulson. He rubbed his fingers against the side of his jaw, lost for moments in the dry sandpaper sound of his callused hand rasping against whisker stubble.

"I'm stuck," he finally answered. "As far as

physical evidence in the Kellogg murder you know exactly as much as I do. An unidentified, blunt-edged instrument was used to eviscerate and mutilate the body. No clues. No footprints. No hank of hair found clutched in his fist. No reason why Kellogg should have been out there in the first place. Allegedly he told Kate Hall, his live-in girlfriend, that he was leaving town earlier that day.''

Paulson's pale eyes blinked at him from behind the polished lenses. ''So you're taking the psychological angle. Possible motives. Pathology.''

Finnerty nodded. One of the knots in his chest seemed to be loosening. He'd gone too long, he thought, without trusting or respecting anyone enough to ask for help when he came to a dead end.

''The way I see it,'' Finnerty said, ''we've got two ways to go: either Kellogg's killer was a psychopath who didn't even know the guy, or it's someone who knew Kellogg and who had a reason, no matter how bizarre, to make Kellogg his victim.''

''If it was a random killing, a 'psychopath' as you say, then what makes you think the murder will be an isolated incident?''

''I don't. And that's what's scaring the bejesus out of me.'' Finnerty pushed himself upright in the chair. ''A psychotic killer loose in Stony Cliffs. Mother of God, imagine it. Then I catch myself wishing the bastard, whoever he is, was just passing through.'' Finnerty was disgusted with himself for that, for wishing it was all somebody else's problem.

''Then what about the people involved? Do any of them seem to have a motive? Any signs of pathology? Delusions? Group collusion?''

Finnerty slowly shook his head. ''Could be 'yes' to everything, could be 'no.' Maybe that's where I could use your help, figuring out what makes these people tick.''

''I've taken another look at the body, too,'' Doc

Paulson told him.

Finnerty raised an inquiring eyebrow.

"You know the weapon used to disembowel was edged, but not sharp. I've studied the bruising at the edges of the wound. I think I can state fairly surely that the blow to disembowel was made in one fast sweeping motion from crotch up through the sternum. With any instrument, but especially with something blunt, it took tremendous force."

"A woman couldn't do it? Not even a strong woman?"

Doc Paulson's pale eyebrows furrowed behind the round lenses. "It's hard to imagine even a strong man cutting through the breastbone with a dull edge."

Finnerty had seen swords, though, that split a man on the battlefield like a chicken.

"There's something else," Paulson said. "The heart was stopped, I think. I'm guessing, but it appears that the disemboweling happened quickly. Kellogg was still alive when the killer or killers reached into his chest and just . . ." Paulson slowly squeezed a fistful of air as though he were crushing a bunch of grapes.

"Stopped it." He stared at his closed fist, then dropped it into his lap.

"Stopped Kellogg's heart with his bare hand?"

Paulson shook his head. "Not exactly. He used something like a vice or a big, flat pincers. Abrasion on the heart muscle indicates some serration. Irregular, jagged. Something of a cross between toothed pliers and a lobster's claw."

"Jesus."

Did his killer watched the life fade from Ted Kellogg's eyes as he stopped the heart muscle in his chest? Finnerty felt very old suddenly. Tonight, he had to get some sleep at home in his own bed.

"Tell me about the people involved in the case," Doc Paulson said. He leaned back in his chair, propping his sneakered feet, still encased in paper booties from the autopsy room, up on the edge of his desk.

"The study group," Finnerty said, but the telephone cut him off.

Doc Paulson answered it, then passed it to the sheriff.

"It's your office," Paulson told him and Finnerty felt the knot tighten again in his chest.

"Finnerty."

"Sheriff? This is Vern Snider." The deputy sounded uncomfortable. Finnerty could picture him contorting over the receiver, all elbows and awkward angles like a sea bird on land.

"Yes, Vern."

"It's the prisoner, sir. Charlie Luther." Finnerty waited. "Walt went down to check on him like we been doing every half hour, but . . . this last check Walt found Luther hanging by a bedsheet. He tried CPR on him, but it was no go. He's dead, sheriff. Suicide."

Sam answered, sounding sleepy and distant, when Nora knocked on her bedroom door at about 8:30. Nora invited her down to dinner in a voice so inflated with heartiness that it made her uncomfortable to hear herself.

"Come down," she said, more soberly, more herself, talking to Sam through the closed door.

"Okay," Sam said, still sounding passive, faraway.

But after a few minutes she came.

They sat in the small kitchen crammed together around the square wooden table, banging bare knees and bumping elbows. It was the brightest room in the house, lit by a bright bare bulb covered with a white paper lantern that just took the edge off the glare.

In the harsh light they all looked a bit frayed around the edges. Sam's face was puffy, like she'd just woken from a nap. Kate might have been an Irish refugee, someone escaped from the potato famine, pale and thin and tired, skin as white as soap under the red hair.

Nora didn't want to know what she looked like. She could guess. Her eyes felt swollen and gritty from crying, her nose a size too big. She'd rumpled her hair so many times she figured the finger tracks were permanent. She felt pale and fragile and she wished she could go home. She wanted some time to herself to mourn Simon and the lost years that went up in flames with him.

"Great tomatoes," Nora said dropping the comment into the silence like a blob of ketchup on a white plate. "They taste home-grown."

"From the Farmer's Market," Kate explained, not looking up from her plate of macaroni and cheese. It was almost black with pepper.

I give up, Nora decided. She left soon afterwards. Kate had decided to talk to Sam about getting some counseling and she wanted to approach her before the girl retreated to her room again.

"Take care," she and Kate both said to each other.

Nora felt like they needed it.

Rick Cummings stood in the hospital parking lot taking a long, deep drag on a fat joint he'd just rolled. He held the smoke, feeling it burn his lungs while the tightness inside him eased away and the darkness in his head retreated.

Good shit. He congratulated himself for scoring it from one of the orderlies. Good shit.

He exhaled slowly, a thin stream of blue smoke, then took another drag. He felt his shoulders relax, his hips loosen, the top of his head open up to let some air in.

Carole was still in the goddamned hospital and it made him nervous, pissed him off. They couldn't find out what was wrong with her. Damn fat, rich doctors. They had sedated her after the convulsions and now she just wasn't coming back around. She was lying in the bed, a little smile on her face like she'd just been fucked, but she wouldn't wake up. Now they had her hooked to a bottle of clear liquid, a needle in the vein at the inside of her elbow, taped to the soft white skin.

How the hell did this happen? He watched the smoke from the joint hang on the still night air. Salant is too smart to get suckered in like this.

Then he snorted derisively at himself, reconsidering. Smart? Salant thinks through her cunt. How smart is that?

Rick rubbed at his crotch, adjusting himself. He was halfway through the fat joint, stoned, and considering a few beers at Donelly's. The idea that he might run into Charlie Luther there only slowed him down for a minute. He didn't want to talk about anything that had happened last night, didn't even want to think about it. But chances were, neither would Charlie.

Besides, Charlie might not be there, but Gloria would be. It was one of her nights to tend bar and she was a good kid. Rick could count on her for a little sympathy and a free beer or two. And maybe he'd get lucky. This thing with Carole made him nervous. He needed a little relief.

Carole Salant shared her hospital room with a 17-year old girl who'd had an operation that morning to add a chin to her milky, timid face.

The girl's parents had spent the evening settled around the lump in the bed that was their daughter. The mother, plump and with no chin to speak of herself, had watched the movie of the week on the rented television. The girl's father read the newspaper, rustling its pages now and then with quick, nervous movements and reaching up regularly to drag three fingers, comblike, through the long, greased strands carefully arranged to cover his shiny scalp. Both of them warily ignored Rick and Carole.

Rick left the room even before visiting hours were over, before the girl's parents. When he left the couple traded significant glances, their one moment of togetherness that evening.

At 10:17 p.m., alone in the room with the sedated girl, Carole Salant opened her eyes to the dark.

"He's here," she said. And she lay like that through the long night. Perfectly still.

When Jerry Rhine woke up he could hear the faraway rumble of sound that meant his dad was still up, watching television. He sat up, eyes wide and unfocused, scanning the room, stopping without seeing at his He-Man Poster. Moving stiffly at first, then more easily, he clambered to his hands and knees and swung himself over the end of the bunk to climb down. At seven and a half he was too big to use the sissy ladder.

Jerry bent over his little brother in the bottom bunk, noticing with a sense of superiority that Stevie was sleeping with his thumb in his mouth again. He grabbed Stevie's forearm and yanked his brother's loose fist away from his face and the boy's eyes flew open. When his round face began to crumple into tears and his mouth opened to squall, Jerry clapped a quick hand over his face.

"Sssssh! You big baby!" Jerry hissed at him.

Stevie stared at his brother's face outlined by the Care Bears night light. Jerry looked fierce, scowling, but he was just waiting, not about to do anything yet. Stevie relaxed slowly, staring back, and Jerry released his grip, ready to pounce again if Stevie started to yell or cry.

"That's better," Jerry said, nodding approval. "Now we have to get dressed."

"Why?" Stevie asked.

"Because."

"Because why?"

"Because he said so, that's why?"

"Who said so?" Stevie looked around the shadowy, still room. "Daddy?"

"No, you dummy. Daddy's not supposed to know." He was sure of himself, full of stinging scorn for his younger brother.

Jerry slid off Stevie's bed and stood back, challenging. "Well? Are you gonna get up?"

Stevie sat up slowly, mouth in a small, soft O, lower lip pouting forward, brows furrowed by making major decisions in the unknown territory of the night.

"Baby!" Jerry taunted.

Stevie closed his mouth and set it, chin tucking stubbornly back. He threw off his top sheet and edged off the bed. Jerry nodded once, satisfied, then whispered, "We have to be quiet!"

They dressed in silence, Jerry in his jeans and Class of 1995 T-shirt, Stevie in tan corduroy pants and the Hawaiian shirt Grandpa brought back from his last trip. They both sat on the floor to lace up their sneakers, but Jerry was finished before Stevie had even worked the knots out of his laces.

"Hurry up!" Jerry snapped at him, and Stevie worked the shoes up over his heels without undoing the laces at all.

He was pulling the jammed tongue of one shoe back up towards his ankle when Jerry opened their bedroom door to check the hallway. Their parents' bedroom door was closed and a light from the open bathroom lit the upstairs hallway. Downstairs the sounds of the television drifted out of the den and a light shone into the downstairs hall and up the stairwell from the kitchen. The stairs were in half-darkness shaded with exaggerated shadows from the railing and bannister.

Jerry stepped out into the hallway and motioned at his brother, impatient to get moving, and Stevie gave

up on his shoe, scrambled to his feet and came to
stand beside him.

"Where are we going?" he whispered.

"You'll see," Jerry said. "First we have to get out
without letting Dad see us. We can go out the back
door."

Jerry began tiptoeing down the hall, creeping to the
stairs and down, like a burglar in the cartoons.
Frowning, Stevie watched him. Then he caught up
with him and trailed him, cat burglars sneaking away
with their loot.

They stopped in the downstairs hall, reconnoitering
a way past the doorway to the den where their father
sat up late watching boring news shows. Jerry peeked
around the corner of the door, then turned to Stevie
with a solemn nod. They could go ahead. Their father
was in his usual chair, the one whose back faced the
doorway. Jerry tiptoed across the hall into the
kitchen.

When Stevie followed he didn't bother to tiptoe.
Instead, he lingered a little in the doorway looking
wistfully in at the den, beginning to hope now that
they'd be caught. His father was on the recliner tilted
all the way back and Stevie could just make out the
top of his head with curly brown hair, just like his,
and the bare tops of his knees like islands in the blue
light of the television.

"Daddy's asleep," he whispered to Jerry.

Jerry hushed him and glared, motioning him
forward to the kitchen.

Stevie hesitated, giving one last long look at his
father, then he squared his shoulders and followed
his brother to the back door.

Jerry carefully unlocked and opened the door and
quietly let himself out with Stevie on his heels. They
shut the door behind them, then Jerry ran across the
flagstone patio to the driveway, down the driveway to
the street and halfway down the block before he

stopped. Stevie ran a few paces behind him and almost collided with him when his brother stopped suddenly in the middle of the deserted street.

"All right!" Jerry crowed. His chest puffed out with self-satisfaction and he looked down at Stevie with a confident smirk.

"Now let's get going!"

"But where?"

"You'll see, you'll see."

Everything looked different to Stevie. Most of the houses on their street were dark with only a single lighted window here and there where someone sat up late doing something only adults did. There weren't any cars and the sounds were all different. The insects were noisy, droning away, but everything seemed muffled somehow, as though night covered them like a goldfish bowl turned upside down. Stevie listened to their footsteps as they walked quickly towards town and the edge of the campus. The scuff of their sneakers on the streets and sidewalks echoed back like the last sound in the world.

Stevie recognized the direction they took. It was the way their mom drove when she went to pick their father up at his office, the same way they took to go shopping in town instead of at the mall. But the stores and offices were closed, weren't they?

Stevie was too stubborn to ask Jerry any more questions and he was afraid if Jerry called him a baby again he might cry. They walked for hours, he thought, while the streets rolled out around them. Jerry was silent, face set. He seemed to know exactly where he was going and he was in a hurry to get there. He walked fast and Stevie had to trot sometimes to keep up with him.

And then they reached it.

It was the tallest building in the town of Stony Cliffs. The seven-story red brick parking garage across from the Student Union. It towered like a hollow mountain in their path. A short steep ramp of concrete led to its mouth of darkness, with just a chain to hold back whatever waited inside.

"Here," Jerry said. His face was lifted to the blackness beyond the streetlamp's blue haze to the emptiness that gaped from the open driveway.

"Here, what?" Stevie said, staring up at it and shifting from foot to foot. He had to pee, he suddenly realized.

"Here is where we're going, you dumbhead. Inside."

Stevie scowled, squinting into the featureless darkness. "In there? I don't want to." It was his I'm-going-to-cry voice.

"Then don't," Jerry said loftily, "but I am. You can just stay here, all alone." He walked off without looking back, gliding up the ramp with long sweeping steps like a water-strider skimming over the surface of a pond.

Stevie watched the shadow of the doorway move down his brother's back. When Jerry reached the chain and started to slip under it, Stevie shouted at him. But Jerry went on into the dark.

"Jer-ry!" he yelled again in panic and anger at being abandoned. "Wait for me!" And he ran up the ramp, chasing the sound of his brother's sneakered feet. They echoed in the hollow space, moving faster now as Jerry trotted up the slight incline to the ramp's first turn. Stevie had to run to try and catch him.

At least his eyes were adjusting a little to the light. It wasn't quite black, as Stevie thought it would be. Dim light from the streetlamps shone through the open sides of the ramp, over the low wall. Stevie could just make out his brother trotting up the ramp, turning the corner to the next level.

And Jerry started to run, fairly flying up the ramps and across the empty floors. Stevie ran behind him, hands in tight fists, arms pumping at his sides. Both

boys were breathing hard now and Stevie kept losing
sight of Jerry, watching his back disappear around the
concrete pillars that marked the turns. Every time it
happened he was afraid that was his last sight ever of
Jerry. By the time they reached the roof, Stevie was
too tired and out of breath for tears.

He was staggering a little and weaved up to Jerry who
was standing triumphant on the open stretch of roof
with only the stars above him. Jerry's face was turned
up to the night sky, then he started to spin, arms
stretched out at his side, around and around, like a
human top, a small boy of a gyroscope.

Stevie's thumb found its way into his mouth and he
stood in silence, wide-eyed, watching.

Jerry finally twirled to a stop, let himself trip over
his own feet and plop down cross-legged on the concrete.

Stevie pulled his thumb out of his mouth and came
to stand beside his brother. Jerry leaned back on his
palms and grinned up at him, wolfish.

There's something wrong with his eyes, Stevie
thought. But everything had looked strange ever since
Jerry woke him. He stood near his brother, waiting to
see what came next.

"Well?" Jerry barked.

"I want to go home."

"Baby." Jerry jumped to his feet and trotted to the
low retaining wall overlooking the street. Stevie
walked slowly after him.

Jerry had hoisted himself onto the low wall. His feet
hung inches above the ground and he rested on his
elbows and forearms, the upper half of his body
angled over the top of the wall.

"You can look down on the streetlamp," he told
Stevie. "We're way up." He looked over his shoulder,
down at his brother.

"Come up here," Jerry commanded.

Stevie's head was tilted back. He couldn't see the

streetlamp over the wall, but he could judge its position by the streams of cold blue light glowing up over the edge of the wall. He shook his head.

"We're supposed to," Jerry insisted.

Puzzled, Stevie frowned at him. "Who says?"

But Jerry just shook his head. "Come on."

Stevie took a long step back. "No."

"Baby," Jerry mocked and swung up one strong, skinny leg to straddle the wall. One leg hanging towards Stevie, one leg in space, he was like an Indian brave proudly riding bareback. He pressed both palms to the wall in front of him, propped himself onto the balls of his feet and squatted there, eyes down, pious as a matador at prayer.

Stevie took another long step backward.

Then Jerry stood up. He turned to look for a moment at Stevie, head tilted to one side.

"He said so," Jerry said.

And then he turned to face the street and the cool blue glow of the streetlight and he took a long single step into space.

Long after Kate gave up and went to bed, Sam was awake, lying in the shadowed dark, watching the hazy, out-of-focus patterns of leaves, dark against light, forming and reforming on her ceiling. After Nora left Sam knew Kate wanted to have "A Talk," but Sam couldn't seem to care one way or another.

Nothing seemed very important, only the voices trying to reach her, calling her name somewhere at the back of her mind. She kept trying to listen, but they were never clear. What did they want? It was so hard to tell, so hard to think.

Kate had tried to talk to her, questioning her, so tight and nervous, her pale and freckled square hands clenching and unclenching in angular fists, lighting cigarettes. At least, Sam noted with some still interested part of her mind, Kate wasn't drinking.

Her answers to Kate's questions were mostly shrugs

and single words. Yes, she knew Kate loved her. No, there was nothing about Ted that she wanted to talk about. How did she feel about Ted? Sam shrugged and almost said Ted who? It was another time, another life. Nothing was important now. There were no answers to give Kate who studied her so intently, furrows marking the fine white skin between her eyebrows.

Eventually, Kate stopped trying to get her own answers and started trying to get Sam to agree to answer other people. Would Sam like to talk to anyone else? A psychologist, maybe? A counselor who might be easier to talk to about some things?

What things? Sam wanted to know, wondering what could be so important.

Everything, anything, Kate told her.

Sam shrugged. Not particularly.

Kate smashed out another one of her cigarettes and rubbed her forehead. She was giving up. Sam knew the signs. "Okay," Kate finally told her, "we won't talk about it any more tonight, but that's not the end of it. Anything you want to talk to me about, I want to listen to you. Sam, you believe that, don't you?"

Sam had nodded, knowing that was expected of her. If you'd asked her to repeat what Kate had just said, she couldn't have done it.

"I've used up my sick days and I've got to get back to work tomorrow, but I want you to call Nora. She's expecting you to call, okay? Tomorrow, anytime."

Sam nodded again, looking at her own square pale hands on the kitchen table. "Work" was someplace her mother went, but didn't talk about. She worked at the hospital, Sam knew, in radiology where Sam had visited her a few times. That didn't seem to mean much now. It was just a place that swallowed people up, that would swallow up her mother tomorrow.

After they went to bed Sam could hear Kate tossing and turning for a while, but eventually she was quiet. Sam was alone then, drifting in the darkness like a

small boat on the night sea. She thought she'd been
awake through the whole night, but she must have
slept some, Sam decided, because her eyes were
closed and she didn't remember closing them.

She opened them now, feeling as though she were
waiting for something, that there was some reason
she was suddenly awake. Her gaze drifted slowly
down from the ceiling to her closet, directly across
from the foot of her bed. In the dark room, without
her glasses, Sam couldn't focus. The closet appeared
as a deeper patch of shadow. That meant the closet
door was open, she thought, and she started to watch
it now, sure, without knowing why, that whatever it
was would come from the closet.

So she stared, straining to see in the darkness, eyes
getting dry and aching while she tried not to blink.
She wanted it to come soon and be over with.

And finally it began.

A swirling patch of pale green light, something like
mist, started to form a ball the size of a face, the
height of a grown man. She watched the light grow. It
could be shaping shoulders. It glowed like something
in a cave, and the glow spread downwards, chest
high, and was coming closer.

Tap, tap, tap.

Over her head was a small, sharp clicking. It made
tension undulate down her spine like the wave of
muscled movement that drives a snake through the
grass. She was afraid to take her eyes off the green
light.

Tap, tap, tap.

And she had to look up, just a quick glance toward
the headboard of her bed and the sound like finger-
nails clicking impatiently on wood.

Nothing.

She swung her eyes back to the closet. The green
mist was closer now, its shape more definite. A man,
Sam thought, but she was so near-sighted, so handi-

capped without her glasses, that she couldn't tell.

And tap, tap, tap.

A movement at the corner of her eye drew her with a quick twitch of the head to see the thing suddenly beside her.

A small boy's face was inches from hers, resting at the edge of her pillow. He was watching her through hazel eyes that caught green light from the thing at the end of the bed. His pale face glowed with it and with a small, pleased smile, like a boy who's caught a grasshopper and plans to take the grasshopper's legs off, one by one.

He started moving closer, face sliding across the pillow towards her a slow inch at a time, and then he opened his mouth as if to speak. But all that came out was a hiss and a stench like sewer gas.

Sam rolled away from him, scrabbling over her bed on hands and knees, slapping at the nightstand to find her glasses. She snatched them up, swiveling to put her back to the corner, to face the boy and the green mist shaped like a man, finally on her feet and able to see.

But there was nothing there.

One moment Kate was asleep and the next, without any transition, she was alert, mind poised and ready to race, a rabbit trapped in a flashlight's beam. She lay on her side in the bed, legs tangled in her nightgown and the twisted sheet, eyes closed, mouth loosely open on the damp pillow, feigning sleep. But her heart thumped and spasmed in her chest and she knew she wasn't alone.

She concentrated on controlling her breathing, keeping it shallow and steady and quiet, trying to pick up any alien sound. It never occurred to her that the thing in her room might be Sam. She knew it wasn't.

Exposed and vulnerable, the bare skin of her arms

and back prickled and tightened. The tiny hairs stood straight up, testing the air like radar. It was by the feel of her skin, the prickling of her scalp, that she knew she wasn't alone. She lay waiting for confirmation and it came.

After a soft movement on the far side of the bed, something settled, sinking onto the bed beside her, and she felt her body tilt towards it, shifting with the new weight. With a slow easy creaking of the old innerspring, the weight behind her shifted and stretched out the length of her body. It fit the hollows of the worn mattress, shaped itself, without touching her, to the curve of her body in sleep. Familiar, known, impossible.

Kate wanted to turn, to embrace the thing behind her. She also wanted to scream and run from the bed. She lay still, listening, hearing only the sound of her own breathing in the dark. After an endless time she calmed down and reached that placed somewhere between waking and sleep. She gave herself up to dreaming and turned over.

She was alone.

Nora woke with a jolt to the self-righteous buzzing of her alarm clock. She groaned and smacked the snooze alarm, giving herself ten extra minutes before she'd have to consider getting up.

Sprawled on her stomach, pillow over her head, Nora took an inventory of her condition. A dull headache throbbed at the back of her head and her neck muscles were painfully tight, as though she'd slept tensely, frozen in some stiff, awkward position. She was tired, heavy in the arms and legs, still lost in sleep, mind dull and reluctant. She groaned again, tossing off the pillow and turning onto her back. She forced her eyes into a tight squint, open only far enough to let a crack of dull light stab at her sleepiness.

Today was the day she'd meet with Dr. Ellicott.

Like going to the dentist, Nora thought. She wanted to stay in bed.

She pictured Dr. Ellicott as a dentist, wearing a white coat, a little light strapped to his head. She pictured his cluttered office, walls lined with books, walnut desk covered with papers, text, journals, files, and pictured herself, sitting across from him in the red leather chair with a green paper bib hung by a little chain around her neck. She snickered, stretched, yawned and kicked off the wrinkled sheet that covered her, deciding an appointment with Dr. Ellicott was better than a root canal. Probably.

The day seemed to match her mood when Nora rolled up her shades. It was heavy and sullen, the overcast sky hung low and breathless, a solid dull gray without even the promise of a storm or cooling rain to break the humidity.

Nora groaned at the day in general and turned back to the disordered bedroom that was beginning, finally, to feel like home.

"Miss Durant," Dr. Ellicott said by way of greeting. He inclined his head in a courtly, Old World gesture, standing as Nora entered the office and waiting while she settled herself in the red leather chair with her purse and briefcase balanced on her lap.

When he lowered himself, a little stiffly, into his own chair, Dr. Ellicott closed an open file folder on his desk and slid it aside. He wore the summer-weight gray tweed jacket he had worn the three or four other times Nora had seen him. And the same white shirt, dark gray pants and black bow tie.

But she hadn't remembered his light blue eyes as being quite so piercing. Now, forearms resting comfortably on the arms of his chair, head tilted to one side, Dr. Ellicott seemed to regard her with a friendly curiosity that confused her.

"And how are you finding Stony Cliffs?" he asked. "Are you settling in comfortably?"

Should she tell him that her personal life was chaos and people she knew insisted on dying or falling to pieces?

"Oh, fine," she lied, smiling.

But he must have caught the instant of hesitation before she answered or the phony sunniness of her answer. He ignored it.

"No, how could you? The whole community is upset with these tragedies and I know Mr. Kellogg was a friend of yours." Nora frowned at him but he went on unperturbed. "It's a small town with a small town newspaper. They are in the habit of publishing full names and addresses. I recognized Mrs. Hall's name and address as your local reference. I haven't been snooping, although I am, perhaps, being presumptuous in mentioning it."

A little bewildered, Nora shook her head.

"It's a very quiet town, usually," Ellicott told her.

He reached out to grasp the edge of the desk with both hands and pulled himself closer, sliding his chair forward.

"There were two more deaths, you know." He opened a side drawer in the massive desk and pulled out a neatly folded newspaper. "Have you seen the paper or heard the news reports?"

Nora shook her head. "Who?" Her knuckles were slowly turning white while she clutched the edge of her briefcase.

Dr. Ellicott leaned across the desk toward her. "Would you like some tea? Or coffee?" He sounded like a Victorian gentleman anticipating a fainting spell.

Nora shook her head. "Who was it?"

"Two seemingly unrelated incidents," he told her. "A little boy and a prisoner at the county jail."

"A little boy?"

"Seven years old," he told her. "Difficult to believe. The boy's four year old brother says he jumped from the roof of the parking garage across from the Student Union. Understandably, the younger boy is in a state of shock. His testimony seemed unclear, the newspaper said, and police are investigating the possibility of an accident or even murder. But from what the younger brother says, it appears to be suicide. Terrible."

"And the other one? The prisoner?"

"Evidently a suspect in the case of Ted Kellogg. A young man by the name of Charles Luther."

"Charlie?" Nora gaped at him.

"He was being held for questioning and he hanged himself in his cell."

Eyes fixed on him, Nora shook her head slowly, side to side.

"I can't believe it," she said.

"You knew him?" Dr. Ellicott probed, gently.

"Not well," Nora said. "But he idolized Ted. Charlie would never have killed him."

"And the suicide? Would he have done that?"

Nora's stare traveled, unfocused, to the papers piled on Ellicott's desk. "Maybe," she said, in a voice sounding far away even to herself. "Maybe." Then she frowned and looked sharply up at Dr. Ellicott when the question suddenly struck her as strange. In fact, the whole conversation felt strange.

"Forgive me," he said, "I suppose I'm beginning to sound rather odd. There *is* a good reason for my questions . . . or at least I believe it a good reason although to others it, too, may sound odd." He smiled at her, self-deprecating, then leaned across the desk. "I'm working on a theory."

Crackpots, Nora thought. Simon was right all along, the place is a loony bin.

"We are beginning to see a great many similarities with certain instances of mass hysteria throughout history in small towns, you understand. Most of our documented cases took place in European villages, quite frequently in the Middle Ages. These cases were characterized by brutal murders and inexplicable suicides in a rapidly rising incidence. Like an epidemic, you see." He nodded, encouraging her to see the similarities. "And the people involved were good citizens, clergymen, community leaders, sometimes very small children or elderly women and men. 'Possession' was the only answer the old theologians seemed to agree upon."

"But," Nora protested, "the idea still belongs in the Middle Ages, doesn't it?"

"Oh my, no. Why, in Switzerland, for example, in 1969 six people were found guilty of beating a girl to death in order to 'beat the devil out of her.' People still believe in possession." He smiled at her. "I don't. But some people do."

He was waiting for her to ask about his theory, Nora decided. He was the kid who had collected almost all the cards for the Brooklyn Dodgers and he was pleased as hell with himself.

"Then what is your theory?" she said politely.

"Ah . . ." He made a steeple with his fingers and shook his head a little. "I'm afraid it's still in the working stages. It would be premature to discuss it now. Who knows what other events will take place or what the police may discover? Also, there is another factor . . ."

Nora raised her eyebrows, playing the game, prompting him on.

"My sister," he told her, "Irene."

Oh, my God, Nora thought, there *is* a crazy sister.

"I happened to pick Irene up at the airport yesterday. She's just returned from an extended trip to Chicago where she's been helping the police with their inquiries."

Ellicott cocked his pert head at her.

"Irene is an accomplished psychic, you see. She does this sort of thing all the time. Well," he leaned back in his chair, keeping his bright eyes on her face, " 'Death is walking,' she said."

And Nora shuddered violently in the red leather chair.

"Very odd," he said. "Well, shall we discuss your class curriculum?"

Nora nodded numbly and juggled her briefcase open, moving automatically. When she looked up at Dr. Ellicott he was still watching her with the interest of a robin watching a worm.

Nora stared back. "Your sister . . ." she began, but he interrupted her smoothly.

"She'd like to meet you. Will you come to tea this afternoon?"

"Ye—es," she answered slowly with the uncomfortable feeling that she was committing to something more than tea.

"Fine. Four-thirty? Good. And now we really must discuss your course. I have another appointment in half an hour."

13

"Ah, poor innocent. Then no one warned you about Dr. Ellicott?" Michael said over quiche Lorraine in Nora's kitchen. They were making up for lunch missed the day before.

"What's to be warned about?"

"You know, of course, SCC's reputation for esoteric subjects and eccentricity? Folks who are less kind just call us all wacko. Cracked. Bonzo. Bananas. You get the idea."

Nora nodded, chewing, and waved her fork in the air. "So?"

"So Dr. Ellicott is something like the Great Kahuna of Cuckoos."

"Dr. *Ellicott?*" Dignified Dr. Ellicott with his gray tweed and trim white hair? "How? I mean, why?"

"The Great Horned God."

"Michael, I'm afraid you'll have to enlighten me."

"I'll do my best, but I'm afraid I'm rather fuzzy on some of the details. Let me see," he said, leaning back in his chair and picking up his wineglass. It was half full of Burgundy and he swirled it in the air, frowning into it like a fortune teller with a crystal ball. "Ellicott's sound enough academically—or at least he started out that way. An Oxford fellowship way back

173

when and he taught at Harvard, I think, back in the Ice Age. But then he came up with his Big Theory and that was more or less the end of that."

"And the big theory was about the Great Horned God?"

"Right. Are you sure you haven't heard this?" He peered at her suspiciously.

"Just an inspired guess. Wasn't the horned god some kind of primitive hunting god or warrior?"

"Bingo. That's the earliest version of the horned god, anyway. But just like you end up with the Great Mother—the White Goddess—in different forms all over the place, you end up with a guy with horns. There's a paleolithic drawing in a French cave with what may be the first one. They call it the Dancing Sorcerer and it's either someone part human and part stag or a guy in a stag suit complete with antlers. Egyptians had horned gods. And there's the hubby of Hecate. You know Hecate? She was the Greek goddess of both the moon and death, and she ended up getting adopted by witches as their patron saint or however they work it."

"Herne!" Nora suddenly cried, saluting him with her wineglass.

He raised his eyebrows politely. "I beg your pardon?"

"Herne," she explained. "He's the leader of the Wild Hunt in European folklore. That's something like an early version of ghost riders in the sky, and Herne either has or wears stag's antlers."

"Well, there you are. The guy in horns is everywhere. That's the basis of Ellicott's theory."

"Satan has horns," Nora said.

"Yes."

Nora prodded her quiche crust. "So what was Dr. Ellicott's theory and how did it get him exiled to Stony Cliffs? And how do you know all this?"

"Ah," Michael sighed, "I read the book."

"Book?" Nora echoed. Michael was pouring himself more wine, and she finished her glass with a flourish and held it out for refilling. "What book?"

"Dr. Ellicott's book. I think it was called *Secret Society of the Gods* or *Secrets of the Great Horned God.* Something like that." He filled her glass and carefully corked the bottle.

"In other words," Nora propped her chin on her fist, staring at him thoughtfully, "judging by the title, the horned gods were some widespread secret society. Or a small society that became a legend?"

"Lady, you're smart. And very pretty. Did I tell you that yet today?"

Nora felt her face grow suddenly hot. She started pushing her quiche crust around and around in tight fast circles.

"Thank you."

"And I love it when you blush."

Nora cleared her throat and took a swallow of wine before she could look him in the eyes again. "But the idea of this society," she said, "doesn't sound all that cuckoo."

"There's more to it than that. The old bird got onto dangerous ground by implying that these horned sorcerers may have actually had some real power. You know what academics are like. It's okay to theorize to your heart's content, but you're not supposed to go around actually believing in things. I mean, heaven forbid if you should actually *believe* in magic."

"Mmm," Nora conceded. It was okay to believe in ancient astronauts because that, after all, was simply a matter of superior technology. Stonehenge was simply a giant observatory/calendar, and the Russians were working on making telepathy a practical tool for espionage. But if Dr. Ellicott simply believed in magic, his goose was cooked.

"Michael, how did you happen to read a book like

that by Dr. Ellicott?"

"Victor had a copy. My brother was one of Dr. Ellicott's prize pupils."

"Good heavens."

Michael raised one eyebrow at her. "That surprises you so much?" He shrugged. "Victor admired Ellicott for years, until he decided he'd 'gone beyond' Dr. Ellicott. But the old man refused to acknowledge his superiority, even dared to patronize him, Victor said. Of course Victor stopped speaking to him, but he held onto his books."

"Hmm." Nora was poking her quiche crust again, using the fork to make patterns of dots on the moist inner surface.

"I have the feeling you're not going to eat that," Michael said. "In which case, we're ready to clear the table and do the dishes."

He stood up and started stacking plates. Nora gawked at him.

"You don't have to do that," she protested.

"Maybe not, but I'd like to," he said firmly.

So they cleared the table and did the dishes in comfortable silence. Nora was intensely aware of him working beside her, as they bumped shoulders, brushed hands, and lingered over handing each other dishes.

"Well, that's that," she said brightly when the last dish was set in the drainer to dry.

She turned to look up at him, smiling down at her, his face a hand's breadth away from her. What beautiful eyes, she thought. And then he leaned down and kissed her gently. And again, more firmly, reaching out to hold her waist with warm hands still slightly damp. Nora leaned against him, her arms going up to his shoulders, hands feeling the smooth muscle under his shirt, the dark hair curling on his neck. They stayed like that for some time, kissing, exploring the taste and feel of each other until they climbed the stairs to her bedroom to make love.

"It's a good thing you're not ticklish," she said, interrupting his story about his days of playing the drum in his high school marching band. She was tracing the lines of his collarbone, chest and ribs, propped on one elbow and leaning against him as they lay in her bed.

"You mean it's too bad I'm not."

"Nah. Would I want to tickle you?"

"Probably. But I'm not a ticklish kind of guy. Do you or do you not want to know the greatest hazard faced by the drummer in a marching band?"

"Hernia?"

"Horseshit."

"What?"

"Horseshit. You march behind horses in a parade and you know it's there, but with the damn drum in front of you you can't see it. One false step and you're down, just like that, with the damn drum on top of you."

Nora grinned at him. "That's wonderful! I'm developing a whole new respect for drummers."

She walked two fingers around his side. "Ticky-ticky," she experimented.

"Fat chance," he told her. "Nora . . ."

When he didn't say more she checked his face. He was watching her seriously.

"I think I'm in love with you."

"Yikes."

He nodded at her, looking, she thought, sweetly wry. "Really."

"We've only known each other three days."

"How long does it take?" he challenged. "I don't expect you to say anything. I just wanted to tell you. Okay?"

She nodded, biting her bottom lip, afraid she might cry.

"So. You wanna hear about my days as a gymnast?"
But the phone rang before he could begin.

"I'm expecting a call from Sam," she told him. "Do
you mind if I answer?"

"Go ahead," he said and she rolled over him to grab
the receiver.

"Hello?"

"There's an old man," said the voice on the other
end softly, dreamily.

"What? Sam, is that you?"

"An old man, sitting on the stairs." It was Sam,
Nora was sure, but her voice sounded odd, as though
she were talking in her sleep and as faint as though
she held the phone a foot away from her mouth.

"Sam, I can just barely hear you," Nora said
sharply. "Can you talk louder? What is it?"

"I don't know what he wants." Her voice was high,
bewildered.

"Sam, is he in the house with you?" Beside her on
the bed Michael was watching her intently. She
looked back at him, waiting for Sam's answer.

"Yes," Sam said, and Nora nodded at Michael. He
slipped out of bed and began gathering his clothes and
piling hers near her on the bed.

"Someone broke in? Is that what happened?"

"I don't know," Sam answered, her voice suddenly
clear and close on the phone. "Nora, I'm scared."

"What room are you in?"

"Bedroom." She was drifting again, Nora thought.

"Listen to me . . . hang up the phone and then lock
the bedroom door. Then call the police and tell them
to get there fast. Tell them you have a prowler, do you
understand? Sam?"

"He's in his pajamas," Sam said, sounding faintly
annoyed. "And a robe."

"Sam, I'm on my way over. Lock your door and I'll
call the police, okay?"

"Just come," Sam's voice drifted to her, getting

farther away, and the phone went dead.

"Sam?" Nothing. Nora threw the receiver back into its cradle and leaped up. Michael was already fully dressed and looking for his shoes.

"I'll call the police while you get dressed," he told her and Nora nodded, grabbing at her clothes. She rattled Kate's address off to him while he dialed, threw the tangle of underwear, shirt and jeans back on the bed and took two long steps to her closet. By the time Michael completed his call to the police she'd pulled a crinkled cotton magenta dress off its hanger and dropped it over her head, slipped on sandals and taken off down the hall.

Michael caught up with her on the stairs. "I'll drive."

When they reached Kate's house minutes later the cracked front door was off its hinges. Nora ran up the porch steps and threw open the wooden screen door, calling inside for Sam as she came. Michael caught the door as it swung open behind her and they both moved into the hall and stopped.

"Sam!" Nora called, urgent, but the house was sleepy and quiet. She took a step towards the stair, but Michael caught her elbow and glided smoothly around her.

"Let me go first," he said.

Just like in the movies, Nora thought, admiringly, dimly pleased at feeling feminine and protected. She liked the way his back looked, moving up the stairs. She trotted up behind him.

"Hurry up," she said to him, one hand lightly on the small off his back. "Sam!"

Nothing, and they stopped at the head of the stairs to listen to the silence before Nora called again and finally Sam's muffled voice answered, "Here." It came from behind Kate's closed bedroom door. Michael stepped up to it and rattled the knob, expecting it to be locked, but the door opened easily. He

walked into the room with Nora pressing close behind
him, craning over his shoulder.

A blast of dank air rushed past them like a storm
howling through a sewer. It lasted only as long as a
breath and left behind just a trace of foulness in the
sultry August heat of the darkened bedroom.

Sam sat cross-legged at the center of Kate's unmade
bed, still in her nightgown and robe. She had a
rumpled, disoriented look like a small child woken
from a nap. The hair on one side of her head was
creased into a frozen wave that made a little shelf
above her temple, and she blinked towards them,
blankly, behind the big round glasses that rested
halfway down her nose.

Nora took a step toward the girl, but Michael
blocked her, told her to stay still and moved first into
the room. He looked behind the door and into the
closet, knees a little bent, balanced on the balls of his
feet. He even leaned sideways to look under the bed.
Nora watched him with her lower lip caught between
her teeth until he looked up and gave her a short nod.
She crossed the room in a couple long strides and slid
onto the bed beside Sam, but the girl looked at her
like a hostess examining an uninvited guest.

"Are you okay?" Nora asked.

Sam's brows furrowed. "Did I really call you,
then?"

"Yes." Nora kept her eyes fixed on Sam's.

"I thought I dreamed it, like the people saying my
name."

"You really called. What about the man you saw?
Was he real or was that a dream?"

Sam shook her head. "I think he was real. I'm not
sure any more."

The screen door downstairs creaked open and they
heard a loud knocking. "Sheriff's department!" A
voice called.

"I'll go," Michael said. Nora heard him call down to
the deputies and clatter down the stairs.

"Tell me about it," Nora said to Sam.

Sam shrugged, shook her head. "He was on the stairs."

"Where were you?"

"In bed. But I guess I must have gotten up."

"You came out into the hall?"

Sam nodded.

"Did the man talk to you or come towards you?"

"He didn't even look at me. He was just sitting there, on the stairs." *Go away*, Sam had said, or thought she had said. *Go away!* But he hadn't. "I guess I just came in and called you then."

"Are you just getting up, Sam? You know it's after two o'clock?"

Sam shrugged.

Michael called then from downstairs and Nora left Sam and walked out to the landing. He stood at the base of the stairs with two deputies behind him like a pair of guard dogs nervously scanning the place.

"They're going to take a look around," Michael told her.

"Fine."

"And they want to talk to Sam."

"I'll tell her," Nora said and walked back to the bedroom.

Sam stood in front of her mother's dresser, staring into the mirror with the palm of one hand flattening her creased hair.

"I heard," she said when Nora reached the doorway. "But I want to get dressed first. Okay?"

"Okay."

The deputies searched the house thoroughly without finding anything. They talked to Sam only briefly, convinced by now that Sam had been dreaming or maybe just seeking attention.

"But someone might easily have walked in—and out again," Nora insisted, indignant. "Surely you've noticed the front door? It can't be locked because some deputies bashed it in like something out of a

Dirty Harry movie.''

"Yes, ma'am," they had both said, one looking at the floor, one studying the ceiling.

Michael had put a hand across his mouth to cover a grin and turned away. Sam had retreated, embarrassed, to the kitchen.

When the deputies left Nora insisted that Sam at least eat a bowl of cereal. Eventually they all ended up on the living room floor playing Parcheesi. It was an old board that Kate and Nora had spent thousands of hours over through college and the years after. Nora knew most of the stains and scrapes that marked the board like a scrapbook of the past. A faded brown stain on a slide near the yellow "Start" came from a spaghetti dinner cooked by Kate's second husband. Peter was gay and trying to prove he wasn't by marrying Kate, and Kate was on the rebound from Sam's father, drinking heavily. It was the main thing she and Peter did together. But he stopped drinking and decided to come out of the closet. The marriage ended after less than three months.

A raised, wavy ring near the red "Home" came from Simon's glass of dark beer, condensation from the humid air one afternoon during the summer they'd first met. A cigarette burn near the white "Start" marked her first visit to Kate after divorcing Simon. She'd still smoked then, and she smoked a pack of Marlboros while she and Kate drank four full bottles of cheap champagne and played an endless game of Parcheesi. They'd ended the evening singing all the old Peter, Paul and Mary, Judy Collins and Leonard Cohen songs they could remember in fine, dramatic voice complete with vibrato and special effects. The next day Nora had a massive hangover that turned into a bout of flu.

Michael won the first game of Parcheesi, narrowly beating Sam. They were midway through the second game when Nora remembered her tea with the Ellicotts.

"Hey!" she exclaimed, eyes on Sam's reaction. "I just remembered I'm supposed to have tea with Dr. Ellicott and his sister this afternoon." Sam's face snapped closed like a lady's fan, all the animation that had come back to it while they played suddenly vanished. "But," Nora went on after pausing only a couple of heartbeats, "I've decided to cancel it. I'll take a rain check."

"You should go," practical Sam said in a small voice.

Michael didn't say anything.

"Tomorrow. Or next week. Or next month, for that matter. Dr. Ellicott was just doing his duty by inviting me and he'll probably be relieved if I don't come. Don't worry about it."

At the hall phone Nora looked up the Ellicotts' number and punched it, waiting while it rang four times and halfway through a fifth ring when a woman's breathless voice answered.

"Hello, is this Miss Ellicott?" Nora was relieved, thinking it would be easier to give a phony excuse to a stranger. "This is Nora Durant, from Dr. Ellicott's department. Dr. Ellicott invited me to tea with you this afternoon, but I'm afraid I won't be able to make it."

"Nonsense, my dear," the woman had a high, clear voice that warbled a little, not unpleasantly, "Of course you can make it. In fact, I really think you should because there's a great deal we have to talk about."

"But I—"

"Oh, please do come. And bring the girl."

"What girl?" Disarmed, Nora fairly squeaked.

"I don't know," Irene Ellicott answered blithely, "But whoever she is, she's deeply concerned in all this, too. Very deeply. I believe she's in danger, as are you, Nora. So. May we expect to see you? And the girl, of course . . . what *is* her name?"

"Sam," Nora answered, deadpan. "It's short for

Sample.''

"Sample, how unusual. 4:30, then?''

"All right. 4:30.'' Nora was staring at the head of a nail canted at a rakish angle in the edging of a stair at eye level. It reminded her of the mushroom caps in Disney's *Fantasia* set askew as the mushrooms skipped and marched to the music of spring. After she hung up, Nora stood for several seconds just staring at the head of the nail. *Danger?*

She walked back into the living room, trying to sound more confident and matter-of-fact than she felt. "Well,'' she announced, "the plans have changed again. Not only am I going to tea with Dr. Ellicott and his sister, but *you're* going with me!'' Nora pointed dramatically at Sam.

"What?''

"You do own a dress, don't you?''

"Of course.''

"Good, because I don't know what the proper attire is for tea at the Ellicotts, but I'm not taking any chances. We'll both wear dresses.''

"But—''

"No, definitely dresses. They're as old as the Colonel and your grandmother. They'll like it.''

"But why do you want *me* to go?''

"You were invited.''

"What for?'' Sam scowled at her suspiciously.

Nora shrugged. "For your wit and charm. I suppose the news has spread. Miss Ellicott asked for you and who am I to disappoint a little old lady? Besides, how bad can it be? Go get dressed, okay? I still have to go to my place and get changed myself.''

Sam stood up, brushing at the seat of her shorts, and squinted judiciously at Nora in her magenta dress. "Well, that's for sure. You can really tell you don't have any underwear on.''

Michael sputtered into his iced tea and began to cough until Nora leaned over and gave him a hearty whack on the back and he stopped from pure shock. Sam sailed past them on her way upstairs.

"Um, I think I hit you harder than I meant to." Nora bent over to peer into his face. He looked a little glassy-eyed, she thought, but he smiled at her with one side of his mouth, coughed once and cleared his throat.

"Agh." He blinked at her. "How *did* you manage to get Sam invited?"

Nora dropped to a squat beside him. "I didn't. It was very odd, and that's an understatement. I talked to Miss Ellicott, told her I couldn't make it and she said of course I could and to bring the girl. But I hadn't mentioned Sam at all."

"Ah, the psychic Miss Ellicott."

"You knew about that? Why didn't you tell me?"

"Everybody in SC knows. Irene Ellicott is quite a celebrity, although she tries to keep a low profile. I'm surprised you didn't know about her and, honestly, I just didn't think about it."

Nora wrapped her arms around her legs and rested her chin on her knees. "Curiouser and curiouser," she mused. "Miss Ellicott says Sam and I are in danger."

"What? What kind of danger?"

"I don't know. I suppose we'll find out this afternoon. Why? You don't believe it, do you?"

"I don't like the idea of your being in danger," he said, "Even if it's just the dotty idea of some silly old lady in chiffon scarves."

Nora giggled. "With a pince-nez and a rhinestone-studded cigarette holder?"

Michael reached out to touch her face lightly with the tips of his fingers. "Have I told you in the last hour or so how pretty you are?"

Nora rolled her eyes up to the ceiling, pondering it. "With or without underwear?"

14

Nothing was anything like Nora expected it to be.

She had expected the Ellicott house to be small and musty and old-fashioned. Instead, it was large and gracious, a tall two stories of white limestone in a style that combined French elegance and Georgian simplicity. Large, multi-paned windows were trimmed in fresh white paint and white accented the tall bay window of the front room. Dark ivy climbed the walls and made a bed for white weeping birches. The lawn was deep green and well-trimmed and the walk curved through it to the front entrance.

Nora and Sam had been silent, standing together on the front stoop, shifting from foot to foot like children in their Sunday best. And silence nearly over-whelmed them when Irene Ellicott opened the door to their ring.

Nora had to forcibly stop herself from gawking, first at Irene Ellicott, then, with great difficulty, at the house. It was love at first sight. She could hear it in her own breathing, like a child who's found a secret place at Disneyland. It was like being inside a rose. Or a sea shell. Or a mist on the heather.

The house was luminous. It glowed with muted rose, heathery blues and soft mauve. They were the colors of the abstract, impressionist wallpaper in the foyer, the deep rose carpet, the mauve leather chairs, the soft floral print of the couch and love seat. They were the subtle undertones in rosewood tables, delicate writing desk and chairs. They were the colors of the fresh flowers in vases around the living room.

The rooms were spacious, light and airy. The house seemed both contemporary and timeless. And so did Irene Ellicott.

Nora really had expected an elderly eccentric, someone a bit batty with flyaway hair and a wild look in her eyes. Instead, Irene Ellicott had the grace and style of a movie star of the 1930s. She seemed just slightly larger than life—glamorous, sophisticated, with an offbeat flair that had nothing to do with money or status.

Claudette Colbert, Nora thought, or Rosalind Russell.

Although she was in her late 60s, her figure was still trim and lithe. She was wearing a simple, deep blue dress that highlighted the deep blue of her own eyes while it picked out the fine blue veins under the pale skin. Myrna Loy, Nora decided.

Irene Ellicott led them from the foyer to the living room moving with a quick, light step. Dr. Ellicott met them there looking, Nora was surprised to realize, perfectly at home and in place with his black bow tie and gray tweed jacket.

"I hope you don't really want tea," Irene Ellicott said when Nora and Sam were finally settled in the mauve leather chairs across a coffee table from the Ellicotts. "I like tea, of course, but I tend to prefer vodka. Peter hates tea, but he insists it's the natural drink of everyone at the school."

"Dr. Stephens likes it," Peter Ellicott interjected mildly. He held a small snifter of brandy.

"Harold Stephens is an old prig." Irene Ellicott flipped an elegant, dismissing hand. "Anyway, I hope you don't mind if we skip tea and have something with more of a kick to it."

"Spirits," Dr. Ellicott solemnly explained and Nora smiled uncertainly at him.

"Don't mind my brother, dear. It's an old joke and he's being a stinker. What would you like to drink?"

"White wine?"

Dr. Ellicott brought Nora a glass of chilled Chablis and served Sam a Coke. He pushed a small bowl of mixed nuts across the coffee table towards them.

"To spirits and nuts," Irene Ellicott toasted them with her vodka and tonic. "And to life."

Nora took a cool swallow of wine and found Irene Ellicott smiling at her, benign and secretive as the Mona Lisa.

"You expected to be balancing a bone china teacup and saucer and a plate of little cakes, listening to a looney old bird babble about the spirit world, didn't you?" Nora's face betrayed her and the older woman's smile broadened.

"I don't blame you a bit. I would have thought the same thing. Well, I'm not senile, or impossibly eccentric, but I'm afraid it may take, to borrow a phrase, 'a willing suspension of disbelief' to understand or accept what I want to say to you and Sample."

Beside Nora, Sam sat straight and attentive in the mauve leather chair. She was studying Irene Ellicott with the wide-eyed curiosity of a duckling goggling at a water lily. Nora looked at her quickly, then turned her attention back to Irene Ellicott.

"I don't think I really understood what you said on the phone."

"I said you were in danger," Irene said calmly. "You and Sample. Something is very definitely happening in Stony Cliffs and I'm afraid you're at the center of it."

Nora frowned, worrying about the effect of Irene

Ellicott's announcement on Sam. The kid had enough to complicate her life without vague warnings of danger.

But some part of Nora leapt up in agreement. The warning felt right. And things were not as they should be in Stony Cliffs.

Still, "Miss Ellicott—" Nora began firmly, but the woman politely cut her off.

"Please call me Irene. It's so much easier and less formal. Nora, I know that you're concerned that even though I don't look like a crackpot, I may be potty enough to worry Sample needlessly, but please bear with me a little while. Sample . . ."

Sam hadn't taken her eyes off Irene Ellicott.

"Have you felt recently that someone or something is trying to contact you?"

Sam frowned a little at her. "They've been calling my name."

"Ah, I thought as much."

"Who has, Sam?" A dream, Sam had said, like the people calling her name. But who were they, and who was the old man and what kind of danger was Sam in? Nora looked back and forth from Sam to Irene, but their eyes were locked in a steady stare and her question went unanswered.

"You mustn't listen to them. If you don't listen to them, they can't reach you. They can't harm you unless you let them and you simply mustn't let them. Do you understand?"

Sam nodded. "What do they want?"

"That," Irene Ellicott said, shaking her head slowly, "I simply don't know." She traced a small circle with one finger around and around on her glass and breathed a short, sharp sigh.

"So much of the time the impressions I get are only small pieces of the puzzle. The connections aren't clear. The picture isn't complete or logical, and I've had to learn to be patient and take the pieces one at a time. Yesterday, when I returned to Stony Cliffs, I felt some sense of danger hanging like a cloud over the town. There was nothing, though, that I could put my finger on. Later," Irene's blue eyes fixed Nora like a deer frozen by headlights, "Peter was telling me about you, Nora, and another piece slipped into place. Now, here with you both, I know that Sample is a central figure."

"In *what?*" Nora interrupted, bristling, irritated with Irene Ellicott for the vague and threatening mystery of her pronouncements and irritated with herself for beginning to believe her.

"I don't know," Irene said mildly, shrugging. She took a sip of her drink. "Annoying, isn't it?"

"I have a theory," Dr. Ellicott said. "It has to do with one of the more unusual phenomena of mass behavior, the possibility of a species of mass hysteria. It's the violence, you know, the curious excess and, of course, the unpredictability. It's very interesting on a behavioral level, considering the fact that those involved so far don't seem to share a belief system— religion, superstition, mythology, what have you. In fact—"

"Oh, Peter, that's all very nice, but it's so stuffy. The question is, what can we do to protect Sample and Nora?"

"From what?" Nora protested. She felt like she was losing touch with reality, slipping into some Mad Hatter's Tea Party. "What on earth can Sam and I have to do with clouds of danger and mass hysteria? Dr. Ellicott," she turned to the head of her department as to a touchstone for stodgy academic reality, "you think the farmer in that murder-suicide and that little boy have something to do with mass hysteria? But Sam and I didn't know them. There's no connection. And Miss Ellicott, you think we're in some danger? From what? Or who?"

Irene Ellicott turned a mild, thoughtful look on her.

"I don't know. I wish I did, but clairvoyance is generally annoyingly incomplete."

"What makes you think Sam is even involved?"

"A feeling. I see it. Something, some power, is reaching towards her and you seem to be in the way. This thing reaching for you is very unpleasant."

Nora groaned and thunked her wineglass down on the coffee table, harder than she had intended. "It doesn't make sense!"

"Yes, it does," Sam said suddenly, breaking her long silence. Nora snapped around to look at her.

"Voices have been calling me and when I was listening some weird stuff happened like seeing that old man. And there was a little kid in my room with this green thing that just disappeared. I thought I was either dreaming or going crazy or something because it was so hard to think, you know?"

"Sam . . ." Pained, Nora wanted to stop Sam from speculating on frightening, impossible possibilities. But Irene neatly cut her off.

"Nora. Ignoring things will not make them go away." Irene fixed her again with those penetrating blue eyes. "I think you've been trying that unsuccessfully for most of your life and you ought to realize by now that it simply doesn't work." She said it kindly but firmly, and the words reverberated through Nora like the toll of a great bell striking a true note.

Irene turned towards Sam. "Now, what is it you thought you saw?"

Sam twisted a few inches in her seat, dropping her eyes to her untouched glass of Coke. "I don't know."

"Oh, poop, of course you do."

Sam struggled, then blushed. It was the first time, Nora realized, that she had ever seen Sam blush.

"Something in the closet."

"Yes?"

"It sort of glowed. Green. And it was growing and coming closer."

Irene nodded, businesslike. "And?"

"There was a kid who just kind of appeared all of a sudden. He was next to the bed, real close to me. Looking at me."

"Did you get a feeling of unusual cold?"

Sam shook her head.

"Was there a peculiar odor? Something quite foul?"

Sam blinked at her once, eyes owlish behind the big glasses.

"Yes."

"They do that," Irene told her matter-of-factly. "Also the glowing in the closet. What else?"

"An old man. In his pajamas." Sam's chin went up an inch. It was spoken like a challenge, Nora thought, but not an unfriendly one. Sam looked more open, relaxed and alert than Nora had seen her since Ted's death.

Irene nodded. "Calvin Russell, I suspect. It's beginning to seem as though they were driven to act and they're now being used."

"No!" Nora heard the edge of panic in her own voice and she fought to control it, to speak reasonably. "Look, couldn't Sam just have heard about Calvin Russell and the boy and simply dreamed about them?"

"Sample may have learned about Calvin Russell from the news, but don't forget, she saw the boy the same night that he died, before the news had been reported. Nora, you're not helping Sample or yourself by refusing to at least consider the possibility."

Nora opened her mouth to protest, let it hang through a breath, then snapped it shut and tried again. This time she would try to play Irene's game, just to see where it led.

"Okay, suppose someone or something is aiming this . . . this attack at Sam. Why? What can they be trying to get from her? And who or what would do it? And how?"

Irene shrugged, shook her head, and took a long

swallow of her vodka and tonic. "I don't know," she finally said. "What do you think, Sample?"

The girl shook her head. "Maybe if I listened to the voices, I'd find out."

She wants to listen, Nora realized. She wants Irene to tell her it's all right. She won't have the responsibility for it then, and she won't have the guilt—like a new morphine addict given a prescription for the drug, Nora thought, looking carefully at Sam and seeing the temptation of darkness touching her. For the first time, she began to believe that Irene Ellicott might be right.

"Don't listen to them at all," Irene told Sam. "Resist them, and stay in control at all times. You're a very strong young lady. You'll have to continue to be strong. I have a feeling you'll need all your strength. Soon."

15

They didn't speak much on the way back to Kate's house, each of them wrapped in her own thoughts, until they nearly arrived.

"I feel like I should apologize for dragging you into all that," Nora told Sam. When Sam started to protest, Nora held up a hand to stop her. "But I guess I'm glad we went. We need to talk about this. Seriously."

Nora let the Datsun coast slowly to a stop at the curb. She turned off the engine and twisted around to face the girl. "Don't you think?"

Sam's chin was sunk on her chest, her eyes fixed on her lap, but she gave a barely discernible nod.

"What she said was scary, but I thought she made sense." Sam turned to look at Nora. She looked very young and vulnerable, Nora thought, as though her lower lip would start quivering at any second.

"She knew things," Sam said.

Phony, a critical voice answered in Nora's mind, but she had to admit it sounded like sour grapes. It was just too hard not to trust Irene Ellicott. She wanted to, but. . . .

"Oh, hell," Nora muttered, shoving her hair away from her face, damp with the day's sultry heat. "You've got to admit, Sam, it sounded pretty crazy."

Sam turned away again, her lower lip stubbornly firm now. "Maybe. But at least she didn't think *I* was crazy."

"Oh, Sam, no one ever thought you were crazy. Just under a lot of emotional pressure and pretty naturally upset. It seemed like a perfectly normal reaction."

Bullshit, Nora's small internal voice piped up, demanding honesty, *you were frightened by Sam's reactions. And what about you? What's your excuse for writing yourself nasty messages in your sleep?*

"Nuts," Nora sighed. "Okay, I give up. As Irene Ellicott might say, 'Things Are Not Right,' So? What shall we do?"

Sam rocked and bounced against the back of her seat, staring out the window, shaking her hair back away from her face. "Maybe we should tell Mom?"

Nora nodded. "Yeah, I think we should. But it's not going to be easy."

"*That's* an understatement!" Sam snorted.

They left the car without saying anything more, striding up the path in step, heads high, like a pair of recruits to the Queen's Musketeers.

"Mom?" Sam called when they moved through the new front door that had replaced the one splintered by the deputies.

"In the kitchen," Kate called back to them, "having a domestic attack. I'm making meat loaf, for God's sake!"

Sam and Nora started towards the kitchen, moving more slowly now, sheepishly watching their feet dragging towards Kate. They stood together, shoulder to shoulder in the doorway, silent and earnest.

Kate spun around and studied them, hands on hips.

"Okay, you two, what's with the shit-eating expressions? Did I miss some big punch line? Do I have spinach stuck in my teeth? Nora? What's up? How come you two are dressed up?"

Nora met her eyes. "We just came back from the Ellicotts."

"Ellicott? The head of your department?"

"Right. Dr. Ellicott. And his sister, Irene."

"Oh, shit, the swami."

"She has a good reputation, Michael says. And I liked her."

"Michael," Kate snorted.

"Dammit, Kate, you can't go around being hostile to everybody."

"I'm not hostile to everybody. I just don't have any patience with jerks. So what did the spook lady have to say? And why the hell did you have to take Sam with you?"

"I'm not a little kid, Mom. Nora didn't *make* me go with her."

Kate glared down at Sam and then up at Nora, bristling. "Okay. Great. So now you're both in happy harmony with the spirit world, is that it?"

Nora gazed steadily back at Kate, trying to keep her look open, trying to keep it from being a staring match. How could she talk to Kate about Irene Ellicott without increasing the tension? She couldn't, Nora realized. Anything she said would grate now on Kate's raw anger. But Kate would never let it drop, Nora knew. It would never be easier to talk to her than now.

"Irene just got back from Chicago yesterday. She was helping the police with a murder case." Kate snorted but didn't interrupt. "She said that as soon as she got back to Stony Cliffs she realized something was . . . not right."

Kate made another sound of impatience.

"Anyway," Nora summarized, "she thinks Sam may be in some danger. She thinks there's some force that's linked up with these suicides—maybe causing them—and that the same force may be trying to get at Sam."

"Oh, bullshit!" Kate exploded.

"Kate, Sam thinks Irene might be right."

Kate turned to Sam, all contained fury. "Go

upstairs.''

"Mom . . .''

"NOW! Go to your room, shut the door and stay there until I tell you to come out. You hear me?''

Without a word or a look at either of them Sam swiveled on one heel and stomped out of the kitchen.

Neither Kate nor Nora spoke and avoided looking at each other, waiting for the sound of Sam's door slamming to release them.

"I do not want Sam scared by a bunch of voodoo bullshit,'' Kate hissed at Nora, her face flooded a deep, sullen red. "I do not understand how you could drag her into this garbage.''

Nora's eyes narrowed and she felt her own face get hot, her stomach and shoulders knot and stiffen with a sudden flush of rage.

"*I'm* not the one who got her into it!''

Color washed out of Kate's face like a wave rushing away from the shore, leaving the tide's sad debris stranded in pitiless daylight.

But Nora's anger left as suddenly as it had come. "Kate,'' she said, taking a step towards her. "I'm sorry.''

Kate shook her head, turning away, eyes brimming. She pulled a Kleenex from a box on the counter and laughed once—a short, sharp sound, raucous as a crow—then blew her nose.

"When did things get so screwy?'' Kate muttered.

Nora knuckled both her fists into her temples. "Damned if I know.''

"Well . . .'' Kate blew her nose again, then looked up at Nora. "Just what is it your Madame Whosis thinks we should do?''

Nora frowned, considering, then shrugged. "Be careful?''

Kate stared, waiting for more. She smiled slowly, chuckled, then began to laugh, a choking sound, close to sobs, but a real laugh.

After a few seconds Nora joined her until both of them were laughing and crying at once in a flurry that passed quickly. It left them shy but comfortable with each other again. Kate passed the box of Kleenex. They stood together, quiet, mopping at their faces, blowing their noses until Kate jerked her head up to look at the clock.

"Jesus!" She jumped for the stove. "I'll bet the meat loaf's dead!"

And they both laughed again, more quietly and without the tears.

Nora stayed for dinner. The meat loaf was dry, but passable. She and Kate made silly jokes all through it, giggling for no apparent reason to Sam's disgust until she, too, got silly. The girl was defensive when Kate first called her down, but she let it slide in the mood of the evening.

They talked about nothing serious or painful or tense, and Nora left early, getting home just before 9:00.

The sullen red eye of the answering maching was blinking twice. Two messages.

One was from Hal Townsend, the lawyer in Simon's office, asking her to call him back at the office in the morning. Nora gave a little shiver at the sound of his voice, unctuous as a funeral director's and oh-so-sure of himself.

The other message was from Michael, threatening to sweep her off her feet the next day with dinner at a fancy restaurant. She patted the machine, smiling and thinking briefly of calling him immediately but deciding to wait until tomorrow. Right now, she just wanted quiet and time to herself, time to withdraw.

A good book was the answer, she thought, wandering to her newly organized bookshelves. Something purely entertaining.

She chose a battered Rex Stout paperback. Nero

Wolfe, Archie Goodwin and the old brownstone on West 35th Street with a roof full of orchids would be perfect.

She fell asleep on the couch, reading. But the shrill jangle of the telephone startled her awake, and she jammed her glasses onto her nose, checking the digital clock.

12:00 A.M., it read, the numbers glowing on the radio face.

The phone rang again.

"Hello?" It seemed like phone calls at midnight must always be bad news. Unless it were Michael. Would he call at midnight?

When she picked up the receiver, there was static and that hollow silence she was getting to know.

"Hello?" she said sharply, anger rising in her.

Pause. Then a voice that was uneasily familiar.

"Simon wants to talk to you," it said.

"Nora? Simon wants to talk to you." There was just the hing of a teasing laugh in the male voice.

"Who. . . ?"

Then he did laugh—a low, pleased chuckle.

"You're next, Nora."

Silence. A dead line.

Nora threw the receiver back into its cradle, then rubbed her palms on her thighs, breathing hard, rubbing away the warm, sticky plastic feel of the phone and the touch of the voice. She jumped to her feet, expecting the phone to ring again. She glared at it, paced the length of the room and back, and stopped to look at the phone.

"Shit," she barked at it, and the angry sound of her voice made her feel better. She picked it up and dialed Sheriff Finnerty's office.

Deputy Vern Snider was not about to wake up the sheriff over something the woman admitted was not an emergency. And there wasn't much he could do if

she refused to talk to him. About all he could do was
to take her name and number and tell her the sheriff
would get back to her. Finnerty had barreled out of
the office at 11:00. Going home to sleep, Vern
reckoned. No Chinese food tonight.

He didn't have to call Finnerty until 3:25 a.m.

When he called, 16 hours into his 20 hour shift,
Vern dialed the number with mixed emotions, with a
sense of satisfaction that some might even call petty
and vengeful. But what the hell? If Vern Sider had to
be up and out of his sweet bed, why not the sheriff?

And, partly, Vern was just spooked. Everybody
was, and this was Finnerty's job so, shit, why should
Vern try to handle this new business? So he called
Finnerty, trying to sound cool and professional.

Finnerty answered almost immediately, sounding
crisp with his patience worn thin. And Vern started
tripping over himself, using too many words without
saying anything.

On the other end Finnerty held himself still for just
one more second, his voice not giving away the fact
that he was so damned hot and damp with sweat,
lying tangled in a grayed top sheet, a window fan
noisy and ineffectual in the background. His white
undershirt clung to his sweaty chest, and his boxer
shorts were binding in the crotch, twisted and caught
up behind him.

"Pursuant . . ." Vern repeated, trotting out prissy
Tom Robbins' vocabulary, liking the sound of it,
"pursuant to which . . ."

"Jesus!" Finnerty barked at him, swinging his legs
up over the side of the bed. "Just spit it out, Vern."

Vern got ruffled, blew out a breath and gave up.
"There's another one, Sheriff. An apparent suicide.
This one's a woman named Florence Gleason. Or at
least that's what her identification says. I guess it's
hard to tell."

"What did she do?" Finnerty squeezed his eyes

tight shut and reached for the bedroom lamp. He let
them open slowly, seconds after the room flooded
with light. Finnerty squinted at the clock, rubbing at
his damp chest.

"She . . . uh . . . she put her head on the Chessie
track, down where it crosses 37. Just before the
regular freight to Indianapolis passes through."

Finnerty's arm dropped to his lap. He shook his
head twice, a half an inch in either direction.

"The train engineer called it in through radio to
Terre Haute, and the station master down there called
here to relay it."

"And what did he see?" Finnerty asked. He was
standing up now, prodding the pile of his clothing
with one foot, not really seeing it.

"He only caught sight of her at the last minute
'cause of that little hill near the river blocking the
view around the curve. It was too late to stop the train
by the time he spotted her, he says, though he blew
the horn a lot to warn her off. She just stayed there all
by herself, he said. No one holding her down or anything. I sent Al Beasley out there, but I thought maybe
you'd wanna go take a look."

"Yeah," Finnerty muttered, scraping a hand
against his short-cropped hair. "Did you call Doc
Paulson?"

"Not yet."

"Well, get him out there. And the photographer."

"Right. One more thing, Sheriff."

"Yeah?" Finnerty was poised to disconnect, hand
frozen over the button. He stared up at the ceiling of
his bedroom and absent-mindedly noted a hairline
crack in the plaster running the length of the room.

"Some old lady," Vern told him. "She called to find
out if we had anybody in a train accident, maybe
decap . . . decap . . . head cut off. But get this, Sheriff.
She called a few minutes *before* we got the call from
Terre Haute."

"A witness? She wasn't calling to report it?"

Vern made an uncomfortable noise somewhere between clearing his throat and a self-conscious giggle. "She said she dreamt it."

Finnerty snorted. "You get her name?"

"Irene Ellicott."

Florence Gleason's body lay as the train had left it. It was a middle-aged body, early fifties, Finnerty judged, with a square, sturdy build rounded by plumpness, large, soft breasts, elbows cushioned by fat, and knees puffed by arthritis. She wore a flowered housedress and no jewelry. Soft, beige wedgies were jammed on puffy feet.

A beige pocketbook was found next to the body. It held a pale blue plastic comb, lipstick, pressed powder compact, a small package of Kleenex, an old-fashioned snap change purse with $17 in bills and 62 cents in coins. A separate pocket in the handbag held a J.C. Penney charge card and a driver's license declaring Florence A. Gleason. The address was a rural route number, less than a mile away, Finnerty figured.

And there was a note in the purse—one sentence, written in blue ballpoint pen on cheap, lined notepaper. The handwriting was neat and round, with every letter connected, every *i* dotted, and every *t* carefully crossed. Finnerty read the note by the glare of his car's headlights, holding it carefully by one corner pinched between thumb and forefinger.

"When my head leaves my body, it will live."

He read it once and the skin on the back of his neck began to creep, small hairs stirring and rising. He read it again, and between his shoulder blades he felt a cold knot of tension. He stared at it, glowing in the bright beam of light, mind gone blank for long seconds, and then he shook himself and held the note out for Beasley to carefully drop into a plastic bag.

Finnerty watched him take it, then asked, "Where's the head?"

Al Beasley might have grown out of the heavy soil with a farmer's face made hard by generations of fighting weather and the government. The face he showed Finnerty was blank and cold. He jerked his head over one shoulder, up the track.

"It rolled a ways."

Finnerty stepped away from the car, aimed a heavy flashlight up the track and caught a mounded outline in the beam about 20 yards along. He started towards it.

Finnerty didn't realize he'd been holding his breath until he got close enough to see clearly that the head was lying face down on the track. He let his breath out in a rush, inhaling the night air. There was a chilly edge to it, despite the heat of the day before. It was a reminder that fall was coming, like the full moon, big and almost orange, riding low in the sky, shedding soft light on the quiet country. Dull, mostly flat farmland rolled away from Finnerty in every direction, fading into the shadows of the night. He could just make out a dark mass on the horizon that must be trees, probably the windbreak of a farmhouse. Florence Gleason's house?

When he was the length of one long stride from the head lying on the ground between the railroad ties, Finnerty stopped. He played the beam of light over it, studying it, lower lip stuck out in concentration.

The hair was short, curled a little, a faded brown matted now just in a couple spots with dark blood and something with the wet look of oil. The track looked to have been sprayed recently with tar or oil to keep the dust down on the crossing. Finnerty shone his light around. Dirt, gravel and low growing weeds filled the spaces between weathered ties. A sparkle of glass winked in the scanning light.

Behind Finnerty a car pulled up and the sheriff

swung around to watch Doc Paulson and Burt
Johnson climb out of their car with bags and camera
in tow. Al Beasley nodded a greeting, then pointed
them towards the body sprawled by the railroad
track. As Finnerty watched, the two men moved
towards it cautiously, stepping and watching, like
watching a snake by the side of the road. They
stopped a few, respectful feet from it, studying it, sil-
houetted by the glare of headlights. Doc Paulson's
lean, gawky boy's shape curved against the light with
the awkward grace of a grasshopper frozen mid-
flight. His pale hair floated around his head like a
halo, backlit. A step behind him, Burt Johnson was
solid and stocky. They stared, like Finnerty had, for a
long moment before going to work.

Finnerty was watching Johnson snap pictures when
he heard a movement behind him on the track.

He spun fast on his heels, some cold fist knotting in
his gut. Light from his flash swooped around him in a
wild circle, swinging through the shadows, looking
for the head. And it was there, a yard away, just as
he'd left it. But on the other side of it was a big black
dog, watching him. He shone the light in its face and
twin disks of green-gold flashed in the dog's eyes. It
kept staring, watching him coolly, head going up a
fraction of an inch to test the night air. Finnerty's
heart was beating faster than it should. He glared at
the dog and made a rough gesture with the flashlight.

"Get outta here!"

The dog just stared at him.

"Go on! Get away!" Finnerty gestured again with
the flash, then took a step forward. He switched the
flash to his left hand, freeing his right.

The dog backed up a step.

"Beat it!" Finnerty roared it. And the dog backed
another step, then turned and disappeared into the
shadows.

Finnerty nearly straddled Florence Gleason's head,

breathing hard, watching the night like a predator guarding his kill. He swung the light around. No sign of the dog. He shook himself, blew out his breath, changed the flash back to his right hand, stepped back from the head, and turned to the face the clump of men gathered around Florence Gleason's body.

"Deputy!" Finnerty called, "Come here, please."

Beasley jogged down the track towards him. Finnerty handed him the flashlight.

"Keep an eye open here," the sheriff told him. "Got a dog prowling around." He strode down the track to where Paulson bent over the body.

"We need to get cleared out of here as soon as possible," Finnerty told them after nodding and grunting greetings. "Probably going to start getting some traffic through here by dawn or before."

Paulson was studying the mangled flesh of the neck. He nodded, deliberately, understanding the need to hurry. But his face looked paler and thinner than ever, and after a half minute he stood up and walked to the side of the road, taking deep breaths, facing away from the scene.

"What's going on around here?" he asked the night in a voice high and wondering as a child's or an old man's. "What's happening?"

But no one answered him and he didn't seem to expect it. After less than a minute he went back to work.

The sheriff stayed with the coroner as Burt Johnson moved silently up the track to where Beasley guarded the head. A minute later his flash began to punctuate the night in short bright bursts. The smell of cigarette smoke drifted back to them as they finished with the body, turning it over, searching for anything to tell a story like marks of restraint or struggle or the evidence of anyone else present. There was nothing.

An ambulance pulled up along with another car with two men from the office to go over the scene. For what? They didn't know. Finnerty didn't know. Just note everything, he told them.

Doc Paulson let the ambulance attendants take the body and load it on a stretcher bound for the morgue. He stood to one side, polishing his wire rim glasses on his shirt tail.

The sheriff stood beside him. Like two men appraising a fishing hole, they looked off into the night, scanning the horizon.

"How about the blood tests on Luther?" Finnerty broke the silence. He said it casually, like asking about the weather, or what kind of fly to use in a particular hole.

Paulson held his glasses up to look through them. He studied one polished lens, blew on it and began to polish it some more.

"Nothing, so far. No evidence of drugs in the bloodstream. No recent drinking although he seems to have been a heavy drinker." Paulson held the glasses up again briefly, switched to polishing the other lens. "He hadn't eaten anything in quite a while. Two days, at least. He was probably a little light-headed and disoriented, maybe."

Finnerty grunted. Light-headed and disoriented just weren't enough to account for suicide. Guilty conscience? It might be a neat solution, but Finnerty just didn't buy Charlie Luther as Ted Kellogg's killer. And he couldn't see how Luther or any third party might be involved in the Russells' deaths. There was just no evidence for it. But what was Charlie Luther doing out there?

They'd been lucky, so far. None of the media had jumped on Luther's suicide as police brutality or neglect. They were too busy speculating about the Russells and, mostly, about the kid, Jerry Rhine. Little Stevie Rhine, the dead boy's brother, might be able to answer questions tomorrow, his doctor had said. Today, Finnerty amended. Already the sky was beginning to lighten. Maybe the kid could supply some missing piece of information, something that would make sense. Maybe it wasn't suicide. Maybe it was an accident. And maybe some things never did make sense.

That was a thought that shook Finnerty to the foundations of his belief. Things had to make sense and have reasons, even if the reasons didn't seem sensible. Cause and effect. It made order out of chaos. Unconsciously, Finnerty knew he'd been aiming for some connection between all the recent deaths. Could there be one? No. That was nuts.

When Paulson finally finished cleaning his glasses to his satisfaction and breathing the chill night air until he was calm and businesslike again, he nodded, once, and turned. He picked up his bag. "Okay," he told Finnerty and they walked up the track to where Al Beasley waited with his flashlight and Burt Johnson stood watching the moon go down.

No one spoke when they reached the head and Doc Paulson squatted beside it in a silence only broken by the sawing of crickets and a sleepy bird cry. Beasley kept his light fixed on the head with its drab brown hair, and Doc Paulson stretched out a finger to gingerly touch a dark patch matting the hair. He sniffed his finger, nose wrinkling.

"Tar?" Finnerty guessed.

Paulson shook his head. "Machine oil, I think. From the train, maybe. We'll check in the lab. There's something else here that could be tar. And blood from superficial scalp wounds. Scrapes. Some dirt in the wounds."

He studied the back of the head for a couple of minutes, lifting the lank curls to check the scalp and the material matted in the hair. Then Paulson carefully clasped the head in both hands, fingers spread for a sturdy grip and with as little contact as possible, holding it by the firm pads of his fingers. Cautiously, he turned the head over so that the woman's face stared blankly at them.

Florence Gleason's eyes were open. Pale blue, fogged and still with death, they stared sightlessly at the men who crowded around. Her lashes were pale and stubby. A gray pebble, the size of a dried pea, was half imbedded in the white of her left eye at the inner corner. Finnerty had to resist a strong urge to pluck it out. She was a plain woman, ordinary, with a face you might see at the grocery on Saturday morning or the German Club bingo game on Thursday nights.

Randy Paulson carefully placed the head to rest, leaning against the track and balanced on a weathered tie. Her face was tilted up towards them, blind with mouth hanging loosely open. They all stared back into her blank face, the pale skin marked by dirt and scrapes.

And then her mouth yawned open and snapped shut. Yawned again and shut again, like a desperate gasp, like a fish out of water drowning in the night air while they watched. And it opened again, more slowly this time, stretching the moments as it gaped, struggling. Then slowing. Then stopping.

None of them moved, watching her mouth, slack-lipped now.

"Mother of God," Burt Johnson said, and that was all.

16

It was 8:01 a.m. and Sheriff Finnerty rasped a hand across his chin, wishing he'd remembered to buy new razor blades. The blade in his office hadn't been changed since God knew when, and now, if he shaved, he'd have to spend another day with his face scraped raw and pink. The alternative, Finnerty considered, studying his grizzled face in the mirror, was to look like a bum.

He soaped his face, staring into his bloodshot eyes in the mirror. The skin of his eyelids and the bags underneath looked softly collapsed, wrinkles surrendering to gravity. He looked ten years older, Finnerty thought, than he had a week ago. With more nights like last night he'd be an old man—old before his time with hands that trembled and maybe a nervous twitch.

Finnerty looked down at his hands now, one hand holding the razor, the other ready to pull the skin taut. There was maybe the slightest tremor in the razor hand. He stared at it until it steadied. He started to shave with long, sure strokes that left his skin clear and stinging with small, bright beads of blood.

Last night had shaken him, had shaken all of them. It wasn't the first time Finnerty had seen a decapitated body. Just last year a kid on his motorcycle had flipped off a highway overpass. The body and bike had fallen to the highway below. The head, neatly encapsulated in a shiny white helmet, had bounced and rolled for fifty yards down the state road, causing two passing cars to collide in the panic of trying not to hit it.

So Finnerty had seen a head without its body before, but not one whose mouth gaped and snapped at the air—as though it still struggled to speak or breathe or bite.

Finnerty nicked himself and, swearing, plastered a small patch of toilet tissue to the spot. The tremor was back, stronger now, but he stared it down quickly and got back to work scraping the night from his face.

That sudden gut-wrenching violence in the dead muscles had reminded Finnerty of Calvin Russell's body flipped and flailing on his blood-soaked carpet. Connections, again. But like Russell's sudden spasm of movement, Florence Gleason's grotesque convulsion happened only once.

It was enough to leave them all trembling and quiet.

By 8:05 a.m. Finnerty was shaved, face splashed with cold water, hair slicked back with a wet comb, and ready to call Irene Ellicott. The name hadn't rung a bell last night—he was still sleep-heavy with his mind spinning off on the fact of one more suicide—but he had made the connection early this morning. Irene Ellicott—the ghost chaser, medium, psychic or whatever these people called themselves.

Finnerty had first heard of Irene Ellicott at a sheriff's convention in Chicago. One of his tablemates at lunch was Ora Webb, a young sheriff from Chillicothe, Ohio. Ora was a big, good-natured puppy of a man, full of enthusiasm about Miss Irene and the way she'd miraculously led them to find a little girl who had wandered away and disappeared from a family picnic. Teams of deputies and volunteers had searched for the child for two days before Miss Irene was called in. She told them to look for a cave or mine shaft and gave them the general direction and distance. Sure enough, they found the girl, still alive, trapped in a mined-out coal shaft with her leg broken in a fall.

"Geez," Ora Webb had breathed, leaning earnestly across the table towards him, "she's right there in town with you and you don't use her?"

Finnerty had just shaken his head. Privately, he thought all psychics were a bunch of fakers or, at best, nutcases, and if it had been up to him the coal mine would have been one of the first places to be checked. Common sense. Kids were always poking into places where they had no business. But Finnerty didn't want to argue with Webb, and others at their table were listening with interest.

"We tried using some psychics once," one of the other sheriffs said, and Finnerty had settled back in his chair, letting the conversation flow on around him. *He* never would, Finnerty had decided, and that was a fact.

So here he was on the phone with Irene Ellicott— not to use her, mind you, but to find out what the hell her middle of the night phone call had meant.

"I thought I might hear from you, Sheriff." She said it pleasantly enough. Finnerty was listening for any hint of sly satisfaction.

"Oh?" Finnerty thought he had done a good job of keeping any emotion out of his voice, but evidently he didn't. She answered him with a low chuckle.

"I understand. You're probably thinking right now that all you need is a loony old bird calling with psychic predictions."

"I am curious, ma'am, about your call to the station last night."

"Yes, I heard about Mrs. Gleason on the news this morning. Perhaps we should talk."

Finnerty rolled his eyes up to the ceiling, but he spoke mildly. "That, Miss Ellicott, is why I called you. To talk."

"I mean in your office, Sheriff. It would be much easier if I could see you in person. What time shall I come?"

"Miss Ellicott, I'm extremely busy—"

"Of course you are, that's why it's up to you to schedule a good time to meet. When?"

Finnerty sighed. "9:30 this morning."

"Then I shall see you shortly," she said briskly and hung up.

Finnerty was slower to place the receiver back in its cradle. He let his eyes close gently, leaned back in the creaking leather chair, bottom lip stuck thoughtfully out, and rocked a little.

"I had a dream, you see," Irene Ellicott began in explanation.

Finnerty kept his face carefully blank. Too blank, maybe, because she stopped and looked at him.

"Sheriff, let's put all our cards on the table."

She sat in the old brown leather chair across the desk from him looking elegant, comfortable and completely in command of herself. Her graceful good looks had been a surprise to him and he found himself, to his irritation, responding with the rusty manners drilled into him by his Aunt Cissy, old-fashioned manners unused for years.

"I'm listening," he told her. She ought to be wearing a hat, he thought, one of those little things with a feather that women used to wear in Jimmy Stewart or William Powell movies. Like Myrna Loy, Finnerty thought.

She gave him a half-smile. "I believe, Sheriff, that you have the uncomfortable feeling that there's more at work in these deaths than simple coincidence. But I don't think you've been able to put a finger on what it might be and I think that bothers you. I think it bothers you very much indeed.''

Finnerty kept his eyes on hers, his face noncommittal.

She looked almost dreamy, face soft as an Impressionist painting, but her eyes were full of clear and sparkling certainty. ''But you're a man in love with justice and order, aren't you? And now you feel they're letting you down.''

''And where do you come in, Miss Ellicott?'' He had to say it carefully to sound light and mildly curious instead of defensive. She smiled at him again and crossed her legs with a smooth, limber motion.

''I realize,'' she said, ''that I'm an anomaly to you, a factor you'd never normally include in your equations. But doesn't it seem to you lately that two and two insist upon adding up to five? It does to me. Maybe together we can find a pattern in these terrible deaths. Find that misssing element. I think we need each other's help.''

Finnerty let silence settle between them and narrowed his eyes. What the hell was happening to him lately? Getting opinions from a kid hippie doctor and now babbling about dreams with some probably batty old biddy. Because he was going to do it, dammit. And damned if she didn't make him feel as gawky and loose-limbed as a high school kid with his mouth hanging open. She looked that much like Myrna Loy. Hell!

''I can't promise to buy your explanations,'' Finnerty finally told her, ''but I want to hear what you have to say.''

''That's as much as I could expect,'' she said, and her smile was full this time and sunny. And then she told him about her dream. She told it crisply, concisely, with just enough detail to let Finnerty picture it with her, and she told it without dramatics.

It was a clairvoyant dream, she said. She could tell

by the vividness and intensity, and Finnerty quickly
decided to let her explain and not to ask questions. It
happened on a train. Irene Ellicott was riding in a
private car with one other passenger, a woman in her
late forties to mid-fifites. "A little on the frumpy
side," Irene Ellicott said, "but quite pleasant." It was
night and the woman became distraught and grew
more upset by the second. She pulled a slip of paper
from her handbag—a light colored purse, mushroom,
perhaps, Irene said—and pressed it into Irene's
hands.

"She kept looking around the compartment in a sort
of panic, as though she was afraid someone else had
snuck in to spy on us."

The train entered a tunnel and the interior lights
went out. It was completely dark and the woman
began to scream. She was still holding Irene's hands
and she pulled them now towards her face until,
somehow, Irene seemed to be holding her hair
clenched in one fist.

"Her head, then simply . . . came away." And Irene
was clutching it in the dark while the woman's
scream and the roaring of the train clattering through
the tunnel filled the dark, enclosed car. She touched
the woman's face with her free hand, her fingertips
brushing the screaming woman's lips.

"And her teeth closed on my fingers," Irene said.
She shuddered here. "Twice." She looked steadily at
Finnerty. "Her touch jolted me and I woke up. It was
extremely unpleasant. So . . ." She tilted her head just
a fraction of an inch. "I poured myself a stiff brandy
and called here to see if anything of the sort had actually happened. Yet."

Finnerty regarded her, poker-faced. "Deputy
Snider recorded the call from the Chessie station less
than three minutes after yours."

"Allow a few minutes for shock and the relaying of
the call," Irene said, nodding thoughtfully, "and the

woman's death probably happened while I dreamed it."

Privately, Finnerty would have come up with the same time frame, if he were dealing with something reasonable. This was not reasonable. Was it? It had woken him this morning with an ugly start—that image of Florence Gleason's dead mouth snapping on empty air. *Snap.* The head alone, silly and useless. But enough to scare the bejesus out of him and haunt his sleep.

Finnerty thought of May Kwan with a sudden, almost painful longing. He wanted to bury his face in her soft, damp flesh. He wanted to rest his head on her belly and suck the smooth skin where her neck flowed into her shoulder—warm, alive, and a little salty.

His eyes were closed and Finnerty passed a hand across them, rubbing at the tightness in his forehead between his eyes.

Irene Ellicott broke her silence quietly.

"You must be missing quite a lot of sleep lately, Sheriff."

Finnerty, eyes still closed, grunted a kind of agreement.

"Perhaps you should take a nap now," Irene Ellicott said thoughtfully, "while you still have time."

Finnerty opened bloodshot eyes. She was studying him, one finger lightly tapping her lower lip, scanning his face as though cryptic messages flashed and scampered across it. He scowled. He didn't like the feeling.

"Yes," she said, deciding. "They're all linked, I think—Florence Gleason, the little boy, Calvin Russell, Charlie Luther. And Ted Kellogg. And, unfortunately, I'm quite sure we haven't seen the end of it."

"The evidence seems to point to suicide, not murder, in every case but Ted Kellogg's."

"Ah, but there's murder and there's murder."

Finnerty's scowl got deeper. "You mean they may have been driven to suicide? All of them?"

"Something of the sort." She smiled at him again, uncrossed her legs and stood up, preparing to leave. Finnerty found himself automatically, politely, on his feet, too. "I'll be in touch, Sheriff Finnerty."

She started for the door and Finnerty took a few steps around his desk, intending to walk her out and she poised, waiting for him to catch up. At the door, while he held it open for her, she turned, serious, looking up at him with sharp blue eyes.

"And, Sheriff, please keep an eye on the girl."

She walked away before he could ask what girl she meant. But then, he didn't really have to ask.

Nora awakened late with an unremembered dream clinging to her like a dull gray hangover. 10:00 and the sheriff still hadn't returned her call. She was inclinced, almost, to forget about it now. Almost, but not quite. Instead, she started thinking again, as she had last night about calling Irene Ellicott.

Simon wants to talk to you.

Some sick prank by God knows who? Truth? They didn't have the body yet, Townsend had said. Could Simon be alive? Or was it some cross-world operator trying to connect her with her ex-husband in the beyond?

"Shit," she said out loud. It was time to get up and stop thinking for a while.

Just before climbing into the shower she called Irene Ellicott, but though the phone rang a half dozen times, there was no answer.

By the time she got out of the shower her own phone was ringing.

She started to reach for it and snatched her hand back with just that brief jolt of fear that it might be him. *It*. That smooth melodic voice. But the moment of fear made her angry and she grabbed it off the hook to snap "Yes?"

"Hello? Is Nora Durant there?" It was a man's voice sounding a little taken aback, but still full of oily self-possession.

"Speaking."

It was Hal Townsend, Simon's associate in the law office. The reason he'd called, he said, was simply to keep her informed. They hadn't found the body yet and, in fact, there was beginning to be some question now of whether Simon had indeed been killed in the crash.

"Then where could he be?" And Nora thought of the call last night. Simon alive and really wanting to talk to her? "Kidnapped? You think he could have been kidnapped? Or lost somewhere? Injured?"

Townsend cleared his throat. "Possible," he conceded. "And it may have been a . . . voluntary disappearance."

"What, like running away from home? That's ridiculous. Why would Simon do that?"

"Ah." She imagined him running a manicured finger around the inside of his starched, expensive collar. "We have no apparent explanation for your . . . for Simon's disappearance. We simply must realize that in cases like this with, you understand, a substantial life insurance policy in question and no body in evidence we must keep our minds open to all possibilities."

"Collusion. Intent to defraud. Is that it?" She hadn't been married to a lawyer for nothing.

"Oh, no, no," he said, slick and conciliatory, "I simply want you to be aware of some of the delays that may occur in processing your claim."

"*My* claim?"

"Yes, as Simon's sole beneficiary. You were aware of that, of course."

"No . . ."

"Now I'm afraid you can't inherit until a legal death certificate has been filed. And if the body isn't found . . ."

"Stop." *The body.* Like Simon was a thing, a piece of meat.

". . . then there may be a waiting period of . . ."

"Shut. Up." Her stomach knotted like a fist, and she was blind with rage.

"Look. I don't give a damn about the money. And I don't give a damn about your opinions. Or your insinuations. I don't give a damn about you, but I did give a damn about Simon and I don't want to hear you talk about him. In fact, Hal, I don't want to talk to you at all, so good-bye. I'm hanging up now . . . and please, don't call me unless you absolutely have to."

And she slammed the phone down, damn satisfied with herself.

On the top step of her front porch with a glass of orange juice, Nora decided there was a distinct similarity between her front lawn and the weather.

Both were dismal, bedraggled and forlorn. And making her feel the same way.

The thick low cloud cover of the day before had dissipated, but not cleared. Instead, the sky was a dingy white like a soiled sheet hung up over the town. The sun made a brighter smear behind the shreds of leftover cloud, and it all made a backdrop for the barely visible downtown and campus in the distance like a child's discarded play set. Stretched at her feet, the unkempt lawn had the same dull look as the derelict sky.

It was hard not to feel that apathy dragging at her, making her just want to climb back into bed and forget about the effort of trying to make a life for herself.

Nora's exhilaration at telling Hal Townsend to go stuff himself was short-lived. Now she was fighting just to keep herself moving.

There wasn't anything she could do about the dull, sultry heat or the dusty look of the town, but she could, Nora decided, do something about the ragged, wretched lawn. She could volunteer to mow it instead of helplessly waiting for the unreliable nephew to appear.

Nora was fairly certain Mrs. Roberts was home again. She'd heard her landlady moving around in the night—footsteps that creaked down the long upstairs hall, something that bumped gently around the bedroom on the other side of the thin wall from her own, something that made the bed pressed against the dividing wall creak in protest.

It had to be Mrs. Roberts, home from her mysterious disappearance.

Nora plunked her glass of juice down on the porch step and marched around to Mrs. Roberts' front door. She knocked and waited, but no one answered. Windows overlooking the front porch were closed. Pale parchment shades with a scalloped and fringed border were carefully aligned with the bottom of the windows to make a pattern of small fringed triangles.

Nora opened the screen door and knocked harder on the inner door. More silence.

She squatted down then, eye to a dark triangle at the bottom of the window, trying to peer in through the fringe and the sheer ivory curtain behind it. She could barely make out the room inside, all neat and tidy with heavy furniture outlined in shadow. It seemed to be dozing, undisturbed as Sleeping Beauty in her spell.

But if Mrs. Roberts weren't back, what made those soft sounds in the night?

Across the street, a woman thin and gray as a stick was giving Nora a squinty-eyed stare when she stepped off the porch. Nora glanced at her, absent-minded, then looked again and headed in the old woman's direction, putting on her best neighborly smile.

"Hi," Nora said, still only halfway across the street.

Her neighbor watched her come without changing expression. She was still and stiff as the broom she'd been using to flick at the sidewalk. It looked like a prop, clutched in her bony hands. It was an excuse to be outside, watching the rest of the world go by. The woman's short, barrel-chested, bowlegged dog sat panting double time behind her, saliva spindling down from his long pink tongue. He watched Nora come with only a hint of interest in his arrogant pop-eyes.

Had the lady noticed anything suspicious the night before? Nora wanted to know. Cars, lights, people walking around the house, anything odd?

Nothing, the woman said in a high voice that cracked and quavered with suspicion and bad temper. And she should know, because she never got to sleep before 2:00 a.m. Trouble sleeping. Besides, Mary Roberts had already asked her to keep an eye on the place while she was gone, although she had plenty of other things to do besides sit around watching Mary Roberts' house day and night.

Nora thanked her and retreated quickly, back to her own side of the street. The old lady could have missed something like the nephew or a burglar casing the place. Because if it wasn't Mrs. Roberts moving around in the night, then who was it?

When she got back to her place, Nora called the sheriff's office. And this time she got Finnerty.

She told him about the noises in the night from the empty apartment next door and he promised to have it checked out. She told him about the phone calls she'd been getting that seemed to threaten her and Sample. She told him about Simon. She did it all succintly and calmly, and the sheriff wasn't as skeptical or ready to dismiss her as Nora had thought he would be. In fact, he seemed interested and told her he'd be in touch with the state police in Harrisburg.

"Sheriff . . ." Nora began and stopped. She was about to start asking questions about how safe it was for her to stay there. What she was looking for, Nora realized, was permission to run away. But she wouldn't allow it, wouldn't let herself surrender any of the independence she worked so hard to build.

"Never mind."

When she hung up the phone rang before she even had her hand off the receiver. She picked it up, said hello, and listened to that dark, breathless silence that was beginning to seem so familiar.

This time she'd play the game and stand listening quietly to the nothingness on the other end of the line. Around her the kitchen seemed to become a world of its own—small, isolated, silent, suspended in time, as though the room held its breath.

A heavy crash sounded from upstairs, then a second crash, and Nora craned towards the ceiling, listening. The sounds came from Mrs. Roberts' half. She was almost positive.

Crash, again. And Nora disconnected the silent phone, got a dial tone and punched up Mrs. Roberts' number.

One more thudding crash shook the walls and made the ceiling shudder. Then Nora heard the first peal of the telephone ringing through the thin wall. And nothing else.

She listened to the phone ringing through the walls. Once, twice.

It rang five times before she hung up. No answer and no more sounds vibrating through the walls.

And then her own phone rang.

She gasped, jumped, snatched it off the hook and shouted, holding it out like a microphone where she could glare at it.

"What do you want?"

Silence. Then Kate's voice came on, puzzled and wary. "Nora?"

Nora let her breath out, closed her eyes and pressed the phone to her chest.

"Kate."

"What is it? What's going on?"

"Oh, hell, I don't know. Crank phone calls. Weird noises."

"Did you call the police?"

"Mmm. About five minutes ago." And that, of course, was all she could do. No use worrying Kate about it. "They'll be around. Nothing to worry about. So, what's up?"

Kate was calling to see if Nora would have lunch with her at the hospital where she worked.

"It sounds gruesome, I know—hospital cafeteria food—but actually they've got a great deli staffed with enlightened dietitians. Chicken Kiev. Sweet and sour shrimp. Marinated artichokes. Spinach salad. And a pecan pie you could die for."

"I'm convinced, I'm convinced."

They set a time and Kate gave her elaborate directions for twisted shortcuts to the radiology office. After a while, Nora stopped trying to take them down. She'd just ask when she got there.

"I'll find it," she assured Kate. How hard could it be?

After talking to Kate, Nora tried calling both Michael and Irene Ellicott. She couldn't reach either of them.

She stood in the kitchen a long time, then. Listening to the quiet.

17

Things are not always what they seem.

The golden coach is a pumpkin. The frog is a prince. The gingerbread house holds a witch and an oven just the right size to roast a child.

Spend a night in the faerie hill making merry and you'll find a hundred years have passed in the world of men and everyone you loved is long dead.

The beautiful Snow Queen with her luminous eyes and sweet lips has a heart of ice. But the Fool is the wisest and bravest knight of all and helping an ant with his burden may help you win a kingdom.

Everything is light and dark. The reddest apple is poison. Yet what looks like death is only sleep. Even in fairy tales we recognize that things are never simple and it's dangerous to trust our own perceptions.

Always look twice to make sure it's really Granny and not the wolf in that nightdress and bonnet, Nora thought. On the other hand, a handful of beans is not necessarily a bad trade for a cow, not when it gets you to a giant's castle to steal a treasure.

"Did you know," Nora asked Kate over lunch, "that Bruno Bettelheim—*the* Bruno Bettelheim—says that Jack and the Beanstalk is really about penis

225

envy?''

Kate gulped pecan pie. ''Mmmph?''

''Penis envy,'' Nora repeated, disgusted. ''Geez, I can't say that with a straight face to a room full of people. Anyway, it sounds pretty far-fetched to me.'' She bent over her pie, frowning, and gave it two or three testy jabs with her fork.

''*Penis* envy,'' she whined through her nose.

Kate got a wildly gleeful look in her eyes. One cheek was pooched out with pecan pie hurriedly stuffed to the side. ''Oh,'' she said, wide-eyed and earnestly which Nora didn't buy for a second, ''it makes perfect sense. The guy with the best beans gets the biggest stalk . . .'' snicker ''. . . and wins the hen who lays . . .'' Kate started to choke ''. . . golden eggs!''

Nora groaned and shook her head.

But Kate was tickled as hell with the vision, hooting and gargling pecans until her face went beet red and she had to gasp for breath.

Nora made faces at her. Swell, this is what I'm supposed to say to a class of horny college kids. ''Geez.''

Kate slowed down and stopped. ''I'm sorry,'' she said soberly. ''I guess I needed that.''

But that struck her funny, too, and she was off again, bleating and rocking with glee.

Nora watched her, afraid the laughter would turn into tears and pleased to see that it didn't.

''So,'' she finally said when Kate had stopped for good this time, ''how are things?''

Kate shrugged and half-smiled. ''Okay. You?''

''Okay.''

They smiled at each other—fond, shy and grown-up. They were going to be all right. So far, they'd both managed to survive life.

After lunch, Nora shook off Kate's attempts to pass along complicated directions out of the hospital.

''I'll make it fine,'' she said airily. ''I got in all

right." Though she had been late, getting lost and asking directions at every turn.

Kate was doubtful. "The hall connections are weird on this floor because of the courtyards."

"Don't worry, don't worry." Nora waved a hand. "What can happen to me?"

He crouched between the cars, staying in a pool of shadow protected from the dull white glare of sun through high clouds. Heat shimmered off the red and blue and silver metal of the car bodies that hulked over him. A trickle of oily sweat wore a path down from temple to jaw through the soft stubble on his face.

He leaned forward to blink at the building, blinded by light, hiding behind a wine-red fender that burned his hand when he touched it. When he flinched from the hot metal he lost his balance, dropped one knee and the flat of his hand onto an oil slick to catch himself, only barely aware that he'd moved at all. He was concentrating so hard on the building, watching a door and waiting for something. Someone.

Eyes fixed on the door he rubbed gritty oil from his palm across his thigh, scrubbing the sticky slickness into his Calvin Klein slacks.

"Hecate," he murmured like a man in his sleep. The word stumbled out through lips that clung like dying lovers.

She had been sure it was the most direct route. It certainly seemed logical. But there were twists and turns where no one in his right mind would put them or expect them. Dead ends and doors that didn't open. And the place was remarkably empty for a bustling little hospital. There was no one in the corridors Nora could ask for directions. She finally gave up and decided to go out any door she could find and spend her time being lost outdoors in the parking area. At least she'd know which side of the hospital she was on if she could see it and she could find her car.

A heavy metal door at the end of the corridor sported a modest Exit sign and Nora headed for it, relieved and determined to leave the limbo of quiet, pale blue corridors with their splashes of orange doors and bright green signs. It was like a deserted kindergarten, too contemporary for Nora's taste with scant comfort and no cosiness. There were no windows to the outside and only an occasional glimpse of the hospital courtyard. Heading for the door to freedom, the corridor seemed to stretch and grow in front of her. She shoved her weight against the metal door with just a trace of panic and stopped there, eyes closed, drinking in the outdoors like a man coming out of a cave.

"Nora."

She squinted against the glare of light. The voice came from below her, from a man at the bottom of a short flight of cement steps to the parking lot. Unable to see him well, she shaded her eyes.

"Yes?"

He moved up two steps, hovering nervous as a blackbird.

"Alex Thomas," he said and the sound of his own name seemed to calm him. He stood straight suddenly and moved more confidently up the last three steps to join her at the top of the landing.

She could see him now, lit from every angle by daylight bouncing off the white concrete of the hospital and the stairs. She could smell him, too—the odor of flesh in the sun like an animal's body smell, the smell of sweat from heat and exertion, the sharp stink of fear.

"Oh, hello." She was careful, reserved. She didn't know Alex Thomas well, but she knew this was wrong. It was so far out of character that it jarred her. The tracks of his fingers were marked in oily tunnels through his hair.

"Alex?"

He stood in front of her, looking over her shoulder like a starving man staring into a restaurant. His eyes glittered. He looked into hers, blocking her path.

"Yes. I'm here to visit a friend, but this door doesn't open from the outside." He looked lost, Nora thought, like a disappointed child. "I didn't want to walk around to the front."

"Well," Nora said brightly, opening the door further and trying to sidestep around him, "here you are then. I was just leaving."

"You mustn't." He blocked her again, a shadow covering his face as he stepped to one side. He reached for the door she held, his arm adding a wall to the cage that held her trapped at the stairs.

"You must come with me. He wants that."

"Who?" She retreated a step. "Who wants it?"

Light shifted in his face. He smiled, a slow smile with a shadow of his usual urbanity.

"Carole. Carole Salant." He pressed another half-step forward.

Nora retreated a step, back pressed now against the metal bar of the door.

"You said 'he.' "

"Did I? Slip of the tongue. Carole. She's been here for some days now and I know she'd like to see you. She admires you, you know."

"I barely know her." Nora was backing again, sliding against the bar of the door and trying to keep a distance between Alex and herself.

He reached a hand out to her and she pulled back to avoid it, stepping back over the threshold, back into the dimness of the hospital corridor. Alex stepped in beside her, pulling the door shut on the light outside.

"This way," he said, and he took her elbow.

Carole Salant admiring her? That was more than far-fetched. But she hadn't thought fast enough, Nora told herself. She should have made up some quick excuse. Now she was trapped. She felt like she was moving in slow motion through some vague threatening dream.

"I can only stay a few minutes," she told him as they floated down the corridor together. He nodded, as though he understood.

She felt high, Nora realized, gliding along with this soiled parody of the always immaculate Alex Thomas. It was as though he walked in a cloud of unreality that captured and slowed and distorted everything around him.

She made one effort to make normal conversation. "Why," she said through lips that felt oddly thick, "is Carole still here?" Kate had told her about Carole's convulsions, but the way she'd talked, Nora thought they were mostly for the sake of drama. "What do the doctors think?"

"The doctors are fools."

They went the rest of the way in silence.

The bed nearest the door in Carole Salant's room was occupied by a girl with her face swathed heavily in bandages. She wore a blue football jersey for a nightshirt and a striped blue and white cotton robe. She was laying on top of her covers, the bed cranked up to a sitting position, leafing through the latest issue of *Glamour* magazine. When Nora and Alex came into the room she glanced with mild curiosity at Nora and let her eyes linger, then shy away from, Alex.

Carole Salant lay in the bed next to the window, lush body outlined by the wrinkled white sheet that covered her. Even lying still, Nora thought, she had the lazy sensuality of a cat. She filled the room with heat.

As they got close to the bed, Carole turned her blank, china doll face towards them, her dark stare fixing Alex like a stone spear. Their eyes met and locked and nothing else in the room lived. God help whatever came between them, then, Nora thought.

The girl in the next bed shifted restlessly. Nora

stopped moving forward and took a tentative step back, irrationally deciding with a wave of relief that she could just duck out now. They'd never notice.

But she was caught by convention and what one simply can't do—the necessity of being polite. And, besides, she wanted to know what it was all about. In the other bed, the girl slapped her magazine shut and slid her legs over the side of the bed. In the room's silence Nora could hear her feet scrabble into flip-flop slippers. The silence lasted until the girl's footsteps echoed away down the hall.

And then Alex breathed into the silence, a hoarse voice from the moist bottom of his lungs, full of awe.

"He came."

And there was just the hint of smugness about it like an achievement.

Nora shivered when he said it, a finger of cold tracing its way down her spine in the echo of his voice *He came*. Who?

Silence. But Nora determined to break the spell. She took a deep breath, shook herself, stepped forward and broke the silence with a bright, inane voice. Too loud, but she didn't care.

"Hi! Well, how are you?"

Salant's shiny brown eyes broke from Alex's with an almost audible snap. They traveled to Nora's face and she caught their impact with a dull shock that seemed to thud down her spine and fix her feet to the floor. Madness, Nora thought. Mad eyes.

And the curving lips parted. "I am the Angel of Death," she said. "The girl belongs to me."

"What?"

Nora searched the mad eyes in the sweetly innocent face, not able to believe she could have heard right. She looked quickly at Alex.

His face glowed, a soft smile twitching at the corner of his dry lips. He turned to look at her, blindly.

"Yes."

"He will have her." Carole's lips curled around the
words. "He will take her."

"Yes." Desire hissed in the word when Alex
breathed it. He said it to Carole, like a litany. To Nora,
like a judgment.

"No!" Nora denied it and denied them.

"Kellogg failed. I won't," Alex told her.

Nora stepped back, watching him. "Failed at
what?"

Alex grinned nastily at her. "You'll find out."

"Blessed be," Carole said.

"Blessed be," Alex echoed.

"What do you want?" She almost shouted it, voice
too ragged. They both watched her, Carole china doll
blank and Alex wolfish.

"No."

And Nora backed away from them, out of the room,
looking back over her shoulder as she walked faster
and faster down the corridor, wanting only to get
away from them.

"Blessed be."   ·

The words followed her down the hall.

"Daddy, she's doing it again." Four year-old
Cybele's voice wavered and whined and sent a shiver
down his spine like a fingernail screeching down a
blackboard.

The shiver traveled down to the tips of Paul
Vronski's fingertips where his hands rested palm up
on his folded knees. His long legs were loosely twined
in a full lotus. His eyes were closed. He was repeating
his mantra over and over to himself, trying to block
out the sound of Cybele's whining. She knew better
than to interrupt him while he meditated.

"Daddy!"

Cybele was standing arm's distance from her father
who was immobile in the center of the living room.
Her hands were on her hips, her face bright pink

starting to shade to deep red. She stamped one small foot.

"DADDY!"

Cybele stepped back, picked up her teddy bear by one plump arm and swung it full out, smacking her father on the side of the head.

"YOU STUPID!" she yelled as it connected.

Paul's eyes flew open and he snatched the teddy bear out of her hand, throwing it violently from him and lurching forward onto his knees to grab her by the shoulders. She went limp in his grasp, suspended a few inches above the ground, eyes and mouth open wide while the angry red drained from her face.

He could feel his face burning and was aware of his fingers sinking into her soft skin, the light bones so fragile in his tight grip. But for seconds there was nothing else, only fury and the impulse to crumple her and throw her, like the teddy bear, across the room.

But he set her down slowly and let her go.

She stepped back one quick step and stared at him.

"Mommy's doing it again," she finally said.

"Doing what?" He slowly straightened his clawed fingers, flexed and straightened them again. Cybele watched his hands with wide-eyed interest. It was the first time he'd ever touched her in anger, Paul realized.

"You know." Cybele squirmed and looked at her feet. "She's in my room."

Paul sighed and massaged his temples with the palms of his hands in slow circles. "I'm coming," he said. "Go play outside."

"I don't want to." She started to whine again.

"Just do it," Paul snapped, and for the first time in her life Cybele hurried to do what her father told her.

Standing in the bedroom doorway, Paul surveyed the cluttered room. It was crowded with toys, books and games. Dolls and stuffed animals made a wild

scrimmage pile, a tumble of arms, legs and faces.
Posters and drawings covered the walls with images
of Strawberry Shortcake and her friends, unicorns,
rainbows and fat pink bears. A pink T-shirt and the
top of a magenta bathing suit trailed out of the top
drawer in a child-sized white wooden dresser. The
top of the dresser was covered with Tinker Bell cos-
metics, crayons, pages torn from coloring books,
jewelry and miscellaneous treasures.

Cybele's bed was a single mattress on the floor with
a fluffy white cover strewn with the remains of a
doll's tea party. Franny Vronski was wedged between
the dresser and the bed, pressed against the wall and
wrapped around Cybele's giant blue elephant, Fred.
She was humming, very quietly, a tuneless crooning.

Paul stepped carefully into the room, placing his
long bare feet delicately between toys and books,
piles of clothing and dolls. He stepped in front of
Franny and squatted. She didn't look up.

"Franny?"

Nothing.

He frowned at the pale strands of her hair spreading
across Fred's blue plush back. He tried concentrating
on the white skin at the part of her hair, willing her to
look at him. Nothing.

He touched one white forearm lightly with the tips
of his fingers and she twitched away from him.

She broke off humming. "Stop it!" she snapped and
her voice was muffled by the stuffed animal.

"Franny, you have to talk to me." No response.
"You're scaring me. You're scaring Cybele. She
doesn't understand what's going on and neither do I."

She raised her head and glared at him, looking
young and lost.

"It's your fault," she said. "Your fault."

"What is, Franny? What did I do?"

"This!" She swept an arm around the room. "This!
All of it. Why couldn't you just get a normal job and

watch TV and be like other people? Why not?''

He locked his fingers together and bent his head, eyes avoiding hers, studying the square knuckles of his long fingers. "I can't. I'm just not . . . It would destroy me.''

"And what's this? What are we doing here?'' She was breathing hard, hands clutching Fred like a life preserver.

Paul still couldn't look at her. He crossed his arms protectively against his chest, holding himself together.

Franny leaned towards him, confiding to him in a soft undertone. "I think I'm going crazy.''

He looked up into her eyes, searching for the truth behind it.

"I am,'' she said, slowly, nodding into his face.

"Baby.'' He took her forearms and this time she didn't pull away. "I just wanted peace, some peace in my life after all the hassle from parents and teachers. Always somebody wanting something. Always expecting you to push and push and play the game like it's life or death and if you fail you might as well just curl up and die because you're useless. And I just couldn't do it, Franny. I thought you knew that. I thought you could see how destructive their games are. So I thought if only I could find some peace, everything would be all right.'' He was looking over her head now, blind and unfocused, still holding her forearms and remembering. "I tried so many things. And some of them really did help . . . but it was never quite enough. There was always something missing and I thought the group had the answer. You know that. You know all I wanted was to find the star within, the true self. Peace.''

Franny's eyes closed slowly and he could see the blue of her eyes like a bruise behind the fine, nearly translucent skin of her eyelids. The soft curve of her eyeball shifted dreamily from side to side.

"Franny," he said in a wandering boy's voice, "what did you want?" It was, he realized, the first time he'd ever asked her, and he was filled with genuine curiosity and had no idea of what she'd answer.

"You," she said, simply enough. Her head dropped to the elephant's back like a tired child's. "I wanted you to be happy. I wanted a home. I wanted us to be a family."

"Baby." He reached out for her, folded his long arms around her, held her gently and rocked her for a long time.

"The dreams," she said, muffled, into his shoulder. "The dreams."

"I know."

And later she said, "People are dying."

"Yes," he said, holding her tighter. "Yes."

Irene Ellicott met Nora at her front door with a small frown rippling across the fine skin of her forehead.

"You look like you could use a drink," Irene said, stepping back into the foyer. "This way," she said over her shoulder, indicating briskly a new section of the house for Nora.

"I had just left the hospital when I called you," Nora told Irene's back.

Irene looked over her shoulder, looking Nora up and down, but kept walking. "You're not ill, are you? Hurt? Nothing's happened to Sample?"

"No. Kate, Sam's mother, works there. We were just having lunch."

They were passing through the dining room, high-ceilinged and with room to spare even though a massive rosewood table, chairs and sideboard helped to fill the room. Wide French doors stood open to a screened side porch and while Nora's glance drifted wistfully out to the white wicker furniture and lush plants, Irene called over her shoulder, "There's a lovely breeze on the porch. We may as well have our drinks there."

"Fine!" Nora scurried to catch up with Irene, staring around her at the enormous kitchen styled after an English country kitchen with the space of a manor house and all the conveniences of contemporary America.

"Anyway, I ran into Alex Thomas," Nora told Irene.

"Ah, the Beau Brummel of Stony Cliffs. Such a sly, slippery young man. And so disdainful of everything . . . disdainful of life, the poor fool. If I didn't dislike him so much, I'd feel sorry for him. Alex wants SCC to be his empire, and at the moment, Peter is in his way. He treats both of us as though we were tottering on the brink of senility while of course being profusely complimentary. Silly prig."

"Mmm." Irene's description certainly fit the Alex Nora had seen before today. But today was different. "Something's happened to him, I think. He looked . . . crazy."

Irene was getting glasses down from a built-in china cabinet. She stopped and turned to Nora. "In what way?"

Nora shook her head, searching for some way to communicate that sense of sick madness that shimmered from Alex, the way his eyes glittered and the way he seemed to hunger.

"He hadn't shaved in a while or washed or combed his hair. It looked like he'd just stopped . . . stopped taking care of himself, I mean. His clothes looked like he'd been wearing them for days. Grass stains, dirt, grease. He looked grimy and sweaty, obsessed and feverish."

"And how did he act?" Irene was loading glasses and a carafe of chilled white wine onto a wooden tray.

"Odd. And Carole Salant was just as bad. Worse."

Irene handed Nora the loaded tray. "One of the benefits of age," she told Nora. "I can be lazy. Let's get settled on the porch, then I want you to start from the beginning and tell me everything that happened."

They moved out to the porch. Gracious and cool in the sun-dappled shade, it had the lush, self-contained feel of an oasis or a Victorian retreat. Nora took a long sip of wine. Already the episode at the hospital was beginning to seem unreal. Impossible.

"I was coming out a side door," she began. She told Irene about Alex intercepting her, inviting her to visit Carole Salant—because "he" would like it—then bullying her along.

Irene Ellicott has probably never been bullied into doing anything, Nora decided wistfully.

And she told Irene about the terrible energy that flowed back and forth between Carole and Alex.

"I am the Angel of Death," she said. *"The girl is mine."* And Carole's face as she said it came back to Nora with a shiver. She shook herself. "Alex said that Kellogg had failed," Nora told Irene, "but that he would succeed."

"At what?"

Nora shook her head and shrugged. *"Blessed be,* they said."

"Oh." Irene screwed up her face for an instant looking like she'd smelled something rotten. "Hecate." As though that explained it.

"Hecate?"

"Goddess of witches and sorcerers. And suicides."

"Oh."

"Indeed. Peter may be able to make something out of it. All I remember about her is that she's supposed to wander among the tombs and drink the blood of corpses. It's a grisly picture. I always imagined her with legions of the ghosts of suicides tramping along behind her. And dogs. She's also the goddess of dogs."

18

Driving the streets of Stony Cliffs you might notice, if you were apt to notice that kind of thing, that the town had an unusually large number of funeral homes. They existed to fill a full range of expectations from an oddly mixed community. There were the college people, the town people and the rural people.

There was Hoffman's Funeral Parlor in a big frame house on College Avenue. It had stood there since 1847 and the only change in the outside of the building, aside from occasional new paint or aluminum gutters, were the tasteful neon sign and clock added in 1959. The sign spelled out Hoffman's Funeral Parlor in curving blue script and under it hung the big round face of the clock outlined in neon pink. Hoffman's was the funeral parlor of choice for all the German families in Stony Cliffs.

Catholics patronied Nolan & Flannerty's. It was a stately old home from the turn of the century with neoclassical white pillars and a curving driveway off north Wabash Avenue. Inside, the home was filled with furniture upholstered in maroon velvet and trimmed with gilt or heavy wooden pieces carved and dark. Crystal chandeliers, flowers and flocked wallpaper, and fireplaces with marble mantels and electric logs completed the ambiance.

For the "new" people, the college families who sometimes settled for good in Stony Cliffs and the town people who were moving into a newly self-conscious, status-jealous middle class, there were places like Wilson's Sanctuary. It was functional, contemporary and non-denominational—a square and barren concrete building with no windows, landscaped with stately evergreens and dark green ground cover.

Other funeral parlors dotted the town. They were older homes, Victorian style like most of Stony Cliffs, with front parlors converted into viewing rooms and basements acting as embalming rooms. Each tiny place was a family business, supported by loyal groups of families who came back, year after year. The little parlors on the outskirts of town took the farm families through all their generations since the early 1830s. In town, for the businessmen and merchants who weren't moving "up" to Wilson's—and who weren't German or Catholic—there was crisp, tidy Anderson's, fussy Merriman & Fletcher's Mortuary, the Hough Family Funeral Home, Albert E. Conkle Funeral and Memorial Home, St. Pierre Funeral Services or, even, the House of Usher.

The Rhine family were "new" people, outsiders, even though they had lived in Stony Cliffs for 10 years. They had the rootlessness of a small, fairly well-to-do family. His parents lived in Miami. Hers in Arizona. Their few other relatives were scattered. So Stony Cliffs was as close to being home as anything ever would be and they worked hard at settling in. Ken Rhine had earned his tenure teaching math and he'd stay with the school indefinitely, while his wife Cheryl had been elected president of the Art League. Both boys had been born in SC.

Now Jerry Rhine's small, broken body would be buried there.

Norm Treller from the Turners Club had dropped by the Rhine house with a noodle casserole his wife had fixed. He took Ken Rhine aside in the kitchen and muttered to him confidentially that Hoffman's Funeral Parlor would do the best job for him. Even though they were talking about his boy's body, Ken Rhine felt the pleasure of knowing they were really part of the town. He's gotten their sanction. Hoffman's Funeral Parlor.

Cool blue light diffused throughout the sterile room in the basement where Jim Hoffman stood looking down and frowning at Jerry Rhine's body. The parents wanted an open casket service, Jim's dad had said, and Jim, as the only family member in a long line of morticians to have gone all the way to St. Louis for school, would have the responsibility of making the boy look as good as possible.

Fresh from St. Louis, Jim was full of new ideas. He wanted to get rid of the neon sign and the clock that was always seven minutes slow. But his dad and older brother vetoed him. He wanted to do some discreet advertising on television. Vetoed. He wanted to modernize the furnishings in the place and expand the casket line. Vetoed again.

But they'd given him Jerry Rhine to deal with. It might have been a consolation prize or maybe a test. Whatever it was, Jim Hoffman was determined to do an outstanding job.

He'd been studying Jerry Rhine's small face for nearly half an hour, closeted in the embalming room with the smell that clung to him no matter how often or how diligently he showered. He always associated the smell with his father. It had comforted him as a child, but his girlfriend Sara hated it. Half the time, Jim couldn't smell it, anyway. She said she could, but maybe it was her imagination.

He held Jerry's face by the chin, turning his head to one side. His head moved just a bit too loosely, the neck broken in the fall. In the autopsy, Dr. Paulson had neatly carved through the back of the skull but hair, scalp and bone were back in place and he could make sure they stayed that way. Luckily, the boy's hair was thick and a little long. He probably had been due for a haircut and that helped.

There was a broad, bloodless scrape on one high cheekbone, the pale flesh translucent and uneven. But Eunice could fix that. Fat Eunice McEveety had looked the same for as long as Jim could remember, he thought, studying another scrape on the fine line of Jerry's jaw. Eunice could be anywhere from 40 to 65. She was grossly obese and had taken lately to walking with a strong wooden cane. She always wore dresses with an intricate print of tiny flowers and a low cut cleavage that bared a deep crease where the flesh pressed tight together. Jim used to fantasize about grabbing handfuls of her abundant flesh when he was a kid. Even now a kind of fascination with the idea made his prick stir in his pants.

Eunice wore make-up like a whore, but all her clients always looked more wholesome and fresh than they had in life.

Eunice could take care of it, Jim thought, studying Jerry's face, with a little help from some subtle injections here and. . . .

And a small white spider scuttled out from the boy's thick hair, running across the pale forehead to crouch on the boy's eyelid.

''Shit!''

Startled, Jim Hoffman yanked his hand away from the dead boy's face and felt his stomach lurch up in shock.

He felt his face grow warm, embarrassed by his jumpiness. A light sweat dampened, then cooled Jim's face, and he stepped back to the table, closer to the boy, leaning over him to try flicking the spider off his face.

But he couldn't find the spider and the boy's eyelids flared open.

"Damn!"

He leapt back, spooked, then angry at himself for acting like an amateur. The boy's eyeballs were slightly sunken and dull. His head lolled on the broken neck, the torn cheek resting on the cool metal of the tabletop.

Jim took deep breaths to calm himself and regain some of his professional poise.

Jerry's right hand, the hand nearest Jim, twitched.

Jim stared down at it, forgetting to breathe. And the hand jerked like a plastic bobber when a fish is biting.

"It shouldn't be doing that," Jim said aloud. "Not this far along."

The hand jerked again, so hard that the forearm shifted on the smooth stainless steel table.

"That's not right." Jim said it in a mild, wondering protest.

The hand leapt on the table, flopping as ungainly as a fish on the shore. The forearm followed with the mild squeak of flesh against the polished metal.

"No," Jim said calmly, pondering it, taking a single step back. "No, that's wrong. That's definitely wrong."

And then Jerry Rhine's broken back heaved and arched against the cold table and the sheet that covered him slithered to the floor.

"Michael and Kate are the only people here in Stony Cliffs who know about Simon's death," Nora was explaining to Irene Ellicott. She'd been talking for almost an hour, telling Irene everything from the beginning.

Irene nodded. "You must find out if . . ." Her hand twitched sharply and abruptly. It was her right hand and it held a nearly full glass of wine. The clear liquid flew out of it in a sweeping arc.

Both women stared at the hand as it spasmed violently again. With her left hand Irene carefully removed the glass from her own grip.

"Something's wrong," she said in a calm, thoughtful voice. She watched the hand as though it belonged to someone else and she had no idea what it might do.

She's having a stroke, Nora thought, or convulsions or God knows what. "Shall I call a doctor?"

The hand twitched again, more violently this time. Irene stared wonderingly at it and didn't answer.

"Irene?"

"No. This is something quite different. Please be quiet while I concentrate."

Nora put her own glass carefully down on the small table, leaning forward, ready to move if necessary.

Irene's back arched suddenly, throwing her head back, her spine shaping a sharp bow of tension. Her shoulders pulled up, closed around her ears while her head rolled to one side, her mouth hanging slack. Jaw loose, her head rolled and teetered on the point of her shoulder. Her mouth gaped, then worked, soundlessly. Some of the tension left her back and the sharp bow straightened.

Her eyes found Nora.

"It's cold," she said. But the voice wasn't Irene's. "Cold."

It was a child's voice—high, clear, complaining.

Irene's head lolled on her hunched shoulder, her mouth slack, her shoulder a prop to hold the heavy head that threatened to roll to some impossible angle. Irene's eyes were unfocused and dull.

Nora's stomach grabbed and clenched, and the August sun on the garden a few yards away seemed to belong to another world. She faced Irene like a dangerous stranger.

"He's here!" the child's voice announced. And, slowly, all the tension of that *other* slid away to leave the woman limp.

When she started to collapse, Nora sprang out of her chair to grab Irene by the shoulders and keep her from tumbling face forward onto the ground. She leaned Irene carefully back in the chair, frowning with worry at the face that was quiet and peaceful now. She seemed pale, Nora thought, and the fine blue veins beneath the translucent skin were more visible as well as the delicate network of age lines.

Irene's eyelids flickered and opened, vacant for a moment, then quickly filled with recognition and reason.

"Thank you, dear," she said, as though Nora had just opened a door for her. "I'm all right now."

Nora released her grip on Irene's shoulders, took a short step back and studied her doubtfully.

Irene moved her head around tentatively. "Ouch. I seem to have pulled something."

One step at a time, like a cartoon character, Nora backed away to take her seat again, watching Irene stretch her neck and cautiously roll her shoulders.

"It didn't look like a comfortable position," she told Irene drily. In fact, it had looked grotesque, even horrifying. Nora's heart still thudded and careened off her ribs. When she reached for her glass of wine, she saw that her fingers were trembling.

Irene gave her a sharp glance. "I must have frightened you. I'm sorry."

Nora shrugged, wishing she could be as matter-of-fact as Irene.

"I've simply had to get used to it, you see. I'm a very receptive person. Strong emotions and unusual psychic activities somehow seep into my system sometimes if I'm not on guard. It has sometimes frightened me, sometimes saddened or frustrated me. Now, most of the time, I manage to be curious, more than anything, and generally calm." Irene poured herself another glass of wine.

Her hand, Nora noticed, shook ever so slightly.

"What happened?"

"I'm not entirely sure," Irene said. "It was very cold. Something cold—metal, I think—pressed against my back and I was trying to pull away from it. There was an unpleasant odor, very strong, gagging. Chemical. Disinfectant?" Irene tapped one fingernail against her glass and stared into the distance, summoning words.

"There was bright light all around—an unhealthy light. And I wasn't alone."

A long pause.

"Someone was with you?" Nora prompted.

Irene shook her head, stopped, then nodded.

"There was the vague feeling that someone called me into being. It was like being a puppet, but only slightly aware of the strings. And there was someone else. Someone actually outside me, in the room. Someone very frightened."

"Probably me," Nora said.

"No. I wasn't *here* for those moments. I was *there*."

"Oh."

Irene laughed, not unkindly, at Nora's discomfiture. "I'm afraid you'll have to get used to it, Nora, if you're around me for any length of time. Particularly now when these forces, whatever they are, are at work. I seem to be uncomfortably susceptible."

They sipped their wine for a few moments in silence, both of them watching a fat red squirrel perched on the lawn grooming himself.

"*He's here*," Irene said, and Nora shot her a nervous look.

"Just thinking aloud," Irene said soothingly.

"Who do you suppose 'he' is?"

"I have a suspicion."

Moments passed and she didn't say more. Their silence grew, and to Nora it felt dark and full of secrets. The one thought that kept drifting to the surface of Nora's mind was the thing she'd refused to let herself think for days now. It was ugly and impossible and frightening, and she didn't want to think the words much less actually say them. But she heard herself speak.

"Satan," she said quietly, watching her wine glass on the arm of the wicker chair. She turned it round and round in small circles. "Or Lucifer or Beelzebub or whatever it is they call him."

She looked up at Irene with a sad, stricken defiance.

Irene stared at her, looking surprised. Then she smiled and shook her head gently like an adult explaining away a child's bad dreams.

"Oh, dear, no. Victor Sears."

19

"Victor?" Nora stared blankly at Irene who was smiling benignly at her. Like the Good Witch Glinda, Nora thought, explaining how the Ruby Slippers will get Dorothy home.

"But . . . Victor's dead," she protested.

Irene nodded. "Of course. But I believe he's still with us."

"A ghost?" Nora fought the impulse to snatch a quick look over her shoulder. The flesh on the back of her neck chilled and tightened.

"Not in the ordinary sense," Irene said, and Nora snorted.

"I suppose that does sound odd if you're not involved with these things. No, what we usually call ghosts are more like echoes or remnants of personality or emotions. They're traces left behind. There is no consciousness. No volition. Seeing a ghost is like watching a movie. But sometimes something different happens."

"And you think something different happened with Victor?"

Irene sipped her wine and nodded. "Victor was an extremely strong personality. He generated an enormous amount of psychic energy and had an almost overpowering force of will. I believe his will and energy are holding him here and still operating on some level.''

Nora took a sip of her wine and turned Irene's words over carefully, exploring the idea.

''When Alex Thomas and Carole Salant said *He* was here, they meant Victor Sears? He's somehow in touch with them?''

Irene nodded. ''And I believe Victor is responsible for driving those people to kill themselves.''

''But why?''

''I think . . .'' Irene hesitated, interrupting herself and frowning. ''I think Victor is drawing power from them, using their psychic energy to feed his own.''

Nora frowned back at her, ''Like a psychic vampire?''

''Yes, that's a very good description for it.'' Irene looked more enthusiastic, leaning a little towards Nora. ''The idea isn't new, you know. Dozens of cases have been reported, although the so-called vampire was most often a living member of a household. One woman back at the turn of the century even reported her teenage daughter leaving tiny bite marks behind. Today, we're more comfortable talking about the phenomenon in psychological terms. We talk about people who 'drain us' or 'suck the life out of us' emotionally. Victor is one of those people with unusual power.''

Nora was lost in her own thoughts. She wasn't entirely willing to believe Irene's theory. Part of her demanded explanations that would put everything back in the normal, safe, everyday world. Yet to another part of her Irene's explanation made chilling sense.

''Then why did he kill himself?'' Nora questioned. It was a chink, maybe, in Irene's logic.

''Death and rebirth.''

The words rang and settled on the summer air.

Nora listened to the echo eddy around the lush ferns in their wicker stands, not accepting its meaning. She shook her head slowly at Irene.

"Power," Irene said. "The magician must die as an ordinary man and be reborn as an adept. A master."

"That's crazy."

"Is it? All of our major religions are based on the concept of death and rebirth. Look as far back as the Egyptians with Isis and Osiris or the Greek Persephone emerging from the underworld. And then there's Christ. Death and rebirth."

"But . . . did Victor expect a new body? Or resurrection?"

"I don't believe so. I think he is using his present spiritual form to gain psychic power."

Nora pushed out of her chair and paced to the other end of the porch. "I don't know. I'm finding it really hard to believe all this."

Irene remained silent, and behind Nora was only the sound of her hostess pouring herself another glass of wine. Nora stared out at a climbing rose rambling up and over a white wooden arch. To accept the idea of Victor Sears, the *late* Victor Sears, somehow hanging onto life as a disembodied force pulling the strings that controlled half a dozen people, driving some to their deaths, draining life and energy from the living . . . to accept all that would mean changing all her comfortable, lifelong beliefs in how the world worked. It required a leap of faith she wasn't sure she was ready, or even willing, to make.

Silence had settled over them with the hot, sleepy hush of summer afternoon.

"Nora, you're free to believe and think as you like. I've simply told you what I believe to be true, and if you find you can use those ideas to help you or Sample at any time, then I hope you will."

Nora turned and regarded Irene seriously. "Thank you," she said. Then, grinning, she added, "Tell me, is there such a thing as psychic garlic?"

Maybe Alex Thomas was just having a breakdown. And Carole Salant. And the others, who died—the little boy, the old man, the woman on the railroad tracks and Charlie Luther. And maybe Sam was verging on something. And maybe she herself was a little crazy by now, Nora thought.

"Oh, hell," she said aloud, driving from Irene's back to her place. The trouble was that rational explanations began to spread themselves too thin, and the only step by step logical way to explain things was to accept Irene's theory.

Victor Sears was still in Stony Cliffs manipulating people to their deaths. Is that what he was trying to do to Sam? Drive her to suicide?

A block from her house Nora slowed down and took a turn. She didn't want to go home, she realized, not just yet. So she headed for the campus and downtown, wanting to be around people, back in a normal world.

She parked on First Street. It was the main street of Stony Cliffs and ran parallel with the Black River for just over a mile. First Street marked the border between town and campus. On the west side, the river side, were the oldest buildings of the school arranged on the vast green Pentacrest. Huge oak trees with knobby boughs and gnarled trunks made pools of deep shade across the square. The original buildings of the college marked the four corners with one large building in the center. The buildings had high ceilings and tall windows that opened to let hot summer breezes ventilate the old-fashioned class-rooms with their hardwood floors and corniced plaster walls. Some of the classrooms were amphi-theater style with acoustics that echoed and rang. The teachers' offices were claustrophobic, much taller than they were wide.

The warm air drifted in the windows, Nora remembered, with the sound of students shouting to each other, playing frisbee, hurrying or just waiting between classes. And wasps and summer smells drifted in too.

She couldn't wait to begin teaching.

The campus was much bigger than the Pentacrest, of course. A long hill behind the Pentacrest sloped down to the river and a short retaining wall made the perfect seat for students looking out at the water. There were women's and men's dorms, a new art building and museum, a gymnasium, a new science building, and the student union.

On the town side of First Street, the businesses were mostly college oriented. There was the SC bookstore—Nora's excuse for coming downtown. It carried nearly all the books SC teachers ordered for their classes. Next door to it was the Red Hangar. A bar with photos and models of old airplanes and a propellor mounted over the front door, the Red Hangar catered to the rowdier crowd of students.

There was a barbershop with a red and white pole that had been transformed into a hairstyling salon. There was Burlington's Corner Drugstore, which, from the old photographs hung inside, hadn't changed in over 40 years.

Around the corner was Yggdrasil, the alternative bookstore and coffee shop named after the world tree, the great ash tree whose roots and branches in Norse myth hold the universe together.

Nora actually preferred the clutter and disorganization of Yggdrasil, even though she'd ordered from the efficient, sterile SC Bookstore. At Yggdrasil they couldn't, or wouldn't, meet deadlines, didn't give discounts to students buying in quantity, and wouldn't stock all the books Nora requested. So much for Yggdrasil.

Nora checked at the SC Bookstore and found that

the last of her ordered texts had arrived. She spent an hour browsing the aisles, looking at the text lists of other teachers and skimming through the books. By the time she emerged from the fluorescent lights and air conditioning of the bookstore to the end-of-day bustle on First Street, Nora had decided to head for the riverbank. She wanted to sit peacefully, watching the long shadows grow while the river sparkled in the late, golden sun. It almost would be her last chance to enjoy it in relative peace before the start of school. When classes started hundreds of students would make the riverbank a kind of crowded lounge between classes.

She was walking down the long slope of hill behind the Pentacrest, moving between tree shadows and bright sun and squinting a little in the glare of light reflected from the river. Then she saw it, or thought she did—a figure, a familiar silhouette, that flared into shape against the bright, shimmering river and vanished into glare.

Nora stopped, standing in the shadow of a Pentacrest oak, shading her eyes and squinting hard to catch the familiar shape.

"Simon," she said, but she couldn't make him out clearly. A group of students went walking across the area where he stood. She started down the hill faster, taking long, loping strides, a little unbalanced, eyes fixed on the riverbank.

Nora used to wonder sometimes if she'd recognize Simon immediately after two years of not seeing him. She used to think she might mistake someone else for him or hesitate when she saw him. But the shape of him, the set of his back, the way he bounced a little when he walked resonated through her.

Searching, she couldn't spot him, and she began to run, galloping down the last of the hill and onto the riverbank.

"Simon!" she called into a group of people who

blocked her view on the broad sidewalk beside the river. They kept walking, turning off the sidewalk across the grass to the riverbank. The sidewalk swung away from the river and tunneled through a short, steep hill. Nora started to run again, making for the tunnel. It was the only place Simon might be, and she was sure he was there.

It took her only seconds to reach the dark mouth of the tunnel, a shadowed contrast with the river's glare, and she had to stop for the length of a heartbeat to squeeze her eyes shut and get her sight back. When she opened them again she caught only a glimpse of him, a dark shape outlined against the light at the opposite end of the tunnel moving away from her.

She took a quick breath to shout his name, but a sound like thunder exploded around her, a great boom that softened her knees and sent her arms flying up to protect her head and ears. She automatically crouched and cowered away from it while the sound roared around her and a blast of cold stench pushed her off balance, forcing her a step back. It hit her again, sound and stink rolling towards her, and she retreated another step and then another until she was suddenly outside the tunnel, standing in the warm sun surrounded by peaceful silence.

Nora gasped, swung around and stared at the little group of students a few yards from her sitting on the riverbank. They were absorbed in their own conversation.

"What was that?" Nora threw at them.

They turned toward her, mildly surprised, not sure she was talking to them.

"Pardon?" a girl asked politely.

Nora frowned at them. "That booming," she said, "like an explosion."

The girl shook her head.

"We didn't hear anything," one of the boys volunteered.

"But . . ." Nora said and stopped. How could they not hear it? Her ears still rang from the sound. Was it something that only happened in the tunnel? Some acoustical trick? Even so, surely they would have heard it just a few yards away.

She shook her head, waving a dismissing hand, and they turned back to their conversation.

Nora turned back to the tunnel mouth, taking deep breaths and trying to build up courage to race through when two girls, talking and walking close together, appeared at the other end. Nora waited a few seconds, long enough to see that nothing was about to happen, then she ran into the tunnel, brushed past the oblivious students and out the other side.

She stood on a busy street, a main drag between town and the men's dorms, and the sidewalks held clusters of men walking, talking, moving and standing in sun-dappled groups.

There was no sign of Simon.

Finnerty's office was temporarily off-limits to anyone who knew his ass from a hole in the ground.

The sheriff had rumbled into headquarters like a black thundercloud and his men knew better from hard experience than to knock on his door for anything less than an all-out emergency. Tom Robbins was smugly handling anything else that came up.

Behind the firmly closed door Finnerty stood beside his desk, arms crossed on his big chest and head cocked to look down at the file folders neatly arranged there.

Ted Kellogg. Calvin Russell. Charlie Luther. Jerry Rhine. Florence Gleason.

Technically, the only cases he had to worry about were Ted Kellogg and Charlie Luther. And Charlie Luther's was a case for internal inquiries. The inquest on Calvin Russell and his wife Matilda had already ruled, as Finnerty had known it would, that Calvin

Russell had murdered his wife and shot himself.

Little Steven Rhine, Jerry's brother, was still unable to give a statement, according to the boy's doctor, but Finnerty had heard enough to figure that, too, was a suicide. Not an accident, nothing you could explain, but a seven-year old kid who snuck out of bed to walk off the top of the town's tallest building straight into thin air and his death, trying to take his little brother with him.

And Florence Gleason. Again, there was a witness to suicide. The engineer on the train swore she was alone at the railroad tracks, clearly seen in the train's headlight, kneeling with her neck on the rail like a sacrificial lamb.

And Charlie Luther was locked alone in his cell.

Suicides, all of them, and no doubt about it. But Finnerty didn't like it. He didn't like it at all.

He brooded over their names on the file folders, knowing their contents by heart. He picked up Ted Kellogg's file and opened it to study the black and white enlargements of the mutilated body with an impassive eye. There had to be some clue in the grotesque mangling to tell him about the killer.

Finnerty held a photo down at arm's length. Damn. There had to be something there.

Hands and feet were sticking out of the gutted torso in a bizarre arrangement, like something a little kid would do with a broken doll. Finnerty thought he read contempt in it. Contempt for the human body, yes. Contempt for the man? Add the fact that the killer had held Kellogg's still-beating heart. To Finnerty that could mean the killer was after some thrill, some sense of power over life and death.

And what did it all add up to? Diddlyshit. Their investigations had uncovered nothing at all—no clues, no suspect, no clear motive.

The sheriff was still scowling at the photo when his intercom buzzed. Finnerty turned on it a look so fierce that if Tom Robbins had seen it, it would have turned his hot hands clammy.

Oblivious, it buzzed again and Finnerty snatched up the receiver, barking into it. "What?"

"Sheriff," Tom Robbins, sounding nervous but determined, said, "I'm sorry to disturb you, but there's a call on line two I was sure you'd want to take."

"Who is it?"

"Dr. Paulson."

"So? He tell you want it's about?"

"Yessir."

"And?" Robbins cleared his throat, stuttered, and Finnerty, on the edge of a roar, rumbled, "Spit it out, Deputy, or don't waste my time."

"It's Florence Gleason's body, Sheriff," Robbins said. "It's gone."

20

When Nora got back home the small red eye on her answering machine was blinking twice. Two messages.

The first was from Michael, reminding her of their date for dinner and telling her he'd be by at 7:00. A message from Sam followed. She sounded a little self-conscious, talking to a tape recorder, but otherwise perfectly fine. Would Nora like to go bike riding up to the reservoir tomorrow? She could borrow Kate's bike and they could pack a picnic lunch.

But behind the words, almost drowning them out, was a cacophony of sound, and Nora played the message again and again, listening and picking out the sounds, while a slow sweat started to chill her and her fingers, pushing the buttons of the tape recorder, began to tremble.

There was the lost, haunting whistle of a train fading and blending to the howl of a dog. There were voices, men and women both, mumbling, whispering, calling together in a jumbled background babble. Nora couldn't make out the words, except for her own name. She heard it in voices that mocked and threatened. And in another layer of sound she heard what she thought was the same child's voice that had come from Irene's lips.

"*It's cold . . . cold.*" The same complaint and same piping voice, now was slipping between Sam's words.

Bursts of static crackled through the tape like a storm, and a low thrumming vibration made a sound like blood beating in her ears. It shuddered and pulsed under the discord.

Nora played the tape again and again, then turned off the machine with fingers that shook and dialed Sam's number. It rang twice and then the ringing stopped. Silence.

Nora pressed the receiver hard against her ear, listening. There was no sound of breathing or a hollowness. Had someone picked it up?

"Hello?" Nora called into the phone, crouching over it and holding it now with both hands, afraid of who or what might answer.

Silence.

"Sam?"

Silence.

"Sam? Are you there?"

A soft childish giggle. "*Nobody ho-ome!*" A child's voice cried gleefully, then disconnected.

Nora slammed the phone down and took off out the door at a dead run.

She drove the short distance to Kate and Sam's house with both hands clenched fiercely on the wheel. Was Sam safe? Was she too late? She pushed the car forward by pure force of will, parked sloppily a yard and a half from the curb, bolted for the front porch, the closed door, and skidded to a stop.

Out of breath, hot and cold at once, Nora raised a fist to bang on the newly installed front door, then hesitated. She realized she had no idea of what she would or could do. And she was afraid of what she'd find.

She banged on the door.

No answer.

She banged again and called.

Across the street the neighbors' two small boys stood watching her, small mouths hanging open.

Still no answer.

Nora tried the doorknob, expecting it to rattle, locked, against her hand. Instead, it turned smoothly. She opened the door and stepped into the hallway.

The house was still with the sad hush of something abandoned, waiting for someone to come, for something to happen. Nora coughed and clapped one hand over her nose and mouth. The air was thick with a sick stench, a fetid odor that crawled inside the nostrils and clung there.

Nora took another step in and uncovered her mouth to call. "Sam?"

She listened, heard nothing, then stepped further into the gray quiet of the house.

"Sam!"

Overhead, somewhere in the quiet recesses of the old house, she heard a rush of light footsteps, then a door slammed shut.

"Sam? It's Nora!" Pause. "Kate?" Kate should be home by now. It was after 6:00.

Nora moved to the base of the stairs and climbed two steps.

"Is anybody home?"

Upstairs, another door slammed.

Nora held the stair rail, climbed two more steps and paused, head cocked, listening to the quiet house, breathing shallowly through her mouth because the stench was thicker now.

Then the front door slammed shut.

She swung around, grabbing the rail for balance. The hall was empty.

She turned and started going up the stairs, one step at a time, pausing to listen to the silence.

When she was just over halfway up, Nora heard a sound. It came from the living room where her view was cut off by the arch of the doorway. She turned towards the sound, waiting, then crouched a little on the stairs to see what caused it.

It was a quiet sound, slow like a shuffling. *Shuffle, flap.* A tired sound. *Shuffle, flap.* Moving towards her like a nightmare. *Shuffle, flap.*

Nora crouched lower, straining to see what moved wearily and inevitably towards her. Holding the bannisters like the bars of a cage, she twised her head for an angled look.

"Sam?" she called softly, sure that it wasn't the girl and instantly sorry she'd made a sound to call attention to herself, stranded on the stairs in the sick air.

And an old man came into sight, foreshortened from her viewpoint, the top of his balding head visible first with its tender, bare shine. He was looking down and Nora couldn't see his face. He wore a robe over pajamas with leather scuff slippers on naked white feet.

Something was wrong with the way he looked, Nora thought. Something was odd. Then she saw how all the colors were subtly wrong—his robe, his pajamas, the old flesh. He was like a Brownie snapshot, 30 years old and faded. The colors bleached out, pale and forgotten in the family album.

She wanted to call out but couldn't. She watched him shuffle towards her, moving into the hall below with a terrible weariness. And then the stair rail beneath her hands began to shudder.

Nora snatched her hands away and sprang to her feet, watching as the thing began to shake violently, the old wood creaking, layers of paint crackling in protest. And suddenly the whole house boomed like an enormous wooden bell struck with a giant mallet, and the walls and stairs vibrated with the shock. Reaching her palms out behind her to steady herself, Nora touched the wall and felt it tremble to the foundations.

Another boom followed and Nora thought she could tell where it came from this time—Sam's room.

And it beat again, a sound like fever humming in the blood.

Nora's eyes were on Sam's door. It was there. And Sam?

Nora took one slow step up. Below her, the old man was shuffling forward. He was in the hall now, a yard and a half from the bottom of the stairs. Nora looked at him, looked up, then took one more step towards the head of the stairs.

A boom reverberated into silence, pierced then by a pure high voice, a child's voice, singing.

"Jesus loves me, this I know . . ."

Coming from Sam's room.

"For the Bible tells me so . . ."

"Sam?" Nora half-whispered. But Nora knew it wasn't Sam's voice.

"Little ones to him belong . . . They are weak, but he is strong."

Nora climbed a step, then another. Below her and out of sight somewhere in the living room glass shattered. She heard it splinter and crash, shards rustling and tinkling in a brittle cascade of sound.

Up two more steps, she was just short of the top now. And from out of nowhere, from out of the empty rank air came a wave of foul water. It dashed against her face, and she gasped and shook her head, coughing. The water was warm and slick with the same fetid odor as the air, and it dripped from her hair, soaking her clothing.

Another boom, and she staggered towards the rail, grabbing it for balance.

Below her, the old man had reached the foot of the stairs and had placed one slippered foot on the bottom step.

In the living room another crash sounded, a dull sound of wood on wood.

Nora reached the top of the stairs just when all hell broke loose.

The house boomed and crashed, rattling the walls and trembling through the floors as pictures jumped off their hooks and the stair rail waved like grass in the wind. The closed doors to the bedrooms and linen closet flew open and crashed against the walls. Glass cracked and shattered in Sam's bedroom, and a sudden blast of wind hit Nora with a force that made her stagger and flail for balance at the head of the stairs. She caught the bannister and held it while wind swept over her. From the living room came another crash.

The wind stopped abruptly, and a heartbeat later Nora heard a high, thin howl of rage and disappointment begin and build from somewhere out of sight in the living room.

After another beat a second voice echoed the first with a high wail from outside the front door. And then the door swung slowly open.

Kate and Sam stood framed in the doorway, and Sam, eyes squeezed tight shut, head thrown back, mouth open wide and body straight and taut as a wire, was screaming. Her mother stood beside her, staring at her as if she were some changeling who'd taken Sam's place. The terrible scream built and gathered volume in an eerie duet with the long pained scream from the living room until it seemed there was nothing in the house but the screams—and finally, together, they stopped.

Kate reached out to Sam and wrapped both arms around her shoulders, pulling the girl to her. Sam leaned against her, passive and exhuasted, and Kate finally turned her pale face towards Nora.

They were staring into each other's eyes for a long second when a sheriff's deputy suddenly bounded up the porch steps and Kate swiveled towards him.

"You all right?"

She nodded, looked down at Sam and gently pushed her back to see her face. "Sam?"

The girl looked up, opened and shut her mouth once, then nodded and shrugged.

Stepping around Kate and Sam, the deputy called into the house, with his eyes on Nora, still clutching the bannister.

"Phil?"

"Here!" a voice came back from the living room and the deputy moved towards it while Kate and Sam followed.

Nora stared after them, then slowly pried her fingers loose from the stair rail. She became uncomfortably aware of the water that dripped from her soaked hair and trickled down her cheeks and neck to stain her shirt.

Alex Thomas stood in the center of the living room. One of the deputies held his arm, reading him his rights while the other pinned his arms behind him, fastening handcuffs.

Two of the living room windows were broken in and glass covered the floor. A side table, the rocker and a bookcase were overturned and the couch was shoved out of place, its pillows half dumped on the floor. Both the deputy with the handcuffs and Alex were disheveled, panting and sweating. Alex stood and stared in front of him, oblivious as a robot.

"Alex! What the hell is going on here?" Kate finally broke her silence. "What are you doing here?"

A trickle of dark blood ran from one corner of Alex's mouth down his chin. He didn't even blink when Kate spoke.

Sam stood a yard and a half behind Kate and Nora stood beside her, studying her profile.

"You know this character?" the deputy asked.

Nora leaned towards Sam, bending to eye level. "Sam?" The girl blinked twice behind her oversize glasses. "Sam?" She turned her head, slow and wide-eyed as an owl awakened in the daytime.

"Are you okay?"

There was that curious blankness, Nora saw. She was beginning to recognize it now. She'd seen it in Sam first and, just a few hours before, in Irene. But it was clearing a little. Sam was coming back from wherever that distance took her.

"Sam?"

"I'm okay," she finally said, her voice sounding rusty, as though she weren't sure how to move her lips and tongue to produce the right sounds. "Okay," she repeated slowly.

"Just what the hell is going on here?" Kate was demanding. This time she was glaring, hands on hips, at the deputy who had trailed her into the house. She looked at the pocket just over his heart where his name was embroidered.

"Dep. Ralph Cooksey," it read.

Cooksey was tall and smooth-muscled with the easy slouch of a country man who liked midnight hunts for coon and possum more than just about anything and spent his Saturday nights off putting down a dozen beers with the boys at Weller's Truck Stop, listening to the country and western bands while his wife waited at home.

Now he looked down at Kate with dark brown eyes, half-hooded with sleepy lids. She squinted back at him, feisty and offering a challenge.

"Ma'am?" he said coolly, almost bordering on arrogance.

"I would like to know," she said, enunciating each word carefully, "why you are in my house?"

"Just doing my job, ma'am," Cooksey answered, all innocence.

Kate swung towards Phil Jenkins. "Who broke the windows?"

"This gentleman here." Phil nodded towards Alex, passive as a prophet waiting for martyrdom. "I saw him break both of them, then duck inside. We've been keeping the house under surveillance, ma'am, for your protection.''

Kate snorted, letting her eyes travel across the chaos of the room with furniture, broken glass and spilled books littering the floor.

"Now looky here, Ms. Hall,'' Cooksey drawled, interrupting. He didn't like Kate or any of these head-up-their-ass college people. And he especially didn't like anything to do with the Kellogg case. "Deputy Jenkins was doing his duty as he saw fit in the pursuit of law and order. He saw a crime committed— breaking and entering—and he followed up. I come along as back-up after the deputy radioed for assistance. We're just doing our jobs, ma'am.''

Nora watched Kate bite back an answer, angry energy run aground for a moment. Then Kate spun to face her.

"And what are you doing here?''

They were all staring at her now—all except Alex Thomas—and Nora stared stupidly back, feeling accused of some crime.

"I was worried about Sam,'' she said. "There was a message. On my answering machine . . .''

Kate shot a look at Sam.

"I only asked if you wanted to go bike riding tomorrow.''

"I know,'' Nora said it for Sam only. "But there was something in the background.''

"What?'' Kate challenged.

"Voices. Strange sounds.'' Nora kept her eyes on Sam.

"Maybe,'' Phil Jenkins put in, "the wires got crossed somewhere.''

"I didn't hear anything,'' Sam told Nora.

Her eyes were wide and solemn, only a little frightened. Nora shrugged. "Okay.''

Silence. And Nora felt like they were all, in one way

or another, accusing her of something.

"How did you get in?" Kate broke the silence,
sounding uncomfortable.

Nora pulled her eyes slowly from Sam's face. *Be
careful*, she kept trying to telegraph, *be on guard*.

She met Kate's eyes. "The front door was open. I
knocked, then just walked in."

Kate stared at her, then said, "Oh." It was something she'd always done, forgetting to lock doors
behind her.

And then she swung back to Alex Thomas who,
wrapped up in his own dream, stood away from them
all.

"I still want to know why you broke in here, Alex,"
Kate demanded, but still Alex stared vacantly towards
the half-hidden stairs. "Alex?"

"We'll question him down at the station, ma'am,"
Cooksey told her, and holding Alex's slack arm, he
began to walk him out.

Alex moved forward without a struggle until he
stopped suddenly at the foot of the stairs. Eyes
brightening and finally focusing, he gazed up the
stairs, face radiant as a sun worshiper welcoming the
morning sun.

"Blessed be!" he breathed, standing firm when
Cooksey tried to shift him, feet braced against the pull
of the deputy.

"Blessed be!" he shouted up the stairs.

"Son of a bitch," Jenkins muttered under his breath
and took Alex's other arm to add his weight.

"Blessed be! Blessed be!" Alex threw it up the
stairs, part benediction, part a plea for help.

Jenkins and Cooksey gave a solid yank and Alex lost
ground, staggering backwards with them towards the
open front door.

"Blessed be!" he shouted one last time, just before
animation left him as he crossed the threshold of the
front door. The deputies half-dragged him, limp as a

puppet, down the front steps.

Kate, Sam and Nora stood in the entry to the living room, close together and silently watching. They moved together into the entryway to watch the deputies put Alex in a patrol car and drive him away.

And they all moved together to turn and look, still not speaking, upstairs.

21

"Sam, I don't want to have to argue about this."

Half an hour after the deputies left with Alex Thomas in custody, Nora, Sam and Kate were clearing the last of the wreckage from the living room. Kate and Sam were having the kind of conversation Nora thought it best to keep out of.

"Is that clear?"

Sam didn't answer immediately. She was picking up the overturned rocker and folding the blue and white afghan that always hung on the back of it. She was working with the economical movements and pursed lips of a refectory housekeeper faced with the aftermath of a wild Irish wake.

"This is not an argument," she explained patiently. "This is a discussion."

Kate sighed heavily. "Who's supposed to be the mother here?"

"Mom, just because you're my mother doesn't mean I shouldn't get to say anything about my own life."

That's a good point, Nora thought, keeping her own mouth firmly closed. Sam was certainly old enough to have a say in her life.

"It would just be a couple of weeks, Sam. Just until

the police get this mess straightened out and stop bashing in our door and climbing through our windows. Things will be a lot more peaceful for you in Memphis, and you know the Colonel and Gram will love to have you."

"They just had me all summer. Besides, school starts next week."

"It won't hurt to miss the first week or so. I'll write a letter and explain it to the principal." Kate was squatting among the splinters of glass from the shattered windows, carefully collecting the jagged fragments in a paper bag. She had rocked back on her heels to give Sam her full attention.

Sam didn't answer or look at her. Her head was bent over the afghan, tugging at nonexistent wrinkles.

"But it's a new school," she finally said. "Junior high . . . and starting late will be just awful. I'll be behind in everything and I won't know anybody and everybody else will be used to it already. Besides, you don't know how long it might be so I could be weeks behind everybody."

Kate frowned at her.

"Seventh grade *is* traumatic," Nora volunteered, breaking her own resolution to stay out of it. Nora was concerned first with Sam's safety, like Kate was, but the painful trial of adolescence might be a more vivid memory for her than for Kate. Sam deserved the chance to start with as few handicaps as possible.

The publicity surrounding Ted's death would already have marked Sam as the future object of whispered study hall speculation and giggling conferences in the girls' locker room. Add a mysterious absence from school to make Sam the "new" kid, a latecomer to the freshly formed cliques and alliances, and Sam could be devastatingly isolated. Because she was proud and stubborn, Sam might end up in the permanent role of outsider. Seventh grade, Nora remembered, was bad enough without making it worse.

"Anyway," Sam said, fixing Kate with a steady look, "I don't want to leave you alone."

Kate finally gave her a tired smile and shook her head. "We'll see," she said, and she went back to picking up glass splinters with the easy grace of a veteran pick-up-sticks player.

Nora had cleared part of the floor of glass and now she stood up, unfolding a little stiffly, and announced she was leaving. She hadn't said anything about the old man—Sam's old man, she was sure—or the child singing or anything else that had happened to her in the house. She knew Kate well enough to know that, no matter whether Kate believed her or not, she'd be furious. Denial and anger were the way Kate dealt with any threat and neither would do any good.

Nora hesitated at the door, wanting to say something to protect them but not knowing what to say.

"Be careful, you two," she finally said and left with the restless, uneasy feeling that makes dogs howl before a thunderstorm.

"Tell me about Victor," Nora said to Michael over dessert.

He didn't mind talking about his dead half-brother, Michael had said. They had talked about almost everything during a leisurely evening of drinks and dinner—past loves, abandoned dreams, hopes that still kept them getting out of bed in the morning.

Nora gave him an edited account of seeing, or thinking she saw, Simon that afternoon. She had listened to the tape on the answering machine and it was clean of everything except Sam's voice. She didn't talk to Michael about it or tell him what had happened to her at Kate's house, only that Alex Thomas had broken in and was arrested. Nora was thinking, a little muzzy with wine and food and candlelight, that Michael was very important to her very quickly. Who *is* this man? she kept asking herself. She didn't entirely trust her feelings. She was afraid to.

"What do you want to know?" Michael answered.

Nora shrugged. "Anything. I don't know. Did you like him?"

"Hmmm." Michael's bright gaze wandered to his chocolate torte and he began prodding it absent-mindedly with his fork.

"Did I like him?" he said, listening to himself. "I didn't honestly think about it that much. For years he wasn't really a person to me. He was just the genius half-brother who got most of the attention, and I resented him like crazy. We were never what you'd call friends. Other guys' big brothers played football with you or told you dirty jokes or let you help them mess around with cars. Or maybe they pushed you around or ignored you. Or they were just sort of there, like Wally. You remember Wally and the Beaver?"

Nora nodded. "Or Bud on *Father Knows Best*."

"Exactly. Do you realize how many people our age grew up fatally dissatisfied with their own families because they never stacked up to the Andersons or the Cleavers? How could they?" Michael delicately carved a forkful of torte and lifted it to his mouth. "Anyway, Victor just wasn't my idea of a big brother. Most of the time he was sent away to school or special camps so I didn't have much of a chance to get to know him, even if either of us had been interested. By the time we were adults, Victor and I were strangers. When I came to Stony Cliffs I was looking for a more sophisticated version of Wally or Bud, some dream of a brother who'd take the place of all the family I didn't have. I wasn't looking for Victor at all. Did I like him? I can't really answer that."

"But I think you loved him."

He shrugged. "I wanted to. Maybe I did. Anyway, love was something Victor required. If you didn't love him, it was too easy to dislike him. Or despise him."

"Why?"

"He was so extreme—Extremely negative. He was vicious, and bitter, always ready to discourse on the stupidity of just about everyone else in the world, about their narrow-mindedness and lack of perception. What he meant, of course, was that he wasn't being properly appreciated. He really was brilliant, but it was a twisted logic, perverse and cruel. Sometimes I think Victor was firmly convinced he was the only person in the universe—at least, the only one who counted. Other people were tools or objects. He loved to manipulate. He was also incredibly lonely. He separated himself from everyone and everything and then ached with the loneliness of it. Poor bastard.''

Nora was quiet, munching absent-mindedly at her cheese cake and watching Michael dismantle his torte without again tasting it. He could be talking to himself now, she thought. She leaned across the table on her elbows, watching him and learning about him while she learned about Victor.

"And he had a bizarre sense of humor. Bizarre. I don't know what else to call it. Maybe sly or malicious. Totally without pity for someone else's discomfort or humiliation. He loved crude practical jokes that no one else could see any humor in at all. Anything to embarrass. Any nasty barb . . . and Victor could be very sophisticated and witty in his barbs. In one way or another, Victor managed to alienate anyone who ever cared for him at all.''

"Women?'' Nora felt her face flush. "I mean, lovers?''

Michael snorted. "Victor didn't believe in limiting himself, but female was his usual choice. By all accounts, Victor's sex life was the stuff porn epics are made of. He attracted a varied bunch—the self-styled intellectuals from the college, both students and teachers, any age, either sex. They were the lost souls who hang out in Stony Cliffs, stuck in some kind of limbo, never making the transition from college to the real world. There were also the drugged-out chickies from the high school clamoring for a cosmic orgasm to boost them into Nirvana. Those were Victor's favorites. The younger the better.''

Michael tossed his fork down and lit a cigarette.

"Like I said, Victor required love. He needed it. Adoration was even better. And sweetest of all was total worship by some mooning adolescent who'd think Victor was God himself and be only too willing to open her legs for holy communion.''

Michael blew out a long stream of smoke. His face softened when he looked at her, Nora thought, and she liked that. He reached across the table and took her hand.

"You'll be happy to know it doesn't run in the family.''

"He must have been very unhappy.''

"Tortured. But he did it to himself. Sometimes I thought I came close to touching him, to making some real contact, but he'd always manage to slide away with a snide comment or some insult to put me in my place. I should have kept trying, though. The thing that hurts is that I keep thinking I could have done something. I saw the pain and didn't do anything about it. I just played Victor's game and let myself be distracted by his sheer unpleasantness and evasions.''

"You said it yourself, Michael. He did it to himself. Victor was what he was and you couldn't change that. Could you have forced him to get help? I doubt it. He had to want help, to want to change, and you couldn't do that for him.''

They were leaning towards each other, awkward across the restaurant table, hands joined and oblivious of everything around them.

"Hey, lady,'' Michael finally said, "wanna go see my etchings?''

* * *

"Run a check on Alex Thomas's fingerprints," Finnerty said. "See if they match any of the four found on the slab."

Bobby Hunt whistled through his teeth. "Sheriff, you think that devil cult's stealing bodies now?"

Finnerty scowled at him without speaking. He tossed Florence Gleason's file back down on his desk, and it skidded across the other folders, skimming towards Hunt. He caught it, stopping it from sliding over the edge with a clumsy reluctance to touch it, and pushed it back in place.

"What would they do that for?" Bobby Hunt shook his head, wondering. "What do you think they'd do with it?"

"Did Doc Paulson say when Thomas could talk?"

"He doesn't know. Thomas kind of went catatonic after they got him to the hospital. Like that Carole Salant. She's not talking yet either."

"Catatonic."

"Yes, sir."

Finnerty sighed and lowered himself back into the creaking embrace of his chair. "Have the lab run a check on Thomas's car."

"Yes, sir."

"*Now*, Bobby."

The deputy snapped to attention. "Right, Sheriff."

When Bobby Hunt let himself out of Finnerty's office, closing the door behind him with ostentatious care, the sheriff began rubbing the tight space between his eyebrows, the place where the headaches started.

"Oh hell," he said to the empty air. Then he made a phone call.

Irene Ellicott wasn't at all surprised to hear from him.

"Are you sure you don't want me to go in with you and yell boo into your closets?"

"Positive," Nora told Michael. "You'll just scare my moths."

"Or we could just go back to my place. I would like it if you'd stay."

They were standing on her front porch with only the shifting light of a streetlamp shining down through the lush canopy of trees. Her door was open. The house was dark and quiet. Most of the houses in the neighborhood were dark and sleeping.

They'd made love in the loft of his studio apartment. It faced the river, a converted carriage house taller than it was wide and all window looking out on the black water where the moon shivered. The night was cheerful and noisy with the sound of crickets. And all Nora could think of after they'd made love was going home. It was important, going home alone and facing the night. Facing her own fears? For whatever reason, it seemed like the most important thing in her life just then. So she asked Michael, half-asleep in the dark loft, to take her home.

"Sometime," Nora told him, "I'd really like to stay. And sometime I'd like to have you stay at my place. But tonight I'd just like to be here. By myself."

Michael nodded, accepting it and at least looking like he understood something she wasn't sure she understood herself.

"Then, seriously, I'd like to just go in with you and make sure everything's okay. Anyway, it's a good excuse to spend a little more time with you."

Nora hesitated for just a beat, then shook her head. It was long overdue for her to grow up, she thought. If I can't go into my own house by myself without somebody else to tell me it's safe, I might as well give up.

"Thanks, but no. I'm sure everything's fine."

"Famous last words," he said, smiling, giving her one last chance, but Nora smiled back and shook her head.

"Stubborn woman." But he said it with some fond

admiration. "We do have a date for tomorrow, right?" When she nodded, he kissed her, sweet and lingering, and she tried not to cling. Then he left while she waved jauntily from the porch.

Her living room was dark, black compared to the lamplit porch, and still as a sleeper. Nora tried standing still, eyes and ears straining into the dark and quiet, hoping her senses would adjust quickly. Around her the dark seemed to gather and shift. Things at the outer edge of her vision seemed to move and change shape, but never when she looked directly at them.

It always happens when you're tired, she told herself.

The air was thick and humid with just the hint of a cool early morning breeze beginning as an undercurrent in the heavy atmosphere. The light breeze stirred and lifted the curtains hanging at her open windows. Slowly, Nora's eyes adjusted to the darkness and she could make out the dark shapes that brightened somewhat as the curtains flared open and let in light from the street.

She got her bearings and started to edge towards the nearest lamp, telling herself not to be so silly. She hadn't taken a full breath since she came through the door, and her knees felt weak. She kept waiting for something to happen.

"I'm home!" she yelled into the quiet night of the house. She meant it to be cheery, some humor to dismiss the fears. But the quiet of the house swallowed her voice and the silent echo in the air made her shiver.

She listened to it for a quick breath, then stepped and reached into the dark to turn on the lamp.

The bulb flashed. Then it popped and went out.

Blinded by the light, Nora blinked and squeezed her eyes shut against the fresh darkness closing in.

"Damn bulb," she muttered. She was irritated with

herself for the way the skin in the center of her back had chilled, expecting to be touched.

She walked quickly towards the other lamp until she banged her shin on the coffee table and slowed down to move more carefully. When she reached the lamp she turned the knob with only a fractional hesitation.

It lit.

And blew out with a sharp crackle.

Nora froze, staring in the darkness at the shadow of the lamp as though she expected it to change into something out of a nightmare. Coincidence? Maybe something was wrong with the electricity, some kind of overload or something.

She swung around to face the room, jumpy as a spooked horse, as though she knew something rushed at her unprotected back. She suddenly became aware of her own breathing, fast and shallow in the still house. She took half a step back and something touched her bare leg. When she jumped, screamed and swatted at it, Nora realized she'd backed into the trailing vine of her grape ivy plant.

"Stop it!" she said out loud. And suddenly she wasn't sure, hearing her voice, that she was talking only to herself.

The next nearest lights drew her farther into the house, into the dining room where a chandelier on a dimmer made a constellation of lights just waiting to prove that the two light bulbs blowing out at once was just a coincidence. Only, Nora wasn't sure she wanted to test it. It still wasn't too late to just leave.

But she walked quickly into the dining room and reached without hesitating for the dimmer. She turned the dial and the glass candle flames glowed obligingly. And stayed lit.

Nora blew out a pent-up breath and felt the strength rush back into her legs. It *was* just a silly coincidence. She took a few confident strides into the kitchen and flipped on the overhead light, filling the room with brightness.

She bustled around, relaxing finally, poured herself a generous goblet of cold white wine and sipped it as she leaned against the sink. What she really wanted, Nora thought, was to stretch out for a while on the couch with an old black and white late night movie, her wine and a magazine propped against her knees. She wanted to drift into a kid's easy nest on the family couch, safe and secure at home with bright lights and reassuring noise.

But with both lamps out in the living room, that was impossible.

All she had to do was replace the bulbs that had blown out, but searching under the sink, she couldn't find any of the extra bulbs she was sure she had bought.

Downstairs, she remembered. They were in the basement, still in the bag with that other stuff from the hardware store. Nuts. It was always the basement where things waited, crouching behind the furnace, hidden in the shadows, squatting under the riserless stairs waiting to grab a bare passing ankle.

Dammit, Nora's inner dialogue picked up with vehemence, I don't need this. So a couple lights blew out and I have to go down to the basement to get some new bulbs. So what? Very simple. People do it every day.

But she waited to down half her glass of wine before starting the trip to the basement. And she crouched first at the head of the stairs to carefully survey the bleak, bare basement before making her way down. And her ankles tingled all the way down, just waiting for a touch.

Downstairs, the shadows squatted and waited behind the water heater and furnace. But they stayed where they were supposed to be, never moving when she looked at them, and nothing moved at all while she finally found the bag of supplies that held her extra light bulbs.

Nothing except the small white spider that gave a small, secret skitter a few inches up the cool concrete wall.

And upstairs, in a kitchen drawer, the long butcher knives that were an old wedding present began to rattle and shiver together. Their wooden handles clicked and rustled together, and the long blades rang a soft, musical note. On the next floor, the door to one of the unused bedrooms softly shut and the latch clicked into place.

22

Judy Fisher and Brenda Morrison were best friends.

They had met in eighth grade when Brenda's family first moved to Stony Cliffs. Dr. Morrison taught medieval history at SCC and, although he didn't know it yet, this would probably be his last year at SCC.

Dr. Morrison's classes weren't popular. His view of history was dry and lifeless. Instead of pomp and intrigue, passion and drama, his Middle Ages were painted in the arid structure of a changing legal system. Dr. Morrison didn't speculate on whether Richard III was the victim of Tudor propaganda or a black-hearted hunchback who'd killed an assortment of relatives, including his small nephews. Instead, he was more interested in the changing role of Chamberlain. Was William the Conqueror really gay? Dr. Morrison never so much as raised the question although medieval scholars seemed to hint at it. Dr. Morrison was more concerned with William's adaptation of Danelaw. His classes had a record high rate of dropouts and incompletes among the first and second year students. By the third and fourth years, the students knew better than to enroll with him at all. No one ever took a second class from Dr. Morrison.

Judy's father, David Fisher, was an art teacher, and

most of his students called him David. He painted
huge canvases using buckets of paint and push
brooms. The titles of his paintings were always either
one word or at least ten.

"Delbert Discovers the Touch That Shows How
Futile It Is to Expose the Curiosity of the Mind." That
was a David Fisher painting.

David never gave any student a lower grade than
"B," so David Fisher had a waiting list for his classes.
And he had tenure.

"It's *white* magic," Judy Fisher was insisting,
impatiently repeating herself for the umpteenth time
to Brenda. But Judy was used to having to convince
Brenda Morrison of different things. Brenda was
always a chicken.

"I still don't see why we have to do it," Brenda
repeated, just as stubbornly as Judy.

They went through their magic phase a year ago,
back in ninth grade. But nothing much ever happened
and they'd both lost interest. Now Judy was bringing
it all up again, insisting that Brenda join her in a
ceremony of psychic protection. She was so damn
dramatic about it and it was all so silly.

Judy sighed and rolled her eyes up to show the
whites. "I'll explain it again," Judy said heavily, and
Brenda pressed her lips tight together and crossed her
arms over her chest. Sometimes she didn't know why
she was friends with Judy Fisher. But they *were*
friends, best of friends, and so close and busy with
each other that neither of them had any other really
close friends.

"Evil has karmic energy, right? And sensitives like
us are really vulnerable when Evil is present. And it
is, Bren. *Evil is here.*" She said it dramatically, pinning
Brenda with a steady stare, her face glowing in the
light of the four white candles that marked the
boundaries of the magic circle Judy had traced in pure
white sand on the green carpet of her bedroom floor.

Brenda had nervously watched Judy forming the circle, letting the sand trickle to the floor from her closed fist. She knew exactly how her own mother would react to sprinkling sand indoors. But Judy's mother had left her family years before. Sometimes, a couple times a year, Judy got a postcard from Mykonos or Barbados. The ex-Mrs. Fisher traveled a lot.

"Oh, come on," Brenda said, squirming uncomfortably. Her legs were starting to feel cramped as she sat cross-legged opposite Judy. *"Evil?"*

"Well, think about it. Some guy in a devil worship cult gets practically torn apart and all of a sudden people all over SC start going crazy and killing themselves in all kinds of bizarre ways. I mean, on a railroad track! Gross. Even little kids are being afflicted. And old people. So if that's not Evil, I don't know what is."

"I just don't like fooling around with this stuff. It makes me nervous."

"God, you are so dumb sometimes. This is for protection. It's *white* magic. It's the only way sensitives can defend themselves from psychic attack."

Brenda heaved a sigh that made the candle flames bend and shiver and sent shadows swooping around the room.

"I wish your dad were here," Brenda said without thinking. If she'd been thinking, she wouldn't have said it since it was exactly the wrong thing to say to Judy lately. Lately, Judy's father was never home much. He'd found a new girlfriend, one of his students, not much older than Judy herself. It made her sick, she had told Brenda. She thought her father, at 42, was practically prematurely senile. It was a midlife crisis. Even if he was better looking than most of the guys in high school, he was still too old for that dumb chasing around. It would ruin his health. He had bags under his eyes all the time now. Tonight,

like many other nights, he wouldn't be home. Maybe
she'd see him tomorrow. Maybe not.

Judy had to be tough. She was raising herself, and it
was one of the things Brenda had admired about her
when they first got to know each other. Judy was
going through a stage back then of wearing only black
with heavy black eye makeup. She'd stood out like a
sleek young raven, proud and isolated in a flock of
plump cooing pigeons.

"Anyway," Brenda went on, "I don't really think
I'm sensitive."

"Of course you're sensitive. *I'm* sensitive and I
ought to know. Now are you going to act intelligently
or what? Because if you don't do this you're just
asking for trouble, that's all."

"Oh, hell." And Brenda gave in, like she always
did. "Okay, let's just do it and stop arguing about it."

"Finally," Judy said and picked up the small jar of
ointment she'd bought at Paul Vronski's herb and
incense store. She thought Paul Vronski was totally
gorgeous. Brenda said she did, too, even though she
didn't really. She always liked blond guys with
muscles, but Judy thought they all looked brainless
and insensitive. So Brenda kept quiet.

They both agreed that Paul Vronski's fragile, dull
wife was a total disappointment.

Judy gingerly sniffed the contents of the jar of
cream. "Fresh," she pronounced, nodding weightily
as a connoisseur. "Just beneficial, natural herbal oils.
Now . . ." She dipped the tip of her index finger into
the small white jar, just touching the surface of the
greasy ointment, then handed the jar to Brenda. "Just
get some on your finger," she directed, "then we
have to anoint our foreheads."

Brenda took the jar, holding it with the tips of her
fingers, the way she'd hold a plastic spider. She kept
it inches away from her face and sniffed cautiously at
it, nostrils curling delicately away from the pungent

odor. She touched it lightly, just enough to pick up a light film on the tip of one finger.

Judy was frowning at her, impatient to get started. *It's because she needs me.* The thought flickered briefly, dimly, across Brenda's mind. She'd figured that out, without allowing herself to recognize it too clearly, a long time ago. It was the first time anyone had ever needed her. And Judy didn't have anybody else.

She put the jar down, glistening fingertip held out before her like some foreign object, and nodded.

Judy reverently pressed the creases out of the tissue-thin printed paper that came with the ointment. Something for psychic protection she'd told the dumb college student who'd waited on her while Brenda hung around the doorway pretending to read the labels on different spices. They'd gone in twice hoping to see Paul Vronski, but he was never around lately. At least, Judy said, Paul must have mixed the ointment himself and written the protective verse. She thought his hands were absolutely enrapturing. She told Brenda that all the time.

"Okay," Judy said, "now repeat after me. *I anoint myself with the goodness of the earth.*" She read it dramatically and raised a delicately posed hand to her forehead to apply the scented balm.

Silence followed, and she scowled at Brenda. "Come on," she prompted, and Brenda self-consciously muttered the words and rubbed ointment on her forehead.

"I wrap myself in the protection of the universe."

"I wrap myself in the protection of the universe."

Judy was aiming at keeping her voice deep and mysterious, Brenda knew. They'd been practicing it. Her voice sounded dumb, Brenda thought, kind of a drone.

"I trust in its peace and harmony."

"I trust in its peace and harmony."

"I ask the living spirit of the universe to keep me from all harm."

"I ask the living spirit of the universe to keep me from all harm."

That was better. Brenda was listening to herself now, half-detached and distant as someone talking in her sleep. In fact, it felt a little like that. She let her eyes close. Calm. So calm.

"Safeguard me."

"Safeguard me."

She felt herself drift into the darkness within, sinking into a well that had no limits, no bounds. Quiet.

"I am surrounded and enfolded by the Gift of Protection."

"I am surrounded and enfolded by the Gift of Protection."

Blackness covered her like a stone.

"I am joyous, full of life and grateful for this Gift."

"I am joyous, full of life and grateful for this Gift."

Judy rested the backs of her hands against her thighs, closed her eyes and concentrated on looking beatific in the steady gold glow of candlelight. After a couple minutes she jumped to her feet and turned on the overhead light in her bedroom.

"Well, that's it," she said briskly to Brenda and bent over to blow out the candles. Brenda was still as carved rock. "Hey." Judy studied her face, brows wrinkling. "Okay, Bren, that's it."

Brenda's eyes opened slowly and she turned her face up to Judy like a sunflower, wide-eyed and wiped clean of thought.

"That's all there was to it, see? Nothing to make a fuss about. And now I'm starving. It's all this healthy joy, I'll bet, and there's a watermelon downstairs just waiting to get eaten."

Brenda got to her feet, uncurling like a night-blooming vine, and Judy watched her a minute curiously before she shrugged and turned and started for the kitchen. She trotted down the short flight of steps that connected her wing to the rest of the house.

It was a very contemporary house, designed by her father and a short blond architect who wore her hair cropped nearly to the scalp. Her father and the architect had had a brief affair that fizzled quickly. The house, though, blossomed during the passionate interlude. There was something Moorish about it, even though it had the clean, sparse line of the most minimalist designer. The doorways were spacious arches, and the house had shadowy depths within sunlit spaces. It had the feeling of courtyards and sun, the sense of intimate seraglios and private quarters hidden around corners.

Judy's wing included her bedroom, a study area and a lush bathroom with a skylight and sunken tub. Her father's wing was even more luxurious. He and his string of women might disappear to the other end of the house for an entire weekend at a stretch. His studio, included in his wing, had a small refrigerator so they didn't even have to come out for meals. The great room, solarium and kitchen, made up the center of the house and Judy headed straight for it without waiting for Brenda. Brenda had been there thousands of times and she could take care of herself.

Judy slid the large cutting board out of its slot under the counter and set it in place over the sink. She pulled the largest knife in the set from a wooden butcher block and laid it on the cutting board. When she was wrestling the watermelon out of the refrigerator, pushing containers of flavored yogurt, cans of tuna and corned beef out of her way, she heard Brenda come into the kitchen behind her.

"Hey, grab some paper plates, willya?"

When she turned, the watermelon cradled in her arms ungainly as a Great Dane puppy, she turned to face Brenda. Brenda had the knife, her fist closed tight around the handle, her face still curiously blank.

"Geez, Brenda. That is *not* funny." Judy dropped the heavy melon on the counter with a thud. "Then *you* cut the damn thing up and I'll get the paper plates."

She was turning back towards Brenda when the knife came down.

It was aimed at the space between her shoulder blades, but when she turned it only grazed the soft flesh of her upper arm.

Judy grabbed her arm, slick with blood, as she threw herself back, out of the way. She didn't get far. She slammed into the refrigerator, its surface a cold shock against the bare skin of her back in a summer halter top.

Brenda raised the knife again.

"NO!"

Judy slid away, across the face of the refrigerator, and grabbed its handle with fingers that were slick with blood. She yanked it open and hid behind it like a shield as Brenda brought the knife down crashing and clattering against jars of pickles and ketchup on the refrigerator door. Judy shoved it back, slamming it against Brenda's arm, knocking her off balance.

"Brenda!" she screamed, like she was screaming to her for help, and she spun away from the refrigerator, out of the corner she'd been backed into, circling wide around Brenda to run for the door.

But she didn't circle wide enough.

Off balance, Brenda could still swing out with the long knife and cut an arc through the air between them that caught Judy's halter as she ducked past leaving a trail that oozed bright drops of blood on her tan back.

Judy screamed again. *"Brenda-a-a!"* She ran, staggering, into the great room and knocked a slingback chair over in her path. She stopped and swung around at the center of the room, in time to see Brenda fall as heavily and awkwardly as a mechanical doll. She started up again slowly.

"Brenda?" Judy whimpered, taking a step backward.

Brenda started towards her, ponderous as a juggernaut.

Judy took another step backward, and another, retreating farther into the room without thinking, away from the door. Her eyes were fixed on Brenda. She looked so odd.

"Why are you doing this?"

The room was dim, the only light from track lighting scattered around the broad perimeter. Spot lights showered beams on the bold Fisher paintings on the high white walls. The rest of the room melted into shadow.

Judy walked back into the low couch. "What's the matter with you?" she shrieked, voice shrill and cracking, and she reached behind her to grab a throw pillow from the vast pile on the low couch. She threw it with all her might at Brenda.

The pillow hit her in the face, hard enough to make her head snap back. She blinked, but her expression stayed the same—heavy and still as death.

She kept coming.

Judy edged sideways and grabbed another pillow and held it with both hands, eying Brenda and sizing up the distance between them. When it was right, she hauled back and swung the pillow like a club at the knife and the hand that held it.

Brenda's arm swung wide with the force of the blow and Judy followed through by batting down at the arm, pushing Brenda off balance. In control, moving fast, Judy shoved the pillow into Brenda's face like a battering ram delivering a padded blow, driving her back. But the knife arm had swung full circle, down and around like a comic wind-up, and it circled down again as Judy stepped forward to add her weight to the pillow.

The knife swung up and flashed down, the point puncturing Judy's back. It pierced the skin, entered the muscle, but scraped against the bone of the shoulder blade. Judy screamed and twisted under it, dropping the pillow.

She slammed into the couch again and flopped over its back like a man falling overboard. She bounced across the seat and in one quick tumble rolled over the pillows to the floor as Brenda stretched the knife after her, only puncturing a seat cushion.

Judy scrabbled on her hands and knees towards the fireplace, towards a rack of cast iron fire tools.

Brenda climbed clumsily over the couch.

Grabbing too fast, Judy knocked over the stand of fireplace tools. She was sobbing for breath, snatching at the tangle of handles when Brenda stood over her and drove the knife down deep between her ribs.

Brenda pulled the knife free with a sick, sucking sound. She was raising it to strike again when Judy's hand grappling in the mess of tools closed on the handle of the poker.

Judy pushed back up to her knees, swinging the poker around in front of her and letting the momentum of the swing turn her towards Brenda. As she swung she shifted and leaned and concentrated the force of the wild blow, aiming in the last few instants for the arm that carried the knife poised above her.

She connected.

The poker caught Brenda's arm with a heavy, glancing blow at the elbow, enough to make her arm go suddenly limp.

But not enough to make her drop the knife.

Brenda took a step back, eyes traveling to her own arm, looking almost puzzled and betrayed.

Judy leaned against the fireplace, blinking hard to get sweat and a blinding gray mist out of her eyes. She pushed the poker point into the taupe rug and used the poker to struggle to her feet.

Brenda's limp arm twitched. She took a step toward Judy.

Judy's right arm, the arm that had been cut, was weak and wet with blood, and she'd taken the knife between the ribs on her right side. She lifted the poker, feeble and slow as Brenda, as though they were both giants out of a fairy tale in a battle that spanned centuries. She held the poker in her left hand, awkwardly, and swatted with it towards Brenda. She hit her in the elbow again.

Brenda dropped the knife.

There was no sound but Judy's wet, labored breathing.

Brenda folded at the waist, bending towards the knife, reaching for it with her left hand when Judy hit the back of her head with the poker.

It was a weak blow that thumped and slid off Brenda's thick hair. It was just enough to knock her to one knee, wobbling until she steadied herself.

Then she picked up the knife.

Judy stood away from the fireplace, grasped the poker handle with both hands and raised it high and steady over Brenda's bent head.

When Brenda began to bring her head up, face all white and blank, and to bring the knife up, Judy drove the poker down as hard as she could and the sound it made on Brenda's skull was a sharp crack.

Judy crumpled and fell, sliding against the wall of the fireplace, as Brenda fell face forward on the rug.

A bold swath of blood smeared the fireplace's white stone.

Sam went to bed early, but Kate was sitting up, alone in the quiet living room, wading through *Anna Karenina*. Once upon a time Tolstoi had been her favorite author, but now she had trouble keeping her attention engaged. She was determined, though, to finish the book if it was the last thing she ever did.

Her eyes kept wandering to the pieces of brown cardboard, the sides torn from boxes, that she and Sam had fitted onto the broken windows. It made her feel transient, like an Okie, she thought, or a ghetto dweller. Her landlord would be furious. He was already angry about the front door. Probably the only reason old Harold hadn't blown a gasket was that he was making an effort to be considerate—because of Ted. Not that Harold had liked Ted. Or liked her. It would just be the thing to do.

She remembered that when Ted had moved in the sanctimonious old bastard had raised the rent $50 a month. Would he lower it now? Not likely.

Kate started to reread the page she'd been reading for a second time. By the time she got halfway down it, she quit. She clapped the book shut with a sigh and dropped it onto the couch beside her, leaned her head back, eyes closed, and then had to concentrate on not crying.

"Damn." She rubbed at her eyes with her fists, jumped to her feet and headed up the stairs.

From the hallway outside Sam's bedroom, Kate could hear the muffled cries and thrashing that meant a nightmare was in progress. She hesitated, listening for only a minute, before opening the door to look in, but the nightmare seemed to be over. Sam was sprawled on her stomach, arms and legs tangled in the sheet, sticking out at odd angles.

Kate closed the door quietly and went to her own room to find the bed entirely unmade as she'd left it that morning, sheets off to air the mattress. Tired, she briefly considered sleeping on the bare mattress and rejected the idea—too much like the cardboard in the windows downstairs, too much like really letting go and giving up. She had to be careful of letting her life slide into some slipshod disrepair and become a dingy mess outside the sunny structure of life as it should be.

"Jesus Christ," she finally muttered to herself, "just shut up and make the damn bed."

The linen closet was just outside the bedroom door

between her room and the bathroom. Kate crossed to the head of the stairs to flip on the hall light, swung around, and pulled open the narrow door. And there was Ted jammed into the bottom of the closet.

She just stood there looking at the obscene thing crushed and folded into the bottom of her closet. Ted! One bent leg suddenly flopped lazily towards her, and she gawked at it while gravity settled it down and moved his body oh so slowly towards her.

He was wearing his jeans and a work shirt rumpled and smudged with dirt. He was wearing his work boots. Only his chest was torn and wet with dark blood, and the boots stuck out of his chest, and his hands groped, too, from the glistening cavity.

She looked at his face, his head propped at an awkward angle in the dark corner of the closet, and his dull eyes barely caught the light, like a fish in a butcher's case. And a sheet on the shelf above him twitched and rustled forward and Kate looked at him and looked at it and took a step back.

"K-k-k-k-k . . ." It came from inside the closet, she thought, but she couldn't see Ted now because the sheet had slithered out and another followed it and they hung now, suspended, gently waving in the air in front of her like two silly Halloween spooks.

"K-k-k-k-k-ka . . ."

She couldn't breathe, couldn't scream, couldn't blink her dry eyes, and couldn't take her eyes off the sheets, the two white spooks, fanning the air before her.

"K-k-k-katie . . ." It was from the closet, from the thing in there, but not Ted. It didn't sound like Ted.

The sheets shuddered and swept towards her like the wings of enormous bats. One of them brushed her bare arm and she stepped back.

And they moved and glided towards her. And she stepped back again.

"*Leave her alone!*" It was Sam. Chunky, rumpled,

near-sighted, she came charging out of her bedroom to the rescue like the cavalry over the hill. "Stop it!" Sam flailed her fists at the sheets that fluttered and swooped closer to Kate. She tangled in them, grabbed and tugged. "No!"

Kate was at the head of the stairs now and she tried to move towards Sam, but one of the sheets dived towards her and wrapped her in a swift cotton embrace, and Kate screamed and in a panic tried to throw it off her. She lost her balance and fell, rolling, wrapped in the sheet, down the long stairs, striking the bannister and the walls, thudding and cracking against the wooden steps.

When the phone rang at Nora's she'd fallen asleep on the couch with a magazine open on her chest and the television on. The bell woke her with a sick twist of tension in her stomach, and she lurched off the couch to stand next to the phone and watch it ring twice more before she gently lifted the receiver from its cradle.

"Hello," she said, very quietly, very calm.

"Nora, dear, did I wake you?"

It was Irene Ellicott, Nora realized, and she lied politely, "Oh, no. No, I was up."

"You were asleep," Irene contradicted her firmly, "but it can't be helped. I think Sam is in some danger. Sam, and someone close to her."

"Danger?" The old man. The child singing in Sam's bedroom. She should have told them, warned them, but when the police took away Alex Thomas she thought they'd be safe, that somehow Alex had caused it all.

"Yes. A few minutes ago I got a very strong feeling that Sam was frightened and angry. There was a big burst of energy and now nothing. Will you call them?"

Nora agreed and told Irene she'd call her back and

let her know what, if anything, was happening. Then she dialed Kate's number.

It was answered after five rings by a crisp man's voice, totally unfamiliar to Nora, and she repeated Kate's number, making sure she'd called the right place. She had.

"Is Kate there?"

"I'm afraid Mrs. Hall has had an accident. She and her daughter just left in the ambulance."

"Sam? Is Sam all right?"

"She's fine. We just didn't want to leave her alone here."

Nora was talking to an EMT from the fire department, she found out. Both their van and the ambulance had answered the emergency call. Kate had fallen downstairs, the EMT said. She was unconscious. They'd be able to tell more at the hospital after she'd been examined and x-rayed. Nora thanked him, hung up and called Irene.

"I'm going to the hospital," she told Irene. "I'll bring Sam home with me."

"Nora, please be careful. I think things are just beginning."

At 2:00 a.m. Nora and Sam were sitting together, silent, in the otherwise deserted emergency room. Sam was still in her pajamas with her pink chenille robe knotted tightly around her, barefoot, hair rumpled and pushed behind her ears, glasses perched on her nose. It seemed like hours passed before the young doctor on duty came out with the news. Kate had a severe concussion, two broken ribs and a broken arm. Her condition was satisfactory, but she'd be in the hospital for at least three days, probably more.

"Can we see her?" Nora asked, and Sam, at her elbow, added a solemn stare.

The doctor shook his head. "Not tonight. Come

back tomorrow morning. Or *this* morning, I guess I
should say."

"Everything's going to be all right," Nora told Sam
when the doctor left them. She hoped it was true.

At Kate's house two crumpled white sheets rustled
and shivered. The one that lay at the bottom of the
staircase slithered and flowed up the stairs to the
open linen closet. In the bottom of the closet a small
white spider crawled over Ted Kellogg's cheek.

"Yes?" he answered the dark, his voice dry as
fallen leaves. "Yes?"

Alex tensed and strained against the restraints that
held him to the bed. "Yes?" His back arched away
from the cool sheet damp with his sweat.

"Master?" He strained in the dark. "I am yours."
He listened, waiting for release, waiting to be taken.
"I am yours."

On another floor in the hospital Carole Salant's lips
opened with a soft, wet noise. She moaned, low in her
throat, and ground her buttocks into the firm hospital
mattress. Her white hands, hot and moist, closed
around the metal guardrails tightening with every
grind of her hips.

In the next bed the girl with the artificial chin
opened wide eyes in the dark, wishing furiously that
it were the next day so she could go home.

Carole Salant moaned again. "*Oh, yessss,*" she
hissed.

The girl in the next bed squeezed her eyes shut.

Franny Vronski was locked in the bathroom of their
apartment, curled into a tight ball, arms protectively
wrapped around her head. She was jammed into the
tight cool space between the toilet bowl and the wall.

Cybele was awake that night, too. She was

frightened and angry that she was frightened. Angry because Mommy had gotten so funny in the last few days. She wouldn't pay any attention to her at all. She wasn't like Mommy any more. Everything was all wrong.

In the bathroom Franny stared without blinking at a hairline crack in the pink tile. Cybele cradled her big violet poodle Georgette close, then began punching her steadily, methodically, in the stomach.

Randy Paulson sat up quietly smoking a joint in his living room. His wife was asleep and he couldn't remember the last time he'd said more than "good morning" or "good night" to her as they rose and went to bed on their separate schedules. He'd have to do something about it soon, he thought, but right then he couldn't think much beyond getting relaxed enough to sleep so that he could get up early the next day and start again with the endless dissection of the murdered and suicides.

He was looking for reasons—something, anything that made sense out of the stream of bodies rolling in, like brain tumors or some obscure poison that affected the judgement. To find sense in the senseless, Randy Paulson rose to the challenge like a fish to bait.

By the time he got through medical school and his residency in family practice, Randy had thought all he wanted was to be a country doc, getting jars of preserves from his grateful patients and coming to know all of them and their lives. At sunset he could settle back on the front porch and watch the sky change colors. He and Laura could eat good natural foods, raise a garden, have dogs, and get in touch with the universe and all the homely old virtues of small town life.

But Randy started to doubt his own motives when all these mad deaths began. He was appalled by the waste of life and the seeming insanity. But he was also

fascinated. The search for clues seized his attention
like no teenage acne or case of mumps ever could. He
was exhilarated by the sense of urgency, the mystery,
the need to test and enlarge his resources and
knowledge.

He'd been frustrated, he'd been horrified, but he'd
also been more alive and excited in the last week than
he had been in his two years in Stony Cliffs. Things
had been easy for Randy all through college and he
aced courses without even trying. But medical school
was different. For the first time in his life he had to
work for grades. And his residency was even harder,
filled with stress. It had scared him and finally shaken
his confidence in himself. Things had always been so
easy for him. Now what if he couldn't really make it?

Was that why he'd taken the easy way out and
faded into a small-town, small-time life? He took
another drag on the joint. Maybe he was ready for
something more. If he could just get a handle on these
cases, just find the pattern.

He was looking forward to examining Alex Thomas
in the morning.

Irene Ellicott was playing solitaire with the *Magic
Flute* playing quietly in her mauve living room. She
was sitting at her rosewood desk facing out into the
room and taking small sips of Drambuie. Irene
counted out three cards and turned up the Queen of
Hearts with a small sound of satisfaction.

The King of Spades was open and waiting.

Nora didn't bother to stop at Kate and Sam's on her
way home. Sam was just going to bed when they got
back to her place, and they could come by Sam's
home in the morning. Sam could borrow something to
wear, Nora told her, and Sam didn't object. In truth,
neither of them wanted to go back to Kate's house
alone in the middle of the night. They talked only a

little in the car, both of them tired and numbed by the terrible strangeness of everything that seemed to be happening at once.

For the second time Sam shared Nora's bed instead of bedding down on the couch. She wouldn't say so, but Sam was afraid to be alone and Nora didn't suggest other arrangements. They both drifted off into deep, uneasy sleep. It was only Nora who woke up later.

In the bushes on the riverbank Florence Gleason's body stirred and trembled, her movements softly rustling the leaves and slender branches of the weedy shrub she rested in. The fingers of one fist fiercely clutched Florence's hair, and the head in her lap leaned, as though weary, against the soft fleshy pouch of her stomach. One foot, the foot with the bunion Dr. Paulson had cut for her last spring, stirred gently.

23

Sam thrashed and plunged in her sleep like a horse trapped in its stall with the barn on fire. Her nightmarish bucking woke Nora with a start, but before Nora could wake Sam to soothe or offer comfort, the girl subsided and lay still, breathing with the heavy sound of exhaustion.

Nora, though, was wide awake.

It was that limbo before dawn when dim gray light suffuses the sky and seems to glow from the ground, trees, houses, and the air itself. Birds were offering peeps and calls of encouragement to each other to get on with it. An early morning breeze lifted and flapped the shades over open windows while the room brightened and dimmed to the fitful gusts.

Nora slipped quietly out of bed to go to the bathroom. She didn't bother to put her glasses on, so that coming out of the bathroom, the figure she saw in the half-lit hallway seemed at first a fuzzy illusion.

"Simon?" Her voice came out high and disbelieving. He *was* alive. Wasn't he?

She took another step towards him, squinting, feeling vulnerable and self-conscious in her T-shirt and underpants. How did he get in? He was standing outside her bedroom door, his back turned to her,

looking in. Nora got closer, a yard away, a little more
than arm's distance.

"Simon? What's going on?"

And he turned towards her. Eyes wide, he seemed
to be looking through her to some other place. He
looked blind, all wrong. And he was grinning.

Simon used to smile, but he never grinned, not this
teeth-bared forced look. He looked insane, she
thought. He looked like a stranger.

"Simon?" Nora took a step back.

His grin became broader, and Nora had to squint
hard to see if what she suddenly thought she saw was
really there—a fine dark line of red. She stared hard at
it, so hard that when he took a step closer it didn't
register with her. The line of red seemed to crawl up
from his upper lip. His lip split, like a flower opening
in time lapse photography. And the split spread. A
line, then a fissure split his nose, shot up his forehead
and disappeared into his dark, thinning hair.

Nora could only stand rooted, horrified, staring at
flesh that split and curled back, peeling away from
the glistening pink underlayer. The skinned flesh and
hair slithered from the skull and fell to his shoulders
with the soft settling of a hood thrown back. Bared
muscles and blood vessels comprised the face beneath
the face like an illustration in an anatomy book. He
grinned at her still, his brown eyes glowing from the
raw meat of his face.

He shuffled half a step closer and the naked lips
grinned at her.

"You're next, Nora," Simon said.

And Nora swung at him, a full roundhouse punch
aimed at the gleaming red jaw. It struck the air where
the skull should have been and kept going, slicing
through empty space. The punch threw her off
balance, meeting no resistance, but she righted
herself quickly, feisty as a street fighter, both fists
doubled and ready, glaring and squinting around her

in the half-light, blood drumming in her ears.

There was nothing.

"I appreciate your coming down so early," Finnerty told Irene and Peter Ellicott. They were sitting across the scarred wooden desk from him.

"I keep an early schedule myself," Dr. Ellicott said.

Irene smiled without comment. She'd slept a few restless hours on the living room couch and felt as though a layer of fog surrounded her. Her head throbbed dully, just this side of pain. She felt she had to concentrate very hard to stay alert in the battered, drab office.

"The body of one of the recent suicides disappeared from the morgue yesterday," Finnerty began without preliminaries. "Florence Gleason."

Finnerty was watching Irene Ellicott as he said it, but she looked only politely blank.

Dr. Ellicott made a small "tsking" sound.

"We've uncovered some evidence that indicates the body was probably taken from the morgue by Alex Thomas."

Dr. Ellicott raised his eyebrows in an unspoken question."

"Fingerprints," Finnerty said. "Trace of blood and some hairs identified as Gleanson's found in Thomas's car."

"Hmm." Dr. Ellicott seemed to accept Finnerty's evidence and gave the sheriff a quick nod to continue.

"Thomas was arrested yesterday in the act of breaking into the house formerly occupied by Ted Kellogg. Kellogg's girlfriend and her daughter are still living there, but they weren't home at the time of the break-in. They came in just after Thomas was arrested. Unfortunately, we can't get any information from him. The doctor tells me he's in a catatonic state and there's no telling when, or if, he'll come out of it."

Finnerty leaned back in his creaking chair, folded

his fingers over his gut, and studied Dr. Ellicott through heavy lidded eyes. The light, small-boned professor had his gray head cocked like a robin's at a worm hole. He looked back at the sheriff with bright, curious eyes, but left it to Finnerty to bridge the next step.

"What I want from you, I guess, Dr. Ellicott, is some information. Or maybe just your opinions. I want to know if Thomas's actions square up with anything you know about the practice of witchcraft or devil worship."

Dr. Ellicott shook his head as though a promising pupil had just said two and two equals five. "Sheriff," he said patiently, and Irene settled back in her chair, only half-listening. She knew the tone of voice and what would come next.

"Witchcraft has gained, over the years, an ill-deserved reputation largely promulgated by those who felt the ancient religion a threat to their own narrow beliefs. And by the ignorant who are taught to fear anything outside their own realm of experience." Peter Ellicott settled comfortably back into the leather chair—like Alastair Cooke, Irene thought partly fond and partly with irritation. For heaven's sake, she wanted to say, get on with it.

"What we call witchcraft," Peter continued, "is perhaps the oldest religion surviving today, modified somewhat by time and cultural influences but nevertheless a direct descendant of prehistoric worship. It is based upon a very primitive belief system, founded in celebration of fertility personified in male and female figures. It has to do with the harmony of nature, the changing of the seasons, with man's potential oneness with the universe and his ability to effect change through magic. Generally, sympathetic magic, also known as imitative magic involves the principle—"

"Peter," Irene cut him off, "the sheriff does not

want a complete history of the misunderstood practice of witchcraft. He wants to know what's going to happen next.''

Dr. Ellicott turned to his sister with a blandly innocent face, gave a little shrug and turned back to Finnerty.

''Forgive me, Sheriff. Perhaps I do tend to get carried away by the subject, but it is distressing how little of the true practice of the Old Religion is understood. One would like to blame Hollywood, but long before that, notably in the Middle Ages—the Dark Ages—witchcraft began to gain a warped, quite inaccurate image.'' Irene rustled impatiently in her chair and, without looking at her, Peter held an open palm in her direction. ''Don't worry, I'm not about to take off on another lecture. I'm simply trying to make the point that the real practice of witchcraft and the innovations and perversions of various groups and individuals may have very little in common. What Alex Thomas may be practicing—though he should know better than to identify it as true magic or witchcraft—may have nothing whatever to do with the Old Religion. In short, Sheriff, Alex may have been up to almost anything.''

Finnerty grunted and rocked back in his chair. Disappointment with Peter's answer didn't show in his face, but Irene read it in his sudden silence. The sound of his breath as he sucked in a bushel of air through dilating nostrils jarred her back to attention. She felt like she'd been drifting. Falling asleep? Like an old woman, she berated herself. It was unusual and a little frightening. She tried forcing herself to focus on the situation. Alex Thomas stole Florence Gleason's body? She turned the words over in her mind, but they didn't mean much to her.

''However,'' Peter said, abruptly breaking the silence, ''I am quite familiar with several of the distorted systems purportedly based on the Old Way. I

may be able to speculate on some of the possible
motivations. And I do have a theory about mass
suicides.''

Irene suppressed a sigh. Hopefully Peter would re-
strain himself on the subject of his theory. More
worldly than her brother, Irene knew he risked
immediate dismissal as a loony by most people. Irene
judged Finnerty as an open listener, but a hardheaded
man who would first trust what was known—physical
evidence and proven fact.

Finnerty might privately consider Peter's theories,
Irene thought, but in meeting his duties as sheriff he
would opt for the surest pathways. She had a sudden
image of Finnerty as an Old Testament shepherd
leading his flock and the picture made her smile.

''The theory's a lulu,'' she said aloud. ''Let's talk
facts first. Starting with Ted Kellogg's death. Sheriff?''

She stared hard at Finnerty, feeling as though he
were far away, at the end of a long tunnel.

''How, precisely, was Mr. Kellogg killed?'' Peter
asked.

Irene heard him with muzzy fondness. Peter always
had loved facts. He loved the careful process of
research and making a chain of connections, link by
cautious link. What is wrong with me? she wondered.
I can barely stay awake.

Finnerty leaned forward in his painfully creaking
chair.

''Eviscerated,''   he   pronounced   succinctly.
''Weapon unknown. The body was mutilated after
death.''

''Ah. In what way?''

Finnerty flipped open a file folder and frowned
down at its contents.

''I have a photo of the body taken on the site of dis-
covery. it's pretty gruesome.''

''It would help if I could see it, Sheriff.''

Finnerty picked the photo up and silently held it out
towards the professor.

Peter reached for it and Irene watched as shock passed briefly over his face, then turned to careful scrutiny. Good old Peter, she thought, always a trooper. The throbbing in her head had become a not unpleasant buzzing. She watched Finnerty watching Peter, turning to look at her brother when interest and hope spread over the sheriff's face. Peter was nodding, looking like a satisfied magician.

"Tell me," he said, "was the victim's tongue intact?"

Finnerty's eyebrows rose and he leaned forward, forearms propped on the desk. "Cut out. No trace of it."

Peter nodded again.

"The disobedient servant," Peter said. He took a last look at the photo and handed it back.

Finnerty studied it, searching for the clues that Peter had spotted.

"You see? Hands, feet, tongue . . . genitals. A sexual act, probably, that Kellogg failed to perform. Heart? Was his heart in place?"

"Disturbed," Finnerty told him. "Caught and stopped in his chest." The sheriff was studying the photo, comprehension lighting his face. "I didn't see it."

"Hands and feet that wouldn't obey," Peter said. "Heart that was false."

Kellogg failed but I won't. Kellogg failed but I won't. Irene heard the words echo through the fog that moved closer to her. *Someone said that to me. To me? To Nora.*

"Kellogg failed but I won't," she said aloud, dreamily.

"What?" Finnerty asked sharply, and Peter turned to look at her.

"Irene?"

"Yes, dear?" she smiled at him gently, a little impatient at being disturbed.

"You said, 'Kellogg failed but I won't,'" Peter

prompted her.

"That's right. Nora said that. I mean, Nora told me that Alex said it."

"Irene, are you all right? Would you like a glass of water?"

"Don't be silly," Irene said, "I'm not thirsty." She must try to concentrate, but she only wanted to go somewhere quiet, to get away by herself. "It's all right," she told them. "I'm only a little tired."

"We'll be leaving soon. I must get to the office. I'll drop you off at home and you can take a nap."

She smiled at him. Concentrate, she scolded herself.

"Miss Ellicott," Finnerty said, "you say Nora Durant told you that Alex Thomas said it? 'Kellogg failed but I won't.' "

"Yes."

"Do you know what it is that Kellogg failed to do?"

"No. But something . . . I think it's the girl. Sample. Something to do with Sample." A warning of danger clamored somewhere buried in the thick haze that muffled her thinking.

Peter was nodding enthusiastically. "She would be the right age. Thirteen or so."

"Twelve."

"Well, they start earlier these days. Puberty," he explained to Finnerty. "A young girl, virginal, about to enter womanhood, has enormous power. We see it in poltergeists, you know. Many belief systems honor, fear or try to harness the power, according to their individual beliefs. Kellogg may have been appointed some task relating to Sample and failed to carry it out. Alex Thomas would then be responsible."

"What sort of task?"

"Well, judging by Kellogg's punishment, I'd say he was to have sexual intercourse with the girl. Then probably sacrifice her."

Nora had been debating with herself how much to

tell Sam about her encounter with the Simon-thing.

All along she'd been treating Sam like a child, assuming that keeping things from her was protecting her. But perhaps Irene was right. Sam's best protection might lie in knowing exactly what threatened her. It was way overdue to talk about it.

They were up and dressed, sitting down to breakfast when Nora asked Sam to tell her what had happened the night before. Sam had been too upset and exhausted to talk about it when they left the hospital.

"She fell down the stairs," Sam answered, head suddenly bent over her plate. She started pushing a forkful of scrambled eggs around and around.

"Sam, nothing you say is going to sound too weird or unbelievable. Not to me. Do you know why I called last night?"

Sam blinked up at her and shook her head. "It was real late."

"Exactly," Nora nodded. "Not a time I'd usually call. But Irene Ellicott called me, woke me up and told me she thought you might be in trouble."

"Geez." Sam was impressed, but something was still bothering her. She slumped back in her chair and started culling small piles of egg into a neat pattern.

Nora watched her, waiting for more, but nothing came.

"She was right, I guess, huh?"

Sam jabbed a sausage. "It's my fault."

"What is?"

"That Mom got hurt. It's after me, but Mom's in the way so it's going to get her. It's all my fault."

Nora leaned across the kitchen table and grasped Sam's wrist, willing the girl to meet her eyes. "Listen," she said slowly, trying to drive it home, *"it is not your fault.* You didn't ask for any of this. You didn't cause it. What's causing it is that sick thing out there. The enemy."

It was one of the names of Satan, Nora remembered. The Enemy. But if Irene was right, it

wasn't some abstract evil they had to deal with—it
was Victor Sears.

Briefly, she filled Sam in on her conversation with
Irene Ellicott, including Irene's trance and the child's
voice that spoke through her lips. She told her, too,
about seeing the old man on the stairs in Sam's house
and the voice of the child singing. They were Victor's
puppets, if Irene was right. And Nora certainly had no
other explanation for any of it.

Sam had listened to it all calmly and steadily. "That
Victor *was* creepy," she said and thoughtfully bit the
point off a slice of toast.

"Creepy?"

Sam shrugged. "I don't know. Sometimes he just
looked at me, you know, like he was watching. Like I
was doing something real interesting, even if I was
just sitting there. I think he wanted to *get* me."

"Get you?"

"You know, do it." Sam piled some strawberry jelly
on her toast and took a big bite.

Nora stared at her, flabbergasted and a little embarrassed. "Have sex?"

Mouth full, Sam nodded.

"Oh, but, Sam . . ." She was just a little girl, Nora
thought, but an echo of what Michael had told her
made her stomach clench. Victor liked little girls.

"Well," Sam said reading Nora's look, "Cheryl
Peterson did it and she's only in eighth grade."

They want to grow up so fast, Nora thought and
shook her head.

"Not with Victor?" Surely not.

"No," Sam said it scornfully. "With Brad Stevens.
He's real cute. He'll be in high school this year."

"Oh," Nora said faintly.

Sam slathered more jelly on a second piece of toast.
"He wanted me to sit on his lap once. Victor."

"Did you?"

"Gross! No, I'd never do that. Besides, Ted got real

mad and told me to go outside and play." Sam grimaced and shook her head. "Adults are hopeless."

I suppose we are, Nora thought. But good for Ted. "And how did Victor react?"

Sam shrugged. "He just smiled." She did an imitation of him, a small self-satisfied cat smile, full of secrets.

Nora took a bite of her own cold toast, stalling now, wondering what made Victor tick. It didn't make sense to her, any of it. Was Victor trying to get revenge on a little girl who refused to sit on his lap? That seemed insane. She couldn't understand the hatred he must feel, not just for Sam, but for anything human. He thought the world rejected him and now he was getting even. Pure malice.

"We can fight back," Nora said aloud. She gave Sam a brief, edited outline of her encounter with the Simon-thing. "I just got furious, and when I refused to be frightened it disappeared. I don't know if that will ever work again, but it's a good thing to remember."

Sam nodded seriously. "The best defense is a good offense. So, do you think we ought to go looking for Victor?" Her words were brave, but her little face was pale, eyes wide.

"Either we go looking for him, or we wait for him to come after us again. I don't think it will be very long before he tries again."

24

Nora called Irene Ellicott to invite herself and Sam over. They'd decided Irene was the best hope they had—the one person who wouldn't think they were crazy. But the phone call left Nora feeling uneasy, and now, ringing Irene's doorbell for the third time half an hour later, Nora was afraid.

On the phone Irene had sounded distracted and vague, as though every time she spoke she had to come back from some great distance, Nora thought. But when Nora asked her if she were all right, Irene had said she was only sleepy. She'd take a nap, Irene said, until Nora and Sam arrived.

It was hard to believe anything awful could happen on such a glorious day. The air had cleared after the sultry weather. It was hot, the sun high and bright in a deep blue sky, but the air was fresh and clean. On the drive over, Nora's spirits had lifted. She'd been feeling strong and confident, positive that they'd find a way to get rid of the shadows that threatened them. Now she wasn't so sure.

A gust of wind with a cool undertone of fall made the deep plum leaves of a Japanese maple in Irene's front yard shake and toss. In the full-blown roses on the trellis next to the front door, fat bumblebees

hovered and bumped down onto the yellow center of
the flowers, grubbing in the pollen. The hum of the
bees was the only sound until Nora pressed the doorbell for the fourth time. They stood on the front porch
listening to the bell chime inside the quiet house.

Sam shifted from one foot to the other.
''Something's wrong.''

Nora looked down at her standing so stoically, eyes
fixed on the brass knocker on Irene's door. She had a
fleeting urge to lie to the girl, say something reassuring
that she herself didn't believe, but Sam deserved
more than that.

Nora tried the brass doorknob, polished and gleaming like the deep shine of the walnut door. It turned
with well-oiled precision, and she opened it about a
foot and, with a quick look at Sam, leaned in.

''Hello?'' The house swallowed her voice, the word
like a penny dropping on velvet.

''Irene?'' She tried it louder. Nothing.

Nora stepped back, withdrawing from the house to
come back to the daylight and Sam on the porch. ''I
don't like this,'' she told her and the feeling now was
much more than that. Nora just wanted to run, and
she might have if Sam hadn't been there staring at her
so solemnly, trusting her to be strong.

''It might be that Irene just fell asleep and doesn't
hear us. Or she might be in some kind of trouble. I'm
going to go in and look around and I want you to stay
here, okay?''

''But I might be able to—''

''Sam, please just stay here.''

Sam opened her mouth to protest, paused and
snapped it shut. She nodded.

''Be careful.''

''You betcha,'' Nora told her, and she stepped into
the rosy foyer.

It was suddenly another world cut off from the
bright colors, light and sound of outdoors. It was like

being underwater, Nora thought, hushed and muted. No, it was like being inside a nautilus shell and dreaming about the sea. Sunlight dappled the empty living room and she moved towards it.

"Irene?"

Nora's voice jarred the stillness and she tensed, listening for a response.

There was a rustling, she thought, from back towards the dining room. The screened porch? She walked back to the foyer, crossed into the dining room and skirted the massive rosewood table to the French doors that opened to the porch.

Irene Ellicott was there. And she wasn't alone.

Irene sat straight and prim on the wicker love seat, ankles neatly crossed, hands folded and resting quietly on her lap. The other sat next to her echoing her posture and position. It was a woman's body— naked, sagging and headless.

Her decapitated head was carefully propped on her naked thighs, shown off like a prized pocketbook. The lips of the head writhed as if to speak, but the voice came from Irene, yet it was not Irene's voice.

"Nora," she said, and the voice had a soft country twang, "we've been waiting for you."

Irene and the pale corpse stood up, moving together in smooth synchronization, turning towards her in tandem like a pair of figure skaters. The corpse held her head with one hand, her fingers twined in the faded hair. The head rested between her white, pendulous breasts, its filmy eyes fixed on Nora. Irene's curled hand echoed the gesture, clutching only air in front of her deep blue silk blouse.

"Oh, my God," Nora breathed. She wanted to run, but her legs felt suddenly boneless, ready to waver and go out of control.

She took a step back, a small one, but it filled her with hope and struck back at the panic that fogged her thoughts. She could still get away, but she couldn't leave Irene with this obscene thing.

"Irene!" Two yards away, Irene and the head stared calmly at her.

"Irene!" No glimmer of recognition or response illuminated Irene's face.

"Did you bring the girl?" The head's lips moved but Irene spoke the words. In perfect step the two of them moved toward Nora.

And Nora edged away from them, afraid to turn her back. She felt behind her for the edge of the table.

"No."

Irene clucked her tongue. "Naughty," she scolded, "I can feel her. SAMPLE! COME HERE!"

"No!" Nora spun around shouting towards the front door. "RUN!"

"Nora?" Sam's voice drifted back high and plaintive. The front door creaked as the girl tentatively pushed it open.

"RUN SAM!" And two pairs of hands clapped over her mouth, jerking her backwards, off-balance.

Nora flailed, struck the table and caught the back of a chair as the hands pulled her down, back against the two women's bodies. As she fell and twisted to face the tabletop the head was there, lying on its side, eyes watching hers. She threw herself forward, out of their grip, and landed awkwardly to scrabble around and face them, panting hard.

"Sample!" Irene called—and Nora tackled her.

When Irene fell the corpse toppled, crumpled with the same sudden violence. Nora jumped clear of them. They were jumbled together, twitching, the rhythms and connections disturbed like robots with faulty wiring.

"Irene! Irene, come out of it! Come back!"

They were struggling to their feet finally, clumsy as bears, slow as cold honey, but just beginning to regain their easy synchronization. They swayed together and Nora tried again to break the link between them. She grabbed Irene's upper arm, jerked at it and yanked her upright.

But the corpse echoed the move, snapped upright and swung to face her, and together it and Irene reached for Nora's throat with one smooth lunge.

They missed by inches as Nora side-stepped and dodged back and the four outstretched arms tangled in midair. And Nora took one more twisting dodge back and hit the table, stumbling against a chair, as Irene and the thing moved in and trapped her there. The tangle of hands was on her throat now, all of them grappling for a hold and two were icy and two were chill and Nora couldn't breathe, barely think, only see Irene's face with that awful blankness.

"My head! Look out!"

They'd been forcing her back, arching her over the table, the woman and the corpse pressing against her when the pressure suddenly stopped.

"My head!" Irene said again.

The head was lying on the table, Nora remembered.

She threw herself backwards and ground her weight against the thing underneath her. Nora could feel the head under her left shoulder. She could feel the cheekbone under her shoulder blade and the wisps of hair against her neck.

When she flopped back she had grabbed the arms that held her and pulled Irene and the corpse with her to add their weight to hers. They fell easily, caught off guard by the sudden change.

Irene shrieked when Nora landed on the head. She lay on top of Nora, arms stretched towards her throat, her grip broken like the corpse's, and when she shrieked she grabbed the sides of her head with wide-spread fingers. Her fingers clamped onto her own head, while the fingers of the corpse reached for empty air.

She shrieked again, struggling to get off Nora, her mouth working, teeth bared and snapping until Nora felt teeth close on the flesh of her back.

Horror shot through her like an electrical charge and the shock drove her to her feet. She shoved Irene and the headless corpse apart like leaves blasted by a winter wind. She was up and on her feet and she had Irene caught by the elbow. Nora swung her free arm like a club and hit the corpse across the soft, cold flesh of her naked back. The corpse toppled. Holding Irene up, Nora struggled to get her away while she twitched and trembled. On the rosewood table the corpse flopped feebly as a fish drowning in air.

"Irene!" Nora shouted, shaking the fragile older woman, searching her face for any sign that the link was breaking.

She started backing away from the thing on the table, dragging Irene with her. They were almost to the foyer when Irene stopped and stiffened, pulling away from Nora's grip.

"Nora?" It was Irene's voice, uncertain but clearly her own.

"You're back!" Nora grabbed her by both thin shoulders. She wanted to hug her, but there wasn't time.

"Come on, we have to move. We have to get out of here."

"But what—"

"Later, I'll tell you later. First we have to get away from this place."

Still holding Irene's shoulders, Nora took a step backwards and Irene moved with her, but she seemed drained. She almost fell, and Nora had to move quickly to catch her.

Over Irene's shoulder she could see the body still squirming on the dining room table. She started backing towards the door, supporting Irene, with her eyes fixed on the thing. The struggling diminished and the white body started to slither off the polished wood. It fell with a heavy thud to the floor, and Irene tried to turn in Nora's grasp to look, but Nora held her facing forward.

"Don't."

From the dining room table the head stared after them.

Nora kept Irene moving out the front door and down the walk. She was weak and Nora walked beside her holding her up. Nora was relaxing a little as Irene seemed to gain some strength, pulling away to walk alone. But she suddenly gasped and tensed and clutched her left arm. Her blue eyes met Nora's with a wide-eyed look of surprise.

"Heart," she said and her legs suddenly folded.

Nora caught her, just barely breaking her fall. She lowered her to the sidewalk and stared, helpless, while Irene grimaced in pain. The quiet suburban neighborhood was deserted. There were no people on the stately porches and neatly trimmed lawns and no cars humming down the curving street.

There was no sign of Sam.

Without a conscious decision, Nora was on her feet and running back into the house. She ran for the telephone in the kitchen, past the still, white corpse, past the head with its eyes full of sorrow.

She called the ambulance and raced back to wait with Irene until it arrived. Irene was still conscious and the pain seemed to have subsided a little. Her breathing was ragged on the edges and though she tried, Nora wouldn't let her talk. Everything was fine, Nora told her. Everything was going to be all right. But all the time she kept wondering where Sam was. When the ambulance arrived minutes later and technicians swarmed over Irene, Nora hovered in the background just long enough to see her loaded into the ambulance. Then she bolted for her car, ignoring the shouts of one of the ambulance crew.

She didn't know where she was going. She only knew she had to find Sam who was out there alone somewhere and running scared.

Finnerty impatiently paced the hospital corridor
waiting for a report on the girl. Her father, David
Fisher, sat down the hall in the waiting room,
crouched on the edge of his chair over a container of
coffee growing cold in his hands.

Fisher had been unable to give them any information to help clear up what had happened the night
before in his home. He'd spent the night with a girlfriend and come home early that morning for a
change of clothes to find the bloody scene in his living
room.

Brenda Morrison was dead. Judy Fisher hung onto
life stubbornly and tenuously.

Finnerty had taken the call to the Fisher home and
the sequence of events seemed clear enough. In the
kitchen they found the cutting board, the watermelon
and the start of the trail of blood. The sheriff traced
their struggle by the overturned chair in the dining
room, the slashed couch, the scattered splashes of
blood, and the scene at the fireplace. Bobby Hunt had
searched the rest of the house and called Finnerty into
the girl's bedroom.

On her dark green carpet white sand traced a rough
circle and four candles marked its perimeter.
Grunting, Finnerty bent to pick up a sheet of paper
left lying on the floor. He had Bobby Hunt bag the
unmarked jar lying next to it. The sheriff handled the
paper gingerly, carefully holding it by one corner
pinched between thumb and forefinger.

When he read the printed ceremony of psychic
protection a wave of weary grief washed over him. *I
am joyous, full of life and grateful for this Gift,* he read.
And then anger swept the grief away.

Brenda Morrison's short life was over. By every
visible piece of evidence she'd tried to kill Judy
Fisher. But Finnerty saw her as a victim, just as much

a victim as the Fisher girl. Or the kid, Jerry Rhine. Or Calvin Russell and his wife. And Florence Gleason. And Charlie Luther. The list was growing and Finnerty felt helpless. He didn't know what or who the hell was causing the craziness and death in his town, but he planned to stop it. So far, nothing he knew or trusted had worked. He was ready to try anything. Chaos had come.

Now he and David Fisher waited to hear about Judy's condition. Finnerty wanted to know when he could question her. He wanted to understand what final shape madness took in the victims it claimed here in his county. He wanted to know what had happened to Brenda Morrison.

Dr. Bellamy, the surgeon on duty when Judy was admitted, appeared at the end of the corridor. He was still wearing his surgical greens, paper slippers over his shoes and mask hanging loose around his neck. He stopped near Finnerty, leaning against the floor desk across from the elevators. At the end of the hall David Fisher bounced to his feet; cold coffee sloshing over his hands. He trotted towards them, leaving a trail of coffee behind him.

Bellamy looked from Finnerty to Fisher, deep wrinkles of exhaustion around his eyes. He didn't bother with preliminaries.

"She's still in critical condition. She's lost a lot of blood. One lung was punctured, and there's some damage to the liver and internal bleeding. We've done what we could to repair the damage and she came through the operation okay. Now we just wait and see. She'll be in intensive care. No visitors for at least 24 hours. And I mean *none*." He looked pointedly from Finnerty to Fisher.

"But I'm her father!" Fisher protested.

"So you want what's best for her. Right now she needs rest." Bedside manner wasn't Bellamy's specialty, but he made an awkward effort to pat

Fisher's shoulder. "She's a strong girl."

Finnerty started to ask a question when the elevator
doors parted and a small cluster of people, a cart of
equipment and a gurney rolled out. The sheriff,
Fisher and Dr. Bellamy stepped aside to let them pass,
and Finnerty glanced down at the small figure draped
with a sheet on the gurney. It was Irene Ellicott.

She opened her eyes as they passed and they
widened when she saw the sheriff's startled face. One
elegant, blue-veined hand escaped from the covering
sheet and grabbed the oxygen mask that covered half
her face. She was pulling it off when a nurse caught
her hand, making soothing, efficient noises as the
gurney traveled quickly down the hall to intensive
care.

Finnerty's eyes followed the gurney, then he
swiveled and trotted after it, elbowing his bulk
between the orderlies that pushed it.

"I'm listening, Miss Ellicott," Finnerty said, leaning
over so she could see him.

The nurse glared at him. "Sheriff, you can't . . ."

But Irene grabbed the nurse's wrist in a fierce grip.
Under the transparent oxygen mask her lips carefully
shaped muffled words for the sheriff.

"The girl. You must find her. Sample is in great
danger."

Irene's eyes closed and her fingers slid from the
nurse's wrist as the group reached the doors of
intensive care. Finnerty stepped back, out of the way,
as they raced through and the doors swung back
towards him.

"I'll find her," he said while the doors settled back
in place. "I'll find her."

Nora drove in circles searching the area for Sam.
How far could she have gotten? Would she head for
home? For Nora's? For the hospital where her mother
was? For the anonymous safety of downtown SC

crowded with students? She might be headed anywhere. Nora's circles got wider and at every turn she
was sure she made the wrong choice. There was no
sign of Sam.

Sam ran blindly through the strange streets. She'd
lived in SC since she was little and now it was like a
different city. She was lost and nothing looked
familiar. She was afraid she was going to throw up.
Back on the porch, she remembered, she had
wanted to go inside but not to help Nora. She wanted
to go inside because something there called her—a
wordless voice inside her head, something that tugged
at her insides like music. She remembered standing
on the front porch swaying to some beat like a blind
singer and she staggered, running, when she thought
of it. She ran away when Nora called to her, too
scared to do anything else. It was because she wanted
to go in that she had to get away. She wanted to go in
more than anything and she ran.
She had heard her name everywhere. It was a
hissing call on the quiet sunny street. It rustled in the
trees, hummed in the sweet thorny rose vine that
climbed near the door and her ears were filled with it
until she heard it come from inside the house.
"SAMPLE!"
It wasn't Nora. She didn't know who it was. When
Nora said "Run" she was already poised to go. She
was a traitor. She deserted them. Now she was
running and she had to keep running. She didn't
deserve to be with people.
She ran with no direction, no idea of where she was
going or even why. She just had to move. She
stumbled through lush backyards, crashed through
hedges, backtracked around mesh fences and sent the
neighborhood dogs into a frenzy.
She ran up a long driveway past a sprawling red
brick ranch house with a picture window where a

Pekinese ran yapping back and forth across the top of a long couch. She dashed through the backyard of the house, clambered over a split rail fence into a yard full of small children who stopped playing to gawk at her. She ran past them, swerving around their scattered trucks and dolls and tricycles, and ran down the driveway to another unfamiliar street.

Gasping for air now, Sam kept running, moving down one street after another like a small steam engine, chugging and pumping hard. She'd finally stopped thinking and all that filled her now was running and trying to breathe. She cut across a wide sweep of lawn and a lady on the front porch yelled something at her.

She didn't understand the words, but the sound of it made her flinch and swerve, and when she saw a small park at the end of the curving street she headed for it. There was a sharp pain in her side and she was barely moving faster than a walk when she got to the park. A play-fort stood like a beacon over the small square of grass. It was part of an elaborate wooden structure of ladders and small bridges and slides and things to climb on and poles to shinny up or slide down. Gasping, Sam clambered up a heavy wooden ladder, swayed across the suspension bridge and limped across the platform to the enclosed fort. She climbed through its low door on hands and knees and collapsed in a corner.

She only thought about trying to get enough air in the quiet, shady dimness. She didn't hear her name called any longer. She didn't see Nora's car when it drove slowly past.

Nora was lost. Here, all the streets curved and looped on each other running to dead ends, plush suburban courts and circular drives. There were sweeping lawns and elegant homes and gardens, but no people to ask for directions. No one to ask about Sam.

After a frustrating, fruitless run down another dead end Nora finally admitted to herself that she didn't have a chance of finding Sam this way. It seemed to take her forever to find her way out of the area, but she finally made her way back to the street where the Ellicotts lived. Slowing near the house she saw one of the cars from the Sheriff's Department parked in the Ellicott driveway. Should she go in? Should she try to explain that the corpse and Irene had been puppets pulled by the same strings trying, together, to kill her?

Nora touched the gas and moved on.

Finnerty stood beside the rosewood table, studying the corpse of Florence Gleason. Behind him, Vern Snider shifted uncomfortably from foot to foot.

"Jesus God Almighty." Vern gawked at the body on the floor, the head on the table. "No wonder that old lady had a heart attack."

Finnerty ignored him, bending over the body to look more closely at it. A sweet smell of corruption drifted from the body. It made his nostrils curl and the back of his throat close up. What he couldn't figure out was why the corpse had been dumped in this position. He would have been less surprised to find her sitting at the head of the table.

"Get Doc Paulson over here," Finnerty finally said, straightening up slowly. Too many nights on the couch were killing his back. "I'm taking the car and leaving you here to keep an eye on things. Get Burt, too, to take some pictures. Tell Paulson when he gets here that I want to know if the body's been tampered with in any way. And have him check for signs of sexual activity."

"Oh Jesus, Sheriff," Vern said, grimacing at the soft flesh of the body on the floor, "who'd want to fuck that?"

"Just do it, Vern."

Finnerty had issued an APB on Sample Hall, but the sheriff wanted to do some searching on his own. He'd read the report on Kate Hall's fall down the stairs and he didn't like it. Something didn't ring true about her just falling like that. She hadn't been drinking or on drugs. She hadn't been walking in her sleep. There was nothing for her to trip over and the only other person present was her daughter. Did Sample push her? Two weeks ago, Finnerty wouldn't have believed it. Now, anyone could do anything, it seemed. Brenda Morrison was a quiet, even-tempered girl, everyone said. Mousy, David Fisher said, always letting Judy tell her what to do. Not always, Finnerty thought, not always.

At the hospital, they told him Kate Hall was heavily sedated, unable to talk to him. According to their records, Sample Hall was staying with Nora Durant. Did he want the address? Finnerty thanked them. He already had it.

He tried calling Nora's house one more time from the Ellicotts. Each time he had tried before he'd gotten a busy signal. Now he got a recording that said the phone was out of order.

25

It was early afternoon when Nora pulled up to the curb in front of Kate and Sam's house. The fine morning sunshine had been replaced by a patchwork of sullen gray clouds that scudded across the sky on a stiff, gusting wind.

The house looked deserted and one of the last things in the world Nora wanted to do was to go in there. But she left her car and started up the walk, determined but slowing a little as she reached the front porch. She tried the door.

It was locked, but that didn't mean Sam wasn't inside. Nora banged on it and called out.

"Sam? Are you in there? It's Nora!"

She listened carefully for any sound from inside, but heard nothing. She pounded again and called but got no response. That should do it, Nora thought, disgusted with herself because she knew it wasn't enough. She wouldn't be satisfied that Sam wasn't hiding inside the house, afraid or unable to answer, until she'd gone in to see for herself.

"Shit, shit, shit," Nora was muttering under her breath. All those damn stupid heroines running around in their nighties in the middle of the night to investigate strange noises with nothing but a fluttering candle and here I am being just as goddamned stupid.

She smashed a fist against the square of cardboard she'd helped Kate tape in to replace the broken pane of glass. It crumpled and she pushed it all the way out, then reached her hand through to unlock the window.

"Nuts." The window was open and she could get in. She pushed the window up and climbed into Kate's living room, legs swinging in first. She was backing through, her top half still hanging out the window, when a soft sound made her turn and look toward the end of the porch.

A teenage girl in shorts and a T-shirt was sitting in Kate's rocker, watching her. The girl was not quite pretty. Her face was bland and passive, and she had heavy dark brown hair. She was barefoot, her knees drawn up, feet on the edge of the rocker. She and Nora stared at each other for a long moment.

Nora could swear the girl hadn't been on the porch when she approached the house. And she hadn't heard or seen her climb onto the porch while she was there.

"Hi!" The girl smiled suddenly and Nora wished she hadn't. There was something wrong with the way she did it, as though fingers had pushed the corners of her mouth up.

"Who are you?" Nora challenged, uncomfortably aware of her awkward position—half-in and half-out of the window. "What are you doing here?"

"I'm a friend," the girl said and she swung her feet to the ground. Her legs had been hiding a long carving knife gripped in her fist. She transferred it to her left hand and stood up.

"Stop," Nora said in a low voice.

The girl took a step towards her, stopped and cocked her head.

"You'd better tell me where Sample is or I'll have to

chop you into tiny pieces."

Nora shifted her weight, ready to pull back and escape into the house. Out the back door, maybe.

"She's someplace safe," Nora said, hoping it was true.

"Liar!" A child's voice screamed it from behind her and Nora jumped back and around to face the living room.

A little boy stood in the archway to the hall, and while she stared at him he pointed an accusing finger at her.

"Big liar! You were calling her when you got here. You don't know where she is!"

And the girl filled the window, moving in, knife first. Nora dodged to the side, away from her and away from the little boy. It backed her into a corner by the bookshelves.

"That was just to fool you," she said. She started edging to one side while the girl with the knife kept parallel pace with her. Could she maneuver them around to get a clear run to the window? Some part of her mind raced and wrestled with the angles for escape, leaving the rest of her thoughts curiously calm.

"You're dead, aren't you?" She looked at the little boy and the girl. They looked real enough, like Simon and the woman's corpse. Solid or not? She didn't want to find out.

"We're never going to die at all!" the little boy shouted with glee. "He said so!"

"Who said? Victor?" Nora challenged.

"*Him*. The Master!" the boy screamed and the girl nodded solemnly.

"Doesn't he have a name?"

"That's his name, you dummy," the little boy said scornfully. "He's the Master."

"Victor," Nora insisted. "Victor Sears."

"Victor Sears," the girl echoed, and Nora watched

some recognition flicker across her face.

"He killed himself," the girl said. "It was in the paper."

"He killed you, too."

"No, he didn't. That rotten Judy did. She was supposed to be my best friend!" She raised the knife, pointed its tip at Nora and took another step towards her.

Nora edged to one side, this time closer to the window. Their orientation had shifted. The little boy had moved closer, standing beside the girl, and they both faced her now. Nora took a chance and moved a step closer to them.

"But it was Victor's fault," she said. "He made it happen."

And the girl took half a step back, the knife point lowering, a frown starting on her passive face.

"I don't care. I'm going to live forever, now."

"Except you'll never be a senior." Nora edged towards the window. She sat on the frame and leaned conversationally towards the boy and girl. "You'll never go to a prom or have boyfriends. You won't go steady or go to college or get married." She squirmed backwards, feeling her way with her bottom on the wooden sill. "And it's all Victor's fault."

Only the balls of her feet still rested on the floor inside.

"Why should you do what he says?"

"Because he's all there is left!" Brenda Morrison shouted with knife upraised, Jerry Rhine following close behind. She lunged at Nora.

Nora pushed off from the floor like a swimmer in a race pushing off from the side of the pool. She plunged through the window and landed with a heavy thud on her back on the front porch. She barely felt it. She scrambled to her feet in an instant and ran from the porch towards her car.

Nothing followed her.

* * *

Finnerty frowned and rechecked the address scribbled on a torn sheet of note paper. It matched up, but Nora Durant's half-double had the neglected look of abandoned property. The lawn was long and scraggly, scarred with rough clumps of weed and gangling thistle that sprouted knee high. The house could use a coat of paint. One side looked completely closed up, shades drawn over the windows like the closed eyes of a corpse. On Nora Durant's side, at least, half curtains were drawn back to let in the light.

Two of the windows that opened from the living room to the front porch were an easy invitation to burglars. After knocking and getting no answer, Finnerty moved to the open windows.

"Hello?" he called inside through the screen. "This is Sheriff Finnerty. Are you there, Miss Durant? Sample?"

No answer.

Finnerty walked completely around the house, checking for anything unusual, any sign of a break-in, anything at all. But he found nothing, only a black dog who waited for him on the sidewalk beside his patrol car. The dog looked familiar, he thought.

Perhaps it was a neighborhood stray he'd seen around. No. It looked like the dog he'd seen on the railroad track the night of Florence Gleason's death. The same dog? Finnerty shook his head. He couldn't be sure. A big black mutt—there could be a half dozen in town—picked up and abandoned by the college kids who thought having a dog would be fun, until they had to start taking care of it. Poor damn animals had to be put away regularly.

"Beat it," he hissed at the dog, and the animal stared at him with a cold intelligence that sent a chill up Finnerty's spine. He didn't move.

Finnerty scowled and walked around the car to climb into the driver's seat. He pulled away from the curb, driving slowly. He hadn't decided yet where to head next, but the dog at the curb had spooked him. He just wanted to move on.

Finnerty glanced up at the rearview mirror and there was Charlie Luther slumped in the back seat staring out the side window.

The steering wheel swerved wildly in his hands and Finnerty hit the brakes hard. He hit the gear shift, put the car in Park and swung around to look through the wire mesh into the back seat.

Nothing.

Heart pounding, Finnerty hoisted himself a little higher to get a view of the floor behind his seat. Nothing.

He had stopped in the middle of a traffic lane, and a car pulled up and waited patiently behind him, the businessman in glasses driving a mid-size Chevy sitting there like a model good citizen. The sheriff grunted and put the car back in gear, moving forward again a few yards before his eyes were pulled back to the rearview mirror.

And there was Charlie Luther, the fitful afternoon sun shining off his pale hair. Finnerty gasped and hit the brakes again. Behind he heard the other car's brakes squeal in protest.

But again, when Finnerty swung around to look, his back seat was empty.

The sheriff rolled down his window and waved the other car around him. He watched it go, staring out his passenger window and around to the front, watching it disappear down the quiet street before he let himself look up into his rearview mirror.

It showed him Charlie Luther and, as he watched, Charlie slowly turned his head to meet Finnerty's eyes in the mirror. He looked infinitely sad and different somehow, Finnerty thought. And then he knew what it was. Charlie didn't look afraid any more.

"Luther," the sheriff said, and his voice came out as a hoarse croak.

Charlie gave him a small, slow smile.

The smile swung Finnerty around in his seat once more, but as before the back was empty. And this time when Finnerty checked the mirror there was no sign of Charlie Luther.

Finnerty sat for a long time before driving to Kate Hall's house.

When she finally got home, Nora was reluctant to go in. Sam possibly could be there, Nora reasoned. She'd shown the girl where she hid her extra key before they left this morning, and Sam might be waiting for her inside.

Still, Nora sat for a long time in the relative safety of her dusty Datsun gathering her courage and watching her house. She studied its sad state like a housewife would appraise a ragged drifter come round to the back door for a handout. When this was all over, she decided, she was going to insist that Mrs. Roberts start making some repairs. And she'd take care of the yard herself if the landlady would reduce her rent a little.

Across the street her elderly neighbor peered at Nora from curtains opened just a crack and shook her head to herself, wondering what the sheriff had wanted. Something to do with drugs, probably. That's what they were all up to these days. She decided to keep out of it because, after all, Mary Roberts had only asked her to keep an eye on the house. It wasn't her duty, Christian or otherwise, to go warning the neighbors about drug raids. And there was that pesky dog again.

In the next yard a big black dog lay in the shade of an overgrown lilac. He watched Nora through green eyes that shifted shadow and color like a drowning pool.

Nora heaved a sigh and pushed her fists into her temples, grinding them against the tension that gathered there with the heavy beat of blood. She stretched in her seat, opened the car door and got out.

Across the street the black dog rose gracefully to his feet.

"Sam?" Nora stood in her living room calling into the quiet. Around her the house held its breath, a moment suspended in the summer afternoon as though the house kept its own time a world away from people and traffic and everything safely familiar. Like the Beast's great house, Nora thought, under a melancholy enchantment until Beauty set the poor Beast free.

There was no answer from Sam, just the silence of the house.

A light sweat blossomed on Nora's back and on her upper lip. She walked through the living room, into the dining room to the foot of the stairs and called again, not expecting an answer.

But a sharp creak sounded suddenly overhead, a sound like a cautious footstep on a squeaky floorboard. Nora couldn't tell exactly where it came from, either her own second floor or Mary Roberts' upper story. The supports of the old house carried sound like a telegraph, and footsteps next door often seemed to be coming from her own rooms.

Listening hard, Nora climbed the six steps to the small landing where her stairs turned up the blind stairwell to the second floor.

"Sam?" she called for the third time. She had to fight a reluctance to disturb the silence in her own house. She forced herself to climb all the way up the stairs, stopping two steps from the top before coming vulnerable into the hallway that opened in both directions. Any way she looked at the top of the stairs would leave her blind on one side, open to attack from anything that waited.

She listened to the silence for a second, then dashed up the stairs and looked quickly to one side then the other. When nothing was there, she felt silly.

"Honestly," she said out loud and blew away some tension with a deep breath. "Don't waste time."

Nora walked quickly down the hall to her bedroom, looked in and saw it empty, everything as she'd left it that morning. Coming back down the hall, she was already thinking about where next to look for Sam when the door to the small corner bedroom she used for storage swung halfway open and stopped.

Moving carefully to the head of the stairs, just in case she needed to make a fast exit, Nora kept her eyes on the half-open door, waiting for something more to happen.

Nothing.

She waited. And then she stalked the door like a cat, watchfully inching closer, ready to bolt. Outside it, she pushed it open with a quick jab and took a step back to give the interior of the room a speedy scan. There was no one in sight.

There were two walls of windows set close together but nearly all, she'd discovered, painted shut. A couple would grudgingly open a few inches before they stuck and that little bit of air was all that kept the room from being an oven. As it was, the place was stiflingly hot. One wall was lined with boxes of clothes Nora never wore but dutifully dragged with her from place to place. She always meant to sort through them and get rid of things, but she never quite managed it. Other boxes held old photos and letters, cancelled checks, dried flowers, old towels, miscellaneous china, all the unused junk and mixed debris of her life. The fourth wall held a few more boxes and an enormous mirror that had hung there when she rented the place. The heavy frame was darkened, gilt-painted carved wood. The mirror itself was spotted and discolored. Next to it the attic door, usually closed with a sliding bolt, stood ajar.

Nora stepped into the room. She was reaching for the knob on the attic door when behind her the door to the hall slammed shut.

Michael Justin dialed Nora's number for the fifth
time that day. Twice in the morning it had rung
unanswered. At noon he got a busy signal, and
minutes later when he tried calling back he got static
and an angry hissing. The fourth time he got a
recording that said the number was out of order.

He called the phone company, but they couldn't tell
him what had happened to Nora's phone or when it
might be fixed. So he'd just wait, Michael decided. He
had a video tape on the problems of a local landfill to
edit for showing on the cable channel tomorrow
night. It would take him a few hours and getting hold
of Nora would just have to wait.

But he couldn't shake the nagging feeling that it was
urgent to find Nora. Thoughts of her kept distracting
him. He was chain-smoking and making stupid mis-
takes. Now the tape was less than perfect, but he
decided it would have to do because he couldn't concentrate enough to smooth it out without making sure
Nora was all right.

So he was dialing her number for the fifth time. And
he got the recording again.

He used to fall in love a lot, Michael remembered,
back in his early and mid-twenties. But either it was un-
requited love or his relationships brought him pain that
outweighed the pleasure. For whatever reason, he'd
stopped falling in love before he was thirty. He had
comfortable relations with no commitments. Women
regularly fell in love with him and he had practice at
letting them down easily. For years now he'd weaved
through a field of lovers like a halfback carrying the
ball on a 90 yard run for a touchdown—dodging, side-
stepping, twisting away from any hold. Now here was
Nora and suddenly he was in love again. And far from
pursuing him, she seemed to have her own evasive
defense.

He stubbed out his cigarette, turned off the tape machine and grabbed his car keys. If he couldn't reach her by phone, he'd show up on her doorstep.

Nora put all her weight behind one last tug on the door to the hall, but it refused to give. The glass door-knob wouldn't turn, but that simply didn't make any sense since the door could be locked only with an old-fashioned, long-shafted key. The key to that door must have been lost years ago, but it was locked now. It just didn't make sense.

She bent to peer through the broad keyhole. A small white spider was crouched in the opening. It was less than an inch from her eye, and startled, Nora jumped back. A box falling to the floor behind her made her jump again and spin around. A short column of boxes piled against the wall moved as she looked at them.

It was the box on the bottom of the pile that caused it. That box went squat and concave, then filled again, beating like a brown cardboard heart. It squeezed and pulsed again, cardboard side bulging out, and inside it something scratched tentatively at the carton.

The boxes balanced on top of it shifted and slithered out of place, cardboard rustling against cardboard like a dry whisper. It beat again and the box on top slid off. Old letters spilled from the box, scattering at Nora's feet. Wedding pictures of her and Simon scattered from it and swirled to rest like leaves stirred by an autumn wind. They were momentarily still, and then a handful skittered closer to her.

Nora drew her feet back with a gasp and turned again to the door. She grabbed the glass knob and yanked frantically, shoving forward and back as though the door were simply jammed from humidity and thick layers of old paint. She tried driving her shoulder against it to loosen it. She squatted and put her legs and back into pulling it towards her. It didn't even move a fraction of an inch.

The scratching from the box was louder now and more insistent.

Nora gave up on the door and, skirting the photos that lifted and rustled on the floor, she ran to one of the windows that was open a few inches. She jammed up with both palms on the window frame and tried rattling it in its frame. Nothing. She shoved down. Nothing. She moved to the next window, pushing and shoving at the paint-stuck frame in a frenzy. It wouldn't budge.

Above her, in the attic, something thumped. She froze and listened.

But the only sound came from inside the pulsing box. The scratching turned to long, hard strokes against the cardboard.

Sweat trickled and ran between Nora's shoulder blades and dripped from her forehead to sting her eyes. She pushed her damp hair behind her ears and moved to the next window, attacking it with the force of panic. It rose a scant half inch in the frame, paint cracking with a brittle accompaniment.

In the attic whatever moved there thumped again, and this time a slithering, slow drag followed it.

The attic door was still open. Nora slammed the window she'd raised back down, planning to rock it like a car stuck in snow. But first she ran for the attic door and slapped it shut. The paint-encrusted bolt that locked it always stuck. Now it refused to move at all.

She rammed it with the heel of her palm and pain shot up her arm. It wouldn't move. She grabbed the tiny knob and worked at it with no effect, all the time small noises filling the room with menace. There was the rhythmic creak of cardboard bulging to some strange pulse, the scratching, the slip and slide of the last three boxes piled on that beating cardboard heart, the rustle and slither of pictures and letters that suddenly shifted and moved themselves. And the thing in the attic.

Another box tumbled off the pile and suddenly there was silence. Nora stopped breathing to listen to the stillness. Far away, someone called her name. Michael.

The little bedroom where she was trapped was at the back of the house and it sounded as though Michael was out front calling in through an open window. Nora shouted his name with all the volume she could gather.

"Michael!"

She listened again and heard nothing and started to move towards the door to the hall when the box that pulsed and scratched gave a sudden leap towards her.

Other boxes on top and around it tumbled to the floor, their contents sprawling out, bursting out like confetti from a party favor. Old clothes stirred and shimmied out of their folds, rustling towards her like a restless tide. An old, tattered art print of race horses in a paddock by Dufy wavered into motion like a flying carpet rising towards Nora's face.

She swung around then and kicked her foot through one of the closed windows, glass bursting and letting in fresh air.

"Michael!" Nora screamed again, bending towards the window. And then the long shards of glass that hung broken in the frame shifted and chinked together like troops coming to attention.

"Michael!" Nora shouted again, but she took a step back and kept her eyes on the moving glass.

Then she heard him. He was calling her name and running up the stairs when the frozen hall door suddenly burst open on its own accord. Michael was moving through the doorway before Nora could stop him.

She tried to run to him and out the door, but a flight of wedding photos flew at their faces like a swarm of bats with glossy wings, all cutting edges and fluttering confusion. Michael threw up an arm to protect his face and held out a hand to her. She grabbed it,

burying her eyes in the crook of one arm, and
struggled towards him in the storm of paper as though
she were striding through a blizzard.

From the attic overhead came a roar filled with the
fury of a damned river. Sound crashed towards them,
spilling from the attic, and the attic door exploded
open to spew out a torrent of hot, fetid air like the foul
breath of the house itself. The blast blew Nora to
Michael, and like a shipwrecked sailor she gasped
and coughed and clung to him.

And while they swayed together the massive mirror
reared off the wall and crashed against them, then fell
to the floor and shattered. Michael took most of the
force of the blow and Nora felt his body vibrate with
it. He staggered, almost falling, and she tried to keep
them both on their feet. The mirror had glanced off
one of her arms and it now hung limp and useless at
her side.

They were shaken, but still standing, beginning to
shuffle towards the door with the wind pushing them
out. And then the airflow changed direction. It began
to suck at them, pulling them back towards the attic
door. They were fighting it, but losing ground.

And then it stopped.

The room went still again, but only for the space of
one clean breath. Then the box that had beat and
pulsed and scratched was suddenly torn open from
the inside, exploding like a puffball shooting spores.
And there, on the brown cardboard shards of the torn
box, was a Chatty Cathy doll.

She wore a pink and white ruffled gingham dress.
Shiny blond hair framed the round face and the
curving pink smile where the tips of two baby teeth
barely showed. Her eyelids curved down to long
black lashes that rested on the chubby cheeks.

And then its eyelids clicked up and two blue glass
eyes rolled sideways to look at them.

Nora screamed and began to push Michael towards

the door, but he was still stunned by the mirror or just too dazed to move. He stood staring at the doll, shaking his head.

"Hi! My name is Cathy," the mechanical voice of the doll said. And then it sat up.

"Michael, go! Move!" Nora shoved at him with both hands.

He took a step backwards, eyes still fixed on the doll, and Nora pushed him again while the doll climbed awkwardly to its feet.

"I'd like to be your friend," Chatty Cathy said, and one plump plastic leg took a step towards them. And then another.

Michael grabbed Nora's hand then and started to run, pulling her along. They were at the head of the stairs when Nora heard the doll's mechanical voice call plaintively after them.

"No-ra . . . Come back and play!"

They were on the stairs.

"I'm not through with you!" And the house boomed and shook and Michael caught Nora at the landing as she lost her balance and nearly fell.

"Run! Run!" she gasped at him and he half-pulled, half-carried her through the dining room, across the living room and to the front door. Nora fumbled with it, unlocking it, and Michael reached around her to throw it open.

He pushed her through first, out to the porch, and the first thing Nora suddenly noticed was a sheriff's car pulling up, light flashing, and the old lady who lived across the street standing like a portrait of doom in a flowered blue housedress pointing an accusation in her direction.

Michael's hands grabbed her shoulders just as a small, hard voice spoke down by her knees.

"Good-by, Nora," the voice said, and Nora got just a glimpse of Chatty Cathy smiling up at her as Michael's weight drove her to the floor. They were

still in midair when the two front windows behind
them burst with a shriek and crash of shattered glass.
When Nora hit the ground, long arrows of jagged
glass were falling around them like hail.

26

Sam lost track of time in the playground fort. She stayed there until a group of children invaded her sanctuary. There were three of them, two girls and a boy, all much younger than Sam. They came piling into the fort laughing and chattering like a flock of sparrows, and Sam tried ignoring them, but it didn't work.

"Hi! I'm Courtney. What's your name?" the oldest girl asked, plopping companionably down next to Sam.

She was about eight, Sam guessed. She had long, light brown hair hanging in limp pigtails held in place with holders sporting bright pink beads. The smaller girl, a kid sister Sam figured since they were wearing matching pink shorts sets, ignored them both. She threw herself gleefully head first down the slide. The little boy hung behind Courtney and sucked his thumb.

"Well?"

"Sam," Sam said, and it came out sounding rusty.

Courtney grimaced at her. "That's a boy's name."

"It's actually Sample," Sam bristled. "Sam for short."

The little girl wrinkled up her nose. "Sample.

345

That's a silly name."

"Not as silly as Courtney," Sam said, and she stood up with stiff dignity and slid slowly down the slide.

She kept walking when she landed, not looking back. She didn't know where she was going, though. No place seemed safe or good or normal any longer. And it was all her fault.

She should have stayed and waited for Nora, Sam scolded herself. She shouldn't have run when Nora said to because Nora was probably just trying to protect her, and if she'd gone inside maybe nothing bad would have happened to Nora. And what happened to Irene? They could both be dead and she wouldn't know it.

And it was all her fault.

Sam was trudging wearily down the street, eyes on the sidewalk watching her feet moving forward, one after the other, over and over, like they had no connection to her, like maybe they knew where they were going. She didn't notice the old man who stood watching her come down the length of the block until she'd almost walked into him.

"Hey there," he said when Sam was almost even with him. He was standing over a privet hedge with a pair of pruning shears.

Sam stopped with a jolt and stared at him like a trapped deer.

"You live around here?"

Sam hesitated, then shook her head.

"Lost?"

She nodded.

"Well, where you headed?"

"First Street," Sam said. It was the first thing that popped into her head.

The old man frowned. "That's a few miles from here. Where on First Street?"

"Downtown. McDonald's."

It was a straight course but close to four miles. The

old man gave her directions, then asked if she wanted a lift. He told her he had some errands to run, but Sam figured he was lying. He was sorry for her, she thought.

Sam shook her head vigorously.

"That's all right, then. Better not to take rides from strangers. You remember that."

"Yes, sir," Sam said as she would to the Colonel, her grandfather. Maybe she should go back to Memphis like her mother wanted. But then, maybe she'd just bring trouble to her grandparents.

"Thank you," Sam said politely and began to walk more energetically towards town. She was a half block away when the old man called after her.

"You call your mother and let her know where you are," he yelled. "She'll be worried about you!"

Sam half turned and waved, breaking into a trot until the old man was far behind her.

There was enough change in her pocket to buy an iced tea, and by the time Sam got to the McDonald's she could use one.

She sat nursing her iced tea, sucking on the chipped ice and chewing the waxed paper cup until she finally worked out a plan. It was already late afternoon. The day had finally turned dark gray and overcast with a threat of rain sulking in the air. Sam wanted to stop quickly at home, pick up her rain slicker and pack a bag of clothes and stuff. And she wanted to pick up her savings. By the time she got everything together it would be time for evening visiting hours, and if she were lucky she could sneak into the hospital and see how her mom was before she left.

Sam had never met her father. She'd seen pictures of him, though, and once she'd seen him in a TV commercial shampooing some lady's hair. Now she decided it was about time they met.

He wouldn't be real glad to see her, probably. If he actually wanted to see her, he'd have sent for her by now. But she might talk him into letting her stay with him for a while in California. It was so far away, it had to be safe. She could just disappear without letting anyone know where she was going and then her mom and Nora and Irene would be safe. Maybe Victor would just give up.

Finnerty was more shaken by seeing Charlie Luther than he wanted to admit. He sat for a long time, drumming his fingers on the steering wheel, probing at the idea of it like feeling around a loose tooth wobbling in a sore gum. When he raised his arm to restart his engine, Finnerty got a sharp whiff of his own acrid stench. Too many days in the same rumpled uniform, he thought. Past time to take a stop at home for a quick shower and change of clothes before going out to look for the girl. A good stiff shot of brandy wouldn't hurt either.

As Finnerty drove home all his glances at the rearview mirror were quick ones.

Doc Paulson and the ambulance drivers who came to pick up Florence Gleason's body found the front door of the Ellicott house standing wide open. They went in, Doc first, calling for Deputy Snider. They found Florence's body in a heap on the dining room table. Her head watched them come with baleful cow eyes.

Vern Snider never did show up.

Finnerty called the office before leaving his house. Tom Robbins answered the phone. He'd been on 24 hours a day, as far as Finnerty could tell. Complaining, but enjoying the hell out of it, probably. Now he had more news for the sheriff—a story Jenkins and Cooksey had called in that Tom couldn't make heads or tails out of.

Jenkins and Cooksey were dispatched out to Nora

Durant's house after a neighbor called to say she'd seen a strange man climb into the place through a downstairs window. Durant and Michael Justin were coming out of the house as the patrol car drove up and there was some kind of explosion.

"Only they said there was no bang, Sheriff. No noise. The glass in the front windows just blew out all of a sudden. Justin must have known something was going to happen because he tackled the woman and shielded her just before it blew. He caught most of the glass. Damnedest thing is, Ralph and Phil said they looked through the place and couldn't find anything that would cause the explosion. No sign of a bomb. No projectiles. Nothing."

"What happened to Justin?"

"Pretty badly cut up. Ambulance took him in to the hospital. Durant had minor cuts."

"Any sign of the Hall kid?"

"No, sir."

Finnerty scowled, told the deputy where he was going and hung up. The girl should have been with Nora Durant, although it sounded like that would have been dangerous enough. Now she could be anywhere in who knew what kind of trouble.

Trouble from what or whom?

Damned if he knew, but Finnerty had taken a simple leap of faith when Irene Ellicott gave him her message. The girl was in danger. Finnerty snorted, strapping on his gun before leaving the house. Right now it looked like the whole damn town was in danger.

The sheriff's first stop was the Hall house. The place was in a sad and sorry state, he thought, studying it from his car. It looked abandoned and brooding, Finnerty thought.

Finnerty got out of the car, telling himself to keep his imagination in check. What was really worth noting was the broken front window like an open invitation to anyone to come on in. And, from up close, there were signs that somebody had taken the invitation.

He banged on the front door. No answer.

Bending down at the gaping window, Finnerty stuck his head partway into the room.

"This is Sheriff Finnerty," he shouted into the house's late afternoon gloom. "Is anybody there?"

Silence.

Then from what sounded like the back of the house Finnerty heard the faint squeak of a door opening or closing.

More silence.

Finnerty heaved himself through the window and stopped to listen. A floorboard upstairs creaked with the sharp sound of a footstep.

It could be anyone, Finnerty thought. A curious neighborhood kid taking a look around or a junkie, maybe one of Charlie Luther's friends, looking for something to steal.

"This is Sheriff Finnerty," he called again. "I want you to come out where I can see you."

The creak of another floorboard was followed by the sound of a door being gently closed.

Finnerty eased cautiously through the living room to the base of the stairs, listening hard for any other sounds. He slid one foot onto the bottom step, then tested it with his full weight. It gave a sharp creak, a dead giveaway to anyone upstairs, and Finnerty cursed softly under his breath. He was sweating now and he drew his gun with a reflex he thought sure he'd lost. Finnerty took the steps two at a time, gliding up to the top landing for a quick scan of the place.

Four doors faced him. Two open doors led to bedrooms, one was the bathroom straight ahead, and next to it a skinny, closed door with the tail end of a white sheet caught in the crack must be a linen closet.

Like a hound testing the air, Finnerty lifted his head and swiveled on the balls of his feet toward each door. Every sense was keyed to full pitch and he felt a good 50 pounds lighter.

He checked out the closet bedroom first. It was a big, untidy room with a stripped bed and no place to hide but the closet. Finnerty crept up on it and swung the door open with his gun ready, but he had the draw only on clothes drooping innocently from their hangers. He shook some of the tension out of his shoulders and moved on.

The other bedroom—the girl's bedroom, it looked like—was smaller, neater and more full of furniture but not much easier to hide in. He did a quick check of the room, then the closet. The closet door was ajar and Finnerty half expected to find Sam crouched on the floor. But there was nothing, only the girl's clothes hung on pastel plastic hangers.

Finnerty let his breath out slowly, aware of the adrenalin that made his heart beat faster and the tension that made his grip on the gun damp. He went back to the landing, drew down on the linen closet and yanked the door open.

Nothing.

That left the bathroom, if there actually was anyone up here, and Finnerty was beginning to wonder now if the old house hadn't just been settling.

The sheriff stood in the doorway to the small bathroom. From where he stood he could see the whole of the small, white-tiled old-fashioned room. There was no place to hide. Except in the bathtub behind the drawn white shower curtain.

Metal screeched against metal, the curtain rings scraping like nails on a blackboard against the metal curtain rod, when Finnerty swept the curtain back.

Charlie Luther's body hung suspended in midair over the tub. His head was forced to one side by the unseen ghost of the sheet he'd used to hang himself.

His eyes bulged, and his face was tinged deep angry red, almost purple. His tongue was swollen and protruding from his slack mouth.

The body started to revolve, a slow and lazy spin, counterclockwise. After a pause it started back again. Finnerty couldn't take his eyes off the contorted, discolored face until a sharp sound in the doorway made him swing around, gun coming up to ready.

Vern Snider stood in the bathroom doorway. Vern was grinning, but it was no expression Finnerty had ever seen on his face before.

"Surprise!" Vern said.

Finnerty lowered his gun. Slowly. This was all wrong, and the wrongness made his gut growl and the little hairs on the back of his neck prickle.

"Vern. What the hell's going on here?"

And Charlie Luther clapped a pale, freckled hand on Finnerty's shoulder.

Finnerty twisted away from him, springing to one side, but Vern jumped him before he got his bearings and balance. The sheriff let the force of Vern's dive carry them over and the two men slammed into the cool tile wall. Vern's hands were locked around Finnerty's throat and then Finnerty tried driving his forearms up to break the deputy's grip, but Vern had the advantage of height and angle. He kept a good grip, squeezing long strong fingers against Finnerty's larynx, and the sheriff could feel his lungs beginning to empty while he tried to get a breath.

His gun was still drawn, but instead of pulling the trigger Finnerty reached up to smash Vern full in the face with the heavy weapon.

The blow made Vern loosen his grip and Finnerty drove upward again with both arms, breaking Vern's hold on his throat. Blood was streaming from the deputy's nose and driping down his chin. He'd stopped grinning.

With the muzzle of the gun, Finnerty rammed Vern

in the solar plexus and skipped back as Vern doubled over. But Vern suddenly charged him, head aimed at Finnerty's gut. Finnerty side-stepped like a novice bullfighter and Vern's rush hit him in the ribs and spun him to one side. The sheriff stumbled over the toilet bowl, and the force of Vern's charge and his own clumsy fall knocked him into the cool tile, head first.

Vern was on his knees now. One hand clutched his gut as he gasped for air, the other shot out and caught Finnerty behind the knee. When Vern yanked it, Finnerty folded.

They were both twisted at awkward angles, partially sprawled on the floor, partly wedged against the tile wall or porcelain of the tub and toilet. Their legs tangled together, both trying to kick free, trying to push themselves up while they sucked for air. And then a short shrill scream sounded from the doorway.

It was the girl, Sam, standing stiff and glaring at them, fists drawn beside her khaki shorts, indignant and terrified. She turned on her heels and ran.

At the sight of her Vern vibrated like a gong struck with a hammer. He twitched into action, ignoring Finnerty, hoisted himself up by the rim of the tub and staggered through the door after the girl.

"Vern!" Finnerty pushed himself upright and started sliding his back up the tile.

"Vern!" From the bathroom doorway, Finnerty could see Vern starting down the stairs and Sam at the front door working at the lock. It wasn't opening.

"Vern, hold it right there!"

But the deputy kept moving and Finnerty lurched after him, the gun still in his hand, to the head of the stairs. He started to raise the gun but knew sure as shit he wasn't going to shoot his deputy in the back. So he shoved the gun back in its holster, and as Vern hit the bottom of the stairs Finnerty launched himself like a glider from the top, a flying tackle the length of the stairway.

He caught Vern high in the back and the deputy fell straight forward, crashing heavily to the hall floor. His body broke Finnerty's fall with a sickening impact on the wood.

Finnerty rolled off his deputy and blinked up at Sam, the breath knocked out of him. She had the door open now and turned for just a second to look down at him with horror.

"Wait . . ." he tried, but he didn't have the breath. The girl turned and ran.

Next to him on the wood floor, Vern wasn't moving at all.

27

Nora paced in the small waiting room outside surgery. They were still working on Michael and it had been over five hours. The first hour she had spent giving evasive answers to the deputy who questioned her. There wasn't much she could tell him and still sound sane so she just kept telling him she didn't know what had happened. She'd gotten locked into a room upstairs, yelled for help when Michael came and left with him. He tackled her and that's all she knew.

The deputy thought she was holding something back, lying or involved in some weird plot, Nora figured. He kept frowning at her suspiciously and after a while she started to feel furtive and desperate. She finally lost her temper and told him to leave her alone.

At Intensive Care, she checked on Irene and found out she was "in satisfactory condition and stable." That was the second hour and she spent most of it pacing. By the third hour she realized she could see Kate, but by then it had been so long that she was certain they'd be finished with Michael any minute and she didn't want to miss a chance to find out how he was.

355

Nora had been alone in the waiting room through all the hours. It was a small hospital and their routine surgeries were done in the early morning. People passed the open doorway occasionally, gawked in at her and quickly looked away. They were curious but embarrassed visitors and Staff who didn't want to get involved.

For a small hospital in a relatively small community, St. Francis had the chilly atmosphere of a much bigger place. It was a well-endowed microcosm of modern medicine, a compact structure with a labyrinth of halls and courtyards. It had about 150 beds, labs, morgue, radiology, a pain treatment center, a burn unit, surgery wing, intensive care unit, family birthing rooms with Colonial decor and more. It had an affluent feeling, and the university community liked it that way.

The original St. Francis was about a mile away, an old brick, 35-bed structure that now served as a medical history museum which no one visited. The working hospital was in its third or fourth incarnation. Wisely built with a modular design in the 1950s, the hospital now gained new wings and new areas without becoming misshapen, the new additions blending smoothly with the old. The decor in each area of the hospital reflected the best of institutional good taste at the time it was built. Some wings had featureless hospital green walls and speckled beige linoleum, while others had white tile and bold graphics in primary colors painted on the white walls. Some of the latest areas were done in soothing mauves, dusty blues, grays and cream.

The waiting room for the surgery was done in the primary color era. A bright, broad strip of green ran around the room at waist level in stark contrast to the white walls. The furniture was boxy, solid and covered in nubby "natural" fabric that glinted stain-resistant polyester in the light.

Nora was looking out the vertical blinds through a broad picture window with a view of the Black River. It was still early evening, but the day had gone dark and cars already had their headlights on. She watched the pairs of white headlights and red taillights trace patterns on the road across the river, running up and down the hills that crossed the shallow river valley.

Behind her, the squelch of gummed shoes finally coming through the door made Nora swing around.

"Mrs. Justin?" asked a comfortably round, dark-haired nurse.

Nora shook her head. "No. I'm a friend of Michael's. How is he? Is it over?"

"Well, they've finished with the surgery," the nurse told her, "but I couldn't really tell you how he is. You'd have to ask the doctor."

"I'd really like to know. Can you find out?"

"I'll see if Dr. Bellamy will speak to you. But you're not family?"

"We're engaged," Nora said firmly.

The nurse nodded and Nora couldn't tell if she believed it, but it didn't matter. "I'll see," she said.

Family only, as if other people didn't care or didn't count. Nora had seen Peter Ellicott outside Intensive Care and he'd tried cheering her up even though he looked drained and ashen.

"She'll be all right," Dr. Ellicott had said, patting her arm. "The doctor said it was a very mild attack. She's resting now."

They didn't talk about anything else. There would be time later, Nora thought, to talk about everything that led up to Irene's collapse.

So Nora waited. And she waited for the nurse to bring her news or the doctor who had taken the long shards of glass from Michael's body and stitched him back together. They were meant for her, she kept thinking, but she'd only gotten a few small cuts and an inch-long sliver lodged in her calf. The local

anesthetic they'd used on her in the emergency room
was wearing off, but she was lucky. She was a survivor, alive and walking around while Michael and
Kate and Irene were all here.

And she kept thinking about Sam.

The deputy had told her that Sheriff Finnerty had
put an all points bulletin out on the girl. They were
bound to find her, he said, but Nora wasn't so sure.
Sam must be hiding now and she just didn't know
where.

She wouldn't go back to Irene's. She surely
wouldn't go home alone. Once she saw the wreckage
at Nora's, she'd have sense enough not to go in.
Besides, patrol cars were searching that area for her
as well as the area around her house.

Sam would come to the hospital, Nora thought, to
see Kate, and Nora would be watching for her.

It had been only a few minutes when a tall man in
blood-spattered surgical greens came into the waiting
room, and Nora walked to meet him in the center of
the little room.

She was studying his face but was unable to discern
anything except exhaustion. There were dark, wet
patches on his cap, underarms and chest. He smelled
of disinfectant and sharp sweat, but he smiled a
small, professional smile at her.

"He should be all right," the doctor said. "You
were with him?"

He eyed the gauze bandages on her forearm and calf
and the little cut on her cheek.

Nora nodded.

"He's lost a lot of blood but we've given him
several units and he'll be getting some more. There's
heavy laceration with some muscle damage in both
legs, but that should heal up all right. He may need
some therapy to get rid of the stiffness, but he looks
like he's in good shape and he should get full use
back. A few small slivers did some organ damage.

Like shrapnel. Or glass bullets." He pushed his cap off and rubbed his short gray hair into damp spikes.

Nora just stared at him, waiting for the rest.

"We saved the kidney. The actual stab wounds from the larger pieces looked worse than they were. They didn't do any major damage. He's damned lucky. Go on home now."

The doctor gave her a heavy-handed pat on the shoulder and turned away.

"But when can I see him?"

He flapped a hand at her over his shoulder. "Later. Tomorrow, maybe. He's out now and for most of the day tomorrow. Go get some sleep yourself. I'm going to."

It's like being a leper in *Ben Hur*, Sam thought, or a mangy stray dog.

She was hunkered down behind a tangle of shrubs at the edge of the hospital parking lot watching from the shadows as visitors moved in and out of the brightly lit hospital entrance. It was late, she guessed. Visitors were leaving in clumps and streams like kids getting out of school.

Sam had been in the parking lot forever, it seemed. More than an hour, at least. There were just too many people going in and out of the place and somebody was sure to stop a kid. It would be better, she decided, to wait for visiting hours to be over and to sneak in then. At night the lights in the corridors were dim, and there weren't as many nurses around and they'd be busy giving people pills and stuff. She'd wait and keep out of sight.

There was no one she could trust now. No one. The thought thrummed and vibrated at the core of her like the deepest toned string on a bass plucked to the rhythm of her heartbeat. No one to trust. She felt light-headed, curiously detached.

Before, she thought she wanted to go to the hospital

to see her mother, but there was something else now. Someone else. It was getting harder and harder to think. She only knew she had to get inside.

Carole Salant opened her eyes in the shadowy room and sat up, smoothly levitated like a floating girl in a magic act. A cloth restraint held one wrist to the bed-rail like a line anchoring a boat to harbor. She bobbed softly and her IV line trembled and swayed.

"Sample," she said to the empty room, to the one that called her. *I am the Angel of Death.*

One floor above Carole Salant, Alex Thomas slowly focused on the pattern of dots in the acoustical tile of the ceiling above him. They breathed darkness at him with a foul breath.

"Help me," Alex whimpered. And the air around him gathered with a sullen heat.

Around a corner and down the corridor from Alex's room, Nora leaned wearily against the pale green wall outside Kate's room. Kate had slipped from uncon-sciousness to sedated sleep to natural sleep, and Nora didn't want to wake her. Mostly, she would have liked to climb into the next bed and forget everything herself. Instead, she was just waiting in a half-doze on her feet.

When the floor nurse came gliding up like a proud sailing ship in full rigging, she paused just long enough to give Nora a sharp head to toe appraisal and a small frown. Visiting hours were over in ten minutes, she told Nora, though she looked like she wanted to say a lot more.

Nora pushed off from the wall and murmured something conciliatory, "just going" motions. She started walking slowly towards the elevator when the nurse launched herself and moved away without looking back.

But Nora wasn't about to leave. She still expected Sam to show up. The girl might find it difficult, though, to get as far as Kate's room. Since Sam was under the age limit for visitors she would have to find a way to sneak up and it might not be as easy as Nora had first thought. Sam was nearby—she had to believe that.

When Nora appeared in the hospital entranceway, lit with a halo of light by the bright sign over the door, Sam almost jumped to her feet with a shout of relief.

But she didn't. It was enough to know that Nora was alive, that Sam hadn't left her to die when she ran away from Irene Ellicott's. But Nora looked tired and worried and she had bandages on her arms and leg. Nora had been hurt and it was all her fault.

The only way to keep bad things from happening to people was to stay away from them. Whatever happened now, she'd be all alone. It was better that way.

She crouched behind a gray Mercedes in the row of cars in the space reserved for doctors and watched Nora scan the parking lot with one hand shading her eyes as though she were looking out over a desert. When Nora limped down the stairs and started across the lot, Sam swiveled on the balls of her feet to see that Nora was headed for her car. It stood like a shabby green oasis isolated in the empty parking lot under the sickly artificial glare of the lamps.

Nora was leaving.

Nora was fifty yards away with her back turned when Sam made a run for the hospital entrance.

Carole Salant shuffled down the corridor in her hospital gown and a frowsy terry bathrobe. She moved with the vacant determination of a sleep-walker, shuffled past the stairway, then stopped, swung back toward it and pushed open the door to stand for a moment at the intersection of stairs. Then she began to climb. She climbed the stairs with heavy, measured movements, each foot planted flatly in the middle of each cement step.

Alex Thomas was already turned towards the door when she pushed it open. His eyes caught the light like an animal's in the dark and then he squinted and blinked, his face shining with sweat in the light from the doorway, the light that streamed around Salant's dark figure.

"Help me," Alex croaked, and she stepped into the room, the door settling quietly closed behind her.

Nora had half-hoped to find Sam waiting in her car, but the disappointment didn't prevent her from believing the girl was still around the hospital somewhere. She held onto that thought stubbornly. She had to believe that, Nora thought, because if Sam wasn't here, then God only knew where she was.

Nora was trotting back into the hospital when the receptionist tried to stop her.

"Forgot my keys!" Nora called without pausing. She ducked into the nearest stairwell.

Instead off going back to Kate's floor where she was sure the floor nurse would recognize her, Nora went up an extra flight. She was counting on the arrangement of each floor being the same with the ward desk across from the elevator, stairs just around the corner and a storage room next to the staircase.

While she was waiting outside Kate's room, Nora had seen an orderly let himself into the storage room without using a key. Hopefully none of them were locked. That way, she could slip from the stairwell into the storage room and wait there for a while, providing no one needed anything from it, biding her time until the hospital settled in for the night. Then she'd try to make her way unnoticed to Kate's room to wait for Sam. Somewhere in the labyrinth of the hospital, Nora was sure Sam was hiding and waiting.

After about 45 minutes Nora opened the door of the storage room a crack and stepped out. She was wearing a gown and robe she'd found on a shelf in the closet. The gown covered her street clothing and her purse and sneakers were clutched to her chest under the robe. She was hoping she looked like an eccentric patient, not ready to settle in for the night. The bandaged leg would help, and her heavy limp was only partially an act. The anesthetic had worn off completely now, and Nora's whole body throbbed with aches and pains. Fighting the pain and the terrible yearning to just lie still somewhere gave her a kind of tunnel vision of determination. It occurred to her that she might not be thinking clearly, even though she felt incredibly crafty.

She was limping toward the ward desk when the young girl behind it stood up and frowned at her like a babysitter at a child who came down to raid the refrigerator. To Nora, she looked more like a candy striper than a nurse.

"Now, should we be out of bed?"

Nora clutched her purse and shoes to her chest, narrowed her eyes and limped to the desk.

"I don't know about *you*," she said, "but *I* need an aspirin. What do I have to do around here to get one?"

Joni Moore, R.N., the girl's name tag said. Even up close, Nora thought she didn't look more than 16. She blinked heavily mascaraed lashes at Nora, telegraphing pert annoyance.

"Well, all we have to do is press the call button in our room. It lights up in the hall and I come and see what you need."

Nora grimaced at her. "Well, I came to see you instead. Look," she pointed in the direction she'd been walking, "my room's that way, but I'm right here and all I want is a lousy aspirin. Why not just save yourself a trip and give me one?"

The nurse sat down with a self-righteous half-smile. "We have to make sure and only give our patients the medication that's indicated on their charts. I'm sure you'll find what you need waiting for you in your room. And if you don't, you just give me a buzz."

"Right," Nora snapped, "I'll just do that."

Nora began to scuffle away with her fingers crossed, listening for the sound of the nurse's chair squeaking around while Joni Moore pointedly ignored her. She limped to the far end of the hall to another stairway and let herself through the door, hobbled down the echoing stairwell without seeing anyone and slipped out the door to Kate's floor. There was no sign of a nurse or attendant in the hall when Nora cautiously looked around.

She stopped at Kate's door and backed up to it, flattening herself against it and reaching for the handle like a cheap detective in a 1940s B movie, while eying the hallway instead of where she was going.

It caught her off balance when the door was yanked open. Nora stumbled heavily forward, driving her weight onto her injured leg and the shock of pain made her flop forward like a toddler still new at walking. She caught herself on her hands before falling entirely prone. Instead, she sprawled like a spider across the distorted rectangle of light in the shadows.

One corner of light picked out a woman's hand lying limp on the floor. The picture branded itself in Nora's sight in the split second of illumination before the door started to close and the shadow covered it. It was a practical hand with short, square nails, a wedding band and a silver wristwatch. It wasn't Kate's hand.

Before Nora had a chance to scrabble up, rough hands grabbed her from behind and yanked her onto her feet, back against a man's body. One arm clamped across her waist and pinned her arms. A hand with clammy flesh covered her mouth.

Nora struggled briefly, then was still. She closed her eyes, willing them to come to terms with the dark so that she could see. Her heart seemed to be banging against the walls of her chest and she couldn't breathe. It was only seconds before her eyes sprang open. She still couldn't see much in the darkened room. The only light came from faint reflections of streetlamps and moonlight on the river, shining in through the large window.

She could see Kate in her bed, not moving.

Sam and Carole Salant were on the other bed. Salant's heavy body straddled the girl while she half-sat on Sam's thighs. One of Sam's wrists was tied to the raised bedrail and Salant was working on the other one. A band of white covered Sam's mouth and her head was strained up, her eyes wide open and shining at Nora in the half-light.

Carole's white flesh gleamed at her, too, plump legs, back and buttocks flashing from the skimpy hospital gown. She seemed more bloated than ever, an obscene scavenger hovering over Sam who twisted and struggled beneath her helplessly. Salant swiveled slowly and raised one delicate eyebrow in the Madonna face.

"You're next, Nora."

And Nora put all her strength into one tremendous twisting buck against the grip that held her, slithering away from those chilly hands with a sideways lurch that got her right side free. She swung around on the man with his mad, sick eyes and drove the heel of her free hand as hard as she could up under his chin. And Alex's grip on her dropped. He staggered back a step and Nora aimed a wild punch in the direction of his groin, impossible to pinpoint in his baggy hospital gown.

She felt her knuckles connect with the inside of his thigh and quickly compensated with a sliding, glancing blow on the soft testicles.

There wasn't much power behind it, but it was enough to make him stumble back and double over, clutching himself.

The sharp sound of a choking gasp made Nora spin towards the bed, and there was Salant grabbing her throat with both hands while Sam's free fist was drawing back for another shot at her.

Nora lunged to the bed and gave Salant a hard shove in the shoulder with both hands and all her weight behind it. The shove sent her toppling, arms and bare legs flailing. She hit the wall and slid, still choking, to the floor.

But the shove left Nora off-balance and before she could recover Alex was at her from behind, thin arms snaking around her. She kept falling toward the bed and taking him with her while Sam flipped her legs out of the way just in time. Nora twisted toward her while she fell, and Sam grabbed her to help pull her from Alex's half-hold.

The girl was folded in on herself at the head of the bed with Nora and Alex sprawled diagonally on it, Alex trailing across Nora's legs as she wriggled away from him. That's when his hand closed on her bandaged leg and he squeezed and dug his bony fingertips hard into the center of the wound. That's when the bolt of pain filled all her senses and left her for a timeless moment still and vacant.

And that's when Sam must have gotten her wrist free because she dove suddenly across Nora's back, launching herself like a speed swimmer skimming over the water's surface, arms outstretched. What she did was to catch the side of Alex's head and let her weight and outstretched arms ram his head with a muffled clang against the metal foot of the bed.

Nora felt his weight go dead on her, and as she was wriggling under him, the room brightened suddenly with light from the opening door.

"Now what's going on?" The voice was high and old and quavering, a tiny, white-haired nurse, outlined in the doorway, glasses gleaming.

Carole Salant rose then from the floor like a great white beast and lunged howling at the woman. Nora's arm shot out to stop her and grabbed only a handful of gown, but it spun her around and the nurse let out a gasp and a tiny yip.

Salant smashed down at her arm and Nora yanked it out of the way through the bedrail. She slid her legs out from under Alex and felt his body slide down off the bed.

The little nurse had her breath by then and she must have seen the body of the other woman because she started to scream, high and shrill, and it brought Salant's attention back to her.

Nora was finally on her feet, then, with a good grip on Sam's wrist, pulling her along. She wanted to make for the door, to get help, and they stepped quickly over Alex's body, starting to stir a little like a bear waking after winter.

Nora and Salant reached the door and the frail nurse screaming her thin scream at the same time. Salant grabbed the old woman by the throat, fingers like claws, her cherub's face glistening with sweat. And Nora grabbed Salant.

She wrapped her hands around one wrist to pull her off the nurse, but she couldn't break Salant's grip. She chopped at Salant's arms, hacking at the elbow, trying to bend her away from her hold. Nothing. And the little nurse was quiet now except for the sound of the back of her throat working for air that wasn't there.

"Sam!" Nora shouted, and Sam suddenly smacked Salant on the back of the head with one of those kidney-shaped metal pans. It made a hell of a bang, but it didn't do much except startle Salant. Still, it was enough for Nora to get one of Carole's clutching hands off the woman's throat and Nora jumped back to pull her off. And it worked—in a silly, macabre way.

Nora tripped over the body of the nurse on the floor, but she kept her grip on Salant, and when she fell she pulled Salant with her. But Carole still had the nurse held firmly in one hand, and the tiny woman in white fell on top of them so that they were all three struggling in a tangled heap with the woman who lay still on the floor.

Nora was flailing wildly when a pair of hands caught her wrist, and she sensed that it was Sam who grabbed her. Sam yanked at her and Nora kicked out of the pile, wriggling and twisting while Sam pulled, until she was free enough to scramble to her feet.

Sam had the door open then and Nora looked down. Alex was moving to his hands and knees. The nurse was lying still, pale old eyes staring up through thick silver-rimmed glasses. And Carole Salant was struggling up, her head swinging from side to side like a hunting animal.

Nora shoved at Sam, trying to move her through the door where she stood frozen.

"Help . . ." Nora couldn't quite get enough air. "We have to . . . get help."

And Salant was on her feet with her sharp, almost black eyes on them, and Nora gave Sam another good push through the door. It started to glide shut behind them and Nora limped into a run with one hand firm on Sam's shoulder, half propelling her along, half using her for support.

They skidded to a stop at the end of the corridor by the door to the stairs. They were pushing the door opened when they turned and there were Carole Salant and Alex Thomas, leaning together like drunken sailors, shambling towards them.

"Down!" Nora snapped. "Run ahead of me, Sam, you're faster than I am . . ."

Sam had worked the gag loose while they struggled

down the hall. It hung around her neck now like a cowboy's bandanna. "No!" she shouted and coughed, dry-mouthed. She pulled at Nora's elbow, yanking her towards the stairs. "I'm not going without you . . . not like before!"

Nora wanted to argue but there wasn't time. She let the girl yank her onto the landing and then grabbed the metal bannister in both hands and leaned on it. She let her arms and shoulders carry her weight while she slid her hands down and skipped and limped down the stairs with Sam anxiously trotting alongside her.

Above them they heard the door open and the shuffle of bare feet on the concrete steps.

"Door," Nora said and Sam was just ahead of her, skipping to hold the door open for them.

It was locked. A sign above it said "Authorized Personnel Only."

Nora didn't pause but awkwardly swung herself down the steps. The shuffling sounds of Alex and Salant seemed closer but she couldn't waste the seconds to look.

Sam caught up with her easily, her chunky bare legs pumping steadily down the steps to the next landing. She beat Nora to the door and this time it swung open for them. Sam yanked it wide and Nora staggered through, half-running, half-falling.

People lined the hall, crowding around the door. They pressed forward like a nightmare, all sighing together with something like longing as Sam and Nora were swallowed up by the flow of them.

28

They were old—old men, fragile and shriveled, bony and thin-skinned, blue veins marking their pale hands and faces like road maps.

Their eyes and faces were dull and vacant, empty of everything, it seemed, except a hunger that flickered deep in their rheumy eyes. The hunger had them stirring and shuffling towards Nora and Sam and made their mouths work soundlessly and their hands tremble.

It seemed as though the old men were waiting for them, watching the doorway and moving towards it when Nora and Sam burst through. A sound had swept over them, like foul gas escaping a swamp. Momentum carried Nora and Sam until the sight of the old men coming made them stop and stare in mixed horror and pity.

There were old men light as birds, white hair thin and fine as a baby's floating on their freckled skulls. They shuffled forward bent over canes and walkers. They leaned against the wall like men in a storm edging to safety. A few were on hands and knees crawling towards them. Trapped in a chair with a metal feeding tray like a high chair, one of them rocked and beat a soft fist against the barrier. It was the only sound for seconds—the weak pounding of his fist on the metal, the bony feet shuffling bare or in slippers on the cold tile floor, the labored sounds of breathing.

Then a nurse and two male orderlies appeared around a corner of the corridor hurrying towards them.

"Jesus Christ," one of the orderlies, big and black, burst out with, "what the hell are they doing?"

The crowd of them were closing around Nora and Sam like flesh around a wound. Sam shrank closer to Nora who said, "Come on," starting to move them forward through the old men who pressed toward them, reaching out now with bent and swollen fingers. And suddenly the door behind them crashed open and Alex and Carole Salant staggered through.

"What's going on here?" the nurse demanded, aiming it at Nora.

But Nora was pushing through the old men and the others were coming up close behind.

"Help us," Sam said.

The nurse was shaking her head, hands on the shoulders of an old man in a faded plum silk robe.

"Mr. Barkside, you should be in bed. Now you go on back to your room." But he didn't seem to hear or see her. He just kept moving toward Nora and Sam, and the nurse glared up as though it was their fault.

"What is this?"

That's when Alex and Carole caught up to them, shoving through the swarm of old men. Carole caught Sam by the hair as Alex's hand closed around Nora's throat from behind. Sam screamed and the nurse moved towards them quickly.

"Now just a minute," she said, and Alex reached out from behind Nora with one outspread hand and covered the nurse's face with it. He took two steps then, pushing Nora and pushing the nurse, until he got the nurse close enough to the corridor wall to crack her head against it.

"Hey!" the black orderly yelled, and Nora yanked Alex's hand from her throat and pushed away from him.

Salant had switched her hold on Sam to her arm and that was a mistake. Sam twisted away from her and by the time the orderly broke a path through the old men heading towards them, Sam and Nora could duck and slip into the press of bodies around them.

Hands clutched at them and bony arms reached for them, but Sam and Nora kept pushing, brushing them away like the thick growth of a jungle.

They broke through the crowd, stumbled a few steps and turned back to look for just a moment. The old men were clinging to the orderlies, wrapped around them, hands climbing the men's faces, grabbing feebly at them while Alex and Salant were moving through the crush, still coming after them. While they watched, one orderly broke free and grabbed Alex's arm, but Salant drove her nails at his eyes.

"Run." Nora turned her back to them and spun Sam around. "We'e got to keep moving."

"Where are we going?"

"The lobby, maybe. Anywhere we'll find a lot of people."

They reached another stairway and hobbled and raced down it to the bottom of the stairs. There was no sound of pursuit behind them, but Nora wouldn't let Sam slow down. They charged through the door hoping to be in the lobby, the place where there were always people. But they emerged into a quiet, featureless hallway, empty and unpromising in both directions.

The stretch to their right was long. It could have been a trick of perspective, but Nora thought the lights in that direction looked a little dimmer. To their left, the corridor ended with a turn in about 30 yards.

"This way," Nora directed, moving to the shorter stretch. It wasn't that she had any sense of which

direction they should be going, it was just that her leg
was pulsing with pain and her heart felt twice the size
it was supposed to be, banging and thumping against
her breastbone. Left was just shorter.

They came around the corner to face a tall pair of
metal swinging doors. Sam looked up at Nora and
took a tentative step towards them.

Nora shrugged. "Let's try it."

The doors opened into a short passage. Along the
hall were a row of darkened labs, visible through the
doors' glass upper half. At the end of the passage was
another pair of tall metal doors, and they pushed
through.

They were in the morgue.

They didn't realize it at first, but while they stood
staring around them the clues caught their attention
one by one—tall metal and glass cabinets, full of
bottles of chemicals, lab benches, microscopes, name-
less equipment. But more than anything were the
tables in the center of the room. They were like stone
altars, slabs of concave cement with a drain in their
centers. Over them were lights, hoses, microphones,
and instruments on jointed arms. On the back wall
were the faces of giant drawers running from floor to
ceiling. In front of them lay a gurney with a sheet
draped over it. Under the sheet, Nora saw, was a
human body.

They both stared for long seconds while a sudden
silence followed them and filled the room. Nora
shook her head, like breaking a trance, and took a
step backward, pulling Sam with her. They backed to
the swinging doors and pushed against them. But the
doors didn't move.

Nora snapped around then to see what the trick
was, something to turn or lift or press, but they were
simply swinging doors which wouldn't swing. They
were frozen solidly in place, more like a wall then
doors, just like the door of her storage bedroom.

In frustration she beat her fists against it. Nora was hammering against the door when she flashed a look at Sam and noticed that the girl was still standing frozen, staring straight ahead of her at the body lying on the gurney.

"Sam?" Nora reached for her shoulder and tried to turn Sam to face her, but the girl was stiff and fixed in place as a mannequin.

Stepping in front off her, Nora bent to look into Sam's eyes.

"Sam?" But Sam was focused on some inner distance, withdrawn and out of reach, and Nora felt with a chill that ran down her spine that she was alone in the morgue.

No, not alone. There was someone—not Sam—with her. She could feel it, like knowing as you walk down an empty street that someone is watching you.

The only sound in the room was Nora's winded breathing and she fought to contain it, to listen to the cool, sterile air echo in pockets of metal and tile. The place seemed to crowd around her and the presence grew and swelled.

Now she could almost feel where it was, and Nora waited, senses straining, aware of the air against her skin, her eyes wide and painfully dry because she wasn't blinking.

There, Nora thought, and she was staring at the sheeted figure on the gurney. *It's coming from there*.

In the stillness it began to feel like the room was polarized with her at one end and the thing, the other, at the far end of the room. It was waiting for her.

"What do you want?" Nora asked the silence. She was tired of running, tired of the traps and the games. Her voice was calm and controlled, just a little edged with weary impatience like a teacher talking to a child after a tantrum.

Nothing happened for moments, then a hissing slid up to the threshold of her hearing and started to build in volume. It came from the corner where the sheeted figure lay, and it built in volume until it filled the room and transformed, sly and menacing, into a name.

Ss-s-s-s-s-s-s-s-s-s-s-s-ample.

And Sam took a step forward.

"No!"

Nora threw her arms around the girl and hung on while the hissing started again and built and called her again. And Sam took another step forward.

She moved with a slow deliberation and a strength that was more than her own, while Nora hung onto her and put all her weight into holding the girl with her bare feet braced on the cold tile floor. But Sam dragged her another step forward.

"No!" Nora shouted back at the thing in the corner gathering another hiss, and she stepped around in front of Sam to try and block her that way. But it was as effective as standing in front of an avalanche. Nora braced against Sam, trying to drive her backwards, but she was sliding backwards herself, feet working and slipping frantically against the floor. The two of them kept moving slowly towards the unrelenting force in the far corner of the room.

"Sam!" Nora cried out, but Sam was somewhere out of reach.

It was useless and Nora kew it, so instead of trying to stop Sam she turned and ran limping ahead to the draped figure, halting a wary arm's length from it. Its cold presence filled that end of the room. It was the enemy.

"Victor."

Nora named him, and behind her she heard Sam stop moving.

"So . . ."

The voice seemed to float in the air like a falling leaf, melodious and full. He said it like a chess player, confident of winning, acknowledging his opponent's opening move.

The voice hadn't come from the draped corpse—Nora was sure of that—and she searched for its source, hoping he'd speak again. But she didn't need his voice to locate him. She could feel the center of the cold and the malevolence, and then she spotted him.

On the covered midsection of the corpse a white spider crouched, big as a walnut. His eyes were like pale twin emeralds and they flashed and glinted at her with an intelligence and cold malice that made her gut clench. With its emerald eyes the spider looked like some jeweler's bizarre creation, but it was alive. The body shifted gently in the cradle of its high arched legs. And then it was impossible for Nora to focus on the thing. It was like looking at something through a shifting haze of desert air. She blinked and half-squinted, and the thing distorted, then flickered into definition.

It was bigger now—big as a fist.

The spider balanced delicately on the dead man's chest, then scuttled to his groin, stopped and balanced, and Nora involuntarily drew back a step.

It wavered in her sight again, flickered out of vision and returned, big as a man's head. And now the emerald eyes were a man's eyes. Its claws sank into the soft belly of the corpse under the sheet and it stepped gracefully down his thighs to the tabletop, swarming over the side, clambering down the folds of the sheet, impossible to watch, changing as it traveled until, standing on the floor now at Nora's feet, the white spider with the green eyes of a man was as big as a fox. And she retreated another step.

And it flickered and changed and was as large as a big black dog. A glow like moonlight shimmered on his brittle, translucent back.

The green eyes looked up at her, man's eyes in a cruel spider's face, and its jaws worked and it spoke.

"Hello, Nora," it said. The voice was the voice on the answering machine, the voice of her telephone calls.

Nora could feel herself grimace with horror at the
thing that crouched in front of her—a giant spider, for
God's sakes! It was like a recurrent nightmare come
to life.

"Victor," Nora said again.

"Yes, I know, we've established that," the spider
answered. "Here we are at last. Although, you know,
I've been with you before this. You just weren't
paying attention. Stray dogs and spiders go where
they will and no one pays much attention."

A low metallic rumble sounded from the wall of
drawers, then fell silent.

"You're going to die, Nora. You die and the girl is
mine."

The rumbling sounded again, louder this time. It
became a frantic rattling coming from three of the
drawers that shook and trembled in place. On the
gurney behind the spider the sheet rippled and shook.
The body beneath the sheet sat up and the white
covering slowly cascaded from his face and slipped
down his bare chest.

The sound of the drawers shaking became a
crescendo of metal that thundered and echoed and
filled the room with a din like a factory gone mad.

And then the swinging doors flew open, and silence
returned except for the astonished exclamation of the
man who had come walking in.

"Hey . . ." was all he said. He was thin and young
and slouched, wearing blue jeans and a blue Oxford
shirt. He looked familiar to Nora and then she recognized him from the news. It was Dr. Paulson, the
county medical examiner.

He stopped a few yards into the room, frowning at
Sam's back.

"Young lady—" he said. And then a wheeled stool
shot ten feet across the room to crash into his shin.

He yelped and jumped back, clutching his shin with
one hand and hopping away from the stool, looking at

Nora now while she gaped at him. "Jesus," he said.

She wanted to warn him, but before she could say anything a bottle flew from a shelf and whizzed past his face, just missing by inches when he ducked.

The stool smashed at his shins again. He was being driven back into a corner.

And on the table the dead man swung his legs over the side and the sheet slid to the floor. His pale skin with its farmer's tan was whole and unmarked except for some sallow green and purple bruises. He was naked as he stood up.

Nora backed away another step. Behind her, Randy Paulson had his arms up in front of his face. He saw the body moving now and the spider and things were still flying at him with a kind of random disdain. He blocked another bottle and it smashed and splintered against the floor.

The dead man took a step. Then another.

Nora ducked sideways, stepping between two of the autopsy tables, but the corpse didn't change direction. He was headed for the doctor and moved quickly towards him.

One of the dead man's hands seized and gathered the doctor's collar and the other got a firm grip on his waistband. Paulson was struggling now, like a moth beating soft wings against steel tweezers.

The corpse carried him back to the corner wall and smashed him against it twice. Paulson's head hit the tile with two sharp cracks. His body hung limp from the dead man's hands as the corpse stepped back and raised him, stiff-armed, high overhead. Paulson's body cut an arc through the air and crashed, falling into a glass cabinet of chemicals. The glass was smashed and shattered, and bottles rained to the floor with explosive reports. The doctor's body rolled into a sprawling heap of broken glass and puddles of sharp-smelling chemicals. He settled on his side, arms and legs at awkward angles like a discarded rag doll. He wasn't moving any more.

In the wall the three drawers rattled with a thundering sound like applause after a concert.

Paulson's body had crashed less than ten feet from Sam and for the first time now she moved with some uncertainty. Nora was staring at Paulson's still body when she saw Sam turn slowly and look at him and start to shrivel into herself. Sam took a step away from him, away from the frozen spot where Victor had left her.

"Sam!" Nora shouted, and the girl swiveled to look at her. She looked confused and frightened. And panic was beginning to move across her face with returning awareness.

"Nora?" She mouthed it more than spoke it.

"Yes!" Nora hobbled two quick steps towards the girl, but the dead man moved more quickly. He was between them now.

"Stand off!" the spider lilted in a voice like an excited child.

Nora swung around to face him. "Why are you doing this? What do you want?"

"I want you to be dead. Understand? I want you to die."

"Why?"

"Look at it this way . . . I want your lives."

"Because Sam wouldn't be one of your groupies?"

"Tsk, Nora, you *have* been busy. My half-brother gave you that idea, I suppose. Michael was always envious of me, you know."

"He cared about you. You were just too full of self-pity to see it!"

"Oh! You do go on. What a sharp tongue you have, my dear." And the spider's jaws parted while a long, mobile dog's tongue lolled out.

"Nora," he said. So urbane, she thought, so smooth and purely nasty. "You're both going to die. That's all that need concern you. Think of Iago. Act Five.

'Why?' says poor old Othello and our Iago says, 'Demand me nothing and what you know, you know . . .' The rest is silence, Nora.''

And his legs lifted in dainty steps coming toward her.

Nora spun on her heels and ran towards Sam, dodging tables and swerving away from the corpse. Sam spun, too, and followed her example, weaving towards the door like a deft soccer player. A flying bottle crashed against the doors as they moved in on them, and they dodged to one side. When they came together they were at the side of the room across from Paulson's body, a few yards from the door, their backs braced against a crowded countertop.

Metal shrilled against metal, and three drawers in the back wall bucked and slid a little way open and stopped.

''My followers,'' the spider said.

One drawer slid open a few more feet. And another. And the third.

The walking corpse took a step towards them.

Behind them the countertop held a potential arsenal and Nora chose and hefted a heavy iron ring stand, then handed it to Sam. A Bunsen burner made a short club for her and she yanked it free from the rubber hose that connected it to the wall.

''Come, come, Nora, don't be silly,'' Victor scolded. The spider and the corpse faced them only a few yards out of reach. But while the dead man stood as still as a tree, the spider sidled a little and then froze. It was a movement so quick, so smooth that Nora doubted for a moment that she'd seen it. But she had, and perhaps it meant that he was nervous, a little less sure of himself than he pretended. Believing that at least gave her some comfort.

She stepped towards the spider, one long step from the counter to giver herself room to maneuver. The green eyes looked steadily up at her, fixed on her face even while the three bodies in the open drawers sat up.

They moved like three puppets all on one string—Charlie Luther, the headless woman and Simon.

"No."

They swung their legs over the sides of their slabs with a terrible deliberateness, like thick blood dripping from an old wound. Their sheets slithered off and fell to the floor. They were naked and Nora couldn't take her eyes off them. She stared at Simon's white chest but couldn't look at his face.

They stood up.

"No."

"You led me to him," Victor remarked conversationally. "I really should thank you."

"Oh, God."

"Indeed. But really, other than that small favor, you've been quite a nuisance. I'll be glad to . . ."

Nora had reached behind her for something to throw. Her hand closed on a heavy bottle and she threw it awkwardly, left-handed. It crashed to the floor a yard wide of its mark, but the spider skittered a swift few inches to one side when it hit.

Charlie, Simon and the woman jolted into motion, beginning to shuffle towards them, and Sam broke and ran. She tried slipping past the dead man with the beaked nose and sunburned face. He caught her as she ducked by.

"Sam!" Nora feinted towards her, but she swerved instead towards the spider and raised her burner club as she ran. She got close and as he scuttled away she took a wide wild swing that struck the brittle joint of one of his legs. She felt it connect and heard the sharp crack of the cartilage breaking.

The leg jerked and flailed the air with rapid beats until it fell suddenly limp. When the spider skittered out of reach behind an autopsy table, the leg was trailing behind him.

Nora followed him around the table like a housewife chasing a rat but Victor rounded it nimbly, keeping just out of reach. He disappeared around the corner of the table, then suddenly reappeared over the top edge and rushed at her. She jumped away from the table, but not before he swung at her. His sharp claw skidded across her forearm and left a fine, faint line of red dotted with bright beads of blood.

That's when Roy Finnerty pushed open the swinging metal doors, took two strides in and stopped.

"Sweet Jesus."

Nora swung to face him and then back to the spider, afraid to take her eyes off him. He scuttered a little on the table, claws clicking on the concrete. The green eyes flicked from her to the sheriff.

"Vern?" Finnerty took a step towards the walking corpse that held Sam. But the corpse was still and silent as a figure in a Pharaoh's tomb.

"It's not him," Nora said, still watching the spider. "He's just being used, like a puppet."

Finnerty moved farther into the room, taking it all in now, and Nora shifted back and to one side so that she could see him. And he could see the spider.

"My God," Finnerty said, coming up behind her, "what is it?"

"Victor," Nora said, and Sam suddenly screamed.

Vern's broad, bony hand was clamped on the small bulge of Sam's breast. The fingers of his other hand were tangled in her hair, arching her backwards, pressing her face to his naked belly.

Finnerty drew his gun, aiming at Vern in a quick reflex, then scowling in confusion. He was turning the muzzle of the gun towards Victor when the spider sprang at him in a high, graceful arc that brought him hard against Finnerty's shoulder.

The gun went off with a sharp crack that echoed and crashed through the room and Finnerty went down under Victor, hitting the floor hard. Man and spider wrestled for the gun, two of the spider's claws mangling Finnerty's hand and wrist, and the only sound in the room was Finnerty grunting. The spider's sharp claws tore at Finnerty's face and ripped through the heavy brown cotton of his shirt.

Nora watched, staring without thinking, until the sight of dark blood soaking Finnerty's shirt struck her like a slap in the face and brought her back to action. She swung to face Vern, but the corpse was still as a mannequin while Sam writhed and whimpered in his grasp.

Nora rushed to help her, prying the corpse's stiff fingers off Sam's chest. There was a faint smell of him of cold and something sweet. When Nora touched him, her flesh wanted to crawl away from the contact.

Sam had panicked. Twisting away from Vern, jerking against his still grip, she only managed to get her hair more thoroughly tangled in his hold. By the time Nora worked her hair free, Sam was senseless as a rabbit, ready to spring into brainless flight until Nora grabbed her in a tight embrace and held her, trying to contain the fear. In a few seconds, she felt the edge of craziness slip away from Sam and then the shattering of glass made them jump apart.

It must have been the gun, Nora saw, thrown by Victor or Finnerty. It had smashed the still swinging door of the cabinet near Randy Paulson's body.

Finnerty's big hands snapped one of the spider's

legs with a sharp crack, and Vern twitched in place as though a little shock of electricity had run through him. Nora pulled Sam away, back towards the spider and the sheriff.

Blood ran down Finnerty's mangled hand, and it slipped off the slick spider body as he tried for a different hold. Victor had him, then, using his weight to pin the sheriff's good arm and one free claw to hold down his ripped and bleeding right arm.

Victor pressed a claw between the sheriff's lips. He forced Finnerty's mouth open, green eyes bent on him in mad connection. His claw slid between Finnerty's teeth, making the muscles at his jaw bulge.

"When I'm through with you, Sheriff, you'll be a mate for our friend Ted."

And Sam ran at him to deliver a kick like a football pro at the kickoff. Her sneakered foot made a solid connection with the heavy spider body, not enough to send him flying, but enough to unbalance him and break his hold. Nora was only a second behind her, swinging the bunsen burner underhand like a club. One hit and Victor scurried away.

But Vern was moving behind them. And the three still corpses who stood like totems at the end of the room sighed and came forward a step.

Finnerty was struggling up to his elbows, gagging and coughing. Nora grabbed him by the shoulders of his torn uniform, and a sharp grunt of pain slipped out of him.

"Come on, come on," Nora was tugging at him, bare foot slipping in the puddle of his blood. He sat up, clapped a hand to his throat, coughing, and shook his head.

"Get out," Finnerty rasped.

Nora kept tugging at him, trying to get him up.

"Try the door," she said to Sam, but Vern still stood between them and the way out. Maybe Sam could duck around him, but even if she did, Victor might still be able to keep it closed against them. Nora saw the fear of Vern flicker on Sam's face as she eyed the distance around him willing, Nora thought, to try it anyway.

"No, Sam. Wait."

Finnerty was on his knees, leaning forward on his good arm. Nora grabbed him under the arm, squatting a little to get her weight behind it and hoist him up.

"We can't get out," she told him while she hauled at him. "The only way out is to destroy Victor."

Finnerty was on his feet, swaying a little.

"They're moving," Sam said, bouncing a little, ready to run.

Nora kept her eyes on the sheriff.

"Victor?" he repeated it as though it were a word from some foreign language. "The spider is Victor?"

"He's back," Nora said. "He can . . . control things. People."

A bottle flew through the air from nowhere and struck Nora between the shoulder blades.

She yelped and fell towards Finnerty, and he pulled her around beside him, shielding her and using her as a crutch.

"Sample, come here," he said, and Sam looked at Nora before moving.

Nora gave a quick nod and Sam skipped towards them. Finnerty was surveying the room and Nora turned with him.

Victor was back on top of the autopsy table. On one side of his body a segmented leg trailed like a child's pull-toy. A leg on the opposite side was sharply bent, frozen in odd angles and twitching with sharp, uneven spasms.

Simon, the headless woman and Charlie Luther were shuffling up behind him, a determined guard of dead flesh. Vern flanked them, lumbering in like a bear.

Finnerty drew them back, and Nora felt him sway and struggle to recover, his balance unsteady. Where he leaned against her, warm blood made a wet union. She could feel it trickle from her side and drip onto her feet.

"Sheriff . . ." she said, but he shook his head. "Keep moving. We need our backs covered." His voice was low, barely audible.

Pressed together, the three of them shuffled backwards towards the counter. Facing the spider and his guard of corpses, they thought the counter at their backs would offer some protection. But from behind them came a rain of heavy bottles.

Finnerty staggered as one of the bottles hit his head, and Nora's free arm was hit hard enough to send a jangling down her nerves and leave her arm limp. But Sam bent, snatched up a rolling brown glass bottle and heaved it at the spider.

He scuttled to one side, but it crashed beside him and glass burst towards him like shrapnel.

Another yard back was the counter, and Nora slipped her support away from Finnerty and propped him against the counter's edge. Copying Sam she started grabbing anything handy to throw at the spider. Their shots were wide and wild, but they drove Victor off the autopsy table to hide behind it. Then Finnerty's feet slid out in front of him and he slipped to the ground with his head banging on the edge of the counter before Nora could catch him or break his fall. His head lolled onto his chest.

"Nora?" Sam was poised mid-throw, bottle drawn back, watching her wide-eyed.

"He fainted, I think, Sam. He's lost a lot of blood."

Sam's arm came slowly down. Vern had moved around in front of them, naked and white-skinned with hazy eyes that were fixed on some other distance. Victor mounted him from behind, spider's claws pressing the dead flesh, and Nora could feel the spirit draining out of Sam while it suddenly became utterly quiet.

Victor was perched on Vern's shoulder, legs wrapping his rib cage and draping over his arm and shoulder. The spider's unreadable face with its green human eyes watched her from beside the corpse's blank face.

"Hello again," Victor said, and the long pink tongue lolled out like a friendly cartoon mutt's.

"Give it up, Nora, and I'll let you die a clean quick death. We'll crack your pretty bones like a bird in a vise. That's better, though, than some things, isn't it? We could make it very slow." Vern took a long stride forward.

"I win," Victor said.

Nora stared back at the spider face, trying to see the man there, trying to see who Victor had been once.

"No, you haven't," she finally said. "Not in the way you wanted to."

"You're being tiresome."

"You haven't beaten me. Or Irene. Or Sample. Not even an old lady and a little girl. Some victory."

"Slowly, then. With much pain. Did you know, Nora, that the cries of pain just before death are almost indistinguishable from sexual ecstasy? We will have ecstasy, Nora. You and me. And sweet Sam."

"What happened to all your followers, Victor? Where are the hordes clamoring to adore you? To tell you how godlike you are? You're still alone."

Victor slid towards her, edging over Vern's shoulder as the corpse took another step forward. The spider's eyes sparked green light like something surprised in the dark.

"How brave you are," Victor crooned. "And you were such a mouse."

"It's been a long week," Nora answered, watching his claws pierce the dead flesh while anger glittered in his smooth voice.

"Humor? How delightful!"

And a rush of warm, stinking water hit her in the face.

She sputtered and wiped the stuff from her eyes, contacts floating, blinded, choking on the stench.

"People used to say," Victor said thoughtfully, "that I had a rather vulgar sense of humor. Tell me, Nora, have you appreciated it?"

Nora was coughing, shaking her head.

"No, they were right. You are vulgar. You wasted yourself, Victor. Just you. Nobody else to blame." There was something on the counter she could use, she realized. A real weapon. She was facing the spider, but feeling around behind her without trying to hide it.

"Looking for more things to throw?"

And she found it.

Nora spun around, snatching up the Bunsen burner that was a twin to her now-lost club. A long rubber hose still connected the burner to a gas outlet and Nora flipped open the handle of the gas, hearing the hiss of gas escaping and reaching frantically for the thing like the one she'd used in high school chemistry. She pointed the end of the hissing burner at the spider like a talisman and squeezed and released the wire spark maker, trying desperately to get a spark before so much

gas escaped that it blew back in her face and the
flames turned on her.

Only a weak scrape occurred since she was
using her awkward left hand.

Another. And Vern moved towards her. Victor
had seen what she was doing, green eyes fixed on
the burner, and the corpse, slow and clumsy,
shambled towards her.

"Giddyap!" Victor cried, full of glee, and Vern
was almost on her when a bright shower of sparks
flew up and the blue gas caught and flared like a
shield before her.

Vern's hand was outstretched, and flame licked
around the white knuckles and up the forearm,
reaching towards the tip of the spider's claw
resting on Vern's wiry bicep.

The corpse awkwardly swung a bare arm like a
club to strike at the burner, but Nora had already
stepped back, a fencer retreating after the thrust.

Sam came skipping out then, light on her feet,
dancing around the still body of the sheriff. She
kicked at the back of Vern's knee and his leg
folded like a paper fan.

He flopped down onto one knee, unbalanced by
the weight of the spider, while Victor scrambled
to center himself more evenly on Vern's shoulders.

Nora thrust forward again as Vern's knee
thudded to the floor and Victor came into reach.
The spider ducked out of range behind Vern's
head, but two curved claws still dug into his chest
and Nora aimed the flames at their tips. Human
skin charred under the flames, and the spider
yanked back his claws and leapt to the ground.
He scuttered suddenly around Sam, putting her
between himself and Nora's flaming burner.

Vern's body slowly collapsed. The charred flesh
of his chest sent up a wisp of smoke and the
stench of burned meat.

"Sssssssssssssssssssample . . ." Victor hissed.

And Sam stood very still.

"Sam!" Nora urged, but the girl didn't move.

The spider stretched out a claw and laid it gently on the girl's back. He hissed, and a wave passed through Sam. She undulated like grass in a warm wind while Nora stood feeling foolish and lost with her spitting blue flame clutched in her hand.

"Sam!"

The girl was turning now, swiveling slowly towards the spider, and Nora felt sick and helpless.

Then she turned back to the counter, carefully set the Bunsen burner down and snatched up a heavy microscope. Two quick limping steps and she was next to Sam, glaring down at the spider.

She threw the heavy microscrope at him with all her strength, heaving it at the green eyes.

He'd seen it coming, so it didn't land clean.

The spider side-stepped, but not quite far enough. The microscope snapped two more of his legs.

Nora grapped Sam's T-shirt, crumpling a rough fist full of material and yanking the girl off balance.

"Come on! Sam! Come on!"

Sam looked at her then, shame growing on her face when she realized how close she'd come to betraying them both. Tears finally filled her soft brown eyes behind the owl glasses.

Poor kid, Nora thought, poor kid. But there wasn't time for pity.

"Sweetie," she said, "we have to kill the bastard."

When she spoke a wave like a sigh swayed through the three standing corpses. Victor scurried around an autopsy table, awkward now on his broken legs, lurching like a ship on a wild sea. He ran behind the wall of dead flesh, green eyes

glinting at them from between the white thighs.
Like a Greek chorus, they took a solemn step
forward.

And then the lights went out.

Besides her in the dark Nora heard Sam give a
small wail. Nora was completely blinded for a
moment, and then she realized the darkness
wasn't absolute. The Bunsen burner was still
casting its blue light and she squeezed her eyes
shut, then open, blinking furiously, trying to see.

"Sam." She grabbed the girl's shoulder, pulling
her back. There were twin reflections of the
burner light in Sam's glasses. Her eyes were fixed
on the three bodies. They were closer, taking
another slow step.

"Sam, *move!*" Nora said, pulling her shoulder
again, and though the girl let her weight sway
backward until she had to take a step, she wasn't
cooperating.

Then she stiffened under Nora's hold. Hands
clenching to fists at her side, she threw her head
back and shrieked a sharp, shrill scream like a
whistle blast that rattled the broken glass in the
cabinets and reverberated off the metal drawers.
And she broke and ran, away from Nora and the
circle of blue light, away from the closing ring of
bodies, away from the sheriff sprawled on the
floor. She slipped into the darkness, somewhere
into the echoing room, out of Nora's sight.

"Wait!" Nora screamed after her into the dark,
but the three corpses made a barricade between
light and the edge of her vision. They swayed and
were still. Behind them Nora thought she could
catch a glinting reflection of light on the spider's
body.

"Victor!" she called, and light shifted between
Charlie Luther's thin legs. "Me first! Where's your
triumph if you don't beat me?"

She dropped to a crouch, holding the burner on its tethering hose like a short sword of flame. Then something heavy hit her from behind, striking the base of her neck and knocking her flat forward. Glass crashed beside her. Stunned, she was aware for some confused seconds only of the cold floor pressing against her cheek.

He cheats, she thought. And then he was on her.

Claws like grappling hooks flipped her over onto her back and the spider scrambled onto her chest, balanced with claws at her shoulders and hips. She wasn't holding the Bunsen burner, Nora realized, but she could still see so it must be lit somewhere.

One claw closed on her throat—lightly, she thought, with just enough pressure to hold her motionless and breathing shallowly. She blinked up at him, meeting his green eyes so grotesquely human in the spider face, moist and alive in the opal white shell.

"Gotcha," he said, and his long wet tongue slid out to lick a warm, wet trail up her cheek.

Then he screamed.

It was a scream of pain, high and jangled, and his claw clenched reflexively, closing on her throat until he sprang off her. It left Nora gagging, sucking at the air while her heart slammed and ballooned in her chest. She threw out an arm, reaching for air, and hit Sam's bare chunky knee. Seconds later, when she could almost breathe and see and think again, she realized that Sam was standing over her, protecting her. She was holding a long shard of broken glass like a dagger in hands slick with blood. Her own blood, Nora thought. The dark stuff squeezed out between her fingers and dripped across her knuckles.

Victor was circling them, cautiously, about two yards away. Sam's round, determined face turned towards him, following his moves while Nora

coughed and rubbed her throat and started an awkward roll onto her hands and knees.

Victor rushed her, then, while her body blocked
him from Sam. A quick scurry forward ended with a
long slashing swipe that cut her from high on the
thigh to mid-calf. Nora choked on her scream, throwing her legs out of reach, flipping like a fish in panic.
But in the same move she lunged at him to catch one
broken leg. She held him anchored for Sam and her
dagger.

Sam was already dancing around them, looking for
a chance to stab at the spider.

"His eyes!" Nora croaked and coughed and he leapt
almost out of her grasp. "Go for his eyes!"

Sam had to lean awkwardly over Nora where she
sprawled on the floor. Her foot-long shard of glass
thunked against Victor's body, missing his eye by a
hand's-breadth as he bucked away from Nora's hold.
But the point skidded across the bony shell and slid
into his wounded joint where dark fluid swelled up.

The jagged edges of the glass caught on the torn
cartilage of the joint, and Sam shoved down on it,
moving in closer, trying to get a better angle while she
shuffled closer, feet pushing at Nora's ribs and
shoulder.

They were close, all three of them, a bridge of pain
and effort, rasping breath, sweating, grunting in the
still room until Sam's dagger cut the cartilage and
stabbed into the soft interior and Victor screamed. He
leapt free with the pain. The glass broke in Sam's
hand and his useless claw jerked out of Nora's grasp.

Nora struggled to her hands and knees, head
swaying between her arms like seaweed drowning in
the tide.

"Get up! Get up!" Sam's hands were slick when
they grabbed at Nora's shoulders.

Nora coughed and thought she tasted the iron taste
of blood far back in her throat. There was a dog
howling somewhere.

Here. The hollow sound of mourning cascaded around the room, banging against the tile, the metal tables and the concrete slabs. It was Victor.

Sam was tugging at her and shaking her, when all she wanted was to lie down and sleep.

"The burner," she said, listening to herself say it from far away. "Move back. Fire."

Sam pulled her back onto her heels and the movement tore the wound on her thigh. The pain made her move and she was on her feet, unsteady, while the room disappeared in black splotches. A deep breath made it stop. She had a hand on Sam's shoulder, leaning heavily on her. Sam took a step toward the Bunsen burner, lying where she'd dropped it on the tile floor, and Nora moved with her.

But Victor skittered around in front of them, blocking their way. And Vern's charred corpse alone at the edge of the light twitched and jerked.

"No!" Sam shouted at the corpse, commanding it, then shot off again into the darkness.

Nora almost toppled with the sudden loss of support, but she let the momentum of her near-fall carry her on to the burner, just a few yards in front of her.

Victor's howl faded into the stillness of the morgue, but another sound replaced it—the clatter of wheels, Nora realized, small wheels rushing across the floor. And Sam reappeared, rushing out of the darkness rolling a wheeled stool in front of her, sliding it fast as a hockey player driving the puck in front of him.

She ran directly into Victor. Crashed the stool against the spider body, then snatched it up and swung it down like a club. She missed his body, but the wheeled base came down across one of Victor's unbroken legs with a crack like a chicken bone breaking.

His body sagged and listed then, the balance finally broken, and legs more useless than working dragging him down. He couldn't get away.

Sam swung the stool again, sweeping it at him and catching him broadside. He toppled, belly on the floor. A couple of legs scrabbled uselessly at the tile and Sam pinned them with the wheeled base of the stool. She pushed, got her back into it and pushed again.

Victor's broken legs trailed his body like a grass skirt. They made a dry, rattling sound dragging across the floor while Sam used the stool like a push broom to sweep him forward. She was picking up speed, sliding him towards Nora, when one of his good legs angled up and the claw grabbed her wrist.

Sam screamed, but she kept pushing.

Nora was waiting like a goalie at the net. Crouched, burner in hand, she watched them come and calculated how much tube she had, how far she could reach.

"Closer!" she said, but Sam was slowing down.

And Nora turned her back and lunged for the counter, burner still in hand. She turned up the flame.

"Kill it! Kill it!" Sam shrieked and when Nora turned back to them, the spider, pinned at the end of the stool was two long steps away.

She took a step forward and looked down at him, into his green eyes. There was a lush jungle where light and shadow shifted in a mutable pattern of a thousand shades. His eyes were so beautiful, Nora thought, so full of pain and fear. As though, somewhere hidden in the whispering leaves, all the beasts were being slaughtered.

"Nora," he said. And she could only stand there, looking at him.

"Nora!" Sam pleaded. "Do it! Do it now!"

Victor released Sam's wrist and slowly, slowly stretched his claw out towards Nora.

"Please . . ." he said, and whether he wanted her to spare him or turn the flame on him she would always wonder.

She caught him between his green eyes.

The blue flame blossomed, and pale fire burst from the spider's body. His scream pierced their ears like glass.

Sam jumped back and the restraining stool flew through the air to crash ten feet away. Nora and the girl both retreated, backing away with their palms pressed over their ears and the spider's flame making them squint and blink.

Pale fire spread over the spider's body and he shot straight up into the air and stayed there, eye level with Nora, growing brighter. His scream had become a sort of siren note.

Light blurred his outline. His legs jittered in the air like a broken puppet's, and the shriek that came from him grew higher pitched and seemed to come from everywhere at once.

Nora ground her palms against her ears to block it out, but the sound seemed to stab through her flesh and resonate in her bones.

Suspended, the spider's body began to change shape. The blurred outline began to shimmer with a green flame and shift. It was the spider. And its legs drew up and melded and his body stretched and lengthened, sending out a snout, a high-domed head, and a muscular neck. He was the dog.

And he changed again. Torso shifted, length and mass flowing through the legs, and the head and neck differentiated, growing human. A man's shape became bright beaming green, almost too brilliant to look at, and Nora squinted through her fingers at the thing. While she watched he curled forward into a ball, head ducked between his knees, arms wrapped around his shins, and the outline of a man faded altogether.

He became a globe—featureless, just pure light.

The ball rose a few feet, trembled and shivered in the darkness of the lab and began to move. It started to circle the room. Once around slowly, and then it began to pick up speed, racing around the room like a comet caught in a whirlwind until the trail of light became a closed circle.

Nora stared up at the ring of light with wonder and pain, because it was the thing that was Victor, shining up there. He filled the room, and his death scream rang through her bones.

There was rage and fear in the sound, Nora thought, like some terror that waited in a nightmare.

It went on and on while she could barely breathe, and finally, almost imperceptibly at first, the circle of light and the scream began to fade. The shriek lost its edge and the light was a little less bright. It faded more and more, rapidly now, until the circle of light was only a sugggestion on the air and the scream was a faraway whistle.

Then the lights came on.

29

"Simon's body wasn't there at all," Nora said.

She was sitting in her wheelchair beside Irene's bed
with her bandaged arm resting lightly on a pillow in
her lap. Beneath the pillow her heavily bandaged leg
throbbed with the steady reminder that it was past
the usual time for her medication. She had asked her
doctor to cut back on some of the drugs she was
taking.

Maybe, she thought, taking fewer drugs would help
with the nightmares.

"Just a projection, then. One of Victor's tricks,"
Irene told her. Nora nodded. She had realized that,
but it was comforting to hear Irene explain it all so
matter-of-factly.

A full week had crept by, but Nora had only started
giving Irene the details of what had happened in the
past day or so, waiting until the older woman
regained her strength. It had been only a mild heart
attack, it turned out. Irene was recovering quickly.

"It seemed for a while like he could do anything,"
Nora said.

Michael, too, was on the mend, and Nora had warm
thoughts when she thought about the possibility of
their relationship.

"His powers were limited, though. Like a juggler, he had a maximum number of objects he could keep moving at once."

Nora made a hum of agreement. In her nightmares she still saw Charlie Luther. Irene and the headless woman, Florence Gleason, still lunged for her throat and she would wake up, gasping. She would set a blue flame to Victor's green eyes over and over.

"You really think it's over, though?" Nora asked Irene the same question Sam kept asking of her. Nora always answered Sam, "Yes, definitely." But she wanted reassurance from somebody else, somebody who seemed to understand what had happened.

"You forced him to move on, dear. He won't be back."

Was he, in the end, willing to go?

"He was so frightened," Nora said.

"Fear is what kept him here. Bitterness. All negative things. He's shed them, now." Irene fixed her bright blue eyes on Nora. "It's *over*."

"All except for the goddamn paperwork," Finnerty said, wheeling his chair through Irene's open door. "Excuse me. Darned paperwork."

Holy mackerel, Nora thought, he's blushing. And she couldn't wait to tell Sam about it.